Jonathan
KELLERMAN

mystery

headline

First published in the United States in 2011 by Ballantine Books
an imprint of The Random House Publishing Group,
a division of Random House Inc., New York

First published in Great Britain in 2011
by HEADLINE PUBLISHING GROUP

1

Cataloguing in Publication Data is available from the British Library

ISBN 978 0 7553 7446 5 (Hardback)
ISBN 978 0 7553 7447 2 (Trade paperback)

Typeset in Fournier MT by Palimpsest Book Production Limited,
Falkirk, Stirlingshire

Printed and bound in the UK by CPI Mackays, Chatham ME5 8TD

Headline's policy is to use papers that are natural, renewable and recyclable products and made from
wood grown in sustainable forests. The logging and manufacturing processes are expected to
conform to the environmental regulations of the country of origin.

This one's for
Kim Hovey.

1

LIKE A con man on the run, LA buries its past.

Maybe that's why no one argued when the sentence came down: The Fauborg had to die.

I live in a company town where the product is illusion. In the alternate universe ruled by sociopaths who make movies, communication means snappy dialogue, the scalpel trumps genetics, and permanence is mortal sin because it slows down the shoot.

LA used to have more Victorian mansions than San Francisco but LA called in the wrecking ball and all that handwork gave way to thirties bungalows that yielded to fifties dingbats, which were vanquished, in turn, by big-box adult dormitories with walls a toddler can put a fist through.

Preservationists try to stem the erosion but end up fighting for the likes of gas stations and ticky-tack motels. Money changes hands, zoning laws are finessed, and masterpieces like the Ambassador Hotel dissolve like wrinkles shot with Botox.

The Fauborg Hotel was no Ambassador but it did have its charm. Four somber stories of Colonial brick-face, it sat on a quiet block of Crescent Drive in Beverly Hills, wedged between a retirement home and a dry cleaner. A short walk but a psychic universe from the Eurotrash cafés of Canon Drive and the shopping frenzy on Beverly and Rodeo, the Fauborg appeared in few guidebooks but managed to boast one of the highest occupancy rates in the city.

Built in 1949 by a French Holocaust survivor, its design aped the mansions in the American movies that had transfixed Marcel Jabotinsky as a teenager. Jabotinksy's first guests were other postwar émigrés seeking peace and quiet. That same desire for low-key serenity continued with the hotel's clientele, divided between the genteel grandparents of Eurotrash and the odd knowledgeable American willing to trade glitz and edgy and ironic for a decent night's sleep.

I knew the Fauborg because I drank there. The lounge at the back was smallish and dim with nothing to prove, paneled in dark rift oak and hung with middling Barbizon landscapes. The eighty-year-old hunchback behind the bar concocted the best Sidecar in town and Robin likes Sidecars. An assortment of pianists, mostly former studio musicians on pension, worked the big black Steinway in the left-hand corner, never intruding upon the pleasant buzz of conversation and the harmonious clink of crystal glasses. The staff was attentive without being nosy, the snacks were decent, and you left the place feeling as if you'd been recivilized.

Robin and I spent a lot of Sunday evenings in a cracked leather rear booth, holding hands, nibbling on cheese crackers, and inhaling Gershwin.

One Saturday morning in the spring, Robin was delivering a new guitar to an aging rock star who lived in the flats of Beverly Hills and the drive took her past the Fauborg. A sign strung up over the fanlight announced:

LAST NIGHT TOMORROW:
COME CELEBRATE – OR MOURN – WITH US.
THANKS FOR THE GOOD TIMES.

The Family of Marcel Jabotinsky

Robin shouldn't have been surprised; the previous week we'd shown up at a Thai place we'd enjoyed for half a decade only to find an abyss surrounded by chain-link where the building had stood. The month before that, she'd run into an old high school friend and asked how her husband was.

'Which one?'

'Jeff.'

The woman laughed. 'Jeff's ancient history, sweetie. Cliff's recent history but he's gone, too.'

Tissue paper city.

Robin said, 'Not much of a choice, is it? Surrender to the inevitable or risk a whole bunch of mawkish nostalgia.'

We sat on the living-room couch with Blanche, our little French bulldog, squeezed between us and following the back-and-forth.

I said, 'I can go either way.'

She pulled on a curl, let it spring back. 'What the heck, I'll never get a Sidecar that good and it's a chance to put on a dress.'

'I'll wear a suit.'

'I like you in a suit, darling. But not the black one. Let's pretend it won't be a funeral.'

Who knew?

2

WE SHOWED up at nine p.m. The light behind the fanlight was dingy.

Crescent Drive was depopulated except for a man with a walkie-talkie leaning against a parking meter just north of the hotel. Thirties, tall, broad, with short yellow hair, he flashed us a slit-eyed appraisal before returning to watching the empty street.

His suit was black and it draped his bulk uneasily. An interesting bulge swelled his breast pocket, a spiral cord ran from an earpiece down the back of his collar.

Robin whispered, 'If someone needs serious guarding, where are the paparazzi?'

I said, 'Good question. They swarm like blowflies at the first whiff of moral decay.'

'Some flies are kept like pets. Once I was delivering a mandolin to Bite and sat in his kitchen as his publicist phoned the paps to tell them where The Star would be for lunch.'

Something made me turn back to Mr Black Suit. His head jerked away quickly and he studied the sidewalk; he'd been watching us. Despite the theatrical apathy, his shoulders were tight, his profile less animate than Rushmore.

We must've lingered too long because he half turned and stared. Robin smiled and gave a fluttery finger-wave. Her curls were wild, copper-bright in the moonlight, her dress a tight black tulip, set off by red stilettos.

Usually that has its effect.

Black Suit was no exception and he smiled back. Then he stopped himself, returned to reviewing the pavement.

Robin said, 'Guess I'm losing my touch.'

'He's a robot.'

'I used to be good with machines.'

A push of the brass door leading to the Fauborg's lobby plunged us into a sooty, demi-darkness that turned the damson-plum carpeting to soil-brown. All the furniture was gone, no one worked the desk, gray rectangles marked the walls where paintings had been removed.

One thing hadn't changed: the familiar olfactory stew of roasted meat, disinfectant, and grassy French perfume.

The ancient air conditioner thumped the ceiling at odd intervals but the air was close, musty, dank.

Robin squeezed my arm. 'This might be a bad idea.'

'Want to leave?'

'You and me quitters? Not in our DNA.'

Half the light fixtures had been removed from the lounge. The room was a cave. As my eyes adjusted, I made out the overstuffed leather and green plaid seating. Here, too, the artwork was gone.

Same for the big black Steinway with its gigantic brandy snifter for tips. Tinny music seeped into the room from an unseen speaker. An easy-listening FM station. As we stood waiting to be seated, Barry Manilow was replaced by a commercial for auto insurance.

Like pedestrians in a fog, the other patrons materialized gradually. A group of handsome white-haired people in their sixties who looked as if they'd driven in from San Marino, a quartet of well-dressed continental types ten years older, both men wearing ascots.

One exception to the maturity motif: two tables from our usual corner a young woman in white sat alone, checking her watch every fifteen seconds.

5

No one came forward to greet us and we settled behind a scarred coffee table stripped of snacks, flowers, candles.

The insurance commercial ran on. Glass rattled from the bar.

Gustave wasn't bent over the slab of polished oak. In his place, a grim, big-chested brunette who looked as if she'd finally given up on a film career mixed what looked like a standard Martini while consulting a cheat-sheet. The concept of gin with a splash of vermouth seemed overwhelming and she grimaced. Clots of moisture created tiny reflecting pools along the bar-top as her fumbling fingers spilled as much booze as they splashed into the glass. She took a deep breath, reached for an olive, shook her head, and put it back in the bowl, health code be damned.

Her third attempt at carving a lemon twist was partially successful and she handed the drink to a server I'd never seen before. Looking too young to be allowed in a place where spirits flowed, he had floppy dish-water hair, a soft chin, and a dangerously overgrown bow tie. His red jacket was a flimsy cotton rental, his black pants ended an inch too soon.

White socks.

Black tennis shoes.

Ralph, the Fauborg's waiter for decades, had never deviated from an impeccable shawl-lapel tux, starched white shirt, plaid cummerbund, and patent-leather bluchers.

Ralph was nowhere to be seen, ditto for Marie, the middle-aged Savannah belle who split busy shifts and offered naughty one-liners with refills.

Red Jacket brought the Martini toward the young woman in white, plodding cautiously like a five-year-old ring-bearer. When he arrived, she dipped her head coquettishly and said something. He scurried back to the bar, returned with three olives and a pearl onion on a saucer.

As the commercial shifted to a pitch for the latest Disney movie, Red Jacket continued to linger at the girl's table, schmoozing with his back to us. She wasn't much older than him, maybe twenty-five, with a sweet oval face and huge eyes. A white silk mini-dress bared sleek legs that tapered into backless silver pumps. A matching silk scarf, creamy as fresh milk, encircled her face. The head covering didn't fit the skimpy dress; winter on top, summer on the bottom.

Her bare arms were smooth and pale, her lashes too long to be real. She used them to good effect on the waiter.

The watch on her right arm sparkled with diamonds as she consulted it again. The waiter made no attempt to leave as she pulled something out of a white clutch. Ivory cigarette holder that she rolled slowly between slender fingers.

Robin said, 'Someone's channeling Audrey Hepburn.'

The girl crossed her legs and the dress rode up nearly crotch-high. She made no attempt to smooth it.

I said, 'Audrey was a lot more subtle.'

'Then someone else from that era. Hey, maybe she's who Dudley Do-Right's guarding.'

I looked around the room. 'Can't see anyone else who'd fit.'

'Someone that cute all alone?'

'She's waiting for someone,' I said. 'That's the fifth time she checked her watch.'

'Maybe that's why I thought of Audrey. *Roman Holiday,* poor little princess all on her lonesome.' She laughed and snuggled against me. 'Listen to us. The chance to be together and we're messing in someone else's business.'

The girl produced a cigarette, fit it into the holder, licked the ivory tip before inserting it between her lips and half smiling at the waiter.

He fumbled in his pockets, shook his head. Out of her clutch came an ivory lighter that she held out to him. He lit her up. She inhaled greedily.

No smoking in bars has been California law for years. When the girl in white created haze, no one protested. A moment later, someone across the room was also blowing nicotine. Then two more orange dots materialized. Then four.

Soon the place was hazy and toxic and oddly pleasant for that. The commercial ended. Music resumed. Some imitation of Roberta Flack being killed softly.

Robin and I had been ignored for nearly ten minutes while Red Jacket lingered with the girl in white. When she turned away from him and began concentrating on her Martini, he returned to the bar, chatted with the befuddled brunette.

Robin laughed. 'I am *definitely* losing my touch.'

'Want to go?'

'And lower my odds for lung cancer? Perish.'

'Okay, I'll go educate Surfer Joe.'

'Be gentle, darling. He's still wrestling with puberty.'

As I stood, the barkeep said something to Red Jacket and he swiveled. Mouthed an O.

Loping over, he grinned. 'Hey. You just get here?'

Robin said, 'Seconds ago.'

'Great . . . er . . . so . . . welcome to the Fowlburg. Can I get you guys something?'

'We guys,' I said, 'will have a Sidecar on the rocks with light sugar on the rim, and Chivas neat, water on the side.'

'A Sidecar,' he said. 'That's a drink, right? I mean, it's not a sandwich. 'Cause the kitchen's basically closed, we just got nuts and crackers.'

'It's a drink,' I said. 'Any wasabi peas left?'

'There's no vegetables anywhere.'

'That's a bar snack. Peas coated with wasabi.'

Blank look.

Despite Robin's soft elbow in my ribs, I said, 'Wasabi's that green horseradish they put on sushi.'

'Oh,' he said. 'We don't got sushi.'

'We'll just take whatever you have.'

'I think we got almonds.' He ticked a finger. 'Okay, so it's Champagne and a . . . Sidecar.'

'A Sidecar and Chivas,' I said. 'That's a blended whisky.'

'Sure. Of course.' Slapping his forehead. 'I never did this before.'

'You're kidding.'

Robin kicked my shin.

'A Sidecar,' he said, repeating it again in a mumble. 'They just called from the temp agency yesterday, said there's a place closing down, you got five hours to get over there if you want it, Neil. Mostly I work in places with no drinking.'

'McDonald's?' I said.

Kick kick kick.

'That was in the beginning,' said Neil. 'Then I did two years at Marie Callender's.' Grin. 'All the pie you can eat, man I was getting fat. Then I lost that and signed up with the temp agency and they sent me here. Too bad it's only one night. This is a cool old place.'

'Sure is. Too bad they're tearing it down.'

'Yeah . . . but that's the way it is, right? Old stuff dies.'

'We'll take those drinks, now. And those almonds, if you have them.'

'Last time I checked we did, but you never know.'

As he turned to leave, the girl in white slipped on oversized, gold-framed sunglasses with lenses so dark they had to be blinding her. Sucking on her cigarette, she twirled the holder, stretched coltish legs, ran a finger along the side of a clean, smooth jaw. Licked her lips.

Red Jacket watched her, transfixed.

Robin said, 'She is beautiful, Neil.'

He wheeled. 'So are you, ma'am. Um . . . oh, man, sorry, that came out weird. Sorry.'

Robin touched his hand. 'Don't worry about it, dear.'

'Um, I better get you those drinks.'

When he was gone, I said, 'See, you've still got it going on.'

'He probably looks at me like I'm his mother.'

I hummed 'Mrs Robinson.' She kicked me harder. But not enough to hurt. Our relationship's not that complicated.

3

THE SIDECAR devolved to a Screwdriver, the Chivas was a whisky slushy, overwhelmed by crushed ice.

We laughed and I tossed bills on the table and we got up to leave.

From across the room, Neil held up his palms in a *What-me-worry* gesture. I pretended not to notice.

As we passed Snow White, her eyes met mine. Big, dark, moist. Not seductive.

Welling with tears?

Her lower lip dropped, then clamped shut. She avoided my glance and smoked single-mindedly.

Suddenly her getup seemed sad, nothing but a costume.

Neil nearly tripped over himself bringing the check but when he saw the cash, he detoured to Snow White's table.

She shook her head and he slinked off.

A commercial for ecologically sound detergent rasped the smoky air.

When we got back outside, Dudley Do-Right was gone.

Robin said, 'Guess we were wrong about Snowy being his charge.'

'Guess we were wrong about taking a final jaunt on the *Titanic*. Let's go somewhere else and try to redeem the night.'

She took my arm as we headed for the Seville. 'Nothing to redeem. I've got you, you've got me, and despite those killer legs, that poor little thing has no one. But sure, some real drinks would be nice. After that, we'll see what develops.'

'Mistress of suspense,' I said.

She tousled my hair. 'Not really, you know the ending.'

I woke at six the following morning, found her at the kitchen window, washing her coffee cup and gazing at the pines and sycamores that rim our property to the east. Polygons of pink and gray sky cut through the green; intensely saturated color, bordering on harsh. Sunrise in Beverly Glen can be brittle splendor.

We walked Blanche for an hour, then Robin headed to her studio and I sat down to finish some child custody reports for the court. By noon, I was done and emailing recommendations to various judges. A few were likely to listen. As I put the hard copy in a drawer and locked up, the doorbell buzzed.

Shave and a haircut, six bits, followed by three impatient beeps.

I padded to the living room. 'It's open, Big Guy.'

Milo pushed the door open and stomped in swinging his battered, olive-vinyl attaché case wide, as if preparing to fling it away. 'Step right in, Mr Manson, then hold the door for Mr Night Stalker.'

'Morning.'

'All these years I still can't convince you to exercise normal caution.'

'I've got you as backup.'

'That and a Uzi won't buy you a Band-Aid if you ignore common sense.' He marched past me. 'Where's the pooch?'

'With Robin.'

'Someone's thinking right.'

My best friend is a gay LAPD homicide lieutenant with inconsistent social skills. He's had a key to the house for years but refuses to use it unless Robin and I are traveling and he checks the premises, unasked.

By the time I made it to the kitchen, he'd commandeered a loaf of rye bread, a jar of strawberry preserves, a half gallon of orange juice, and the butt-end of a four-day-old rib roast.

I said, 'Hey kids, beef 'n' jam, the new taste sensation.'

He cast off a gray windbreaker, loosened a tie the color of strained peas, and settled his bulk at the table. 'First conundrum of the day: carbs or protein. I opt for both.'

Brushing coarse black hair off a lumpy brow, he continued to stare at the food. Bright green eyes drooped more than usual. Where the light hit him wrong, his acne-pocked pallor was a hue no painter had ever blended.

I said, 'Long night?'

'The night was fine, it was the damn morning that screwed things up. Four a.m., why can't people get their faces blown off at a civil hour?'

'People as in multiple victims?'

Instead of answering, he troweled heaps of jam on three slices of bread, chewed the first piece slowly, inhaled the remaining two. Uncapping the juice, he peered inside, muttered, 'Not much left,' and drained the container.

Contemplating the roast, he sliced, cubed, popped morsels of meat like candy. 'Got any of that spicy mayo?'

I fetched some aioli from the fridge. He dipped, chewed, wiped his mouth, snorted, exhaled.

I said, 'Male or female bodies?'

'One body, female.' Crumpling the juice carton, he created a waxed paper pancake that he pulled out like an accordion, then compressed. 'And for my next number, "Lady of Spain."'

A dozen more pieces of roast before he said, 'Female, and from her figure, young. Then again, this is LA so maybe all that tone came courtesy of surgery, let's see what the coroner has to say. No purse or ID, the blood says she was done right there. No tire tracks or footprints. No jewelry or purse and her duds were expensive looking, some designer I never heard of. Patrice Lerange. Ring a bell?'

I shook my head. 'Robbery?'

'Looks like it. She had on fancy undies, too, silk lace – Angelo Scuzzi,

Milano. So maybe she's European, some poor tourist who got waylaid. The shoes were Manolo Blahnik, *that* I heard of.'

He chewed hard and his jaw bunched. 'Looks like we're talking two killers. The CI's found shotgun pellets and wadding in the wound but also a .45 cartridge on the ground and the slug behind her, exactly where you'd expect it to be after blowing out the back of her skull.'

He ate more roast, contemplated a rare piece, put it aside.

'The major damage was to the face with a little pellet spray at the top of the chest. But they left her hands intact, so I'm not sure the face thing was hiding her identity, just plain old evil.'

'Your money or I shoot,' I said. 'On second thought, I shoot anyway.'

'Goddamn savages . . . I know the face can mean personal, but this could come down to a really ugly jack. Hollyweird at night, all those spacey Euro types are wandering the streets, thinking they're gonna catch movie stars. If she was a tourist, she could've wandered into the wrong neighborhood.'

'Where was she found?'

'The Palisades, less than a mile short of Topanga. Bad guys had any consideration it woulda been the sheriff's problem.'

I said, 'That's a ways from wrong neighborhoods, and expensive clothes don't say naive tourist. Maybe she got waylaid on the Strip, or somewhere else on the Westside.'

'Wherever she started, she ended up far from the city. We're talking mountains, ravines, open space, not much traffic. Maybe that was the point. She was left just off the road, a spot where the descent isn't that steep. I'm figuring the bad guys walked her out of the car, took her goodies, had target practice.'

'Bullet and pellets.'

'All in the face. Almost like a ritual.'

'Who found her?'

'Some eighty-nine-year-old retired Unitarian minister combing for fossils.'

'Fossil hunting at four a.m.?'

'Three fifteen a.m. to be exact. He likes to do it when there's no traffic, brings a flashlight, takes his time. Only thing he ever sees is animals – raccoons, rabbits, coyotes – and they're not into archaeology. He said the entire area used to be submerged under seawater millions of years ago, he still finds stuff. He had two spiral seashells in his sack, some petrified snails, too.'

'But no shotgun or .45.'

'I should be so lucky. No, he's righteous, Alex, really shaken up. I had an ambulance brought just in case but they said his heart was strong for his age.' He drummed the table, wiped his face with one hand, like washing without water. 'One mile south it'd be tan-shirts yanked out of a beautiful dream.'

'What were you dreaming about?'

'Not getting yanked out of bed at four a.m.'

'Lately you've been kind of bored.'

'Like hell I have. That was Zen-serenity.'

He ate more roast, topped with extra aioli.

'Spicy.'

'So what can I do for you?'

'Who says anything? I came to visit the dog.' Reaching into a pocket of the windbreaker, he drew out a nylon chew-bone. 'This okay for her?'

'She prefers truffle-marinated elk ribs, but it'll do in a pinch. She's out back with Robin. I've got some mail to catch up on.'

'Had your breakfast yet?'

'Just coffee.'

Swinging his attaché onto the table, he flipped it open, drew out his cell, downloaded a screen of thumbnail photos. Enlarging one, he handed the phone to me. 'No breakfast, nothing to lose.'

The body lay on its face, supple-limbed even in death.

Wind or impact had lifted the hem of the dress nearly crotch-high, but the legs hadn't been spread, no sign of sexual posing.

Short dress. The flow of white silk.

14

Same for the blood-and-gore-splotched white scarf that swaddled what had once been a face. One backless silver shoe remained in place.

What had once been the face was a clotted horror.

Milo said, 'You just turned a really bad color. Sorry.'

'Any idea what time she was killed?'

'Best guess is midnight to four and the old guy was there by three fifteen, so that narrows it.'

'I saw her from nine to nine thirty. She was young – twenty-five or so, sat ten feet from Robin and me. Extremely pretty, big dark eyes, but I can't tell you about her hair because it was completely covered by the scarf. She was wearing a diamond watch, carried a white silk clutch, smoked a cigarette in an ivory holder and used a matching lighter. A few minutes in, she put on rhinestone-framed sunglasses. She seemed to be waiting for someone. There was a theatrical aspect to her behavior. Robin thought she was channeling Audrey Hepburn. No need to show Robin these pictures.'

He inhaled deeply, placed his hands flat on the table. 'Where. Did. This. Happen?'

I described the Fauborg's final night.

'Hotel swan song,' he said. 'Hers, too. Oh, man . . . so maybe she was staying there and I'll get a name from the register.'

'Good luck but doubtful, no one was working the desk and the place looked cleaned out.'

'Someone'll have a record.' He scratched the side of his nose. Sweat stained the table where his paw had rested. 'This is weird, Alex.'

'All the cases we've worked, maybe it was due.'

'Anything else you want to tell me?'

'There was a guy out in front with a Secret Service thing going on – black suit, white shirt, black tie, two-way radio, what looked like a gun bulge. Robin and I assumed it was for her benefit because no one else in the bar looked like they needed protection.'

'Why'd you figure she did?'

'We didn't, she was just the most likely candidate. It's not that she

15

projected vulnerability – maybe she did. She also looked like someone who should be famous but neither of us could place her. She kept checking her watch but when we left no one had showed up. And Mr Black Suit was gone so maybe his gig had nothing to do with her.'

He pulled out his pad. 'What'd this guy look like?'

I told him and he scrawled. 'The waiter might know if anyone showed up. He was paying pretty close attention to her. Some temp named Neil. She vamped for him and he bought it pretty hard.'

'When was closing time?'

'I don't know. You're wondering if they were both there till the end and he tried to pick her up and something went bad?'

'Her clothes and the watch say she was way out of his league but some guys don't convince easily. Give me a detailed physical on this amateur.'

4

DEAD PEOPLE don't answer questions. Sometimes the same goes for dead businesses.

Milo's attempts to get info from the former owners of the Fauborg Hotel proved fruitless. Marcel Jabotinsky's heirs had relocated to Zurich and New York and London and Boulder, Colorado. The hotel had been unoccupied for two months with most of the fixtures sold at auction and the records dumped. No one knew a thing about the temporary staff who'd worked the bar's final night.

A niece in Colorado thought the evening had been coordinated by her cousin in Scarsdale. That woman denied any involvement but believed that an uncle in Switzerland had hired an event-planning outfit.

'Waste of money far as I'm concerned, but Hermann's senile and sentimental.'

Hermann didn't answer his phone. Cold calls to local event co-ordinators pulled up nothing.

I said, 'Neil said he got the gig through a temp agency.'

Plenty of those on the Westside. Brite-Quick, the twelfth company Milo reached, admitted supplying two people to the Fauborg at the request of Madame Estelle Jabotinsky of Park Avenue.

'She sounded pretty old,' said the owner. 'If I'm remembering correctly, the deal was to honor the guy who built the place or something. But she didn't want to spend anything and all she'd go for was two people.'

'Could I have those two names, please?'

'They in trouble?'

'Not at all.'

'Let me emphasize,' said the owner. 'We background-check, they had to come up clean.'

'That's great. The names?'

Sherree Desmond, forty-three, bartender, address in Mount Washington.

Nelson Neil Mutter, twenty-two, waiter, Gower Street, Hollywood.

No criminal history for either. Sherree wasn't fond of paying parking tickets. Nelson who preferred Neil had just applied for a temporary license, requesting reciprocity from DMV Nebraska.

Nebraska said Mutter had been driving since the age of sixteen, maintained a clean record.

'Careful driver,' said Milo. 'Given the state of her face, that doesn't mean much.'

We drove to Mutter's address on Gower. The building took up a third of the block, rising five off-white stories and shading its neighbors. Newish construction but already shabby, with rain streaks smirching the windowsills and stucco peeling at the corners. Potted plants, satellite dishes, and assorted junk filled narrow balconies. Nearly a hundred units behind the iron security gate. With no alphabetization, it took a while to find *Mutter, N* on the button-studded panel.

Unit 105, shared with *Adams, T* and *LaScola, B*.

The door pickets offered a glimpse of a cramped lobby and a red-door elevator. A female voice answered Milo's button-push. 'Yes?'

'Nelson Mutter, please.'

'Sorry, he's out.'

'This is Lieutenant Sturgis, LA Police. Any idea when he'll be back?'

'Is Neil okay?'

'Far as I know, ma'am. I need to talk to him. Where is he?'

'Um . . . I think he went to the Seven-Eleven to get some drinks. Or something.'

'You're his roommate?'

'One of them.'

'Could you come out for a second? Or you can beep us in.'

A beat. 'I'll come down.'

The girl was black, gorgeous, with round gray eyes, apricot curls, and a slim body encased in a hot-pink unitard. Sweatband just under the hairline. Sweat on her cute little button nose. Her arm muscles glistened.

Milo flashed the badge and she opened the gate.

'Thanks,' he said, 'Ms . . .'

'Tasha Adams. I don't really know Neil, we've just been rooming together.' Not a trace of irony.

'How long have you been roomies?'

'A little over two months. It's a one-bedroom, Brenda – my friend – and I share, Neil sleeps on the sofa bed in the living room. We don't charge him a full third. He's really neat, so it's been okay.'

'How'd you guys get together?'

'Craigslist,' said Tasha Adams, as if any other method was prehistoric. 'Brenda and I are dancers, we came out from Chicago to audition for *Rock On*. We got hired then the show got canceled in preproduction but we already signed the lease and besides, we still wanted to try to break in somewhere. Brenda's got a job teaching little kids ballet but I'm living off what I earned last year teaching modern. Neil pays on time and he minds his own business. Why do you want to talk to him?'

'A temp job he did last night.'

'That hotel.'

'He told you about it.'

'He said he finally got a gig through the temp agency but it was only one night, he might have to go back to McDonald's or something.'

'When did he leave the apartment this morning?'

'Hmm,' said Tasha Adams. 'I'd have to say forty minutes ago?'

'Going to the Seven-Eleven.'

'That's where he usually buys his drinks.'

'Beer?'

'No, soda. Neil's straight as they come.'

'What time did he come home last night?'

'I'd have to say . . . eleven?'

'Could it have been later?' said Milo.

'Hmm . . . actually it was probably earlier . . . yeah, for sure, *Teen Cribs* was still on – but almost over. So just before eleven.'

Milo scrawled.

'Is there something you should be telling me?' said Tasha Adams. 'He does live with us.'

'A guest at that hotel ran into some trouble last night, Tasha. Neil's not a suspect, we're just gathering information.'

'Trouble,' she said. 'Like someone – oh, there he is. Hey, Neil, these guys want to talk to you. They're the police.'

Nelson Mutter in a T-shirt, baggy shorts, and flip-flops stopped short. He studied Milo, then me. Mouthed, *Huh?* In one hand was a plastic Dodgers' cup big enough to wash a family of parakeets.

Milo waved him over, shook his hand. 'Neil? Lieutenant Sturgis.'

Mutter kept looking at me.

I said, 'Nice to see you again, Neil.'

'Chi-vash,' he said, as if downloading a memory file on a balky computer. 'Lots of ice. You're police?'

'I work with the police.'

Tasha Adams said, 'It's about your gig last night, Neil.'

'Huh?'

Milo said, 'Let's all go inside.'

As promised, Mutter's personal space – what there was of it – was spotless. The sofa bed was closed up, graced with three floral-print pillows. Mutter's wordly possessions filled two duffels placed to the left of the couch. A glimpse into the single bedroom offered a view of exuberant girl clutter.

Milo said, 'Sorry to displace you, Tasha, but we need to talk to Neil alone.'

'Oh. Okay.' Pouting, she entered the bedroom but left the door open. Milo went over and closed it, motioned Mutter to the sofa. 'Make yourself comfortable, Neil.'

'Can someone tell me what's going on?' Directing the question to me.

Milo said, 'Sit, please,' and when Mutter complied, settled next to him. 'Last night you served a woman in a white dress—'

'The princess,' said Mutter. He blushed scarlet. 'I mean that's what I called her. I mean in my head, not out loud.' To me: 'You can see that, right? She was kind of like a princess?'

I said, 'Sure.'

'Yeah. She also talked like one – did you hear her talk?'

'I didn't.'

'Just like Princess Di. Or someone like that.'

'British?'

'Totally. *Oh-right. Yes, of cawse. Aw-lihvs, please.* Like class, you know? I couldn't believe someone that class was getting flaked on.'

I said, 'She told you she'd been flaked on?'

'Uh-uh,' said Mutter, 'but she kept looking at her watch and the whole time no one showed up. Why would someone flake on someone that class and hot?'

'The watch,' I said. 'Pretty sparkly.'

'Oh, man, total bling. She okay?'

'Did she give you her name?'

'Uh-uh.'

'Did she pay her tab with a credit card?'

'Uh-uh, cash.' He pinched his upper lip. Grubby nails were bitten raw.

'How many drinks did she order?'

'Just two. Hendrick's Martini, twist, *aw-lihvs* on the side – also one of those little onions. Only we didn't have Hendrick's so I asked her if Gilbey's was okay and she said *Cuhtainly.*' He repeated the word, pumping up the drawl. 'Why are you guys asking about her?'

'She had a misfortune, Neil,' said Milo.

'Like a robbery?' said Mutter. 'Oh, man, that watch? How about her sunglasses? She put on these sunglasses and I figured they were rhinestones but maybe they were diamonds, too.'

I said, 'You knew the watch had real diamonds because . . .'

'I – because I just figured. I mean it looked class and she was class.' Looking from me to Milo. 'I didn't figure her for rhinestones.' Shrug. 'But maybe the sunglasses were.'

Milo said, 'Sounds like you paid a lot of attention to the watch.'

The color left Mutter's face. 'No, I'm just saying.'

'Saying what, Neil?'

'She kept checking it and it kept flashing, you know? Also, it was the only bling she had. Except the sunglasses.'

'No rings, no earrings.'

'Uh-uh, not that I saw.'

'How late did she stay at the Fauborg?'

'Maybe another half hour.' Mutter turned to me. 'I mean after you and your lady left.'

I said, 'You're sure no one showed up to join her.'

'Totally.'

'When did your shift end?'

'Ten.' Mutter frowned. 'Sherree – the bartender – got paid to stay later, like till twelve, but they didn't want to pay me for longer than till ten.'

I said, 'I left around nine thirty so if she left half an hour later, that would be ten.'

'Guess so.'

'That means you and she walked out around the same time.'

'Uh-uh, she left before me,' said Mutter. 'My shift ended at ten but then I had to change out of that stupid jacket and clean the tables, then I had to walk to my car, which was like three blocks away in a city lot because the place had no parking.'

'What street you park on?' said Milo.

'Same street as the hotel but down near Wilshire.'

'Crescent Drive.'

'Yeah.'

'You have a parking stub?'

'Why would I?'

'You didn't see her when you left?'

'Nope.'

'Where'd you go after you got your car?'

'Where?'

'Where was your next stop, Neil.'

'There was no stop,' said Mutter. 'I drove here.'

'What time did you get home?'

'Around . . . probably ten forty. Tasha was up watching TV.'

'What was she watching?'

'Teen Cribs.' He lowered his voice, smiled. 'Lame, but she likes it. Sometimes I watch with her 'cause I can't crash until she and Brenda are finished with the couch.'

'Kinda inconvenient, Neil.'

'I only pay two hundred a month. I don't find a real job soon, I'm gonna have to head back to Omaha. What happened to Princess?'

'For someone without a steady job, a diamond watch could solve a lotta problems.'

Mutter's eyes bugged. 'Oh, no, no way, no way, no way. That's not the person I am, even when I worked for Mickey D I didn't take an extra sesame seed, just what we got with the employee discount. Uh-uh, no way.'

He crossed himself. Protest had firmed and deepened his voice. His chin seemed stronger, too, as if proclaiming his innocence had triggered a burst of testosterone.

Shaking his head, he said, 'Uh-uh, no way and I don't know why you're saying that, why would you say that?'

'You were among the last people to see her.'

'You can check my stuff, there's no watch or nothing. You can put me on a lie-detector, whatever.'

I said, 'Did you notice anyone else at the bar who looked shady?'

'Buncha old people,' he said. 'And you guys.'

Milo and I remained silent.

'This is psycho,' said Mutter. 'I served her two drinks, she tipped me twenty bucks and she left.'

I said, 'Did she give you any details about herself?'

'Nothing. That was the *thing*.'

'The thing?'

'She was like super-nice and sometimes when people are like that it's 'cause they want you to pay attention so they can talk about themselves. Not so much at Mickey D's, people come in and out real fast. But at Marie Callender's I was always hearing stories when I served the pie. But she was just nice to be nice.'

'She didn't want attention,' I said, remembering the theatrical posing.

'It kind of makes sense if she's someone famous. Not like stupid-famous – like brats on *Teen Cribs*, got their own house, Game Boys, rides.'

'A different kind of famous.'

'Like a princess but nobody knows her unless she wants, you know?' said Mutter. 'First time I saw her, that's what I thought. She's probably famous but I don't know enough.' Smiling. 'She was nice and really hot. Hope she gets her watch back.'

5

WE LEFT Mutter sitting on the sofa bed and drinking his Big Gulp.

Milo slipped behind the wheel of the unmarked. 'Unless Tasha's lying for him, the time frame clears him.'

'He was good for one thing,' I said. 'Her accent. So maybe it will come down to a waylaid tourist.'

'Let's see what Big Brother has to say about recent entries of young, cute UK citizens.'

He put in a call to 'Ralph' at Homeland Security, got a voice-mail litany that necessitated six button-pushes, finally left a vague message about 'the British invasion.'

I said, 'They've got that kind of data at their fingertips?'

'So they claim. All part of the war on terrorism – 'scuse me, the alleged struggle with alleged man-made disasters. Now let's work on my disaster.'

At West LA station, we climbed the stairs and passed the big detective room. Milo's closet-sized office is well away from the other D's, at the end of a narrow hall housing sad, bright interview rooms where lives change.

Closet-sized allotment; he claims the privacy makes it worthwhile. Grow up in a large family, you appreciate any kind of space.

His lone-wolf status began years ago, when he was the only openly gay detective in the department, and continued as part of a deal cut with a previous police chief, a man with a media-friendly demeanor and slip-pery ethics. Working a long-cold murder case handed Milo enough info to ruin the boss. The barter got the chief honorable retirement with full pension and earned Milo promotion to lieutenant, with continuation as a detective and none of the desk work that went with the rank.

The new chief, brutal and statistics-driven, learned that Milo's close rate was the highest in the department and chose not to fix the unbroken.

When he closes the door to the office, it starts to feel like a coffin but I'm getting used to that. I've been slightly claustrophobic since child-hood, a souvenir of hiding from an enraged, alcoholic father in coal bins, crawl spaces, and such. Working with Milo has been therapeutic on many levels.

I wedged into a corner as he wheeled his desk chair inches from my face, swung long legs onto the desk, loosened his tie and suppressed a belch. A sudden reach for a pen knocked a pile of papers to the floor. On top was a memo from Parker Center marked *Urgent*. When I moved to pick up the sheaf, he said, 'Don't bother, it's all trash.'

He pulled a panatela out of a desk drawer, unwrapped, bit off the end and spit it into the wastebasket. 'Any additional wisdom?'

I said, 'Mr Walkie-Talkie intrigues me. Not a friendly sort. And his being gone doesn't mean much, he could've ducked somewhere.'

'Bodyguard turns on his charge?'

'Or his charge was the person she was waiting for and he'd slipped away to attend to the boss. Someone she was eager to be with from the way she kept looking at her watch. Someone she was intimate with.'

'Girl in designer duds and a diamond watch wouldn't hang with Joe Sixpack. Some rich guy confident enough to keep her waiting.'

'And Black Suit could've chauffeured the two of them – his clothes would fit a driver, too. Or he followed them in a separate vehicle. At some point, the date went really bad and the two of them shot her. Or the plan all along was to kill her. Either way, finding him might help and I got a good look at him.'

'Lots of private muscle in town, but sure, why not.'

Booting up, he searched, printed a list of LA security firms, made a few calls, got nowhere. Plenty of companies left to contact, but he swung his feet back to the floor. 'Wanna see the crime scene?'

On the way out, he picked up the fallen papers, checked the urgent message, tossed everything.

'Chief's office keeps bugging me to attend ComStat meetings. I've dodged most of them, including the one today, but just in case they bust me, let's take separate cars.'

He drove me home, where I picked up the Seville and followed him back to Sunset. We sped west and after a brief ride north on PCH, he hooked east and climbed toward the northwestern edge of the Palisades.

He turned onto a street lined with stilt-houses defying geology. The residences thinned, vanished as the road narrowed to chasm-hugging ribbon furling the green mountainside. The sky was clear. The world was as bright and pretty as a child's drawing.

It took a while for him to stop. I parked behind him and we crossed the road.

He stretched, loosened his tie. 'Nothing like country air.'

I said, 'The ride from your office was thirty-eight minutes, allowing for the stop at my place. Beverly Hills is farther east, so even with less traffic at night, we're talking about that much time. If Mutter was accurate about her leaving the Fauborg around ten and the time of death was closer to midnight than two, she was done quickly. That could indicate a premeditated abduction and execution. If, on the other hand, the TOD's closer to two, the killer had plenty of time to be with her and we could be looking at something drawn-out and sadistic. Any ligature marks or evidence she was restrained?'

'Not a scratch, Alex. If there was any disabling it wasn't hard-core. Wanna get closer?'

Like movie sets, crime scenes are elaborate but short-lived creations. Scrapings are taken, plaster casts harden, shells are searched for, bagging and tagging and photography ensue at a steady pace. Then the vans drive off and the yellow tape is snipped and the blood's hosed away and everyone goes home except the flies.

No flies, here, despite lingering blood on the dirt, dried to rust-colored dust. But for a slight depression where the body had rested and stake-holes for the tape, this was lovely California terrain.

Under last night's skimpy stars, it would've been ink-black.

I recalled Princess's face, the carefully crossed legs. The posturing, the blinding sunglasses. Smoking with aplomb.

The spot where Princess had been found was a plateau just steps off the road, invisible to motorists. You'd have to walk the area to know about it. Maybe fifteen feet by ten, dotted with low scrub, pebbles, twigs.

I said, 'Not a scratch also means she wasn't rolled or dumped, more like laid down gently. That also points to a prior relationship.'

I paced the area. 'It was a warm night, love under the stars might've sounded like a good idea. If she got out of the car ready to play, there'd be no need to restrain her.'

'Instead of kissy-poo, she gets boom? Nasty.'

'Nasty and up close and personal,' I said. 'The darkness could've shrouded the gun, she might never have known what hit her. Can I see your phone again?'

He loaded the pictures. I endured every terrible image. 'The way she's lying, she was definitely positioned. And except for that spillover on top, she's pristine below the face. This was no robbery, Big Guy. Maybe the watch was taken because her hot date gave it to her in the first place.'

'Bad breakup,' he said.

'The worst.'

Milo sniffed the air like a hound, jammed his hands into his pockets, and shut his eyes. A pair of raptors, too distant to identify, circled high above. One swooped, the other continued surveillance. The first bird shot up and nosed its mate with *Look-what-I've-got* exuberance and the couple glided out of sight.

Something else had died; brunch was on.

He said, 'Robin also get a look at Black Suit?'

I nodded.

'And she's an artistic girl. Think she could do me a drawing?'

'I suppose.'

'There's a problem?'

'She's better than average but drawing's not her thing.'

'Ah.'

'Also,' I said, 'I haven't told her anything.'

'Oh.'

Up on the road, I said, 'I'll have to tell her eventually, so sure, let's ask her.'

'If it's gonna upset her, Alex, forget it. If you can describe him in enough detail, I can get Petra or one of our other sketch-demons. And if one of those rent-a-goon outfits gives me a lead, I might not need any talent at all. Let's get outta here.'

I walked him to the unmarked.

'Thanks for the cogitation,' he said. 'The whole intimacy thing, that's feeling right.'

'Ask Robin to draw.'

'You're sure.'

'Go for it.'

He shrugged. 'Whatever you say. I know you like to protect her.'

'She's on a project with a deadline, I didn't want to distract her.'

'Sure,' he said. 'That was it.'

I followed him back to the station, where he called a few more security companies with no success. I used the time to check for messages.

Despite the joys of mechanization, I keep an answering service because I like talking to actual people. Lucette, one of the more durable operators, said, 'Hey, Dr Delaware. Looks like I got . . . five for you.'

A family court judge I'd never heard of wanted to confer about a custody case. His surname had lots of consonants and I had her spell it.

The second call was from a Glendale pediatrician who'd interned at Western Pediatric back when I was a psych fellow. She wanted advice on a failure-to-thrive infant that might be Munchausen by proxy.

Lucette said, 'The other three are all from the same person, came in starting at nine, half an hour apart. And I'm talking thirty minutes precisely. Ms Gretchen Stengel.' She read off the number. 'The first two were just her name and number, the third was kind of a strange conversation. If you don't mind my saying.'

'Strange, how?'

'She sounded pretty nervous, Dr Delaware, so I asked her if it was an emergency. She went quiet, like she had to think about that, finally said she couldn't honestly say it was an emergency and nowadays she needed to be honest. To me that sounded like some kind of twelve-step thing, you know? But you know me, Dr Delaware, I'm just here to help, never put my two cents in.'

The last time – the only time – I'd met the Westside Madame was almost a decade ago.

Restaurant on the trendoid stretch of Robertson just below Beverly Boulevard. A few storefronts north of Gretchen Stengel's short-lived boutique.

Her play at legitimacy. Lack of crime did not pay.

I'd been tagging along with Milo as he worked the death of a beautiful young woman named Lauren Teague who'd once been part of Gretchen's call girl stable. Gretchen had just finished serving two-thirds of a thirty-two-month sentence for tax evasion. Still in her thirties, she'd come across prematurely aged, sullen, unkempt, quite likely stoned.

Her arrest and trial four years previous had been nectar for the media and every wrong turn in her life had been retracted, probed, and aspirated like a surgical wound.

She'd grown up rich and privileged, the daughter of two high-powered lawyers at Munchley, Zabella, and Carter – a firm since diminished and eventually destroyed by malfeasance and corruption, so maybe character issues had laced the family's chromosomes.

Education at the Peabody School, summers in Venice and Provence, frequent-flier status on the Concorde, socializing with celebs and the people who created them.

All that had distilled to drug and alcohol abuse by adolescence, six abortions by age fourteen, dropping out of college to take on self-abasing roles in bottom-feeder porn loops. Somehow that had led to a seven-figure income running beautiful, fresh-faced girls, some of them Peabody alumnae, out of the better lounges and hostelries of prime-zip-code LA.

Gretchen's trick-book was rumored to be hours of fascinating reading but somewhere along the line it vanished and despite rumors of LAPD enmity, her eventual plea bargain was a sweetheart deal.

Now she was calling me. Three times in one morning. On the half hour precisely; shrinks and hookers are both good at sticking to timetables.

Not an emergency. I need to be honest.

That did sound like rehab-talk.

Milo slammed the phone down, studied the single-spaced list of rent-a-cop outfits. The place his finger rested said he'd barely made a start.

'This is gonna take time.'

'If you don't need me—'

'Yeah, yeah, sure, go have a life, someone should.'

On the way home, I phoned the judge and the pediatrician. The custody case sounded ugly and probably futile and I begged off. The failure-to-thrive lacked any hallmarks of Munchausen by proxy and I gave the doctor some differential diagnoses and suggested she get gastro and neuro consults on the baby but continue to keep an eye on the parents.

That left Gretchen Stengel.

Eager to talk to me. But no emergency.

I shut down the hands-off, put on music, took the long way home.

Wonderful sounds filled the car. More than music; Oscar Peterson doing impossible things with a piano.

LA rule number one: When in doubt, drive.

6

Robin cried.

Wiping away tears, she laid her chisel down, stepped away from her workbench. Laughed, as if that would reverse the emotional tide. 'No sense staining a nice piece of Adirondack.'

A finger traced the edge of the spruce slab she'd been shaping. The beginning of a guitar top. Spec job, no deadline.

I said, 'I figured you'd want to know. Sorry if you didn't.'

'I'm being a baby, she was a total stranger.' Spots appeared on sawdust and she swiped at her eyes again. 'Damn.'

Blanche waddled over and nosed the shavings. I bent down and petted her. Her eyes remained fixed on Robin.

'When did it happen?'

'A few hours after we saw her.'

'That's crazy,' she said. 'How'd you figure out it was her?'

'Milo came by this morning, showed me crime scene photos.'

'How'd she die?'

'Shot.'

'Where?'

'That's important?'

'You know me, baby. I code the world visually.'

Exactly.

I said, 'In her face.'

She flinched. 'How vicious. Such a beautiful face. And now you're on it?'

'Mostly I've been tagging along.'

'Sure, I'll draw, but I don't know if I can come up with anything good. If I don't, I'll sit down with a real artist.'

'I could do that.'

'So can I,' she said. 'I'd like to do something.' Leaning on her bench. 'Poor, poor thing. It's like we were predestined to be there, Alex.'

I put my arm around her.

She said, 'Whenever they want me, let me know.'

'Okay.'

I kissed her.

She said, 'You didn't tell me earlier because . . .'

'I needed to digest it, myself.'

'Sure. That explains it.'

'I—'

'I love you, too, baby.' She walked to her drafting table. 'I'm going to give it a try, right now.'

Four attempts were crumpled. Examining the fifth, she said, 'This'll have to do.'

Spare but accurate likenesses of the girl in white and the man in black. More than enough for the evening news.

I said, 'A-plus.'

'More like C-minus. It's just lines and shadows, I didn't capture a whit of their personalities.'

'I'm not sure we saw her real personality, Rob.'

'What do you mean?'

'When's the last time you saw someone use a cigarette holder? It felt like she was playing a role.'

She climbed off her stool. 'That *was* high drama, wasn't it?' She studied the drawing some more, brushed a curl of eraser lint from the girl's mouth. 'I'm not happy with these. They're missing something.'

'I'm sure Milo will be happy.'

'Let me sit down with a real artist and work on it until it's perfect, Alex. I've got a few people I can call. Ask Milo if it's okay to bring in a civilian.'

As opposed to us.

She frowned at the drawing of the man. Lifted the drawing of the girl. 'Playing dress-up for some bastard who keeps her waiting then ends up doing *that*.'

'Or he stood her up and she met someone else. At this point, anything's possible.'

'I knew there was something off about him.' Jabbing the drawing on the table. 'He looked so hostile. If he was a real Secret Service guy doing an actual job, you could understand that. You'd want that. But being part of some sick drama? Creepy, definitely creepy. If Milo's okay with it, I'll call Nigel Brooks, see if he'll help with some real drawing. Better yet, Sam Ansbach, portraiture's his thing, he's just back from a show in New York.'

Frowning. 'On the other hand, Sam's not exactly a law enforcement fan, what with that restraining order his ex foisted on him, stupid mixup put him in jail for three days. So Nigel, first.'

She phoned Brooks's Venice studio. Out of town for a month.

'I'll try Sam, worst he can do is say no.'

'Maybe we don't need a civilian,' I said. 'Petra Connor used to be a professional artist.'

'Good point, I've seen her work, she's good. Fine, arrange it, and I'll head over to Hollywood. Once Milo gets both their faces on the news, maybe he can solve this quickly.'

Milo was still at his desk. 'Great, hold tight.'

Minutes later: 'Petra's in Atlanta for a conference but she told me there's a new Hollenbeck guy named Shimoff – a fellow Alexander – did some training at Otis before joining the department. Is Robin up for it if he's available today?'

'Raring to go.'

'So she took it okay.'

'She's a tough girl,' I said. 'No progress with the security firms?'

'No one owns up to a Fauborg gig. Jernigan called from the coroner's just before you did. Our princess was a natural brunette who enhanced herself with dye. No sign of strangulation or stab wounds or blunt-force trauma, death due to exsanguination as a consequence of gunshot wounds. Autopsy's in the queue but swabs from all intact orifices bear no semen, blood, or signs of trauma. As to the state of her mouth, the damage is too great to rule anything out. But Jernigan's not feeling a sexual attack. She did think it weird that two guys shot her at the same time in the same relatively small target area. Said that felt like a firing-squad execution. And that got me wondering: Some enraged boyfriend wants to blast her away and take back his watch, why share the fun? I can see bringing muscle along for security, but when the time came to pull the trigger, why not go solo?'

'Could be cowardice,' I said. 'Or lack of experience. Someone unaccustomed to firearms might want reassurance.'

'Ready aim fire,' he said. 'Or it could be some kind of sick game. Okay, let's get those faces out there, maybe someone'll come up with an ID. By the way, I checked out those designers – Lerange, Scuzzi. Both are high-end but kind of obscure. And not carried in any local outlets. A few stores in New York stock individual pieces but none of them could help much. That and Princess's Brit accent says I shouldn't give up on a foreign visitor but the Homeland Hoohahs haven't called back yet. So as of now, I'm majoring in art appreciation. Let's see about this Otis guy.'

Ten minutes later he left a message. Detective I Alexander Shimoff had a day off but could meet Robin anytime until nine p.m. at his home in the Pico-Robertson district.

I'd missed his call because I'd been talking to someone else.

7

GRETCHEN STENGEL answered her phone after one ring. 'I'm me, who are you?'

Her voice was low, hoarse. The tail-end of each word faded.

'This is Dr Delaware returning your call.'

'Doc,' she said. 'Been a while, huh?'

'What can I—'

'You do remember me.'

'I do.'

'Been told I'm hard to forget,' she said.

I waited.

'All those years ago, huh, Doc?' Coughing. 'Not exactly good times.'

'No one likes visits from the police.'

'The unspoken message: especially a pimp.'

I said, 'My messages tend to be spoken. What can I do for you, Gretchen?'

She barked laughter, slid into a coughing fit, caught her breath with a sharp intake of air. 'Now that we're BFFs, may I call you Doctor?' Giggling.

I didn't answer.

She said, 'I can see you sitting there, with that stony shrink look.'

'Pure granite.'

'What – oh, ha, funny. Okay, sorry for being a wiseass. It's just that I get that way when I'm dying.'

She coughed some more. 'I don't mean like some fucking comic bombing. Dying literally. As in the cells will soon go sleepy-bye.'

'I'm sorry.'

'Trust me, I'm sorrier than you. Springing it on you was a little naughty of me, huh? But there's no easy way. Like when cops go tell families someone's been murdered. Your gay buddy must love that, no?'

I didn't answer.

She said, 'I've been watching a lot of cop shows. Seeing it from the other side's perspective has been educational.' Sigh. Throat clear. 'Anyway, I'm on the way out. Kaput.'

'Would you like to come in to talk about it?'

'Not a chance,' she said. 'There's nothing to say. I lived what they call a high-risk life. Cleaned-and-sobered-up for seven years but kept dating Tommy Tobacco. My lungs never stopped bitching at me to quit, I didn't, so they got pissed and cultivated a nice little bumper crop of tumors. I went through one course of chemo, asked the oncologist if there was a purpose to any of it and he was such a pussy, hemmed and hawed, that I got my answer. So I said, screw that noise, time to exit gracefully.'

There's nothing to say.

She gasped. 'Feels like I just ran the marathon. Not that I ever did that. Did anything healthy.' Laughter. 'You're a good shrink, I feel better already.' Inhalation. *'Not.'*

'What can I do for you, Gretchen?'

'Meaning why if I'm going to be snotty am I bugging you? It's not about me. It's my kid. One of the first things I did when I got out of rehab was find a nice anonymous sperm donor. Don't ask why, I don't know why, it just seemed like the thing to do. Kind of easy, I didn't even need to lie about how big his cock was. Anyway, the result was Chad. So now I've got a six-year-old male BFF and I'm going to fuck up his life by bailing and I don't know' – gasp – 'what to do about it. So I figured, why not you? So what do you do with a six-year-old? Play therapy? Cognitive behavioral therapy? For sure not existential therapy, I mean Chad's big angst is not enough TV.'

Ragged laughter. 'Been reading psych books, too.'

'I'd be happy to help. Before I see Chad, you and I need to talk.'

'Why?'

'For me to take a history.'

'I can give you that right now.'

'It needs to be in person.'

'Why?'

'It's the way I work, Gretchen.'

'Into control, huh?'

'If it doesn't work for you, I'll be happy to—'

'It works, it works fine,' she said. 'When do we do this history?'

'Are you healthy enough to come to my office?'

'Mobility's a day-to-day thing. But don't worry, if I cancel, I'll still pay you, I know you guys are big on that.'

'If you're not too far, I could come to you.'

'Like a house call?' she said. 'You're punking me.'

'Where do you live?'

'BH adjacent, got a nice little condo on Willaman off Burton.'

'Close enough. What's a good time?'

'Anytime. It's not like I'm flying to Paris.'

I checked my book. 'How about tomorrow at eleven?'

'House call,' she said. 'You're really going to do that.'

'Unless you have a problem with it.'

'My only problem is I'm going to be shutting my eyes forever, and who knows if Hell really exists,' she said. 'Hey, does this mean you're going to charge me for drive time, the way lawyers do? Nice way to pump up the hourly.'

'The hourly will be the same.'

Silence.

'Sorry,' she said. 'That was assholishly ungrateful. I've never had much of a filter and cancer's no mood enhancer.'

'Tomorrow at eleven,' I said.

'Besides no filter, I'm also a control freak who wants everything buttoned up to the max. What is the hourly?'

I told her.

'Not bad,' she said. 'Back in the day, I had girls giving blow jobs for more than that.'

I said, 'Free enterprise is a many-splendored thing.'

She laughed. 'Maybe you're not as stiff as I thought. Maybe this could work.'

8

AT SEVEN thirty p.m., Milo, Robin, and I arrived at the Shenandoah Street apartment of artist-turned-cop Alexander Shimoff.

Shimoff's flat was on the ground floor. He stood outside his door wearing gray sweats and drinking from a half-gallon bottle of ginger ale. Thirtyish, with a prematurely gray Caesar cut, he was built like a tennis player, had facial bones just a bit too large for the pale skin that cased them.

Milo made the introductions.

Shimoff smiled and shook with a slightly limp hand. No real accent to his speech but a slight stretching of syllables suggested birth in another country.

Standing in the living room were a young, rosy-cheeked platinum-blond wife and two little girls around four and six. The kids were curious but compliant as their mother hustled them to their room, talking in Russian. Shimoff's easel, drawing table, and weathered oak flat file took up half of the meager space. Most of the rest was given over to games and toys. A big-screen Mac sat atop the file, along with brushes in pots and an array of pencils and pens. A nearly completed painting – dead-on replica of Picasso's *Blue Guitarist* – occupied the easel.

Milo whistled appreciatively. 'You could get into serious trouble for that.'

Shimoff's grin was lopsided. 'Only if I put it on eBay for ten bucks.'

He turned to Robin. 'I looked up your website. Beautiful instruments. Someone who can do that, my guess is they can draw pretty good.'

'Not good enough,' she said.

'Show me what you've produced.'

Robin handed him the sketches of Princess and Black Suit.

Shimoff studied them for several moments. 'If the proportions are okay, this gives me plenty to work with. Describe them like you would to a stranger. Start with the guy because he's the easy one; once we're in the groove, we'll work our way to her.'

Milo said, 'Why's he easier?'

'Because women are complex.' Shimoff climbed onto his stool, faced a blank piece of white Bristol board, flexed his neck as if preparing for a wrestling match. To Robin: 'Even though we're just doing the face, tell me how tall he is.'

Robin said, 'Six one or two. Heavily built, but not fat.'

'Football, not sumo,' said Shimoff.

'Not a tackle. Maybe a halfback. Thirty to thirty-five years old, he could be of Nordic or Germanic extraction—'

'Could be or probably?'

She thought. 'There could be some Celtic in there – Scottish or Irish. Or maybe Dutch. But if I had to bet, I'd say Nordic. Definitely nothing Mediterranean and that includes northern Italian.'

'You drew the hair light. We talking blond?'

'It was at night. What I saw was pale.'

Shimoff touched his own steely coif. 'Plenty of good-looking silver dudes. But you'd bet on blond, right?'

'Right.'

'Eye color?'

'Couldn't tell.'

'He's blond, we'll go with anonymous pale.' Scanning her sketch. 'The eyes, you got them as kind of piggy.'

'They were piggy,' said Robin. 'But wide-set, maybe even wider than

I drew them. Squinty, which could've been him trying to look tough, or they really are squinty. One thing I remember now that I didn't include is he had a heavy brow — a shelf right here. Low hairline, too. His hair didn't stay down like yours, it stuck up.'

'Mousse or gel?' said Shimoff.

'Quite possibly. No sideburns, he clipped them way up here. Pug nose, possibly even smaller than I showed.'

'Possibly broken?' said Shimoff. 'Fits with the football build.'

'Good point,' she said.

'Pug as well as high-bridged.'

'Not as high as Milo's but definitely on the high side.'

Milo measured the space between his nose and upper lip with two fingers. Shrugged.

Robin said, 'His ears were really close-set.' She frowned. 'I keep remembering things I omitted. He had no lobes. And they were a little pointy at the top. Right here. Elfin, I guess. But there was nothing cute about him. The lips I got pretty accurately: the upper really was this thin. Almost invisible and the lower was full.'

Shimoff picked up a pencil. 'Wish they were all this easy.'

He worked slowly, meticulously, stepping back from the drawing to take in a long view, rarely erasing. Forty minutes later, two likenesses had materialized. To my eye, stunningly accurate.

Robin said, 'What do you think, Alex?'

'Perfect.'

She studied the drawings. 'I'd lift her eyebrow a bit on the right side. And his neck could be a little thicker, so there's a bulge where it feeds into his collar.'

Shimoff tinkered, sat back, appraised his work. 'Beautiful girl. Now back to Picasso.'

Milo said, 'Picasso looks finished to me.'

Shimoff smiled. 'You are spared the pain, Lieutenant.'

'Of what?'

'Being an artist.'

Milo called LAPD Public Affairs from the Seville, put the phone on speaker.

'Got a couple artist renderings I need on the media A-sap. A Jane Doe 187 and a possible suspect.'

The PA officer said, 'One second,' in a voice that said nothing mattered less.

For the next four minutes a public service announcement on domestic violence took the place of live speech.

A new voice said, 'Hi, Lieutenant Sturgis. This is Captain Emma Roldan from the chief's office.'

'I was just on the phone with—'

'Public Affairs,' said Roldan. 'They passed along your request, it will be prioritized appropriately. You should be notified as to its disposition by noon tomorrow.'

'All I asked was for a couple of drawings to be—'

'We'll do our best, Lieutenant. Good night.'

'Anyone else calls PA, PA handles it. I call PA, you handle it.'

'Chief's standing orders,' said Roldan. 'You get extraspecial treatment.'

The next morning at ten thirty, just as I set out for Gretchen Stengel's place, Milo called in.

'Princess's face will be flashed on the news tonight but no dice on Black Suit. I have failed to establish sufficient cause linking the two of them and unnecessary exposure of an innocent individual could have dire legal consequences. Let's hope she pulls up some tips. One thing for sure, she ain't royalty. If Homeland Security can be believed.'

'No princesses on holiday in SoCal?'

'Just the ones born in BH and Bel Air. They did send me passport photos of young women loosely matching the description, I followed up and everyone's alive. I faxed Shimoff's drawing of Black Suit to the security companies. Nada. All this futility's making me hungry. You up for lunch?'

'When?'

'Now.'

'I've got an appointment at eleven.'

'Seeing patients again?'

I hummed.

'Got it,' he said. 'Much as I enjoy your company, the gastrointestinal tract will not hold out, so we go our respective ways. Sayonara.'

9

LITTLE SANTA Monica Boulevard turns into Burton Way past Crescent, so cruising by the Fauborg on the way to Gretchen's was preordained.

Two jagged crumbling stories stood where there'd once been four. A skyscraping crane hovered above the ruins, a steel mantis poised to strike. The colossal machine idled as hard hats purchased nutrition from a roach coach. A man wearing an orange *Supervisor* vest noticed me as he chewed his burrito.

'Do something for you?'

'Just looking. I was here the other night.'

'What was it, some kind of old-age home?'

'Something like that.'

'Real piece a shit,' he said. 'Going down like paper.'

Gretchen's building was four intact stories of sage-green, neo-Italianate exuberance dressed up by gnarled olive trees planted in gravel. *Il Trevi* in gilt topped the sales sign out front. Fifteen luxury two- and three-bath units (*All Sold! See Our Sister Project on Third Street!*), the apartments rimmed an atrium fenced with iron but open to street view. A stone fountain burbled.

I was buzzed up to Gretchen's top-floor unit without comment. She waited in her doorway, wearing a pink housecoat and fuzzy white mules and breathing with the aid of an oxygen tank on wheels. A plastic tube dangled from her nostrils. She pulled it out and it hissed like a snake.

Showing me brown, eroded teeth, she gripped my hand between both of hers and squeezed.

Her skin was cold and papery. The housecoat billowed on a wasted frame but her face was bloated. What remained of her hair was white lint.

I'd researched her last night. Despite the passage of time, she pulled up more hits than ten years' worth of Nobel Prize winners. Various bios listed various birth dates but each put her at barely into middle age. She looked seventy-five.

'Beauty fades,' she said, 'but obnoxious lingers. Come on in.'

Her living room was twice the size of Alex Shimoff's but ten times as many toys piled in the center gave it the same cramped feel.

Walking three steps to the nearest couch winded her. She stopped to reinsert the air line.

She eased herself down on the sofa. I pulled a facing chair three feet away.

'House call from a shrink, this has to be a first. Or maybe I'm being my old narcissistic self and you do this for everyone.'

I smiled.

'Don't do that,' she said. 'Give that blank, neutral shrink smile and make me sweat for every damn sentence. I'm working against a bit of a deadline.' A sharp, white knuckle rapped the side of the tank. 'Pun intended.'

I said, 'No, I don't do it for everyone.'

She clapped her hands. 'So I *yam* special!'

Where the room wasn't snowed by toys it was bland furniture, generic rugs, floral prints on the walls where crayon drawings weren't taped. Drawn drapes turned the space a gray one shade darker than Gretchen's complexion.

'Chad's artistic,' she said. 'Smart, too, I lucked out in the sperm department. They used to use med students as donors, now, who knows? All I learned about my personal masturbator is that he's of English–German descent, taller than average, and free of genetic diseases. For the first year I kept imagining him – different hims, actually, the images started flipping like cards. What I ended up with was Brad Pitt mixed with Albert Einstein. Then Chad started talking and became a real person and it was just the two of us, I stopped thinking about my silent partner.'

She scanned a couple of drawings. 'What do you think of Chad's artwork? I'll put money you don't find anything neurotic or psychotic in them.'

The drawings were age-appropriate for a six-year-old boy. Many bore *Mommy I love you*s.

'Brilliant, huh?' said Gretchen.

'Excellent.'

'We started with crayons, then he was too good for crayons so I got him these incredible pencils from Japan. That's what he used on that peacock – over in the corner. Go look.'

Searching for that drawing put her kitchenette in view. Cans of spaghetti, boxes of cookies, bags of chips. The refrigerator was veneered with photos of her and a round-faced, dark-haired boy. In the early ones, Gretchen still looked like Gretchen.

The peacock battled with a dinosaur. From the blood and the feathers, score one for the reptile team.

'Vivid,' I said.

'You messed up your line. You were supposed to say, *What an excellent mom you are, Gretchen, to produce the next Michelangelo.*'

'You're doing great as a mom, Gretch—'

'Because it's all about *me me me,*' she said. 'I'm a me-ist, that's always been my diagnosis. "Narcissistic personality disorder with histrionic elements." Oh, yeah, "exacerbated by substance abuse." You agree?'

'I'm not here to diagnose you.'

'That's what the shrink my defense team hired said I was. Narcissistic and a junkie. The key was to make me look intensely screwed up so I could avoid responsibility. I wasn't supposed to read the report but I insisted they show it to me because I was paying for it. It makes sense to you?'

'Legally, it was yours—'

'Not that,' she said. 'What the turkey wrote about me. "Narcissism, histrionic, dope." That fit your diagnosis?'

'Let's talk about Chad.'

Her eyes fluttered. She fiddled with the air hose. 'Just tell me this: How *narcissistic* am I if I devote the last six years of my life to my child? How *histrionic* am I if I never show him anything but a calm, happy face? How big of a dope fiend am I if I've been clean and sober for seven fucking years?'

'Good point.'

'But I'm stuck with that damn diagnosis. In my head – like that bastard passed a sentence on me. Like it's my eye color and I'm stuck with it.'

She cleared her throat, coughed, swooned, adjusted a valve on the air tank. 'I wanted to kill that shrink. Judging me. Now I'd be happy if what he put down was my only diagnosis.'

I nodded.

'Yeah, yeah, up and down goes the head,' she said. 'Been to a lot of you guys, my parents didn't give up on me till I was fourteen. I have to tell you, most of your colleagues were losers. So how could I respect their opinions? Know why I picked you? It wasn't because I remembered you from when your gay buddy hassled me. I mean I did remember, but that wasn't the point. Know what it was?'

'Not a clue.'

'A woman I used to do yoga with, one of the few people who still has the balls to keep visiting me, referred you. Marie Blunt.'

Marie, now an A-level interior designer, had once been a showgirl. The court had asked me to evaluate her kids for custody. The show-girl years had come out, but nothing more. Now I wondered if she'd dabbled in Gretchen's world.

'Silent treatment, Doc. Yeah, yeah, you can't admit you know her, I get it. But I'm sure we can both agree Marie's a saint. Even her idiot ex recognizes that now, but she's too smart to take him back. She said when the court hired you to do her child custody, she freaked out because he had all the money, she was scared you'd be corrupt like everyone else and take his side. Instead, you were fair and managed to get both of them not to victimize the kids. No mean feat, considering the ex is a total rat-bastard.'

I crossed my legs.

She said, 'Nonverbal signal to annoying patient: Quit avoiding what we're here for. Fine – oh, yeah, let me get you your money up front. I'm sure you don't mind cash, do you? I'm a cash gal from way back.' Winking. 'Old habits and all that.'

'Let's deal with that later,' I said.

'No, let's deal with it now.' Hard voice. So was her smile. 'I want to make sure I don't forget.' She touched the side of her head. 'I forget a lot, could be tumors migrating into the old noggin, huh? Or maybe there's just not much worth remembering in the first place? What's your take on my encroaching senility, Doc?'

'It's—'

'Yeah, yeah, you don't know me well enough. Okay, payment with a smile coming up.'

Rising with effort, she hobbled through a doorway, was gone for several minutes, came back with a thick, bright red envelope that she thrust at me.

Unless it was packed with singles, way too thick to comprise a session's worth. I put it on an end table. 'In terms of Chad—'

'I *told* you, this is all about little old narcissistic addictive *me*. Count the moolah, make sure I'm not shorting you.'

I opened the envelope, flipped through a collection of fifties. Enough for twenty sessions. 'This is way too much, Gretchen. Let's go session by session.'

'What, you think I'm going to kick tomorrow?'

'No,' I said. 'It's the way I do business.'

'Well, let's do it differently – be flexible, you know? If we go session by session, you can leave whenever you want. My situation, I need a commitment.'

'I'm committed to helping you. How you pay me won't make a difference.'

'Yeah, sure.'

I didn't respond.

She said, 'You're different from anyone else? Then why the cashmere
blazer and the English slacks and those cute loafers, what are they,
Ferragamo?'

'I like stuff as much as the next guy, Gretchen. And that's irrelevant.
I'm here for Chad and you don't need to buy me in advance.' Taking a
session's worth of cash out of the envelope, I resealed it, placed it beside
her.

'I don't believe you. You want to feel free to leave.'

'If that was the issue, I could refund unused dough and book on you
at any time. Now, how about we stop wasting time and talk about Chad?'

She stared at me. Gasped. Let out a strangled laugh.

'Jesus, I got myself a serious one.'

The urge to prattle never left her but I kept steering her back to a struc-
tured history. Starting with Chad's birth and continuing into the toddler
years, preschool, and the boy's current placement in one of the most
expensive grade schools in the city, an intimate place originally based
on psychoanalytic theory but now eclectic. I'd lectured there a few times,
thought it was overpriced, no better than any school, but not harmful.
If need be, the director could be counted on.

No need for that now, but it might be interesting to see how Dr
Lisette Auerbach's impressions gibed with Gretchen's description of
Chad as a meld of Louis Pasteur, Leonardo da Vinci, and Saint George.

Despite her troubled past and her foreshortened future, Gretchen
could've been any proud, nervous, overprotective, overindulgent
Westside mom.

'Oh, yeah,' she said, 'he's a killer athlete, too. Soccer and basketball.
Mr Cup in Hand must've been some kind of stud. Brad and Albert *and*
Pelé.'

I said, 'You contributed half of Chad's chromosomes. You also created his environment.'

'Three cheers for me. I'm just hoping some of those chromosomes don't mess him up. Like my ADD, my propensity to—'

'Gretchen, what specifically are you concerned about?'

'What do you think?' she shouted. 'What to tell him.'

'What have you told him so far?'

'That I'm sick.'

'Did you name the sickness?'

'No. Why would I?'

'When kids don't have facts they sometimes supply their own.'

'And?'

'Their fantasies can be worse than reality.'

'What can be worse than the fact that I've got fucking cancer and am going to screw him up royal by abandoning him?'

'What measures have you taken for his care?'

'What a way with words you have,' she said.

'Have you planned?'

'Hell, yes. My plan is my sister. I have two of them. Katrine's a bigger asshole than me, total washout, but Bunny's solid gold. Maybe being the middle child helped her avoid family shit in some way. Whatever made her who she is, she's great and she's taking Chad.'

'Where does Bunny live?'

'Berkeley. Her husband's a physics professor, she teaches English, both her kids are off in college. Chad always likes visiting her and Leonard, they've got a funky house in the Berkeley Hills, nice view of the Bay. Got a great dog, mutt named Waldo, Chad loves him, too.'

She sniffed. Caressed her oxygen tank. 'From their backyard you can see the Golden Gate Bridge.' She teared up. 'Bunny will be a great mom for Chad. Better than me.'

'Have you talked to Chad about living with Bunny and Leonard?'

'Why would I even bring that up? It would freak him out!'

'You think he's unaware of how ill you are?'

'I think he doesn't pay much attention as long as he gets his attention.'
I stayed silent.
'You think I'm full of shit.'
I got up and touched the tank. 'This isn't hard to miss, Gretchen.'
She burst into sobs.

She allowed me to dry her eyes. Grabbed me around my neck and held on for a while before sinking back, wheezing.

'Thank you. For not letting go. Everyone lets go.' Sniff. 'No one takes care of me, I'm going to be lost.'

'I can talk to someone about hospice care.'

'That's not what I mean, I've done that already, there's a service, visiting nurses, they're totally into pain control, all that good stuff. I meant . . . whatever . . . why not more dope?'

'What then?'

'People don't like me,' she said. 'I'd say it was my fault, but it's always been that way. As long as I can remember.'

'I like you.'

'Fucking liar.'

'You do make it kind of hard.'

She glared at me. Burst into boggy laughter. 'Oh, you are something. Stud of the psyche.'

I took her hand. 'It sounds as if you've done everything practical that you need to do. But my hunch is Chad knows a whole lot more than you think he does. I can meet with him to try to get a sense of what's on his mind. If there are fallacies, we'll correct them—'

'What kind of fallacies?'

'Sometimes kids blame themselves for a parent's illness.'

'No way, impossible, he'd never do that.'

'You may be right but it's worth exploring.'

She squeezed my knuckles. Slid out of grasp. 'But I may also be *wrong* because what the hell do I know about kids and you've worked with thousands, right? You really think Chad's blaming himself?'

'I don't think anything but it needs to be looked at.'

'Okay, okay . . . but I do need a guarantee that you'll be here for me. *That's* why I wanted you to have the money up front, I need you . . . need you . . . *tethered* to me. 'Cause let's face it, money talks, bullshit walks.'

Snatching the red envelope, she dropped it in my lap. 'Take it, dammit, or I won't sleep at night and you'd be harming a poor pathetic terminal cancer patient.'

I picked up the envelope.

'Thank you,' she said. 'Not for that. For drying my damn eyes.'

10

THE GIRL in white was scheduled for the evening broadcast but got cut. Heavy news day: two separate actresses beaten up by their boyfriends.

The following morning at nine a.m., Milo and I sat in my kitchen watching a network affiliate flash the drawing for ten seconds.

He said, 'Blinked and missed it,' went and helped himself to a half-gallon milk carton from the fridge. 'With their ratings, no big deal. 'Bout as useful as underwear on an eel.'

But before he began gulping, his cell beeped Handel's *Messiah* and he listened, wide-eyed, as Detective Moe Reed delivered a message so loudly even I could hear.

'Anonymous tip, sir, saying you should check out a website called SukRose dot net.'

'Sounds exotic, Moses. Spell it.'

Reed said, 'S-U-K, rose as in flower, dot net.'

Milo hung up and repeated that.

I said, 'Before he spelled it, I heard *sucrose* as in sugar. Maybe as in daddy?'

He put down the milk and left the room. Was seated at my computer before I reached my office.

SukRose.net's home page flashed purple and gold with bright red lettering.

'Classy,' he said. 'What it lacks in subtlety it makes up in vulgarity.'

SUKROSE.NET
FOR UPPER-CRUST SUGAR DADDIES
AND STAR-QUALITY SWEETIES

Why we are a cut above the rest.

You've seen the others. Perhaps you've experienced them. And found out that making promises and delivering upon them are two separate things.

Nowhere but at SukRose.net will you find Sugar Daddies pre-screened for financial, medical, as well as moral net worth.

Nowhere but at SukRose.net will you encounter Sweeties who really are sweet – brainy, sophisticated, lovable, and loving young women who desire more than the superficial and respond from the depths of their beings.

Nowhere but at SukRose.net will you personally benefit from rigorous geographical screening. Sure, it's a big country. But not for discerning Sugar Daddies and Sweeties.

That's why SukRose.net limits its membership to two clusters of meticulously researched zip-code databases: the elite environs of New York City and the elite environs of Los Angeles. And if that sometimes means a transcontinental flight on a Daddy's Gulfstream while sipping Moët & Chandon and nibbling on beluga caviar?

Well, you know the answer: C'est la vie.

So cross our gilded portal and learn what SukRose.net has to offer. No obligations to potential Daddies who want to browse. No obligations ever to Sweeties. If you pass our rigorous screening, consider yourself accepted at one of the most exclusive clubs in the world.

ENTER

'Brainy *and* lovable,' he said.

I said, 'And oh-so-loving when they respond from the depths of their beings. Who knew discussing Proust would be so popular?'

56

'Free browsing, let's partake. Not that either of us would fit the bill.' Laughing. 'For different reasons.'

The first page that came up in the Sweetie database was bordered by photos of a gorgeous young woman with long legs and golden, wavy hair.

Headshot, bikini shot, black-leotard ballet shot, bending over a pool table flashing cleavage, leaning on the rail of a boat flashing cleavage, sitting on a couch flashing cleavage.

Identical toothy smiles in every image. Impish combination of wholesome and corrupt.

SukRose Sweetie #22352

Codename: Bambee

Age: 22

Residence: Western Elite

Height: 5'5"

Weight: 111

Body Classification: Sylph (low body fat but endowed where it counts.)

Eye Color: Amber

Hair Color: Blond

Education: Dance school

Occupation: Yoga instructor

Habits: Social drinker, nonsmoker

Profile: Moved to LA from a cute little town in a not-so-cute flyover state where no one was like me because I loved the deeper and better things in life and they made me feel like a faun stuck between the buffalos. I love to dance any kind of dance and travel any kind of travel am always open to exploring the karmic interplaying between physical, cosmic, and intellectual spheres. Favorite food: Sushi but it has to be super-fresh!

*Favorite music: John Meyer. Maroon 5. Favorite read: So, so, so
many books cuz I love to read but I read an old copy of
the Bridges of Madison County I found in an airport at least
a gazillion times, guess I'm a hapless romantic! I'm fit,
energetic and flexible – in every way. Adventurous too and
open to anything. Well, almost. LOL. But that leaves a lot
of possibilities.*

*Seeking: A Daddy who appreciates the finer objects of life – and
me! You can spoil me with delicious gifting or play poker with me or
I'll just watch a football game with you if that's what
makes you purr like a Ferrari. Any game's fine with me
if you play your cards right.*
XXXOOO BAMBEE

**To Contact This Sweetie: You must first log on and receive your
Platinum Daddy account number. All Major Credit Cards and PayPal
accepted.**

Next page: green-eyed brunette, 23. Codename: Sherbet. Occupation: model. *Love Jane Austen movies and sex. Not necessarily in that order LOL.*

Codename: Surfrgrl, 24. *Pilates coach and fitness fanatic. Abs of titanium, glutes to match. Vegan but not afraid of all meat LOL. Love to position myself for opportunities. Yours.*

Leilani, 21. *Interior designer but you can decorate me to your hearts content, I do all kinds of layouts.*

Milo said, 'Such wisdom. Maybe Harvard should open up a West Coast branch.'

'For the Western Elite.' Anonymous tip. No sense wondering about the source but I had good reason to surmise.

We read a few more profiles before Milo phoned Deputy DA John Nguyen, described the site, and asked why it wasn't prostitution.

'Didn't know that kind of thing troubled you, Milo.'

'Only when it relates to a pretty girl getting her face blown off.'

'Ouch,' said Nguyen. 'Okay, let me take a look – got it right here on my screen – nice colors . . . okay . . . okay . . . okay . . . like the pictures . . . okay . . . okay. Nope, my friend, not even close. The courts dealt with the issue years ago. Even when sex is offered as part of a transaction – and it can be a lot more overt than what these bimbos are advertising – as long as other services are offered in addition to sex it's kosher. As far as the law is concerned, these girls are selling companion-ship and flattery and shared good times and if that gets carnal, no big whoop. Think of it as an alternative to marriage.'

'Always knew you were a romantic, John.'

'Even if it was considered prostitution, do you see Vice bothering to prowl cyberspace when we can't even clear the streets of diseased crack whores? Whoa!'

'What, John?'

'This one. Nice. These are some fine-looking chicks.'

Milo printed SukRose's home page, called a downtown detective with computer skills named Darnell Wolf, and asked for a street address for the site.

'Kind of busy now, Milo. Turns out compliance with the new stat system by detectives is only forty percent.'

'That's your problem?'

'I'm supposed to make it more user-friendly for all you John and Jane Waynes.'

'Try using large block letters and monosyllables, Darnell. Meantime, I'm that rare bird who appreciates what you do, so get me an address. Stucco and soil, not cyber.'

'Fine, you'll need to give me a little time,' said Wolf. 'Minutes and hours, not astral projection.'

Milo reread the home page. 'Ah, the finance of fantasy. From what you described, Princess would fit perfectly.'

I said, 'So would a Sugar Daddy rich enough to hire a goon like Black Suit.'

'Guess their prescreening for moral net worth didn't work too well.' He folded the page, slipped it into his attaché case. 'If they did anything at all, it was probably one of those basic felony checks.'

His phone jumped on the table.

Darnell Wolf said, 'That was easy, man, you could've done it yourself. Company's listed in a basic California business directory, so they're not trying to hide their existence. The parent corporation's called SRS Limited and it's registered in Panama but they have offices on West Fifty-eighth Street in New York and right here on Wilshire.'

He read off the address.

'Much obliged, Darnell.'

'I checked out the site.' Wolf gave a low whistle. 'Made me want to be rich.'

11

THE WESTERN Elite branch of SukRose.net was housed on the third floor of a steel-and-blue-glass office building on Wilshire, five blocks east of the Beverly Hills–LA border. I knew the place; it had once been reserved for health care professionals. Now the tenants were divided among physicians, dentists, psychologists, chiropractors, and a host of ambiguously named businesses, many with *Tech* in their names.

The interior hallways were clean but tired, with brown carpeting vacuumed to burlap at the seams, walls and doors painted a glossy pinkish beige guaranteed to depress. Just in case your mood survived all that, ashy fluorescent lighting finished you off.

The door to Suite 313 was marked *SRS Ltd* and locked. No one responded to Milo's knuckle-rap. He fished out a card, was about to slip it through the mail slot when a female voice called out, 'Hey, guys!'

Two women bounced toward us from the elevator. Each carried a Styrofoam take-out carton. From the aroma of lemongrass as they got closer, Thai.

Both were young, with olive complexions, strong noses, and pretty, full-lipped faces under lush black hair. The taller, thinner one wore a fitted black silk blouse over low-rise black slacks and red sandals with four-inch heels. Her companion, round-faced, curvier, and firmly built, sported the same combo in chocolate brown.

Tall swung her food. Short said, 'Hi.'

'Hi. I'm Lieutenant Sturgis, LAPD.'

'Lieutenant. Wow,' said Short. 'Finally.'

'Finally?'

'We figured it would happen eventually,' said Tall. 'Given the nature of our business. But don't worry, we're legal, nothing sleazy. In fact, we're allergic to sleaze – it makes us sneeze.'

Shared laughter. Both girls flipped their hair.

'C'mon in, guys, we'll tell you all about us.'

The setup was a small reception room, unstaffed and empty, and two larger offices, each furnished with antique carved desks, tufted pink-suede couches, and a bank of flat-screen computers.

'How 'bout we use mine?' said Tall. 'There's still hot coffee in my Krups.'

Short said, 'Sounds good,' and ushered us into the left-hand office. Drapes were drawn and she opened them to a view of taller buildings on Wilshire. 'Make yourselves comfortable, guys. Black, or cream and shug?'

'Nothing, thanks.'

Tall settled behind her desk, checked her computers before turning to us. 'I'm Suki Agajanian and this is my sister, Rosalynn.'

'Hence, SukRose,' said Short. 'Everyone calls me Rose.'

I said, 'When I heard it, I assumed it was a play on sucrose – sugar.'

Rosalynn Agajanian ticked chocolate-nailed fingers. 'Carbon twelve Hydrogen twenty-two Oxygen eleven. Or, if you really want to impress someone, blah blah blah glucopyranosyl blah blah blah fructofuranose.'

Milo said, 'I'm beyond impressed. Suk and Rose, huh?'

Suki Agajanian said, 'Our parents named us for a joke. Daddy's a biochemist and Mom's a molecular physicist. The line was we were their sugar babies.' Her nose wrinkled. 'Growing up, we thought it was lame, despised when they grouped us together as a dyad.'

'You're twins?'

'No,' said Suki. 'I'm twelve months older. She —' pointing — 'is the whoopsie baby.'

Rosalynn pouted, then giggled. 'You play, you pay.'

'Anyway,' said Suki, 'we made limoncello out of lemons when we started the business. Perfect name, don't you think?'

'Perfect,' said Milo. 'So business is good.'

'Business is *great*,' said Rosalynn. 'We incorporated just over a year ago and already have over ten thousand names in our data bank.'

Suki said, 'Actually, closer to twelve thousand at last count.' She clicked a keyboard. 'Three thousand six hundred eighty-seven Daddies and seven thousand nine hundred fifty-two Sweeties. Not including any that signed up today.'

I said, 'Who runs the New York office? Sister Honey?'

Both girls laughed.

'No, that's just a mail-drop,' said Rosalynn. 'Our uncle Lou has a luggage store in the building and he picks up correspondence for us. We did it to look bicoastal. It means paying some New York taxes, but we thought it would be worth it and it has been.'

'You incorporated in Panama.'

'Sure did,' said Suki. 'Our brother's a tax lawyer and he said we need to be careful not to appear as if we're evading taxes but there'd still be some advantages to an offshore registration.'

'We're going to pay a *ton* of taxes this year,' said Rosalynn. 'A heckuva lot more than we ever considered a good income.'

'God bless the Internet,' said Suki. 'Our expenses are minimal, it's just the two of us, the computers and the rent and whatever freelance consultations we use for technical stuff. The bad part is we don't have much in the way of deductions, but the other side of the coin is our profit margin's huge.'

'We'll pay the taxes, we're not greedy,' said Rosalynn. 'We're well aware that our business model could be finite if other people catch on and competition grows fierce. The obvious end goal would be to sell to a bigger company but for the time being we're happy with what we've got. And we're totally glad we took it upscale.'

'Fendi, not Loehmann's,' said her sister. 'For a school project, it's sure worked out fantastic.'

'School project,' said Milo. 'Did you get a good grade?'

'A.'

'Where?'

Rosalynn said, 'We both went to Columbia for undergrad and when Suk got an MBA from Wharton, she had to come up with a novel business model for her honors thesis. I'm no tech freak but I have done two years of grad school in neuroscience at the U, so I can handle the basic stuff.'

'And your brother handles your legal affairs.'

'Brother Brian. He's the oldest. Brother Michael, he's the youngest, is finishing up at Columbia with a BA in econ. He's looking for real estate investments for us. For when it ends and we go passive-income.'

Suki clicked another keyboard. 'Three new Sweeties just came in, Rosie.'

'Yes!'

Milo said, 'You weren't surprised we showed up.'

'My assumption,' said Suki, 'is you came across us while doing some sort of prostitution cybercrawl. Since that psycho Craigslist killer in Boston, there've been clamp-downs on adult services. But we're not adult in *that* sense. We do not buy, sell, or coordinate sexual contact. We're simply a conduit for meetings of the mind.'

'Or various body parts.'

Rosalynn said, 'Before we began, we vetted extensively. The courts have already considered the issue of multiple services and—'

'We know,' said Milo. He leaned forward. 'Sorry to disappoint you but your guess is wrong.'

'About what?'

He showed them his card.

Suki's eyes widened. 'Homicide?'

Rosalynn said, 'Another Craigslist psychopath? Damn. But not on our database, I can assure you, no way. We screen carefully. By that I do not mean just some boilerplate records search like other sites do. We check every single criminal database that's available to us. We even scan court records for civil suits.'

Suki said, 'Which is in our best interest, anyway. Who wants some litigious jerk making your life complicated?'

I said, 'Anyone who's been in civil court is excluded?'

'Of course not, that would eliminate just about everyone with money. What we do – what Brian does – is evaluate to see if there's a clear pattern of duplicity, any sort of major financial impropriety or habitual obnoxiousness. What we call pond pebbles – the kind that trip you up when you're swimming in a lovely, pristine stream.'

'Like at our place in Arrowhead,' said Rosalynn. 'Two acres, we just got it.'

She played with Milo's card. 'So, who got murdered?'

'A young woman, who we've been led to believe advertised on your site.'

'Led to believe?' said Suki. Her hands flew to a keyboard. 'Give me a name and I'll let you know either way.'

'We don't have a name yet.'

She sat back, spun her chair a couple of times. 'Then why in the world would you think she was a Sweetie?'

'We've been informed that she was.'

'By who?'

'I can't say.'

The sisters looked at each other. Each shook her head, as if ruing the delivery of bad news.

Suki said, 'Guys. C'mon. That kind of bluff is not going to cut it.

Even if it is true, your informant could be a competitor bad-mouthing us. Or someone we rejected trying to get back at us.'

'Or just an annoying jerk hacker,' said her sister. 'The Internet brings them out.'

'Did they give you their name?' said Suki. 'So we could at least evaluate their veracity?'

'Anonymous tip.'

Both girls laughed.

Suki said, 'Like on TV, huh?'

'They're for real,' said Milo. 'They solve murders.'

'Anonymous tip,' Rosalynn repeated. 'I know you guys are just doing your job, but obviously following up on something like that would be tenuous, to say the least. Who's to say there's any validity to it?'

'Only one way to find out,' said Milo. 'Furnish us with a list of Sweeties, including headshots.'

The sisters studied each other. Silently calculating who should handle the situation.

Finally, Rosalynn said, 'You seem like nice guys, but why on earth would we turn over our entire data bank on the basis of something so far-fetched?'

'Because it could help solve a murder.'

'Could-should-might-maybe?' said Suki. 'The cost-effective potential is pathetic. Especially considering the multiple assaults on privacy that kind of excavation would entail.'

Milo opened his case, removed a death shot of Princess, and passed it to her.

She stared for a second, pushed it away. 'Okay, you've grossed me out, that's utterly repugnant. However, even being grossed out doesn't stop me from raising the cardinal question: If she doesn't have a face, how could you possibly match her to someone in our data bank?'

Rosalynn said, 'Let me see it, Suk.'

'Trust me, you don't want to.'

'If you saw it, I need to see it, Suk, otherwise I'll be hungry for dinner by seven and you won't have any appetite and we'll get on a different schedule and we'll be messed up for days.'

Suki played with her hair. Passed the photo.

Rosalynn stuck out her tongue. 'Beyond repugnant. Hard to believe it's real, there's almost a special-effects quality.'

'It's real,' said Milo.

'I'm just saying. It's so gross, it's almost like it's phony.'

Suki said, 'We respect the police, our great-great-grandfather was a police chief in Armenia. But without a face – it's beyond tenuous, it's *remote*.'

Rosalynn held the picture out to Milo. He took his time retrieving it, searched the case, and came up with Alex Shimoff's portrait.

Suki Agajanian frowned. 'If you have an intact face, why did you show us that *monstrosity*?'

Her sister said, 'Obviously for shock value, Suk, in order to jolt us into compliance. You don't need to manipulate us, guys. We're on your side.'

Suki said, 'We're not First Amendment–obsessed dweebs ready to fight you in court for every shred of data. Give us a name and we can tell you in seconds if she was one of ours. If she was, we'll also tell you who she linked with. But absent a name, there's nothing we can do and no logical reason for us to release our data bank. Like we told you, it's almost twelve thousand names, most of them Sweeties.'

Milo said, 'I'm a patient guy.'

'You'd go through that many photos? That sounds incredibly inefficient.'

I said, 'Do you subdivide by personal characteristics? Our victim was blond with dark eyes.'

'We do subclassify,' said Rosalynn, 'but that won't help you because nearly eighty percent of our Sweeties are blond so we're still talking thousands.'

'Apparently, fair hair connotes youth and vitality,' said Suki, fluffing her own raven coif.

'Same for small noses,' said Rose, wrinkling her aquiline appendage. 'Anything that evokes childhood in an overall sexually mature package does the trick with the male animal.'

Her sister laughed. 'Apparently guys are all pedophiles at heart.'

I said, 'What percentage of your blondes have dark eyes?'

'Uh-uh,' said Suki. 'You're not getting in through the back door.'

Milo said, 'Five four, a hundred and five.'

'We don't categorize by weight because it fluctuates and people lie and we don't want to be held to anything. Plus, we're not running a meat market.'

I said, 'More like a gourmet deli.'

Both sisters stared. Broke into simultaneous smiles as if a cluster of shared neurons had fired.

'I *like* that,' said Suki. 'Maybe we can figure out a way to work it into our promo.'

'Gourmet deli,' said Rosalynn. 'It's a little overtly oral, but yeah, maybe some variant would work – the haute cuisine of romance.'

'We could do the slow-food angle, Rosie. Look at the ratings chef shows pull in.'

'Gourmet deli . . . food . . . for the soul.'

'Sublime *nourishment* for body and soul.'

'Satisfaction for body, *mind,* and soul.'

'Encompassing the entire realm of the senses.'

Milo said, 'How about nourishing some curiosity?'

'Tell you what,' said Suki. 'We'll check with Brian.'

'Fine, we'll wait.'

'Oh, no, sorry,' said Rosalynn. 'These kinds of decisions can't be made impulsively.'

Her sister said, 'Brian's the last person you'd call impulsive.'

'Aw c'mon, girls,' said Milo.

'You're so sweet,' said Suki. 'But I'm so, so sorry, we can't. In the end it's in your best interests, as well. Well-organized decisions work out better for all concerned.'

'Infinitely better,' said her sister.

She followed us out of the suite.

Milo said, 'Call as soon as you've talked to Brian.'

'You bet. And if you know someone who'd profit from our services, be sure to clue them in. We really are the best.'

12

CHAD STENGEL said, 'Mommy's going to die.'

It was four p.m. and he'd been home from school long enough to have a snack and watch a couple of videos.

We were in his room, a sky-blue alternate universe filled with books, toys, costumes, art supplies. When I arrived he was sitting next to Gretchen in the living room, pretending not to notice as she introduced us. Before she finished, he left.

She said, 'Has a mind of his own.' Smile. Cough. 'I know what you're thinking, big mystery where that came from.'

I smiled back. But she was right.

When I entered the room, he was lying on his back in bed, staring at the ceiling.

I said, 'Hi.'

'Hi.'

I sat down cross-legged on the floor. He blinked. 'You'll get dirty.'

'Should I sit somewhere else?'

He pointed to a chair lettered *Chad* on the splat in gold script.

'Do you know who I am, Chad?'

'A doctor.'

'I'm a psychologist, the kind of doctor who doesn't give shots—'

'We s'posed to talk about feelings.'

'Mommy told you that?'

'Aunt Bunny.'

'What else did Aunt Bunny tell you?'

'Mommy's afraid to talk.'

'About what?'

'She's going to die.'

He crossed husky arms over his chest. His face was a soft white sphere dotted with freckles. A grave little boy, broad and solid with a low center of gravity. His oversized yellow Lakers T-shirt was spotless. Same for baggy knee-length skater's pants and red-and-black Nikes. Dark hair styled meticulously hung to his shoulders. Eighties hairband coif on a six-year-old.

His eyes were a tone shy of black and active. Looking anywhere but at me.

'Aunt Bunny told you Mommy was going to die.'

The arms clenched tighter. 'She's sick. It doesn't stop.'

'Mommy's sickness doesn't stop.'

'Aunt Bunny said.'

Instead of completing the sentence, he snatched up an action figure from a collection of dozens. One space ranger in an army of miniature centurions poised to do battle, green-scaled, fanged, plated with steroid muscles.

'Aunt Bunny said—'

'I didn't give it to her.'

'That's true.'

Silence. His mouth tightened into a sour little knot.

'Aunt Bunny told you the truth, Chad. You didn't give Mommy her sickness.'

A low, gravelly noise rose from his tiny torso. The sound an old man might make when grumpy or congested or waking up tired.

'You're not sure?'

'The teachers are always saying stay home if you're sick. So you don't give it.' Tossing the action figure to the side, the way you'd fling lint. It hit the wall, dropped silently to the bed. 'She stays home.'

71

'There are different types of sickness,' I said.

Silence.

'The sicknesses your teachers talk about are colds. The sickness Mommy has you can't get from anyone else. Ever.'

He retrieved the green warrior, tried to pull off the head. Failed and discarded it again.

'Do you know what Mommy's sickness is called?'

'I gave her a cold.'

'Colds are different. You can catch colds from someone else if they sneeze on you.'

'One time I was real sick.' Touching his abdomen. He tossed the green figure across the room. It hit the wall, fell to the floor.

I said, 'One time your tummy hurt?'

'Before.'

'Before Mommy got sick.'

Grunt. 'I was coughing.'

'Mommy coughs.'

'Yeah.'

'There are different kinds of coughs, Chad. You didn't give Mommy's sickness to her. I promise.'

Rocking on stubby feet, he got off the bed, dropped to his knees as if praying, searched underneath the frame, and pulled out a drawing tablet.

Professional-quality Bristol board. A handwritten note on the cover said *To My Genius Artist, Your Worshipful Ma-mah* in loopy, oversized red script.

Chad let go of the pad. It slapped carpet. He touched his belly again. 'I threw up.'

'When your tummy was—'

'Mommy throws up. All the time.'

'People throw up for all kinds of reasons, Chad.'

He kicked the drawing tablet. Did it again, harder.

'Even though everyone keeps saying you didn't give Mommy her sickness, you're worried you did.'

His toe nudged the pad.

'You don't believe anyone.'

'Hunh.'

'They're telling you a lot,' I said. 'Over and over.'

'Hunh.'

'Maybe that's making you worried. Everyone talking so much.'

He stood, snapped small hands upward in a boxer's stance. Kicked the bed hard. Did it again. Five more times.

Threw himself to the floor and pummeled the carpet with both fists. Jumped to his feet again and watched me.

I did nothing.

'I'm gonna draw.'

'Okay.'

'By myself.'

'You want me to leave.'

'Yeah.'

'Would you mind if I stayed a little bit longer?'

Silence.

'Chad, how about I just sit here and don't talk while you draw.'

'Unh-uh.'

'Okay, then I'll tell Mommy we're finished for today.'

Scuttling on his knees to a box in the corner, he grabbed a red marker, dove down belly-first, flipped the tablet open, and commenced drawing circles. Large, red page-filling circles that he began filling in laboriously.

Big red bubbles.

'Bye, Chad. Nice meeting you.'

'*Unh*. No!'

'No?'

'You draw, too,' he ordered, without looking up. 'We'll draw fast.' Ripping his circle drawing out of the tablet, he tore out the following blank page and thrust it at me.

'Draw!'

'What color should I use?'

'Black.' He punched air. 'We're going fast. I'm gonna win.'

Ten minutes later, he'd announced victory fourteen times before announcing, 'This time you go.'

I left him, found Gretchen in her living room, exactly where we'd left her.

'So?'

'He's a great kid.'

'I don't need you to tell me that. What's going on in his head?'

'Nothing out of the ordinary.'

'I don't believe this,' she said. 'Jesus, it's not like I'm going to be around forever, I need meat and potatoes – put *out*! Why the hell else would I pay you?'

'He's going through what any kid would go through.'

'Meaning?'

'Anger, fear. I'm not going to tell you anything dramatic right now because there's nothing dramatic to tell.'

'Thought you were the master shrink.'

'One thing to be aware of,' I said. 'Everyone's been telling him he didn't give you the illness. That's better than not dealing with it but sometimes too much repetition can make kids anxious.'

'He said that?'

'I deduced it.' I smiled. 'Being a master shrink.'

'Well, I sure as hell didn't bug him about it. I told him once, maybe twice to make sure it sank in, 'cause that's what the books say. Who's everyone?'

'Who else has talked to him?'

'Just Bunny,' she said. 'Oh, shit, I told Bunny to tell him, what, she overdid it? Typical. Only reason I included her was so he'd get a consistent message. And because one day she'll be his . . . she'll be the one to . . .' Burying her face in her hands, she moaned, 'Oh, God.' Looking up: 'Would you just please goddamn hold me!'

I was doing just that when Chad came out, holding a page full of black circles.

'You love her?' he said.

Gretchen pulled away, swiped her eyes frantically. 'No, no, honey, we're just . . .'

'You're sad. He wants to make you happy. Maybe he loves you.'

'Oh, baby, you're so smart.' She spread her arms. 'No, he's a friend, he's helping. And you know what I really want? For *you* to be happy.'

Chad stood there.

'C'mere, honey, give Mommy a hug.'

He walked over to me and held out the drawing. 'For you.'

'Thanks, Chad.'

'You can come back. We'll make Mommy happy together.'

Gretchen swooped him to her breast. 'I *am* happy, honey, you make me *so, so* happy.'

The movement had pulled the air hose from her nostrils.

A hiss filled the room.

Chad said, 'Put it back. So you can get better.'

'Anything you say, sweetie boy, smart boy. Anything.' Plugging the line back in, she said, 'Now come up on my lap and I'll tell you a story.'

'No,' he said. 'I'm too heavy.'

'You're—'

'I'm big. I'm heavy.' Turning to me. 'You can go, I'm helping her.'

Two hours later, Gretchen phoned and spoke to me in a new voice: low, measured, soft around the edges.

'I don't know what you did but it was amazing. Until now he's been pulling away from me, when I try to talk to him he ignores me. After you left we hung out and he was my snuggle-bunny again. He even let me tell him stories about when he was little. It was awesome. Like having my baby back. Thank you, thank you, thank you.'

'I'm glad, Gretchen.'

A beat. 'I'm not sure I like the flavor of that.'

'Of what?'

'Your tone,' she said. 'Tentative. Like don't get too happy, bitch, it could all come crashing down?'

'If I were you, Gretchen, I'd avoid interpretation. I'm glad it worked out. He's a terrific little boy.'

Silence.

'You're a tough one to read,' she said. 'I can't tell if you're playing me. For all I know you're watching porn on your computer while we talk.'

I laughed. 'Too late in the day for multitasking.'

'But it is true, right? We had one good day but it could go back to the way it was and he could start shutting me out again.'

'Kids have moods like anyone else. There's no way to predict.'

'Seize the day, huh? Shut the fuck up and stop thinking about me, me, me and enjoy what I've got.'

'Sounds like a plan,' I said.

'Just answer one thing for me: Can someone be a terrible person but still a good mom?'

'You're a good mom, Gretchen.'

'You didn't answer my question.'

'From my perspective, you're a caring, skillful mother.'

'I didn't mess him up too bad?'

'Chad's a normal kid going through a tough situation. From what I've seen so far, you're doing a great job so don't beat yourself up.'

'Okay, okay – so when are you coming back?'

'Let's give it a few days so Chad doesn't feel overwhelmed.'

'Like everyone shrinky-dinkying him to the point where he wants to upchuck.'

'You do have a way with words,' I said.

'Actually, words were never my thing, Doc. I flunked English in high school. Along with a whole lot of other stuff. Being stoned all the time and never studying ain't the pathway to academic stardom.'

'But it sure was fun at the time.'

She laughed. 'It's more than the training, isn't it? Send some asshole to shrink school, you end up with an educated asshole. Which, now that I think about it, sounds like a good title for a porno. Analyst Anal Adventures: Educating Ruby's Ruby Asshole.'

I said, 'In terms of Chad's next appointment—'

'Stop being *inappropriate*, Gretchen. I may be a compassionate therapist but my patience isn't endless.'

I named a day.

She said, 'Okay, okay, okay, fine. Bunny may be here, it's about time for her next nosy-pants visit. She's decided she needs to be my early-stage hospice provider, even though I keep telling her I'm fine.'

'But you don't stop her from coming.'

'Right now,' she said, 'she's the only person who loves me.'

'Not counting Chad.'

'Yeah, yeah, I'm talking someone who can actually help me. With the nasty stuff, the disgusting stuff. 'Cause eventually, they tell me it's going to get gross.' Her voice caught. 'You should probably meet her, anyway. Seeing as she'll be taking over.'

'Sure.'

'You're a peach,' she said. 'I'm even starting to think you might be for real – sorry, I need to control that evil mouth, there are nice people out there, I just never met them.' Shrill laughter. 'Me, me, me – okay, here's something about *you:* As a token of my appreciation, I'm going to pay you a bonus.'

'Out of the question, Gretch—'

'Hold on, before you brush me off, smart guy, I'm not talking money. What I'm going to give you is better. Information. As in for Sturgis with his current case, the one that was on the news this morning.'

I didn't speak.

She said, 'Aha, now I've got his attention! Okay, here's the deal: I was waiting to see how you did with Chad today so I'd know whether or not you deserved another – a *special* treat. And guess what: You passed the test.'

'Gretchen, if you've got information for Lieutenant Sturgis, you need to tell him directly.'

'You're not pals anymore?'

'Bartering is unethical.'

'I'm not bartering, I'm offering you a freebie on that girl whose face was on the news. Everyone knows when the cops can't ID a victim they're screwed. For Sturgis to put her face up on TV, he's screwed blue and I just might know who she is.'

'I hope you do, Gretchen, but I can't be your middleman.'

'Why not?'

'I owe you undivided loyalties and you owe me no payment other than what we already agreed upon.'

'Now you're being a stiff.'

'Now I'm being your therapist.'

'It's not payment, it's a bonus.'

'Look at it this way,' I said. 'If I had a patient who owned a jewelry store, I wouldn't take a Rolex for my services.'

'Why not?'

'It's wrong.'

'I don't see it,' she said. 'I think you're being a total stiff.'

'Be that as it may.'

'You have no desire to hear what I have?'

'I'm sure Lieutenant Sturgis does.'

'I don't want to call him,' she said. 'I can't stand him.'

The meeting between her and Milo had lasted all of twenty minutes. Frosty, but not conspicuously hostile.

'It's up to you, Gretchen. See you in a few days.'

'I tell you I might know how to ID a dead girl and you don't give a shit?'

'What you and I do isn't about me.'

'Period.'

'Period.'

'So now I need to call that rude fat fag, personally,' she said. 'Man,

78

you should work for the IRS, talk about a bunch of rigid morons. Speaking of which, I need to talk to you about something else, yeah, it's back to me, me, me, can I have another appointment for me, me, me? Sometime when Chad's in school and before Bunny gets here and starts to run my world?'

'Let's talk right now.'

'Only if you charge me, Mr Ethical. Gretchen learned from her previous profession: Only chumps give freebies.'

'You advanced me a lot of money,' I said. 'Let's consider it a draw on your account.'

'Ka-ching ka-ching – hey, what if I don't live long enough to get my money's worth out of you?'

'What's on your mind, Gretchen?'

'Is your phone secure?'

'Far as I know.'

'Hmm . . . yeah, why would anyone give a shit about a shrink? No offense. Okay, it's about those sub-scum suck-ass parasites aka the IRS. When they nailed me on that tax bullshit, part of the deal was I'd pay back everything I'd supposedly evaded. I liquidated all kinds of shit, lost all of my real estate.'

'But . . .'

'Exactly,' she said. 'I saved up for a rainy day. What I need to make sure is that after I bite it no one comes after Chad's trust fund. What my advisors-to-remain-anonymous are telling me is that by itself the IRS won't do diddly 'cause they're stupid, couldn't find a fart after a bean dinner. But if the damn LAPD gets on my case again and sics the Feds on me, everything could get royally fucked up. This is my kid, I can't let that happen.'

'Why would the cops go after you?'

'Why, indeed.'

'You're back in business?'

'Well,' she said, 'let's just say I do a bit of consulting. Have been for a while. Which is how I came across your little informational treat – correction, the fat fag's little treat. Reason I'm bringing this up now is because you've got connections to the cops.'

'My only connection is—'

'Fatso, yeah, yeah, yeah, but *he's* got a direct line to the top. As in the *Top*.'

'Not really, Gretchen.'

'No? How many lieutenants get called into the chief's office like he does?' She giggled. 'Makes you wonder if the chief's got a secret life, maybe likes to suck the big one. You ever pick up on anything like that?'

'What do you think I can do for you, Gretchen?'

'It's not what I think, it's what I *need*. You have to grease me with Sturgis so when I'm gone the department doesn't molest my kid's future.'

'Is that the reason you called me in the first place?'

'What? I hurt your feelings? No, I called you because someone I trusted said you were righteous and knew your business. Then I thought of you and Sturgis and hit on a new idea. Which, now that I think about it, you're obligated to go along with. 'Cause Chad's your patient and this is about Chad and if you fail to protect him, what does *that* say about your ethics?'

I thought about how to answer that.

She said, 'It's not that complicated. Your job is to help my kid, so do it.'

'I don't see Sturgis having that kind of influence but if it comes to that, I'll do my best.'

'Promise?'

'Promise.'

'On the grave of Freud?'

'Adler, Jung, and B. F. Skinner, too.'

'If it comes to that, tell Sturgis I was a good mother. Otherwise he finds out I'm gone, he'll go have a six-course meal.'

'I doubt that, Gretchen.'

'What, he's a sensitive, mushy-hearted marshmallow, not a big fat bully who ruined my lunch and all I was trying to do was recuperate from prison?'

'I'll do everything I can for you, Gretchen. Promise.'

'Fine. Now go tell him SukRose was a baby step, it's time to look for a scumbag named Stefan.'

Pronouncing it Ste-*fahn*.

I thought: *Stefan who?*

I said: Nothing.

She said, 'Don't you want to know his last name?'

'I'm sure Sturgis does.'

'Man, you're a tough one, got those balls of titanium. Ever consider donating sperm?'

13

MILO SPLASHED truffle oil into the pan. Thirty bucks for a two-ounce bottle. He'd entered the house flourishing the receipt and announcing the price. Then he showed me a photocopied driver's license.

Eight eggs from my fridge, scrambled with milk and chives and mushrooms, reacted to the enrichment with a quick, sharp sizzle. The earthy aroma of upper-echelon fungus filled the kitchen.

I said, 'First time you've ever cooked.'

'I'm that kinda guy. Emotionally flexible.' Humming. 'Too bad Robin's not here. It's really her I owe, but we might as well fuel up.'

It was nine in the morning. He'd arrived freshly shaved, hair slicked, wearing his version of haute couture: baggy blue suit bought for a funeral ten years ago, white wash-'n'-wear shirt, discouraged blue tie, black-leather oxfords in lieu of the colorless desert boots.

Dividing the eggs into two heaps, he carried the plates to the table, was chomping away before he lowered himself into a chair.

I was more interested in the license.

Black Suit aka Steven Jay Muhrmann. Six two, two fifty-five, brown, blue, a POB in Hollywood that Milo had marked *defunct*.

'His latest utility bill was sent to Russell Avenue in Los Feliz, but he's got no registered vehicle, no record of recent employment that I can find.'

The picture had been taken five years ago when Muhrmann was twenty-nine and favored a dark mullet. The license had been suspended one year later and never reinstated.

Angry glare. No one likes waiting in line at the DMV but Steven Muhrmann's bullnecked scowl suggested more than a long queue was at play.

I said, 'Friendly fellow.'

Milo put his fork down. 'Julius Child offers you tableside service and you don't even lift a fork? This is a celebratory breakfast, as in I now have a suspect with a real-life name. Eat before it gets cold.'

I took a bite.

'And?' he said.

'Delicious. No job, no car says Muhrmann's an un-solid citizen. Any criminal history?'

'Coupla DUIs lost him his license, at the second he also had what the arresting officer thought was traces of meth in a baggie but turned out to be steroid powder. Despite the unfortunate absence of violence, I like him. Because he makes his mommy nervous. She's the one tipped me off. Phoned this morning at seven and said the girl on the news was someone her son might know. I didn't need to press her for details but she sounded like she wanted to get something off her chest, I figured an in-person would be better. What I did get was that she'd last seen him eight months ago, was calling himself Ste-*fahn*.'

Pronouncing it exactly as Gretchen had. Before Milo showed up, I'd been wondering how to deal with her tip. Some deity was kind.

He said, 'This *is* the guy you saw, right?'

I nodded. 'Mommy sells out Junior. What's this world coming to?'

'More important, Mommy's pretty sure she saw Princess with Junior. Princess never actually came in the house but when Mom walked Ste*fahn* to the car, she was there. He introduced her as "Mystery." Mom said she thought it was "Ms Terry," but Stevie corrected her. Girl never said a word, Mom thought she looked a little sad. Or maybe just shy.'

'Any guns registered to Stefan?'

'Nope and I didn't press Mom, didn't want to overload her before we meet in person. Which is due to happen in an hour, she lives out in

Covina. That gives us just enough time to wolf down this repast. Ingest, lad, ingest.'

East Dexter Street in Covina was a thirty-minute cruise on the 10E followed by half a dozen quick turns onto sun-bright residential streets. Harriet Muhrmann's house was no different than most of her neighbors': a one-story fifties ranch the color of coffee laced with too much cream. White-painted lava rock girdled the width of the structure. Crescent-shaped windows were cut into the brown door of the double garage. Eight monumental date palms columned the driveway. The rest of the landscaping was velvet lawn and neat little pockets of impatiens and begonias. The block was silent.

A sisal mat trumpeted *Welcome!*

The woman who stood waiting for us in the doorway was trim with mannish gray hair, a long pleasant face, and soft eyes behind gold-framed glasses. She wore a cinnamon turtleneck, brown jeans, white deck shoes.

'Ms Muhrmann?'

'Harriet.' She looked up and down the street. 'Better come in, we don't want to alarm anyone.'

The door opened directly into a twelve-by-twelve living room. Brown-velvet couches compressed grape-colored carpeting. The TV, stout and gray-screened, was a borderline relic. A bookshelf held paperback best-sellers, souvenirs from theme parks, a collection of ceramic deer, framed snapshots of cute little kids.

Harriet Muhrmann walked to her picture window, parted the drapes an inch, peered through. 'Make yourselves comfortable. Coffee or tea?'

Milo said, 'No, thanks. Are you worried about something, ma'am?'

She continued to look out the window. 'This is a nice block, everyone's concerned about their neighbors. Anything different gets noticed.'

We'd arrived in the Seville.

'Does your son visit often, Ms Muhrmann?'

The curtain slipped from her fingers. 'Stevie? No, but when he does, sometimes people do ask me about it.'

'Stevie concerns them.'

'They're concerned *for* him.' She turned, gnawed her lip. 'Stevie's had his problems. I should tell you that right after I called you, I had my regrets. What kind of mother would involve her son with the police? I respect the police, my husband was an MP in the army, but . . . I don't know why I did it. But seeing Stevie's face on the news. That girl. I just felt it was my duty.'

'We appreciate that.'

'If it *was* her.'

'You seemed pretty sure it was.'

'I know I did,' she said, 'but now I'm not sure. There are so many girls like that.'

'Like what, ma'am?'

'Beautiful, skinny, blond – the kind who want to be actresses.' She moved away from the window, picked up the smallest ceramic deer, put it down. 'Have I gotten Stevie in massive trouble?'

'Not in the least, ma'am. Our goal is to identify our victim and if Stevie can help us with that, he'd be doing us a giant favor.'

'So you don't suspect him of anything.'

'We had no idea who he was until you called.'

'Okay,' she said. 'That makes me feel better. But I have to tell you, she still could be someone else. You see them everywhere, gorgeous girls. Gorgeous people, period, I don't know where they come from. Doesn't it seem to you as if people are getting better looking?'

'In my job,' said Milo, 'I don't see people at their best.'

Harriet Muhrmann flinched. 'No, of course not – you're sure I can't get you something to drink? A snack? I've got honey-roasted peanuts.'

'No, thanks, ma'am, we just ate. So people in the neighborhood worry about Stevie when he comes to visit. Has he been ill?'

'Do we need to talk about Stevie, Lieutenant? The main thing is that girl might – or might not – be the girl I saw him with the last time he was here.'

'Eight months ago.'

'About. It wasn't a scheduled visit, Stevie just dropped in.'

'And she waited out in the car.'

'Some girl did. I didn't even know he was with anyone until I walked him out.'

'He called her Mystery.'

'Obviously that's not her real name. To be honest I thought it sounded like a stripper name. But I didn't say anything, just "Pleased to meet you" and held out my hand. Her fingers barely grazed mine. Like she didn't want to be touched.'

'Did she say anything?'

'Not a word, all she did was smile. Kind of a spaced-out smile.'

I said, 'As if she was on something?'

Her mouth twisted unpleasantly. 'The thought occurred to me.'

'You've noticed that before in Stevie's friends.'

She trudged to a chair, sat down. 'You're cops, you knew right away what I meant about the neighbors worrying. Stevie's had a substance abuse issue since fourteen. His dad spotted it, Glenn thinks like a cop, maybe too much like a cop. He's in Eye-rack now, as a contractor. Doesn't even tell me what he does.'

I said, 'Glenn knew what to look for.'

'I used to think he was being paranoid but he was right. He confronted Stevie immediately and there was hell to pay.' Slumping. 'It wasn't an easy time for our family. Stevie wasn't the least bit remorseful. His excuse was everyone did it. Including Brett – his older brother. That got Brett mad and the two of them nearly beat each other senseless. Glenn watched, I nearly fell apart.'

She hugged herself. 'Our dirty laundry doesn't matter to you.'

Milo said, 'Sounds like Stevie was a bit of a challenge as a kid.'

'The funny thing is, he started off as the easy one. It was Brett who gave us conniptions, he was a hellion from day one and Stevie was so sweet and quiet. When Stevie was little, I used to say thank God I've got one who *sits*. So now Brett's an optometrist in San Dimas, has four kids, doing great. Sometimes I think they're programmed from conception and we have no control over what happens to them.'

I said, 'When did Stevie fall in with the wrong crowd?'

'Junior high. A *real* wrong crowd, it was like someone flipped a switch.' Her mouth trembled. 'Unfortunately, we could never figure how to flip the switch back. And it wasn't for lack of trying. Or expense. One thing that really irritates Brett is all the money we've spent trying to help Stevie get his life together. So maybe that's where Stevie met that girl.' She laughed. 'Sorry, that was kind of confusing.'

I said, 'Maybe he met her in rehab.'

She stared. 'Yes, that's what I meant. Glenn says it's the dumbest thing, making a rehab buddy, druggies need to get away from other druggies. But the way she looked that day – spacey. Maybe, don't you think?'

'Sure. How many rehabs have you paid for?'

'Three. After the third didn't take, we said enough, Stevie needed to take responsibility.'

'Has he?'

'Well,' she said, 'he seems to be supporting himself. He's bright, you know. Tested way above average except for some problems paying attention. The high school counselor wanted to put him on Ritalin but Glenn said no way, the last thing a druggie needs is legal dope.'

Milo said, 'What kind of work does he do?'

'All kinds of things. Glenn had a friend worked at the Wilmington docks who got Stevie a tryout unloading ships – that was a couple of years after high school, when Stevie was drifting. Stevie's always been super-strong, we thought it would be perfect and everything seemed to be going great. Then Stevie's supervisor found him smoking pot while driving a forklift. After that he . . . what did he do? . . . construction. He's worked a lot of construction jobs. I'd say construction's been his main thing.'

'Carpentry?'

'Framing, digging ditches, driving a trash truck.' She smiled. 'He did some door-to-door sales – magazines, that kind of thing. Sold clothing that he bought at thrift shops to vintage stores. One time he got hired by a company that guards shopping malls. They put him in uniform and a hat. His hair – he had real long hair back then – had to be bunched up in the hat and he looked like he had an oversized head. Glenn used to say putting a doper in that position was having the fox watch the chicken coop. But Stevie was okay as a guard, he never got into trouble. I guess he got bored with it 'cause he quit. Bored with us, too. One day he just picked up and moved to LA.'

'When was that, ma'am?'

'Six, seven years ago.'

'Until then he was living with you?'

'He came and went.' Her eyes compressed 'Why all these questions about Stevie if you just want to find that girl? Who I'm not really sure, now, was the same one.'

'A man fitting Stevie's description was seen near the girl on the night she was killed.'

Harriet Muhrmann gasped.

'Ma'am, I'm being truthful when I say that does not make Stevie a suspect. But we would like to talk to him in case he can identify her. Because right now, she's just a Jane Doe and that makes our job really tough.'

'I'm sure it does but there's nothing more I can tell you about her.'

'At the very least, we can rule Stevie out and be out of your hair.'

'Well, that would be nice but there's nothing more I can tell you.'

'That time – eight months ago. Was it a social call?'

She bit back tears. 'I can't hide anything from you guys, can I? No, Stevie needed money.'

'Did you give him any?'

She picked at a cuticle. 'His father *cannot* know.'

'There's no reason for us to talk to his father unless he can supply details you haven't.'

'He can't, Glenn's been in Eye-rack for two years, on and off. And trust me, all he'd tell you is Stevie's a doper and a disappointment.' Her eyes misted. 'Glenn's a good man but he's not always a kind man. But I understand where he's coming from.'

That sounded strangely detached. What I'd heard from so many parents of troubled kids after hope gave way to despair.

Milo said, 'So you gave Stevie some money.'

'Usually I make him show me a time card or a pay stub, something to show he's been working. Or at least trying to find work. That time he didn't have anything but he claimed he was working on getting a part in a movie. As Ste-*fahn,* that would be his stage name. I said what kind of movie? He said an independent production, if everything came together he'd be in great shape, just needed something to tide him over, he'd pay me back with interest.'

She sighed. 'He caught me on a day when I was tired and missing Glenn and getting over the flu.'

I said, 'How much did you give him?'

'He asked for four, I gave him two.'

'Thousand,' said Milo.

'I know, I know,' said Harriet Muhrmann. 'But Ste-*fahn* does sound like a movie name and that girl was pretty enough to be an actress. Actually, that's what I figured her for.'

'How many times have you seen Stevie since then?'

'None. And yes, he never paid me back. But it was my money, not Glenn's, so I can do what I want with it, right?'

'Of course.'

'You won't tell Glenn? Please, that would be horrendous.'

'There'd be no reason to do that. So the purpose of Stevie's visit was—'

'To use me,' she said. 'So what else is new, I'm a mom. But he loves me, he's always sweet to me. It's just his problems get in the way.'

I said, 'You're worried the money went for drugs.'

'I didn't ask, he didn't tell.' Her eyes clamped shut. 'Do you suspect Stevie of harming that girl?'

Milo said, 'There's no evidence of that.'

'He's never hurt a woman. Never.'

'Do you have a phone number for him?'

'He has no landline, just a cell. But it's been discontinued.'

'What car was he driving eight months ago?'

'One of those little ones, I can't tell them apart.'

'What color?'

'Dark? Honestly, I can't say. It was a long time ago and I wasn't paying attention to auto paint.'

'Would it be possible to have a list of his rehab programs, ma'am? In case he did meet Mystery at one of them.'

'You're asking me to betray Stevie's privacy.'

'It's about her, not him,' said Milo.

'Hmm. Well,' she said, 'Glenn would say absolutely, it's my duty to help you to my utmost. He's all for law enforcement, thinks you guys are – okay, hold on.'

She was gone a few seconds, came back with a bowl of peanuts. 'To keep you busy while I search.'

Her second absence stretched several minutes. 'Here, I've copied them all down. Now I have a date in San Dimas to visit my grandchildren, so if you'll please excuse me.'

Milo said, 'Thanks for your time, ma'am. One more thing: The last address we have for Stevie is in Los Feliz.'

'Okay,' she said.

'Is there a more recent one?'

'I didn't even know about that one so I'm obviously not the one to ask. May I have that address – on second thought, forget that. If Stevie wants to reach me, he knows where to find me.'

At the door she said, 'When you see him, give him regards from his old mom.'

14

As I drove back to LA, Milo called the Agajanian sisters.

Rosalynn said, 'We're still talking to Brian about how best to help you.'

'It just got simpler,' he said, 'search for a girl who called herself Mystery.'

'If you already know who she is, why do you need us?'

'What we know is that she called herself Mystery.'

'Hmm,' she said. 'I'll talk to my sister and brother.'

'How about just plugging "Mystery" into your data bank.'

'It's not that simple.'

'According to Brian?'

'Brian protects us,' she said. 'I'll get back to you.'

'Sooner would be better than later.'

'When I have something to tell you.'

He bared teeth. Ground them. Expelled the next sentence in soft little puffs. 'Thank you, Rosalynn.'

'My pleasure, Lieutenant.'

Steven Jay Muhrmann's last utility bill, still unpaid, had been mailed to a gray frame bungalow on Russell Avenue east of Los Feliz Boulevard. A small, warped, covered porch jutted like a wart on the façade. Dust served in lieu of a lawn. The block was shared by other small houses, most subdivided into flats. The exceptions were Vlatek's Auto Paint and Body, a Volvo-Saab mechanic, and a peeling black stucco box advertising secondhand clothing. Toxic stink and the sound of metal pounding metal emanated from the body shop. Even under a blue sky the neighborhood would've been drab. A late-settling marine layer turned it funereal.

The gray house had no doorbell. Milo's knock elicited footsteps from within but it took several more raps for the knob to turn.

Three people in their early twenties looked out at us, groggily. The air behind them smelled of body odor and popcorn.

Lanky, faux-hawked sandy-haired man.

Lanky faux-hawked black-haired man.

Pretty bespectacled Latina with massive curls twisted into twin barbells.

T-shirts, pajama bottoms, bare feet. The décor I could see was guitars, amps, a drum kit, heaps of fast-food refuse. A giant bag of U-Pop Movie Corn nudged a Stratocaster.

Milo introduced himself.

Black Hair yawned. Contagious.

'Could you guys step out for a second, please.'

Moving like robots, the trio complied. The girl stepped in front of her companions and tried to smile but ended up yawning. 'How could there be a noise complaint, we haven't even got started?'

'No one complained about anything. We're looking for Steven Muhrmann.'

'Who?'

He showed them the DMV shot.

Black Hair said, 'Mean-looking dude-o.'

'Got that stormtrooper thing going on,' said Sandy.

'I was gonna say he looks like a cop,' said Black. 'But that would've been rude. Actually, you guys *don't* look like cops. More like . . . hmm, maybe *you* do. You're big enough.'

The girl nudged him. 'Armand, be nice.'

Black picked something out of his eye. 'Too early to be nice. Are we excused now, Officer?'

Milo said, 'Steven no longer lives here?'

'We don't know Steven,' said the girl.

'We know Steven Stills,' said Armand. He strummed air. 'By reputation. Something's happening here and it sure ain't clear.'

'How long have you guys been living here?'

'Three months.'

'Rent or own?'

Armand said, 'If we had a record deal and the dough to own, it wouldn't be a dump like this.'

Sandy said, 'Bel Air's the place for me. Be a Bel Air hillbilly.'

Black said, 'Trust me, it's overrated.'

'That's 'cause you grew up there.'

Milo said, 'Who's the landlord?'

Sandy said, 'Some company.'

'Could you be a little more specific?'

'What did *Steven* do?'

'Name of the company, please.'

Sandy said, 'Lisa?'

'Zephyr Property Management,' said the girl. 'I'm the primary on the lease.'

Sandy said, 'The bass player always gets the best roles.'

Milo said, 'Do you have a number for them, Lisa?'

Use of her name made the girl flinch. 'Sure, hold on.' She went inside the house, returned with a business card.

Leonid Caspar, Property Manager, cell phone area code that told you nothing about geography, POB in Sunland.

I said, 'When you moved in, was anything left behind?'

Sandy smirked. 'Like a clue?'

'A clue would be great.'

Lisa said, 'Don't pay attention to them. No, sorry, Officer, it was empty and freshly painted. The guy from Zephyr said the last tenant had stiffed him for three months' rent.'

'Boo on Steven Mermaid,' said Armand.

'A pox on Steven Mermaid,' said Sandy.

Lisa said, 'Stop being assholes, guys. Both of you go shower.'

The boys bowed and turned to leave.

Armand said, 'The bass reigns supreme. In Paul McCartney we trust.'

Leonid Caspar answered with a hoarse, 'Yeah?'

Milo filled him in.

Caspar said, 'That one. No employment history to speak of, credit rating worse than the State of California. So why'd we rent to him? Because we're stupid. Plus, he gave us a year of rent upfront and damage deposit.'

'Once that ran out, he split.'

'What can I say, Lieutenant.'

'How many months did he stiff you for?'

'Two – no, says here three. Almost four, really, my son can't add. Oh, boy. So why'd we let him go that far? 'Cause we screwed up, let him slip through the cracks. We manage twenty-six buildings here and in Arizona and Nevada, all of them thirty units minimum, except for that dump on Russell. My wife inherited it from her grandfather, it was his first investment, helped him start up the company so it's like a family big-deal. Up to me, we'd sell it but she's sentimental.'

'Did Muhrmann leave anything behind?'

'Let's see . . . says here just trash. Lots of trash, we had to pay for hauling. So technically, he owes us for that, too.'

'Did you ever meet him, Mr Caspar?'

'Never had the pleasure.'

'How'd he connect with you?'

'We advertise in local papers, on Craigslist, other onlines. What'd he do, scam someone else?'

'Who in the company dealt with him?'

'You sound serious. More than a scam?' said Caspar. 'He did something serious?'

'We'd just like to talk to him, sir.'

'So would I. I put it out to collection but no one can find him.'

'Was the year's worth in cash?' said Milo.

'That's what it says here. I know what you're thinking but it's not our responsibility to figure out how they come up with payment.'

'Cash literally or a money order?'

'It's listed as cash.'

'How much are we talking about?'

'Rental was eight a month, times thirteen is ten four, we rounded off the damage deposit to six, made it eleven even.'

'Eleven thousand in cash,' said Milo.

'You're trying to tell me he's a dope dealer?' said Caspar. 'I get cash from all types. Unless someone tells me there's a problem, it's none of my business.'

'To qualify he had to give you prior addresses. Could I have them, please?'

'We didn't bother with priors because he told us upfront his credit was zero.'

'What about references?'

'Let me check . . . yeah, there's one. C – as in cookie – Longellos.' He spelled it. 'Says here she confirmed he worked as personal assistant, was honest, faithful, true-blue.'

'She,' said Milo.

'My note says Ms C. Longellos.'

'How about her number, Mr Caspar?'

Caspar read off a 310. 'You find him, I wouldn't mind if you let me know.'

'Happy to help,' said Milo. 'I'd be even happier if one of your employees actually met him face-to-face and called me by the end of today.'

'Sure,' said Caspar. 'Quid pro whatchamacallit.'

C. Longellos's number placed her in Pacific Palisades.

Not in service.

No current DMV records for that address existed but the data bank coughed up the two-year-old DUI conviction of a woman named Constance Rebecca Longellos. Forty years old, POB in Encino.

I said, 'Another under-the-radar devotee. Maybe Harriet Muhrmann's instincts were right and alcoholic misery loved company.'

He flipped through his pad. 'Stevie's most recent rehab was about two and a half years ago, place called Awakenings, in Pasadena.'

He consulted his Timex. 'Traffic's gonna be unfriendly all the way east, but we could make it out there in maybe an hour, catch dinner before heading back. Remember that fish-and-chips joint on Colorado I was looking for last year when we worked the dry ice murder, turned into Thai, I was bummed? I've been back there and it's pretty good Thai. You game for driving?'

'Sure.'

'Be sure to put in your gas voucher.'

'You're into quaint rituals, huh?'

'What?'

'I haven't gotten reimbursed for the last three batches I sent in.'

'Why didn't you say anything?'

'It seemed petty,' I said.

'Shit. I was assured by His Arrogance's office that you'd be fast-tracked.' He snapped his phone open. 'Bastards.'

Before he could punch in the chief's speed-dial code, an incoming call was heralded by a few bars of *Eine kleine Nachtmusik*. This year, classical, last year, seventies rock.

'Sturgis.'

A young male voice said, 'You're a policeman?'

'Last time I checked.'

'Oh . . . you're sure?'

'This is Lieutenant Sturgis, what can I do for you?'

'My name is Brandon Caspar, my father said I should call you about a tenant at our property on Russell.'

'Steven Muhrmann,' said Milo.

'Yes, sir.'

'Appreciate the call, Brandon. What can you tell me about Mr Muhrmann?'

'I only met him once,' said Brandon. 'When I gave him the key. That was almost a year and a half ago so I don't remember much, except he was a little . . . I don't want to say scary, more like not friendly. Kind of . . . trying to act like a tough guy.'

'Act how, Brandon?'

'It's nothing I can put into words, know what I mean? He just snatched the key out of my hand, didn't want me to give him the information about the unit we usually give. Where the circuit breaker is, the water main, the meter. He said he'd figure it out. When I tried to tell him I always explained to new tenants he said, "Well, now you won't." Not joking about it – like he could kick my butt if he wanted, you know?'

'Hostile,' said Milo.

'He *could've* kicked my butt,' said Brandon. 'He was big – not fat, buffed, like he lifted. This big, big neck.'

'Was he alone?'

'Yeah, in the house he was,' said Brandon Caspar. 'But later, when I left him with the key, I saw a girl in a car, parked in front. I wasn't sure she was with him but I thought maybe she was 'cause she seemed to be just waiting. So when I drove off I looked in my mirror and she got out and went into the house. Then I started wondering if we had something to worry about. The terms of his lease were pretty strict because it was a cash deal: solo residency, we didn't want to get into a crash-pad situation.'

'Or a dope house.'

No answer.

Milo said, 'Your father was concerned Muhrmann might be a drug dealer because Muhrmann paid eleven thou upfront in cash.'

'I know, I'm the one took the money.'

'He handed it to you?'

'No, it got dropped off at the office. But I found it in the mailbox.'

'Dropped off by who?'

'We assumed him, I mean that kind of money you'd want to handle it yourself, right?'

'That kind of money I wouldn't drop it in the mailbox.'

'It's a locked box,' said Brandon. 'Goes right into the office.'

'What kind of car was the girl sitting in?'

'Some little compact, didn't notice the brand.'

'What did she look like?'

'Hot.'

'Could you be a little more specific?'

'Long blond hair, great body. Kind of like Scarlett Johanssen. Or another one, an old one Dad likes. Brigitte something.'

'Bardot?'

'Yeah.'

'Scarlett or Brigitte.'

'Hot and blond,' said Brandon. 'I only saw her from a distance.'

'But that was enough to know she was hot.'

'Some girls, you know, they've just got the look, you can spot it from far away.'

'If I fax you a picture would you be able to tell me if it's a match?'

'I don't know.'

'Is there anything else you remember about this girl, Brandon?'

'Nope. Why?'

'We're curious about her. Nothing.'

'Nope, sorry.'

'Okay, thanks.'

'I did have an impression, though, sir. About both of them. You interested in impressions?'

'I sure am, Brandon.'

'With him being all pumped and her being hot what kind of flashed in my head was porn stars. We get that all the time. Offers for short-term rentals, mostly at vacant apartments out in the Valley. The money's great, but Dad won't go for it, too religious.'

'But Dad doesn't pay much attention to the house on Russell.'

'You got that right,' said Brandon. 'Calls it his albatross. To Mom it's some kind of shrine, but she doesn't have to deal with renting it or fixing it up.'

'You wondered if Muhrmann was renting the place for shoots, that's why all the cash up front.'

'My dad would be pissed, so I drove by around a week later to see if anything weird was going on, but it wasn't.'

'What were you looking for?'

'Lots of cars, vans, people going in and out, anything weird. I even asked Vlatek – the guy who owns the body shop. He said nothing different was going on since Muhrmann moved in, he never even saw Muhrmann.'

'Sounds like you did a little detection work,' said Milo.

'I was curious,' said Brandon. 'Dad likes me to be curious.'

15

As we headed for Pasadena, I said, 'Muhrmann told his mother he was trying out for a movie and C. Longellos had a POB in the Valley. Maybe the kid's instincts were good.'

'Maybe it's my day for insightful citizens. Let's see if your fellow mental health pros are half as good. If they are, we celebrate with Thai.'

The address listed for Awakenings, A Healing Place, was a triad of whitewashed fifties ranch houses turned into a compound by vinyl picket fencing, not far from the Santa Anita Race Track. Deadbolt and buzzer on the gate, drought-friendly plants in the yard.

No signage. Milo double-checked the address. 'The numbers match.'

We got out of the car. The drive had taken over an hour. Both of us stretched. Quiet block of well-tended apartment buildings and a few other single dwellings. Did the neighbors have any idea?

The faintest odor of equine sweat and waste spiced the cooling air.

I said, 'Maybe they also treat compulsive gambling.'

'Drop your line where the fishies are swarming? Smart marketing. But with all the fancy outfits claiming to fix your head, you'd think Ms C. Longellos would want something swankier.'

'Green acres, tai chi, therapeutic massage, past-lives regression?'

'Toss in vegan cuisine and I'm sold.'

I said, 'On the other hand, a profile this low could be perfect for people with serious secrets.'

We waited to be buzzed through the picket gate, walked up a brick path that led to the center house, and entered a tight, uninhabited lobby backed by a pebble-glass reception window. The receptionist who'd let us in had kept the window shut. To the left, a black door was fitted with security hinges.

Tight procedures because the clientele was unpredictable?

The lobby smelled sweet and acrid and frightening, like a public health clinic during a mass vaccination. Hard uninviting furniture sat atop rust-brown linoleum. The walls were tongue-and-groove wood painted cigarette-ash gray. Seeping through the chemical aroma was the rancid bite of greasy food left too long in steam tables.

A whiteboard to the right of the window listed an all-day schedule of group and individual therapies, psychological and physical.

The session of the moment: *Face Your Self with Focus: Constructive Mindfulness, Beth E. A. Manlow, MD, PhD.*

Milo muttered, 'My butt's falling asleep out of empathy.' He tapped the window.

A lock turned, the pane slid open. A pretty Asian woman, hair tied back in a blue-black bun, said, 'How may I help you?'

Milo's badge flash was followed up by Steven Muhrmann's photo. 'Recognize this fellow?'

'Sorry, no, I've only been working here two months.'

'Could we please speak to someone who's been here awhile – say, two or three years?'

'May I ask what this is about?'

'A serious crime.'

She touched her phone. 'How serious?'

'Serious enough to bring us here. Who's the boss around here?'

'I'm going to page our director, Dr Manlow.'

'Says on the board she's in session.'

'If she is, she won't answer, and we'll just have to see what to do. I'm still learning the regulations, so bear with me.'

She took care to slide the window back in place softly. A few seconds of muffled conversation preceded her reemergence. Smile of relief. 'Dr Manlow will be down in a moment. If you'd care to take a seat.' Motioning to the hard chairs.

Before our butts lowered, the black door swung open. The woman who marched through was forty or so with thick, wavy chestnut hair, wide aqua eyes, and a longish face of a porcelain hue and consistency that suggested sun phobia. Full lips, thin beakish nose, a smidge too much chin for ideal beauty.

An attractive woman made more so by confident posture.

She wore a cinnamon cashmere sweater, muted brown plaid slacks, bitter-chocolate crocodile pumps. A leather day planner matched the shoes. So did the leather pen case hanging from her waistband, along with a cell phone and two beepers, one topped by a strip of red tape.

Enough gear to give her the cop swagger but she strode forward without an errant twist of hip or leg.

No jewelry. The risk of being snagged?

'I'm Dr Manlow.' Glassy, girlish voice but authority in her inflection.

'Thanks for seeing us, Doctor. Milo Sturgis, Alex Delaware.' He handed his card over. Most people skim. Double-Doctor Beth E. A. Manlow put on gold-rimmed glasses and read carefully before slipping the card into her day planner.

'Homicide. Who's been murdered?'

'A woman we're still trying to identify.' Milo showed her the sketch of Mystery née Princess.

Manlow said, 'Sorry, she's not one of our patients. At least not for the past five years since I've been here.'

'You remember all of your patients by sight?'

'I've got an eye for details and it's only been five years. I saw this rendering on the news, it didn't ring any bells then and that holds for now. Annie said you showed her a picture of a man.'

Milo produced Muhrmann's photo.

She stared, removed her glasses, shook her head. Resignation, not denial.

102

'What's his connection to your case?'

'You know him.'

'Tell me the name you've got for him.'

'Steven Muhrmann.'

She nodded.

Milo said, 'What can you tell me about him?'

'Why are you interested?'

'He knew the victim.'

'He knew her, that's it?' she said. 'Or are you saying he's your suspect?'

'Would that make a difference, in terms of how much you're going to tell us, Doctor?'

Manlow tapped a foot. Pulled a thread from her sweater, frowned as she coiled it around her fingers. 'Let's talk in my office.'

The black security door opened to a narrow hallway that terminated in a transparent window laced with steel mesh.

A red *No Admittance Without Authorization* sign hung below the uppermost of two deadbolts. Just in case you missed that, a white placard read *Personnel and Inpatients Only Beyond This Point.*

Manlow's office was just inside the door. As we entered, I glanced through the mesh, caught a glimpse of another, longer corridor paneled in knotty pine. A woman sat on the floor reading. Another woman worked a crossword puzzle. At the far end, a man stretched, touched his toes, rotated his neck.

Everyone in street clothes, nothing clinical about the ambience. But something about the way the three of them moved – slow, measured, mechanical – said frivolity had long been left behind.

Manlow's office was modestly proportioned, walled with bookshelves, file cabinets, and a collection of mounted diplomas. Elizabeth Emma Allison Manlow had earned a BA from Cornell when she was still Elizabeth Emma Allison, an MD from UC San Francisco, and a PhD in neuropharmacology from Stanford. Internship and psychiatry residency had both been served at Massachusetts General. A fellowship certificate in cognitive behavior therapy had been granted by an institute in Philadelphia.

She'd finished her training six years ago. This was her first and only job.

No family photos. I liked that. With a true pro it's all about the patient.

Milo said, 'What kinds of conditions do you treat here?'

'Substance abuse, exclusively.'

'Not gambling?'

'Pardon?'

'Being so close to the track.' Milo repeated his line about fish and fishing.

Beth Manlow smiled. 'Maybe we should develop a program for that. No, we concentrate on addictive chemicals. And that doesn't include overactive sex hormones, either, because sex addiction, in my opinion, is a monumental crock.'

'Tell us about Steven Muhrmann.'

Manlow's smile chilled. 'Are you familiar with rehab programs?'

Milo said, 'Not really.'

'Most of them suck.'

He laughed. 'Don't hold back, Doc.'

Beth Manlow said, 'Look, one thing this work has taught me is that to be effective, you have to grasp reality firmly. This is a very tough business and success rates, as defined by five years with no relapse, are all over the place – from two percent to seventy-five.'

He whistled.

'Precisely, Lieutenant.'

'No one really knows what works.'

'We know a few things,' said Manlow. 'But you're right, there's much to be done in the way of establishing criteria for success. And let me assure you that anything approaching the seventy percent figure is likely to be either an outright lie or based exclusively on self-report, which is a fancy term for bragging. That's not to say most facilities are moneymaking rackets, though some are. It's really the nature of the beast that we stalk: Addiction isn't a sin nor is it simply a set of bad habits, though bad habits inevitably follow addiction. The crux of the problem is that when people get hooked on a narcotic substance, their brain chemistry changes. We can detoxify addicts during acute phases and we can teach them to reverse destructive patterns of behavior if they're sufficiently motivated. But I've yet to see anyone claiming to undo the basic addictive biology.'

Milo blinked. Clicked his tongue. A signal I'd never seen before but decoding was easy. *Take it, pal.*

I said, 'Sounds like a chronic disease.'

'Precisely, chronic care is the best-fit model,' said Beth Manlow.

'And this relates to Steve Muhrmann because—'

'I gave you that little speech because I need you to be realistic about what I can tell you. We are one of the best facilities in the country but we do not turn a profit, nor do we aim to. Awakenings was started by a man who lost two children to addiction and sought to prevent the same tragedy in other people's families. Solon Wechsman passed away five years ago and left an endowment that funds this place, but only partially. I was hired after he died and a bit of financial freedom allows me the luxury of brutal self-appraisal. Our success rate – accurately determined – is thirty-six percent. It may not sound like much but I think it's pretty good. It's like being an oncologist – a cancer specialist. If you've allowed someone several constructive years, you've accomplished something important.'

'You're saying Steve Muhrmann was one of the sixty-four percent.'

'I can't talk about him or any other patient specifically. But I won't tell you you're wrong.'

'Did he create special problems when he was here?'

She shook her head. 'I can't get into details.'

'Can you say what he came to you for?'

'All I'm going to tell you is that for the most part patients come to us volitionally. But a few are sent to us.'

I said, 'Muhrmann had a couple of DUIs and the court imposed treatment.'

'In a perfect world,' said Beth Manlow, 'everyone would have sufficient insight to know when their engines needed a tune-up. In our world, some cars need to be towed in.'

'Have you found any difference between mandated patients and those who come on their own?'

'My preliminary data say there is a difference.'

'Court-appointed patients are more problematic.'

'Let's just say they're less focused on long-term solutions.'

'Clean me up, sign a paper, send me home.'

She shrugged.

I said, 'Did Muhrmann show any tendencies to violence?'

'I'm not going to answer that,' she said. 'But don't interpret my reticence as a yes.'

'Was there anything about him you found troublesome in terms of aggression?'

'I can't tell you that, either,' she said.

'Maybe you just did.'

'I wouldn't assume anything. Now, if there's nothing more, I need to lead a group in—'

I said, 'Constance Longellos.'

Manlow smoothed her thick hair. Stood, straightened a diploma that had been hanging straight. 'I really do need to get going, the group's waiting. It's not a bad thing for addicts to learn to delay gratification, but no sense pushing it.'

As she headed for the door, I said, 'Ms Longellos served as a reference for Mr Muhrmann, so he could rent a house. Like Muhrmann, she was convicted of drunk driving. That could be grounds for rapport.'

Manlow tapped the door frame.

Milo said, 'The girl on TV was seen with Muhrmann hours before she ended up with her face blown off.'

Manlow's knuckles blanched. 'Gory details are supposed to shock me into an ethical lapse? I'm a physician, that kind of thing doesn't bother me.'

'Does it bother you that a former patient you were unable to help may have gone on to commit murder?'

Manlow's pale face colored at the peripheries, hairline, jaw points, and cheekbones reddening like an oxidizing apple filmed in time-lapse.

One of her beepers went off. The one without the tape. Snatching it from her waistband, she read the number. 'I need to go right now. I'm going to buzz you out and I suggest that a return visit will not be useful for anyone.'

16

MILO STOPPED to stare at the ranch houses before slipping into the passenger seat. 'Place calls itself Awakenings but Manlow admitted most of the patients go back to sleep. Including Steve-o. The way she got squirrelly about Longellos tells me there was a hookup. And that Muhrmann was a problem child. So what constitutes a problem in a place like this?'

'Chronic noncompliance,' I said. 'Or consorting with another patient. In this case an older woman with problems of her own.'

'Consorting,' he said. 'Love your knack for the genteel. Yeah, maybe he *consorted* with DUI Connie. Who can't be found anymore.' He grimaced. 'The Caspar kid described Muhrmann as hostile and aggressive. Maybe women he consorts with don't fare well. But Dr Manlow wouldn't come out and say he was dangerous.'

'Maybe he wasn't when he was here. One good thing, we're developing a time line: Longellos and Muhrmann get busted around the same time, Muhrmann's out for a year or so when he uses her as a reference for the house on Russell. By that time, he and Mystery are hanging out, maybe to shoot a porno. He has eleven grand in cash but comes to his mother eight months ago for more money. She gives him two, which he probably uses for dope, because once his upfront rent's paid off, he stops paying. Whatever his relationship with Connie Longellos, he kept seeing Mystery. Maybe for sex, maybe for business, maybe for both. Which could tie in with that scene I saw at the

Fauborg: some sort of fantasy game involving the two of them and a third party.'

'Mystery's hot date,' he said. 'We've been assuming a man, but what if this Connie was part of the threesome? That could explain two weapons when the time came for Mystery to go. A woman might not have enough shooting experience to do it on her own.'

'But she might get a charge out of being part of a firing squad.'

He thought about that. 'Sick. Okay, Thai time, but make a stop first.'

'Where?'

'I see it, I'll tell you.'

We'd traveled half a mile on Colorado when Milo said, 'Here.'

Twenty-four-hour photocopy place. Dime-a-page faxing.

He phoned Brandon Caspar at Zephyr Properties, told him to be on standby, then slipped the drawing of Mystery into a machine.

Moments later, Brandon called back.

Milo said, 'Probably? You're not positive?' A beat. 'No one's asking you to place a bet, Brandon, just go with your gut . . . no, we're not even close to charging anyone with anything so don't worry about going to court . . . yes, I do remember Brigitte Bardot . . . yes, I can see the resemblance but what I want to know is . . . okay, I'll settle for most probably.'

Clicking off, he said, 'Unless you're starving, forget Thai.'

'Lost your appetite?'

'More like putting it on hold. I was hoping the kid would give me a positive ID and I could get Muhrmann's face on the news.' He snatched the drawing out of the fax machine.

Back in the car, he said, 'What the hell, nothing ventured.'

As I aimed for the freeway, he called Public Affairs, hung up squeezing the phone so hard it squeaked.

'As far as they're concerned I've still got insufficient cause but even if I did have enough, the chance of getting more media time would be slim to none. 'Cause that would violate the *one*-time rule.'

I said, 'You get one shot per case?'

'Unofficially, no, but apparently hell yeah. Unless it's a big-time serial killer task force or something the department views as especially media-worthy.'

'Celebrities in trouble?' I said.

'That would work.'

'You'd think O.J. would've been a lesson.'

'Yeah, right. Every idiot wants to be a star or at least fuck one.'

'How about some cheap rationalization? Going public on Muhrmann too early could drive him underground.'

'There's always that risk,' he said. 'But Muhrmann's not some sixteen-year-old gangbanger who's never been on a plane. For all I know, he's already out of sight. Also, the two-killer scenario might mean he's got a partner willing to finance an escape.'

'Homicidal Sugar Daddy.'

'Or Mommy, if it's elusive Connie or someone like her. Did SukRose mention anything about that?'

'Not that I remember.'

'Either way, there's a name in the Agajanians' database that would bust this thing wide open but I can't access it because Big Brother Brian's a damn attorney.'

He looked up Brian Agajanian's office number. Huge firm in Century City. Mr Agajanian was out, his secretary had no idea when he'd be back. When Milo identified himself, her voice closed up and her promise to pass along the message took on the sincerity of a diplomat's dinner banter.

A DMV search produced Agajanian's home address in Glendale, off the Brand Boulevard exit.

Right on our way as we sped west on the 210.

'Talk about karma,' said Milo. 'Let's yank this guy's leash, see how good a guard dog he really is.'

The house was a two-story Spanish perched atop a hillside covered with verbena. Evening was settling in. As the contours of the mountains receded, freckles of city light asserted themselves.

It took a steep hike to get to the paved mesa that served as Brian Agajanian's parking area. Two vehicles rested up there, leaving no spare space. We left the Seville down below and climbed.

Milo started to huff at the halfway point. 'There better be gain with pain.'

By the time we reached the top, he was breathing hard and, in between exhalations, muttering a low mantra of rage.

Agajanian's wheels were a steel-gray Lexus RX SUV with a *Baby On Board* sticker. Two kiddie seats took up the back. Video screens were built into the headrests. Behind that, an immaculate white Porsche Boxster sported *BRY ATT* personalized plates.

'Proud of himself,' said Milo, catching his breath. 'Having the capacity for shame is probably too much to ask of him.'

He jabbed a bell circled by a small, lacquered wreath of pinecones and maple leaves. A pretty, buxom redheaded woman in a red top and black leggings came to the door holding a sleeping infant wearing a pale blue hybrid of swaddle blanket and pj's that evoked Swee'Pea.

'Oh, I thought you were . . . ?' An anticipatory smile gave way to anxiety.

'Ms Agajanian? Los Angeles Police Department. We need to talk to Mr Brian Agajanian.'

'I thought you were my mother,' she said. 'She'll be here soon. There's nothing wrong, right?'

Milo said, 'Nothing at all. We just need to talk to your husband. Is he here?'

Stepping back into a spotless travertine entry hall, she hugged the baby to her breast. '*Bri*-an!'

A tall, thin, black-haired man with an arched nose and a barbered goatee trotted in. He wore a white T-shirt, blue sweatpants with a white stripe running down the leg, yellow-and-black running shoes. 'Everything okay, Mel?'

She pointed.

Black eyes swung to us. 'Can I help you?'

111

'They're the police, Bri.'

'What?' Addressing the question to us, not his wife.

She said, 'They're the—'

'Go back inside, Mel.'

'Is everything okay?' Rocking the still-dozing baby.

'Of course. Go back inside.' His glare dared us to contradict him.

Milo said, 'Everything's peachy.' The baby stirred. Mel Agajanian cooed, 'Sh-sh, sh, sh,' and rocked the child.

Brian Agajanian's eyes slitted. 'Put him to bed. I'll take it from here.'

Once she complied, he stepped out of his house, strode to the outer edge of the flattened parking area, stopped an inch from the drop. One misstep and he'd be plummeting through a slalom of verbena. Folding his arms across his chest, he studied each of us, pretended to care about the darkening sky, then the lights below. Young man but the black hair was thinning and deep furrows scored his cheeks before confronting beard hairs. 'This can't be about what I think it is.'

Milo said, 'That's a pretty complex sentence, Mr Agajanian.'

'Okay, here's a simple one: What's. This. About?'

'A name in your sisters' data bank.'

Brian Agajanian punched a palm. 'Unbelievable. For that you disrupt my privacy and scare my wife?'

'Think of it as a friendly visit.'

Agajanian's arms crossed his chest. His pinched expression said he was wearing the tightest sports bra in the universe. 'I know you have a job to do but this is really outrageous.'

Milo snapped open his attaché case and brandished a photo. Close-up of the bloody swamp that had once been the face of the girl called Mystery.

'Yech.' Brian Agajanian swayed, canting dangerously toward the hill-side. Milo braced his left arm.

Agajanian shrugged him off, careful to keep his movement slow and easy.

Milo said, 'You looked like you were losing your balance.'

'I'm fine,' said Agajanian, averting his eye from the image. 'That's disgusting, there was no need for that. Why didn't you just call my office?'

'We did. Your secretary promised to call you right away but we never heard back.'

'I was working outside the office, haven't checked messages.'

'Outside, as in your sisters' office?'

'Outside is all you need to know. Now, you really should go. This is totally inappropriate.'

Milo said, 'If we had reached you on the phone would you have given me that poor girl's real name?'

'What makes you think this will be effective?'

'I always go for the personal touch.'

'What did you say your name was?'

'Sturgis, West LA Division.'

'And you're a lieutenant.'

Milo smiled. 'And you're an attorney.'

Agajanian said, 'Lieutenant Sturgis,' as if caching a weapon.

Milo said, 'If you'd like to enter it into your PDA, I'd be happy to wait.'

'That's okay, I have a good memory.'

'Does that include this poor girl's real name?'

Agajanian didn't answer.

Milo said, 'I also need the name of anyone your sisters hooked her up with—'

'My sisters don't hook anyone up, they've created a social networking site.'

'Where people pay them for the privilege of hooking up.'

'It's not a fine point, it's the crux, Lieutenant. There's no genuine agency here, meaning SukRose is not a party to any transaction and as such—'

'They're aiming to be the eBay of May–December romance,' said Milo. 'I hope they make billions. Meanwhile, give me names for one particular May and any Decembers in her past so we can find out who turned her into hamburger. At the least, we'll be able to notify her family so what's left of her – her *components* – are not stacked indefinitely in a refrigerated closet—'

'I *get* you, Lieutenant Sturgis. But no, sorry, can't help.'

Milo loomed. 'Why not?'

'Why not? Because SukRose could conceivably end up incurring legal responsibility for any ensuing personal damage brought about by your investigation. Then there's the general matter of privacy and—'

'I get *you*, Mr Agajanian.'

'Meaning?'

'You were always a good student but the sight of blood grossed you out so instead of becoming a doctor where you might actually be able to help someone, you chose a profession where you get paid to turn simple things complicated by creating a foreign language called lawyer-speak that you can then charge poor suckers to translate.'

Arcing a thumb at the Boxster's personalized plate, Milo winked. 'Life is good, huh?'

Brian Agajanian's jaw dropped, then slammed shut, tightening to compensate. 'I'm not going to stand here and justify my profession. Some things *are* complicated and your situation falls into that category.'

Milo dropped the death photo into his case. 'Suit yourself, Brian. Have you discussed with your sisters the fact that the less you tell us, the more public exposure their company's going to get? But not the right type of exposure? As in tomorrow's six o'clock news letting the world know that one of their Sweeties ended up murdered and they've refused to help furnish evidence?'

'That,' said Agajanian, 'would incur consequences of its own.'

'You bet it would, Brian. If I'm a rich geezer looking for a nubile hard-body I'm not gonna turn to a website where a hard-body got turned nasty-mushy and the police are snooping around.'

'That's my point! Your snooping is potentially deleterious to the survival of—'

'What's deleterious, Brian, is your letting things get to the point where everything's out in the open.'

'*You're* the one ripping it wide open.'

'Business is business,' said Milo. 'Mine is putting away bad guys and if your sisters are taking money from a murderer to whom they supply girls – directly or indirectly – you think that's gonna help their business? It's in their best interests to clear this up. One way or the other, I'm gonna find out who killed that poor girl and why. The only question is do Suki and Rosalynn end up part of the problem or part of the solution.'

Agajanian's chest heaved. He stared at the sky.

'Brian?'

'They end up neither, because they're not involved any more than the phone company's involved when someone makes a crank call.'

'We subpoena phone records,' said Milo. 'Have no problem getting compliance.'

'Then maybe you should subpoena us.'

'Suit yourself, Brian. Meanwhile, my Public Affairs Division tells me there's a TV reporter doing a story on computer dating sites, real pushy type, chafing at the bit to learn more about your sisters.'

'My sisters have done nothing wrong.'

'If you say so. We're finished, go enjoy your family.' Milo turned to leave.

Brian Agajanian said, 'You're telling me there's been a specific request to cover SukRose?'

'What started out as general interest got specific when news of this poor girl's murder got out.'

'You didn't purposely direct this reporter to my sisters?'

'Nope.'

'But if I don't comply, you will.'

'Brian, the less media contact I have, the better. But once the wheels start spinning, it's hard to put the brakes on.'

'This is wrong. This is totally wrong.' Agajanian tapped a foot, looked out over the rooftops of houses beneath his. 'Okay, I didn't want to get into this but maybe it'll prevent you from wasting your time and ours. Trust me, there is *no* possible connection between my sisters' client and your victim's murder. None, whatsoever.'

'One client,' said Milo. 'You're saying she only hooked up with one Daddy?'

'I'm saying you're wasting your time looking at *any* client of my sisters. You have my personal assurance in that regard.'

'That so?'

'Cross my heart.' Agajanian's smile was smug. The joy of regaining the upper hand.

Milo said, 'Well, here's my personal assurance, Brian: If you want your sisters' business to thrive, you're gonna need to cut the crap and stop dancing around and give me two names. Hers and her date's. Once you do that, I'm out of your hair.'

'What if you decide to get back into my hair?'

'Then you'll need one helluva comb.'

'Very funny—'

'It's not funny, Brian. Nothing's funny. A poor girl got her face blown off and even if I had a sense of humor to begin with, I lost it. You've got ten seconds to decide before those wheels start spinning.'

Agajanian's Adam's apple rose and fell. He licked his lips.

New smile. Tight, cold, focused.

Milo said, 'Nice talking to you, Brian.'

Agajanian said, '*Should* SukRose choose to help your department in the pursuit of their investigation and *should* SukRose at some point require confirmation of that help, I need a guarantee that said confirmation will be forthcoming without undue delay or obfuscation. Furthermore, the police department must pledge to do its utmost to shield SukRose from unwarranted media exposure, excepting such exposure that SukRose solicits in pursuit of its own legitimate interests, not to exclude film, television, or printed media adaptation.'

'You want to write a screenplay?'

'Just buttoning down details, Lieutenant. Finally, it is *imperative* that SukRose not be identified as the source of the information you are seeking in any way that exposes the company or its principals to civil or criminal liability.'

That sounded like a motion he'd drafted and memorized. To my ear, meaningless, unenforcable pap.

Maybe he needed to face-save at the next family reunion.

Milo smiled. 'You're a good brother, Brian. And that all sounds fine to me.'

Brian Agajanian breathed in deeply, closed his eyes. 'The name in our files is Tara Sly.'

'Sly as in—'

'Clever, tricky. And that's all I know about her except for what she listed on her page. Women don't pay a fee so we don't collect personal data from them. Therefore I have no address or financial information to give you, only the email address she was using at the time, which is taracuteee@gmail.com. I tried to send an email there and it got kicked back as an inactive account. And yes, she did connect to only one client but as I told you he's irrelevant.'

'Because he's a saint?'

'Even better,' said Agajanian. 'He's deceased.'

'His email got kicked back, too?'

'I checked him out in public records, found the death certificate. Natural causes.'

'Thorough, Brian.'

'No need to thank me.'

'I'll thank you once I get a copy of Tara Sly's page as it was when she posted it on SukRose. Same for the late, lamented Sugar Daddy and his personal information.'

'I just told you, he's dead,' said Agajanian. 'Nine months ago.'

'I'm a thorough guy, Brian.'

Agajanian flexed a biceps. 'You cannot tell his family you found him through SukRose.'

'Wouldn't think of it.'

'Fine, fine.' Agajanian's face was wet with sweat. '*If* you promise me that's the end of it.'

'Cross *my* heart, Brian.'

'Wait here, I'll bring it to you.'

'Thank you, Brian.'

'I still don't know why you'd care about a dead guy.'

'Old habits,' said Milo.

17

SukRose Sweetie #21667
Codename: Mystery
Age: 24
Residence: Western Elite
Height: 5'6"
Weight: 113
Body Classification: Sylph With Curve Bonus
Eye Color: Brown (Chocolate)
Hair Color: Blond (Honey)
Education: AA communications
Occupation: Model, Actress, Personal Care Speciliast
Habits: No bad ones. Least I don't think! LOL.
*Nonsmoker but I don't mind if U light up a big juicy Cohiba in
fact I like the aroma.*

*Profile: California Girl all the way, luv the whole state top and
bottom and middle cuz let's face it clouds are a drag and sunshine's
great for the mood and even for the skin if you don't overdo cuz it
puts in a glow. Why not be happy when happy makes everyone else
happy is my montra. Adventure and freedom are my thing. Specially
freedom. But adventure doesn't come too far behind. I luv to travel
but to be real honest haven't done as much as I would if I had a
good friend who also luvved to travel. Favorite food: Mexican if*

there's no cruelty in how they make it and who says Mexican
can't be vegan their great with veggies. Favorite music: Pink,
Lifehouse, Lady Gaga, Katie Perry, The Thermals, Maroon Five.
Favorite read: Elle, Marie Claire, Architecture Digest, People, Us.
Guilty Pleasure: The Enquirer. I like yoga and Pilates and really
anything that centers me and lets me explore. I like to take long
walks they can be slow or airobic. I'm all kinds of physical but also
I'm spiritual and I luuuuuuv animals but if you have allergies we
can just go to the zoo and look at them from far away. Anything
that's fun for U is fun for me. I like to please
so please let me please.

Seeking: A Daddy of any age who knows how to be strong but also
gentle, spiritual but also practical, kind but also a leader who
embraces change. I'm not one of those people who thinks money
has to give you headaches or mess up your life it's all about
balance and why not enjoy the world if no one gets hurt? I want an
adventure with the right person and I don't close doors I like to
open them.

Flanking the profile were four photos.

One was a torso-shot of the girl I'd seen at the Fauborg wearing the same white dress, minus the scarf. Serious set of mouth, as if she was trying to get a point across. Her hair was drawn back and crowned by a network of elaborate braids. No diamond glint at her wrist or anywhere.

Two other photos were swimsuit poses. White thong bikini, long, windswept hair, collarbones in sharp relief above perfect cleavage, lips slightly parted. Rocks and ocean in the background, heart-shaped sunglasses reminiscent of Lolita.

The fourth had her in a dark pin-striped suit, perched on a desk and smiling coyly.

Long, lithe body, sweet unlined face, huge, soft, vaguely unfocused eyes. Even in the bikini shots, they managed to project a hint of innocence bordering on bewilderment.

A man looking to play Henry Higgins would be attracted.

So would a power freak out for total domination.

Milo said, 'She was a cutie, wasn't she,' and reread the profile. 'Vegan Mexican joints and animal shelters, there's an investigative lead. Hell, maybe I'll find a place that saves fuzzies and ladles out cruelty-free menudo and we can grab lunch along the way.' His eyes dropped to the bottom of the bio. 'She wasn't much for spelling or grammar, was she? Guess the sisters don't edit much.'

I told him what I'd seen in her eyes.

'Little Miss Helpless? Yeah, that could get you in trouble.'

He turned to the second page.

SukRose Daddy #2198
Codename: Stylemaven
Residences: Western and Eastern Elites
Education: More Than I Needed
Occupation: Gloriously Nothing
Habits: Fine spirits and wine but in moderation, ditto Cohibas
and other premium Cuban cigars. Premium is my benchword and
don't get me in a discussion of the embargo (can you spell 'patently
absurd?')

Profile: A rich productive life redolent of been-there-done-it could
have caused me to sink into the grand ennui and renounce the value
of future exploration. Instead, I chose to embrace my good fortune
and make creative, constructive, cohesive use of my freedom by
embracing adventure and embarking on a trajectory of emotional,
physical and spiritual collaboration with an
equally fortunate woman.
Shallow is for planting vegetables; if you have no interest beyond
the superficial, look elsewhere. I've developed a strong ethos rooted

in the credo that while relational stability forms the bedrock of societal continuity, without change and novelty, it remains just that: sterile, inanimate. Rock. Life is not about the mineral, it's about the animal but not in a vulgar sense. I'm referring to libido the way Herr Professor Freud intended it: a vibrant, soul-enriching life force that forms the raison d'être of our very existence.
Without passion, connection, synchronicity, there is only existence, not life.

Seeking: A woman who understands all this.

At the bottom of the printout, Brian Agajanian had printed in firm block letters:

MARKHAM MCREYNOLD SUSS

Below that: two bracketed dates documenting Suss's sixty-eight-year life span.

The county certificate had been issued eight months ago, twenty-six days after Suss's demise from natural causes.

Milo called and verified the certificate number.

He returned to Tara Sly aka Mystery's profile. 'A guy pushing seventy trying to keep up with that? I keep picturing natural causes as getting literally screwed to death.'

A few more calls verified that no one else with Suss's name had a current driver's license or residential address in California or New York.

'How does he come across to you, Alex?'

'Like a guy who considered himself brilliant and wanted everyone to know it. I can see him attending top schools, possibly being attracted to intellectual pursuits, but putting it aside to make money.'

'Coulda been a cognitive contender so he tries to bowl the Sweeties over with syntax and vocabulary? Like the girls on the site would care.'

I said, 'Maybe he needed to think they did. To make it more than it was.'

'From the way he goes on, you'd think he was looking for Madame Curie. So who does he hook up with? Little Ms Luuuuuuv with the helpless eyes.'

I said, 'Hey, they both like cigars.'

'There's a foundation for a meaningful relationship. Any other impressions?'

I had another go at Suss's braggadocio. ' "Stylemaven" might mean he made his money in a fashion-oriented business. Tara claimed to read *Elle* and *Marie Claire* so that could've provided another basis for rapport. And they both talk about adventure, so that might have attracted him . . . "newfound freedom" could be due to a recent divorce. Or retirement. Or he was married and lying. The rest of it is pretty much puffery.'

'She bullshits, he bullshits, both of them read between the lines. 'Cause the real *raison d'être* for all the game playing is old guys trawling for young chicks willing to close their eyes and pretend they're boffing a stud.'

He slipped the printouts into his case. Looked up Tara Sly in the databases. Nothing.

'Big shock, no way that's a bona fide name. Think it was an in-joke, as in *I'm craftier than I seem?*'

I said, 'That's a little abstract unless she was a lot smarter than her prose suggests. Also, *Sly* could be fake but *Tara* could be real, because *Ms Tara* could easily morph into *Mystery.*'

'How does Muhrmann figure in?'

'He could've provided protection for a share of the profits.'

'Your basic pimp-hustler.'

I said, 'In this town they call it producing.'

He laughed. 'I'll make you a star, kid, and all you have to do is engage in geriatric sex and squeeze every golden egg out of the goose.'

'Unfortunately, the goose had the poor manners to die. Muhrmann hitting his mom up for money shortly after supports his involvement.

It also fits with what we saw at the Fauborg being an audition for a new goose. Instead Tara ends up with no face, maybe because the mark was a predator with a script of his own.'

'If Muhrmann and Tara were looking for another Daddy, why didn't they just go back to SukRose?'

'Maybe an opportunity came up elsewhere. Or they did return and Brian Agajanian is holding back on any other hookups because he doesn't want the site drawn into a publicity nightmare. SukRose claims careful screening of members but Brian just told us they don't collect significant data on the girls. If they're not much more discerning with the men, it wouldn't be much of a challenge for a slick psychopath to get in.'

He phoned Agajanian. The attorney swore that Markham Suss had been Tara Sly's only Sugar Daddy. 'The door's already been opened, Lieutenant. I have no reason to play games.'

Milo didn't answer.

Agajanian said, 'What do you want from me?'

'The truth.'

'You have it. One client. Period. If there was another and he killed her, I'd want you to know because I'd want you to catch him because the last thing we need is some nutcase using us. She had one Daddy and that was Suss. One. Uno. *Mek* – that's Armenian. Okay?'

Milo rolled his eyes. 'Your sisters claim they screen everyone.'

'They do. A criminal background check is run on every candidate.'

'So you ran one on Tara Sly.'

'And it came back clean.'

'I'd expect that, Brian, seeing as Tara Sly's not her real name.'

Silence. 'That's not our responsibility.'

Milo said, 'Ever think of working for the federal government?'

'Look, Lieutenant, in the last analysis we can only go by what they tell us. We've never had a problem.'

'Until now.'

'We still don't have a problem. Markham Suss died nine months ago.

Last time I checked people can't murder from the grave. We've co-operated fully. Why do you have to keep pushing your weight around?'

'Bulk is my secret weapon,' said Milo. 'Makes lunch tax-deductible.'

He clicked off. 'Okay, let's assume Muhrmann and Tara were doing some kind of dinner theater at the hotel. If the production went *real* wrong, Muhrmann could be a second victim, not a suspect. That would sure fit two killers, Mr Bad Date brought along help in order to subdue a big, aggressive man.'

'Makes sense.'

He yanked his tie loose. 'Makes sense but it would also mean bye-bye prime suspect and back to square one. The elusive Ms Longellos isn't jumping out at me as someone I need to pursue. She hooked up with Muhrmann at Awakenings, wrote him a reference, big deal. Okay, let's head back to civilization. I saw some chicken in your fridge this morning looked fine, so Thai will just have to wait for the privilege of entering my digestive tract.'

Robin was in the living room, snuggling with Blanche and reading.

Milo bowed and kissed her cheek. He looked down at the dust jacket, grinned at the title. *Trouble.* 'Someone already wrote my autobiography?'

'It's a novel, darling.'

'So is my life,' he said. 'Filed under Horror or Comedy depending on what day you catch me.'

'No progress on that poor girl?'

'More like anti-progress.'

'Tell me.'

'Trust me, you don't wanna know.'

'Trust me, Milo. I do.'

Blanche let out a soft, breathy bark.

'Outvoted,' he said and proceeded to summarize.

Robin said, 'Mystery. A girl who sells herself to the highest bidder is anything but mysterious. How old was she?'

'Her profile says twenty-four.'

'Pathetic.'

She got up, hugged me. 'You guys eat yet? I made spaghetti with porcinis, there's plenty left.'

I said, 'The gourmet here prefers cold chicken.'

Milo said, 'The gourmet will eat spaghetti with porcinis and like it.'

'You can have both,' said Robin.

'You are a wise, wise woman.'

The two of them headed for the kitchen but I veered to my office and cybersearched *tara sly*.

That pulled up MySpace pages for three separate women, one of them *tarra*. None was the girl who called herself Mystery.

I tried variants: *torra, terri, sligh, sleigh,* with no success.

Plugging in *markham mcreynold suss* was more productive: nine hits, most from business and trade journals covering the sale, twenty-five months ago, of Markham Industries to a private equity group based in Abu Dhabi.

A garment manufacturer with headquarters in Los Angeles and factories in Macao and Taiwan, Markham specialized in bottom-grade women's undergarments and panty hose designed to look expensive. The company had been established in 1946 by Alger and Marjorie Suss, postwar transplants to LA from Ohio, where the couple had built up a small chain of dry-goods stores in Dayton, Columbus, and Akron before Marjorie's chronic bronchitis spurred a move westward.

Her designs had formed the basis for the new concern based upon a conviction that only a woman could understand what made a 'female foundation garment' comfortable. Eventually, that practical sensibility gave way to 'cutting-edge concepts combined with low-cost materials' under the direction of Alger and Marjorie's son Markham.

'This is a business based on sensory gratification not durability,' he was quoted in *Barron's*. 'There's no reason a bra or a pair of panties should be expected to last forever. Women want style, they want class, they want that intangible but inexorable feeling of tactile sensuality that enhances feelings of femininity. To that end, polyester works as well as silk.'

A black-and-white photo of Suss's parents said they could've posed for *American Gothic* if Grant Wood had been looking for more dour. Markham's resemblance to his father was obvious. Both men were bald with distinctive faces: long, lean, lantern-jawed, thin-lipped. But where Alger's prim visage radiated self-denial, Markham's triumphant smile trumpeted bon vivant.

Alger looked as if he lived indoors. Tara Sly's Sugar Daddy was flamboyantly tan.

Markham Suss's high-dome pate, sun-splotched and naked save for white wisps curling above heavy-lobed ears, connoted nothing but advanced age. The same went for snow-puff eyebrows and a bulbous nose. But all that surrendered to crinkly bright eyes and an impish, boyish upturn of lip. The end result was a handsome man of a certain age projecting youthful exuberance.

Perhaps exuberance had something to do with the sum he'd gotten for his company: eighty-four million dollars, all cash.

When asked by *LA Trade Quarterly* whether he planned another venture in the rag trade, Markham Suss's reply was unqualified: 'Not a chance and I'd give you the same answer even if I wasn't encumbered by a noncompetition clause. I'm going to embrace my good fortune and make creative use of my newfound freedom.'

Those same sentiments had found their way to his SukRose profile.

For all his bravado, just another man fighting mortality and shouting *Look at me*?

I turned to the nonbusiness references.

Two cited Markham and Leona Suss as donors at charity functions. The beneficiaries were a retirement home for screen actors and an inner-city arts program.

The third was a *Beverly Hills Courier* social-pages item citing a benefit for breast cancer at the Crystal Visions Art Glass Gallery in Encino.

That one featured a full-color illustration.

Markham and Leona Suss, flanked by two sons and daughters-in-law, had posed in front of an array of vitreous abstraction.

Tara Sly's Sugar Daddy wore a navy blazer, aqua T-shirt, and indigo jeans. Trim man but the shirt stretched over a paunch that he seemed to flaunt.

Leona Suss was tall, bony, black-haired, around her husband's age. Her pink leather jumpsuit was body-conscious. Enormous horn-rimmed glasses distracted from the rest of her face.

The tendency for son to favor father continued with Dr Franklin Suss, bald, lean-but-potbellied, dressed identically to Markham but for a maroon T-shirt. Clutching his arm was Dr Isabel Suss, a short, compact brunette in an olive-drab pantsuit.

The genetic train ground to a halt at Philip Suss, who appeared around the same age as his brother. Several inches taller than Markham and Frank, he sported a full head of dark wavy hair, a thicker, broader build, and a flat belly. A rust-colored caftan-type garment hung nearly to his knees.

His shapely blond wife was attired in an orange sari embroidered with gold thread and was identified as the owner of the glass gallery.

Connie Longellos-Suss.

I searched using her name as a keyword, found nothing. Tried *crystal visions* and learned on an art glass site that the gallery had closed six months ago.

I ran searches on both sons, learned about Isabel in the process. She and Franklin practiced together as dermatologists in Beverly Hills.

If Philip Suss was gainfully employed, the Internet hadn't found out.

Printing what I needed, I made my way to the kitchen.

Milo was forking spaghetti onto three plates. Blanche nibbled daintily on a Milk-Bone. Robin poured red wine.

She said, 'Perfect timing, dinner's on, baby.'

I said, 'And I brought dessert.'

18

ROBIN WAS the first to speak. 'People find each other on the site by surfing randomly through profiles. But Muhrmann managed to hook Tara up with his cougar girlfriend's father-in-law?'

I said, 'It's possible Daddies can narrow their searches using keywords. *Cohiba* comes to mind.'

'What's a Cohiba?'

'High-priced Cuban cigar. Suss mentions enjoying them and Tara says she's a nonsmoker but she doesn't mind if her date lights one up. Given what we know, that does seem like conspicuous branding.'

Milo crumpled a still-clean napkin. 'Muhrmann and Connie used Tara as a lure for Suss. Wealthy family, it has to be something financial.'

Robin said, 'Get your hooks in the old guy and start siphoning cash.'

I said, 'Connie's got a motive. Her gallery went under half a year ago but she had to know well before then that she was failing. Brother Frank's a doctor but brother Phil doesn't seem to have a job.'

Robin said, 'Maybe Phil's job was at the underwear company and he felt betrayed when Daddy sold out.'

'Money plus revenge,' said Milo. 'A wealth of riches.'

The three of us returned to my office where I searched *markham industries*. Most of the hits reported the sale, seen as a coup for Markham Suss. But predating those was the catalog of a garment trade show in Hong Kong listing the company's executive staff.

**Markham M. Suss, President,
Chairman of the Board, Chief Executive,
Chief Operating Officer
Leona A. Suss, Vice President and Chief Financial Officer
Franklin D. Suss, MD, Materials Consultant
Philip M. Suss, Design Consultant**

Milo said, 'Daddy takes four titles for himself, no mistaking who's in charge. Officially Mommy handles the money and maybe that's real. Or she gets a salary to stay out of Daddy's hair. The boys get bullshit titles, maybe a stipend.'

I said, 'What I find interesting is that even though Franklin has a career of his own, he tops Phil's billing. That could turn out just to be alphabetization. But if it's a sign of favoritism, Connie's anger quotient just got kicked up.'

Milo said, 'Frank's a skin doctor, for all we know he got paid to certify polyester as dermal-friendly. Phil, on the other hand . . . yeah, it's interesting.'

Robin said, 'Those kinds of jobs are pretty common in rich families. Nice way to avoid estate and gift tax.'

Both of us turned to her.

'When my father got sick, he told me he wanted me to inherit as much as possible but he knew that no matter what he stipulated in the will Mom would hold everything back for herself. So he incorporated his cabinetry business and made me a majority partner. That gave me legal possession of his tools, his benches, and a whole lot of wood he'd been stockpiling, plus some cash he put into the company account. Without all that, I could've never started my own business.'

I said, 'How'd Mom react?'

'We never talked about it but I know she was mad, because when I asked for my old bedroom suite that Daddy made for me when I was seven, she said Daddy made sure everything was built-in because he wanted it to remain with the house. I knew he'd just put in elbow bolts for earthquake safety, but what was the point?'

She shrugged. 'The point is money's always mixed in with ego. A family with big money can be a powder keg.'

Milo said, 'Frankie and Philly as consultants. Reminds me of the rooster who was pestering the hens so they castrated him and turned him into a consultant. One question, though: If Phil was getting serious dough through the company why would Connie lose her gallery?'

I said, 'It's not what you make, it's what you keep. Or it's possible Phil had the means to save Connie but chose not to. Maybe their marriage had run into problems due to Connie's alcohol issues. If he found out she'd hooked up with Muhrmann in rehab, that could've been the tipping point.'

He said, 'Yeah, that would squelch spousal enthusiasm.'

'Connie was in a position to know that her father-in-law was looking for love in cyberspace. She and Muhrmann decided to use Tara as bait. And what Robin just said about ego beefs up the motive: On top of financial gain, Connie would be sticking it to the entire family.'

He took a bite of chicken, chewed slowly, enjoyed a pasta chaser, then another. When he put his fork down, he seemed distracted. 'How does any of that lead to Tara getting her face blown off? If Markham were still alive, I can see a power struggle as motive. Tara realized she was doing all the dirty work, demanded a bigger share – or tried to go it alone and cut Connie and Muhrmann out. They got pissed, expressed it with a .45 and a shotgun. But with Markham dead, there's nothing to fight over.'

Robin said, 'Unless Markham left some serious assets for Tara in his will and Connie coveted them.'

'Fooling around on the side's one thing, Rob. Putting it in writing's a giant step into scandal.'

'Exactly why he would've done it as a message from the grave. In his profile, Markham made a big deal about creativity. Setting up his mistress and wreaking havoc on his family could've been his last project.'

I said, 'With Markham dead, Tara would've still had value to Muhrmann and Connie if she agreed to help them snag another Daddy. But what if she refused? And what if her resolve was strengthened precisely because Markham had bequeathed her substantial assets? Connie and Muhrmann would be doubly frustrated. And that syncs perfectly with Muhrmann hitting his mother up for cash right after Markham's death. Tara got confident and cut him off.'

'Overconfident,' said Robin. 'She had no idea who she was fooling with.'

Milo put his fork down. 'Thank you, Nick and Nora . . . none of it feels wrong.' He hauled himself up. 'Guess it's time to learn more about this lovely bunch.'

19

Samantha 'Suki' Agajanian's red Audi TT Roadster zipped into the lot behind her building at ten thirty-five a.m.

Milo knew the car was hers and that her real name was Samantha because he'd spent the early-morning hours researching her and her sister.

Preceding that with a look at the Suss family, using the Web and property tax rolls.

No additional financial details had surfaced following the sale of the company. As a privately held corporation, Markham Industries had done a good job maintaining its privacy.

One surprise: Philip and Franklin's shared birth date made them twins.

''Bout the least identical I've ever seen,' said Milo.

Despite the dissolution of Connie's gallery and her possible fling with Steven Muhrmann, she and Philip remained married and living together on Portico Place, not far from the Encino Reservoir. The POB she'd cited in her reference for Muhrmann was a mail-drop a few miles away, long since rented by someone else and the proprietors didn't remember anything about her.

Drs Franklin and Isabel Suss were in their tenth year of paying taxes on a North Camden Drive house in the flats of Beverly Hills. Before that, they'd lived in a smaller place on Roxbury, south of Wilshire.

Leona Suss was the sole occupant of a two-acre estate on Hartford Way, just north of the Beverly Hills Hotel, and of a condo in Palm

Desert. Both properties had been purchased by a family trust twenty-seven years ago.

None of the Susses had ever been married to more than one spouse. 'Too much goddamn stability, it's un-American,' said Milo.

The Agajanian sisters, on the other hand, had each been divorced in their twenties, twice in Rosalynn's case. The founders of SukRose.net had been truthful about owning a Lake Arrowhead cabin but their city digs was a shared Hollywood Hills rental, just south of the bird streets.

Rosalynn drove the same model Audi as her sib, in silver. Columbia, Penn, and the U verified both women's educational claims. One parking ticket each, paid punctually, comprised their contact with law enforcement.

The slot I'd found at the far end of the parking lot allowed us to watch Suki as she headed for the building's back door, pressing an iPhone to her ear. She smiled as she listened, smiled as she talked. Switched to texting and kept up the mirth. A tailored tweed jacket bisected firm, generous buttocks, and skinny jeans made the most of her legs. Five-inch red stilettos caused her to teeter every few steps but the occasional loss of balance did nothing to shake her good cheer.

As if she'd put in a bid to purchase the universe, fully expected it to be accepted.

We waited until she'd disappeared into the building, spotted her entering the elevator. She looked up from her phone just as the doors began closing. Saw us and raised a perfectly plucked eyebrow as we stepped in.

Milo gave a small salute.

She returned to her mini-screen.

The lift stopped at the second floor. Two of the other riders exited, leaving behind an older woman in a baggy plaid coat and bad makeup who looked ready to discipline someone. She'd been standing close to Suki, moved quickly to put maximum space between them. Sniffed, as if the younger woman was emitting anything but Chanel No. 5.

Ding. Floor three.

Suki hesitated.

Milo said, 'Ladies first.'

The old woman said, '*Someone* get a move on.'

Out in the hallway, the texting continued.

'Morning, Suki.'

'Morning.'

'We need to talk.'

'I don't think so. Brian gave you what you need.'

'Brian gave us basics. Since then, life got complicated.'

'For who?'

'That depends.'

She looked up from the screen. 'I don't appreciate being pressured.'

'That sounds like something Brian told you to say.'

'No. It's how you're making me feel. I don't deserve it.'

'Let's go talk in your office.'

'Do you have a warrant?'

'I can get one but I sure hope it doesn't come to that, Suki. For your sake, because once the process starts, it takes on a life of its own. As in your business gets closed down for as long as it takes our techies to replicate your hard drives and scour your records.'

'No way you can do that.'

Milo clicked his tongue. 'That's what they all say, Suki.'

'This isn't Syria or Iran,' she said. 'You need grounds for a search.'

'We have grounds,' he said. 'No matter what you've seen on TV, murder cuts through the smog.'

'No way,' she said, but her voice faltered.

'The sad thing, Suki, is we probably don't even need your hard drives and going through them is going to be a major pain. All we're after are the answers to a couple of simple questions, so how say we all do ourselves a collective favor?'

'You just said everything was complicated.'

'But you can make it simple again.'

The door to a neighboring office opened. Two men in fitted suits and open-neck shirts came out laughing.

'Morning,' said one.

Suki's return greeting was barely audible and both men studied her as if she'd rebuffed them at a club.

'Whoa,' said one. 'Time to move on.'

As they boarded the elevator, the other said, 'Was that the police? Weird.'

Suki mouthed, *Damn*.

Milo said, 'Let's talk in your office.'

'Fine. But no promises.'

SukRose.net's dark, empty suite gave way to fluorescence as Suki punched wall switches on the way to her office. Vacuum tracks and an orangey-chemical smell said the space had been cleaned overnight. But the aroma of last night's Mexican takeout fought to be noticed and the crew had left packets of hot sauce next to one of her computer screens.

She frowned, brushed them into a trash basket, and looked past us.

The computers hummed. Hardware and software collaborating to align rich men with young female flesh.

I supposed it wasn't that different from what had constituted marriage for centuries, before the ideal of romantic love went from fictional device to social norm. And who knew? Maybe the concept of soul mate would one day reduce to bytes and bits.

Right now, a beautiful girl with a missing face made it feel *wrong*.

As we'd waited in the lot, Milo had asked me to begin the questioning. *You know how I feel about that math science crap.*

I said, 'Suki, how random is your process?'

'You'll have to be more specific about what you mean by "process."'

'Matching Daddies with Sweeties.'

'The *process* is we provide data and people find their own way.'

'All by themselves.'

Her eyes shifted to the left. 'That's what I just said.'

Milo walked to her window and parted the drapes. The blade of light that shot through was harsh and white.

She kept her eyes on him until he returned to his seat. 'What were you looking at? Are there more of you out there?'

He said, 'Great view. You've got yourself a really sweet setup here.'

He has a way of making pleasantry sound ominous. Suki Agajanian swallowed. 'Whatever.'

I never enjoy lying glibly but I'm better at it than I'd like to think. 'Suki, we had some math types examine your site. The consensus is that for you to succeed in a competitive field, the likelihood of random sorting as your dominant mode is about the same as sticking a monkey in a room with crayons and paper and expecting it to produce a Shakespearean sonnet over a long weekend.'

She swayed from side to side. If she were a boat, she'd be taking on water. 'Is that so?'

I nodded.

'Then your so-called math types don't know what they're talking about.'

'You're saying you never narrow searches in order to maximize compatibility.'

Her eyes repeated the same journey portside. 'There are steps we can take if people request. So what?'

'What kind of steps?'

'Constructive focus.'

'Zeroing in on common interests.'

Nod.

'Favorite foods and such?'

'Deeper than that,' she said. 'Values, experiences, intellectual pursuits.'

I tried to imagine a deep conversation between Markham Suss and Tara Sly.

'In order to zero, you use word-search software.'

She held out two palms. 'Uh-uh, no way I'm going to get into technical aspects. Wouldn't do it even if we were already copyrighted – and we're looking into that. Because anything can be modified and ripped off.'

'We're the last people you need to worry about stealing your stuff,' I said.

Her arms crossed over her chest. 'Nope, no can do. Now, if there's nothing else you—'

'So we agree that random surfing for true love might be fun in theory but narrowing the focus works significantly better.'

'Significance is a statistical concept,' she said. 'You mean importance.'

'Okay, focus is important.'

'I guess that depends.'

'Do you word-search routinely or is it an option?'

She didn't answer.

I said, 'My guess is it's a paid option, the geezers get a do-it-yourself base-rate or pony up additional dough for assisted loving.'

Suki Agajanian's crisscrossed arms tightened, folding her shoulders inward, as if someone had laced her into an oppressive corset. 'Relationships aren't a joke.'

I said, 'They're anything but. Do you charge per word, or is it a package deal?'

'I don't see why you'd care about that.'

'Are Sweeties and Daddies both eligible for assistance?'

'Everyone finds their own way, that's the beauty of—'

'Daddies pay to enroll on the site but Sweeties don't.'

'Brian already told you that.'

'So if there is an extra for-fee service only Daddies get to use it, correct?'

Long silence. Petulant nod.

I said, 'Sweeties fend for themselves.'

She said, 'Trust me, they do fine for themselves.' Sweat beaded her pretty Levantine nose. She dropped her arms, laced her fingers. A knuckle cracked. The pop made her jump.

When your own body scares you, you're easy prey.

I said, 'Obviously, you see where we're headed.'

'Obviously I don't.'

'Cohibas.'

She wheeled back in her desk chair. Hit an obstruction and came to a jarring halt, braced herself on the desk-edge. 'We did absolutely nothing wrong.'

'No one's saying you did, Suki.'

'Then can you please leave so I can go about my business? I've got a ton of emails to deal with.'

'As soon as we have the exact dates Tara Sly and Markham Suss registered with you.'

'Uh-uh, no way, I can't do that,' she said. 'Not before I consult with Brian.'

Her iPhone lay on the desk. Sparkling pink case, like a toy you might give to a three-year-old girl. I held it out to her.

She didn't budge.

'Call him, Suki, so we can all go about out business.'

'That's everything you want?' she said. 'Just dates and then you'll leave me alone?'

'You bet.'

She laughed. 'Then you really wasted your time cause the dates are right out in the open, at the top of each profile.'

Exactly.

Milo pulled out Stylemaven and Mystery's ventures in creative writing. 'According to this, Mr Suss registered twenty-three months and four days ago.'

'If that's what it says.'

'And Tara aka Mystery came on real soon after, three days to be exact.'

'Okay.'

I said, 'How much do you charge for keyword prompts?'

'You asked me that already.'

'Don't recall any answer, Suki. And frankly, we don't get why you'd want to be evasive if paying extra for prompts is a policy that all new

Daddies learn about when they enroll. Unless it isn't and you fool with the fee based on some hidden criterion. Like how much you think they're good for.'

'No! Everyone pays forty dollars for three words and each additional word is twenty each.'

'Per month?'

'Per two months but they can change the prompts if they're not getting results and there's no extra fee.'

'What percentage of your members opt to pay for any prompts?'

'I don't know.'

'Is it the majority?'

'We've never counted.'

'Quants like you and Rose?' I said. 'That's hard to believe.'

She sagged. 'It's about half.'

Quickie math made that serious income.

She said, 'Now can I get to my emails—'

'Half the Daddies pay for advanced searches while the Sweeties rely on their wits.' I smiled. 'So to speak.'

'You'd be surprised,' she said. 'Some of them are smart and educated.'

'Tara Sly must've been really smart to snag her Daddy that fast,' I said. 'Though you'd never know it from her spelling and grammar.'

'Whatever.'

'Either that, or she had ESP.'

'What do you mean?'

'You don't know?'

Another eye jog.

I said, 'Take a guess how many words she and Stylemaven matched on.'

Silence.

'Five, Suki. *Adventure, freedom, embrace, spiritual*. And, most strikingly, *Cohiba*. Our math types say the probability of that happening by coincidence is infinitesimal. What we're thinking is Mystery wasn't surfing for some theoretical Daddy. Right from the beginning she set out to get Stylemaven. That would be no big deal if Sweeties had access to Daddy profiles before they registered. All she'd have to do is read about his interests and match them. But that would wreak havoc with your site and turn it into one big linguistic competition. So you keep Daddy profiles off limits to anyone without a username and a password. Unless you mess with *that* rule for a fee.'

'We do *not*.'

I said, '*Adventure, freedom, embrace,* and *spiritual* are words that probably come up a lot on SukRose. Especially *spiritual,* everyone claims to be spiritual. But even so, a four-way match would be quite an accomplishment. Toss in a low-frequency word like *Cohibas* and Tara having ESP sounds real good. Unless you sell data to Sweeties under the table and of course you don't do that.'

'We don't, I swear.'

'Then it's really puzzling, Suki. We randomly sampled a whole bunch of your profiles. Guess how many times *Cohiba* or *Cohibas* showed up on anyone's other than Stylemaven's and Mystery's?'

Silence.

'Any guess but zero would be wrong, Suki.'

'Okay, so what?' she said. 'Someone with a username and a password showed his profile to her.'

'Another Sweetie sharing the wealth?' I said.

'Yes.'

'All those girls competing for a few choice rich guys and they'd hand over freebie data just to be nice?'

She shrugged.

Milo said, 'We have an alternative explanation.'

'What?'

He showed her an enlargement of Steven Muhrmann's DMV photo. 'He look like a sharing type to you?'

Suki Agajanian's mouth dropped open. 'Him?'

'Well, look at that,' said Milo. 'A spontaneous reaction.'

She gaped.

141

He said, 'Obviously you've had the pleasure.'

'Stefan whatwashislastname – Moore,' she said. 'What does he have to do with any of this?'

'His real name's Steven Muhrmann.'

'I knew him as Stefan Moore.'

'How do you know him, Suki?'

'He worked for us, okay? Only for a short time, no big whoop.'

'When?'

She clicked keys. Gasped. Sat back and stared at the ceiling. 'Oh, shit.'

Milo said, 'The date, please, Suki.'

'Right around the same time.'

'As . . . ?'

'As him registering. Stylemaven – Suss.'

'The date,' he repeated.

She read it off woodenly.

Milo said, 'That's two days after Stylemaven came on and one day before Mystery registered.'

'*Shit.*'

'How long did he work for you, Suki?'

'Less than two weeks – hold on.' Click click. 'Guess I don't have a record but it wasn't long, maybe a week, a week and a half.'

'Looks like he used his first day on the job to access your database.'

'No way,' she said. 'He didn't even have computer skills.'

I said, 'And you know that because . . .'

'He told us, upfront.'

'What an honest guy.'

'*Shit.*'

'I'll bet he made a big deal about being a computer dummy, Suki. I'll bet you and Rose were impressed by all that upfront honesty.'

She closed her eyes. Massaged her brow. 'I've got a crazy headache.'

I said, 'His ignorance of computers made you feel comfortable. No way he could mess with your data.'

She sat up straight. 'That bastard – but no way, he'd never be able to get into the profiles, we're security-paranoid, you want to know how paranoid we are? We double-encrypt everything, use layers of firewall, it's like the Pentagon – Brian says the Pentagon should be as secure. We do *everything* to maintain the integrity of the data because without our data, we're toast.'

'What exactly were Stefan's duties?'

'He was a gofer, ran errands, took deliveries.'

'Did he answer the phone?'

'Sometimes.'

'When?'

'What do you mean?'

'Was he limited to when you and Rose were here or did he work the phones when you went out to lunch?'

Silence.

Her whisper was fierce. 'Oh, fuck.'

I said, 'You never bothered to turn the computers off because Stefan was a computer dummy.'

The sound that she made next was hard to characterize. Part laughter, part cackle, part bronchial congestion. 'Shit, shit, shit, how could we be so . . . no, no way, I can't believe . . .'

I said, 'Did you fire him?'

'No, he quit.'

'Did he give a reason?'

'He just stopped showing up.'

'So he didn't officially quit, he just flaked. Because his real job was over.'

Her head dropped as if yoked by sudden, crushing weight. 'I am so sorry. But you're not saying that caused . . . what happened to her. You're not saying that, right?'

Milo said, 'One way or the other Tara Sly got aimed at Markham Suss. If Stefan ripped you off, that's one thing. But if you broke your own rules and took a bribe to guide the process, that's a whole different kettle of scrod.'

'No, no, we'd never do that, there's nothing personal going on here, everything's done online.'

'Romantic.'

I said, 'You had no idea she matched him that precisely?'

'Why would we? We don't look at that kind of thing.'

He said, 'How about after we came in with Tara's picture? You didn't get curious.'

Her jaw swung from side to side. 'Sure we did but all we learned was she only matched one Daddy and that was good, we figured at the worst we'd give you that and you'd leave us alone.'

'The fact that they registered within days of each other and hooked up nearly immediately didn't impress you?'

'I swear,' she said. 'That didn't even register with us, we were just trying to cover our – to stay out of a mess. We're *sorry*, okay? And we never connected it to him – that bastard. Why would we? He came across like a dummy. Even now, you can't prove he had anything to do with it – that our data was even corrupted.'

'A five-word match, Suki? Cohibas.'

'What I said, another girl shared.'

Milo and I didn't speak.

'Okay,' she said. 'It could also have been a glitch.'

He said, 'What kind of glitch?'

'Programming errors, it happens, we fix them. But really, it could've been another girl. Maybe they traded.'

'Like baseball cards,' said Milo. 'Hey, here's an idea for a spin-off: Daddy and Sweetie cards, collect them all, kids.'

'What*ever*.'

' "Gee, Tara, I was surfing with my username and password and just happened to come across this rich old dude who has a thing for Cuban cigars and I thought, hey, that's perfect for you, you love rich old dudes who stink of tobacco and talk about karma, here you go, honey. And once you get your very own username and password you can return the favor – and, oh yeah, homegirl, here's four other words you can stick

144

in your profile to form a mathematically improbable coincidence because I ran a careful word-search in order to maximize your success." ' He slapped his cheek. ' "Oops. You lost your face." '

Suki Agajanian's eyes filled with tears. 'I *said* I was *sorry.*'

'Then how about you channel all that remorse into action, Suki. As in no more delays and legal bullshit and you tell us the address Stefan gave when he applied for his ten-day job.'

'Of course, no problem.' Click. 'Here it is.' She printed a single sheet.

The same defunct mail-drop Connie Longellos had given to Muhrmann's landlord.

Milo said, 'Where's the rest of his job application?'

'That's it, I promise. I know it looks skimpy but we were working day and night to accomplish the important things, didn't have time to get all official with him – and like I said, he was barely here.'

'How'd you find him in the first place?'

'He found us,' she said. Leftward eye slide. Her lips vibrated. She'd never pass muster as a psychopath.

'How'd he find you?'

'Slipped his name and number under the door with a note saying he was looking for office work. He said he'd interviewed downstairs, someone told him we needed a gofer.'

'Who downstairs?'

'I don't know.'

'You never verified.'

'We were *busy.* We thought we needed *help.* Once we got set up and he was already gone, we learned the computers could do everything a person could do except better. That's the beauty of eBiz, you keep overheads to a minimum.'

'Bunch of smart kids, you and Rose and Brian,' he said. 'Anyone else in the family involved?'

'Michael – our baby brother – did some Web design for us, he's artistic, but that's it.'

'Tell us everything you remember about Stefan Moore.'

145

'He was okay,' she said. 'Polite, didn't say much.'

I said, 'He kept out of your way and you were busy so that was perfect.'

'Yes. You're not saying he's the one who . . . oh, God!'

Milo said, 'What we're saying is we've got a dead girl on our hands and ol' Stefan was seen in her proximity the night she died. That makes him what we call a person of interest.'

Her head dropped again. 'This is a shit-filled nightmare.'

'For Tara Sly it was a nightmare, for you it's an inconvenience, Suki.'

She looked up, dark eyes blazing. 'You don't get what I'm *saying*. Any of this gets out and we're complete and utter toast and it couldn't come at a worse time.'

'Business is tough?'

'Just the opposite, business *rocks*. We've been fielding some serious buyout offers that could be huge, so please, please, please, don't go public with any of this. *Please*.'

Milo said, 'We'll do our best, Suki. If you've told us everything you know.'

'I have! I swear to God!'

'Let's go back to something Brian claimed: You don't collect personal data on Sweeties once the initial criminal check comes back clean.'

Moment's hesitation. 'Basically . . . okay, we keep addresses and phone numbers, no reason not to. I'll give you Mystery's. Will that work for you?'

'Excellent, Suki. You'll also give us her real name.'

'I would but I don't know it.'

'Come on—'

'It's true, I'm being totally honest with you now, I *want* to be honest, there's no reason to hold back.'

'You do a criminal check but don't probe for real names.'

'We go by what they tell us,' she said. 'We're not the FBI, we shouldn't be expected to have . . . what do you call them – dossiers.'

He stared at her.

'I swear.'

'All right, Suki. Let's have her address and phone number.'

'Okay, okay, okay.' Click click click. 'Oh, God.'

'What?'

'Blank space,' she said. 'It's been deleted.'

'By who?'

'No way to tell.'

'When?'

'Can't tell you that, either.'

'Looks like your database is far from incorruptible. Better fix all that before the buyout offers are finalized.'

She shot us a crooked smile. 'I'm going to be sick.' Announcing calmly as if introducing her next piece at a piano recital.

By the time she reached the door she was retching.

The bathroom she ran to was close enough for us to hear.

Truth in advertising.

20

SUKI AGAJANIAN returned from the lav pasty-faced and hunched, limp hair tied in an unruly knot.

'Don't worry, I'm fine,' she said, as if we'd expressed concern.

Milo said, 'Now what else are you going to tell us?'

'I swear there's nothing, guys. It's not like I actually met her. Or him. To us they're just names.'

We waited her out.

She said, 'I swear.'

'One more question: Did anyone else named Suss log onto your site?'

She hesitated, threw up her hands, typed. 'Negative.'

'What about Longellos?' He spelled it.

'Negative.'

'Okay, Suki, we're leaving now but if we find out you held back on anything—'

'I haven't,' she said. 'That would be poor judgment and I'm known for good judgment. We're going to button things down even tighter from now on, but no one ever accused any of us of being stupid.'

'Let's hear it for the Agajanian kids,' he said.

'We're achievers. It's nothing to be ashamed of. Now, I really need to get to those emails.'

We left her at her desk, texting with one hand, typing with the other. But before we reached the door to the hallway, she was running toward us, barefoot. 'Could I ask you one thing – you don't have to answer but

I really need to ask. How'd you actually connect us with her? Tara. Whatever her real name is.'

'Just what we told you,' said Milo. 'Anonymous tip.'

Ashen innocence gave way to a crafty smile. 'C'mon, guys, really.'

'Really.'

'That doesn't make sense. Who'd want to screw us like that? That's totally sneaky and low.'

Milo said, 'Anonymous tips are our bread and butter.'

'That's so sad.'

'What is?'

'People messing with each other.'

He winked at her. 'We love our job anyway.'

As we walked to the elevator, he said, 'Truth is, I've been wondering about the tip myself, trying to figure out who else knew about any of this. With all the trouble Muhrmann and Tara and probably Connie Longellos took to cover their tracks, you'd think they wouldn't confide in anyone else.'

I kept my voice even. 'You'd think.'

In the car, he said, 'Rich family, it's all gonna boil down to mow-ney.'

I said, 'How about this for a soap opera: Suss fell quickly into lust, started out paying Tara a monthly allowance, no big deal for someone with his net worth. Then he became emotionally involved and upped the stipend. With Stevie and Connie and Tara splitting the proceeds, that kind of progress was in everyone's interest. But the goose keeled over unexpectedly, the income stream dribbled out, and not only did Tara refuse to hook up with another Daddy, she wanted a lump-sum payment to finance her retirement, threatened Connie she'd tell the rest of the family about the scheme. That would mean more than lost income to Connie. It would spell disaster.'

'Swimming with the sharks,' he said. 'Stupid delusional kid. But who was she waiting for that night at the Fauborg?'

'Maybe Connie.'

'You said she looked like she was out on a date.'

'Yes, I did.'

The elevator arrived. Empty. Once we were inside, he searched for cameras, found nothing but didn't speak.

When we were back in the parking lot, he said, 'Connie's relationship with Tara was more than business?'

I smiled. 'It happens.'

'A threesome,' he said. 'Tara, Connie, and Steve-o, sex and money all meshed up together. Oh, man, that's more than a soap opera. More like a reality show.'

'American Idolatry?'

We both laughed.

I said, 'One more thing: Tara's ambitions could've been fueled by promises Suss made to her, as in permanent relationship.'

'Leaving his wife for his bimbo?'

'Whether or not he meant it, it wouldn't have seemed outlandish. Check out the society photos in any Westside throwaway. Geezers with arm candy.'

'Then he dies and she's nothing but an ex-chippie. Yeah, that could motivate some serious foolishness.'

'In order to keep her believing, he bought her some bling.'

'The watch.'

'Jewelry would be attractive to Tara, because it's relatively liquid and she could sell it privately without paying taxes. She wore the watch in front of Muhrmann but what if Suss gave her a lot of other baubles that she kept from him and Connie? If they'd found out, there's yet another motive to punish her.'

'So the date at the Fauborg was a setup from their perspective. But what was Tara expecting?'

'A night of fun.'

* * *

In the car, he said, 'They plan to kill her, why go public at a hotel and risk being seen?'

'Muhrmann never went inside, it's only a fluke that we noticed him. Neil the waiter told us no one appeared during his shift, so maybe Connie never showed and Tara left and met up with Muhrmann. He told her there'd been a change in plans, Connie had rented a party pad in the Palisades. They drove to a predetermined spot where Connie was waiting and the two of them finished her off with a .45 and a shotgun. They went for overkill because Tara's extortion had made it personal. Obscuring her face had the added bonus of making it tough to identify her. And it worked. We still don't know who she really is.'

'Rub it in . . . okay, let's do some drive-bys, see where these people bunk down.'

We took Laurel Canyon into the Valley, picked up the 134 west to the White Oak exit, headed south and crossed Ventura Boulevard, and climbed into the hills of prime Encino.

Portico Place was a gracious stretch of big houses shielded by healthy shrubbery and high gates. Phil and Connie Suss's address matched one of the grandest constructions: two towering stories of hand-troweled, tile-roofed, ocher-stucco Tuscan Revival set off by meticulously shaped date palms and brandy-colored bougainvillea and preceded by a cobbled motor court. Filigree double gates revealed a white BMW 3 series and a bronze Lexus convertible.

Milo said, 'Mama and Brother Frank go for 90210 but Phil and Connie sure ain't slumming. Pretty good for a guy with no obvious income.'

He eased a soft whistle through his front teeth. 'Nothing like the lucky sperm club.'

We watched nothing happen for nearly an hour before returning to the city.

Drs Frank and Isabel Suss resided in 90210 but their house on the 500 block of North Camden Drive would've fit any middle-class suburb.

The one-story ranch was painted pinkish beige. A skimpy front yard was mostly concrete. An older Honda sat in front.

'Two doctors,' he said. 'They're probably gonna be at work.'

During the twenty minutes we sat there, the only action was a neighbor's uniformed maid walking a mouse-sized Chihuahua.

He said, 'Kinda downscale for two skin docs, no? I thought Botox brought in the bucks.'

'Maybe they don't care about the material world.'

'Numbing faces for fun? The way things are going, I'll believe anything.'

From the look of her real estate, Leona Suss cared plenty for the material world.

The three-story brown-brick Georgian evoked Monticello. If Thomas Jefferson hadn't run out of cash. The property was thirty car lengths wide, cordoned by matching brick walls topped by verdigris metalwork. Granite medallions carved into camellia blossoms punctuated every ten feet. Smudges of moss were too perfectly spaced to be accidental. Topping the grille, variegated ivy streamed gracefully through coppery spikes, loops, and finials. Pruned to the precise point where light peeked through but privacy held fast.

A copper pedestrian gate offered glimpses of the front acre. No parking area, just shaded patches on lawn and brick walkway cast by specimen pines, sycamores, and cedars. Half the lot spread to the left of the house, offering glimpses of boxwood parterres, columnate Italian cypresses, rose gardens spitting color, a lattice pavilion.

I coasted along the west side of the property where automobile access was provided through a ten-foot slab-steel gate set nearly flush with the street. An exquisitely laced Chinese elm spread to the right. Something in the tree caught sun and glinted.

Security camera tethered to a stout branch, nearly concealed by foliage.

We returned to the front, looked for another camera, spotted it winking from the largest cedar.

Milo said, 'If little Ms Tara ever caught a glimpse of this, she'd be inspired. Want to take bets ol' Markham showed it to her?'

I said, 'Too bad for her.'

His cell played Schubert. He plugged into the hands-off, barked, 'Sturgis.'

A woman barked back louder: *'Jernigan!'*

'Hi, Doc.'

Female laughter. 'Hi, Lieutenant. I've got the autopsy report on your victim without a face. There was some alcohol in her system but nothing incapacitating, maybe a drink or two. No narcotics or prescription medication. Death by gunshot, no stunner there. My guess is the bullet entered before the shotgun pellets because we got a nice clean track through the brain and if she'd been blasted with shot initially it would've been like shooting the bullet into soup. No evidence of sexual assault, she's never had a baby, but there was some substantial endometriosis, which could be genetic, or the result of scarring due to an STD. There's also some fibrosed tissue in and around her rectum, so at some point she probably engaged in anal sex fairly regularly. Other than that, her organs were healthy.'

'Thanks, Doc.'

'That's the science part, Milo,' said Jernigan. 'Now here's the gut-feeling part: The wound pattern still bothers me but I can't say it's based on anything other than a little cognitive twinge. Assuming she got hit with the .45 first and the impact knocked her off her feet, there should've been more shotgun damage. She'd be prone, dead or close to it, and totally vulnerable to an overhead blast. But the pellets didn't overlap with the bullet wound as much as I'd expect. In fact, the most severe sprinkling of shot is almost totally in line with the bullet along the vertical axis. Almost as if your two bad guys fired simultaneously.'

'Firing squad,' he said.

'That's the image I got. But a skillful squad, the two of them standing side by side, coordinating perfectly. The shotgun damage was far from tight. The pellets pierced her sinuses as well as the lower part of her frontal lobes. But used up close, a .410 could've taken her entire head off. And there's no way I can see, short of standing on a ladder, that the shotgunner could've hit her straight-on once she was down.'

'Precision murder team,' said Milo. 'Maybe at the next Olympics.'

'It's creepy, right? Almost a ritualistic quality to it.'

'Like she was being punished.'

'I suppose,' said Jernigan. 'You know what it's usually like with sick stuff. We get up-close strangulation, a knife ballet. This is harder to characterize. There's that calculated execution thing going on but possibly also something darker – something Delaware might be able to help you with.'

'Funny you should mention him.'

I said, 'Alex here.'

'Oh, hi,' she said. 'So what do you think?'

'It fits perfectly with our current best guess for motive: money as well as revenge.'

'Great minds,' she said. 'When you learn more, keep me in the loop because this one's got me curious.'

Milo said, 'Love your optimism, Doc.'

Clarice Jernigan said, 'Without optimism there isn't much point, is there? Bye, guys, time for me to meet a few more wonderfully compliant patients.'

We walked up to Leona Suss's gate.

Milo said, 'Firing squad. Now that she's planted that in my head it's gonna stay there.'

We were trying to figure out a next step when a black-and-white SUV pulled up behind the Seville, gunned its engine, went quiet.

Beverly Hills PD Suburban. A young uniformed female officer got out, studied the Seville's rear plate, hitched up her belt, studied some more.

Milo gave his mini-salute. She wasn't impressed.

Small woman. Five three, tops, narrow-hipped, small-busted, and open-faced, with a long brown ponytail.

'Looks about twelve,' said Milo, digging into his pocket. 'Maybe she's selling Police Scout cookies.'

The cop confided something to her radio. Adjusted her belt again and came forward, one hand on her baton.

The open face was freckled, lightly made up except for generous eyeliner and mascara turned to gritty paste.

Borderline Goth; go know.

W. Bede on her badge.

'Gentlemen. That your Cadillac?'

I said, 'It's mine.'

'License, registration, and proof of insurance, please.' A too-husky voice tightened the cords of her neck. Straining, as if she'd taken lessons in authoritative but missed the final.

Milo flashed his badge and his card. 'Will this do, Officer?'

Bede's teal-green eyes seemed to enlarge as her pupils contracted.

She said, 'LA Homicide? Nothing came up at roll call about any joint investigation.'

'There's an investigation,' said Milo, 'but it only touched upon your fair city a few minutes ago.'

'Touched? I'm not . . . sure what that means.'

'The occupant of this house is someone we might eventually want to talk to.'

'This house?' As if owning eight-figure real estate exempted you from suspicion.

Milo said, 'Mrs Leona Suss.'

'What's your interest in her?'

155

'She may know certain individuals of interest and we wanted to make contact with her.' Smiling. 'Top of that, Officer, we get to hang out in nice places. But you're used to that.'

Bede's posture relaxed and her eyes crinkled. Wholesome farm girl in tailored blues. 'You'd be surprised, Lieutenant. We get alarm calls, ninety percent are false but we do walk-throughs anyway. You'd be amazed at the crap people call decorating in Beverly Hills.'

'Big money, no taste.'

'Ain't that the truth.'

'Did Mrs Suss call us in?'

'Five minutes ago, the non-emergency line.'

'Good response time.'

'That's why people live here.'

'What was the complaint?'

Bede smiled again. 'Two males loitering in an old car.'

'A Ferrari woulda made a difference?'

'Probably.'

'Maybe someone should tell her there's old and there's classic.'

Bede stepped back, appraised the Seville. Did the same for me. 'You do keep it up pretty nice. You get it on a confiscation? When we invoke RICO we get all sorts of cool stuff. Just added a Bentley used to be owned by a San Diego dope dealer who made the mistake of transacting here. The right plainclothes assignment comes along, someone's going to be riding pretty.'

She glanced back at the mansion. 'I do need to have contact with the complainant. What do you want me to tell her?'

Milo looked past her. Silk drapes had parted behind a ground-floor window. Woman holding a cat.

Tall, thin, with short black hair, she wore a body-hugging champagne-colored velour tracksuit and oversized, white-framed sunglasses.

Milo said, 'Some variant of the truth will work fine, Officer Bede. You want, we can take it from here.'

Officer W. Bede said, 'No, I need to make contact for my report.

Okay if I tell her you're kosher, doing an investigation, but I don't add details? Then, if she wants to talk to you, it's your game.'

'Free country.'

'Nothing's free in Beverly Hills.'

21

LEONA SUSS stepped through her gate, cradling her cat in the crook of one arm.

Officer W. Bede said, 'Ma'am, turns out they're LA police.'

Leona patted Bede's shoulder. 'Thank you, honey. I'll be fine.'

Bede frowned. 'I'll be off, then, ma'am.'

'Have a nice day, dear.'

Bede's Suburban roared off.

Leona Suss said, 'They're hiring babies nowadays.' A limp-wristed, bangled arm dangled toward Milo. 'Hello, fellas.'

'Lieutenant Sturgis, ma'am. And this is Alex Delaware.'

'Leona. But you already know that.'

Her smile was so wide it threatened to split her face, sacrificing the lower half to gravity. She'd been tucked, but a while ago and with a light touch. The stretch-lines punctuating her jaw and her mouth and her forehead had begun to relent. The end result wasn't unpleasant, hinting of what she'd been at thirty.

A nice-looking woman for any age. When she removed her shades and exposed almond-shaped, purple-blue eyes, that got upgraded to beautiful.

Angular, porcelain-skinned, finely boned, she reminded me of someone . . . Singer Sargent's Madame X.

Milo said, 'Sorry to bother you, ma'am.'

'Oh, you're not bothering me, not at all.' A sunny, plummy voice fought the severe image. 'I wouldn't have even known you were here but Manfred grew alarmed.' Hefting the cat. 'He's better than any dog and considerably cleaner. The bonus is, I never had to buy him, he just showed up one morning meowing like the little panhandler he is. I gave him fresh albacore and cream from Whole Foods and we've had a wonderful relationship ever since. I don't like dogs. Too clingy. How long have you fellas been here – what do you call it, surveilling?'

'We just got here, ma'am.'

'Then Manfred was at the top of his game. He began mewling and when I wouldn't put down my Candace Bushnell, he commenced worrying the front drapes like a little maniac. When *that* didn't work, he raced clear over to the side drapes, then back to the front. Finally I put down my book. Right in the middle of a juicy chapter. I checked the closed-circuit monitor and there you were in your charming old car. We owned one just like it, back in . . . seventy-six.' She stroked Manfred. He turned his head toward the mansion.

'With that car,' said Leona Suss, 'there was no way to know you were police. They tell us to call when something's out of the ordinary, so I called.'

'You did the right thing, ma'am.'

'Of course I did,' said Leona Suss. 'Now let me guess, you're here about her.'

'Who, ma'am?'

'Tara.' Cross-continental smile. 'My late husband's final bit of senior-citizen recreation.'

'You know her.'

'I know *about* her.'

'And you know we're here about her because—'

'Because I saw her on TV,' said Leona Suss. 'That drawing. I mean I wasn't certain, but the resemblance was striking. I didn't call about it because, really, what could I offer? Mark's been gone nearly a year, what connection could there be?'

I said, 'You knew what she looked like.'

'Mark showed me her picture. Bragging, the poor idiot. She gave him several pictures. Swimsuits and such. He was quite proud of his accomplishment.' Leona Suss offered another bifurcating grin. 'As if it had to do with anything other than money.' Laughter. 'You two look rather shocked. I didn't know policemen were shockable.'

Milo said, 'Well, ma'am, you managed.'

Leona Suss guffawed. The cat shivered. 'Mark and I had a rather open relationship, Lieutenant Sturgis. Not in any smarmy sense – it's complicated. I suppose you should come in. What do you think, Manfred? Shall we entertain the shockable Los Angeles police even though we're Beverly Hills folk?'

The animal remained impassive.

'Manfred doesn't appear to object. Come on in, fellas.'

The house opened to a white marble rotunda backed by a double stair-case of the same glossy stone that Leona crossed at racewalk pace. She led us to a collection of cavernous, antiques-filled areas, any of which could be characterized as living rooms, chose to seat us in a hectagonal space painted delft-blue with contrasting cream moldings.

Gold-braided apricot upholstery was printed with scenes from ancient China. Blue-and-white porcelain abounded. Despite the warmth of the day, a gold onyx fireplace glowed electrically. All the case goods were deep mahogany. What looked to be genuine Georgian and Regency. Three large paintings framed in carved gilt graced the walls. Two depicted nineteenth-century, filmy-gowned women sitting in exuberant gardens. Over the mantel was a pastel-hued landscape of an imaginary English countryside. I looked for signatures, found them.

Soft music – something new age, maybe an imitation of whale calls – streamed from unseen speakers. A pair of maids in white nylon pantsuits stopped their tidying as we entered. One was gray-haired and Slavic, the other African.

Leona Suss said, 'Would you ladies mind shifting to another room, please – the library hasn't been dusted in far too long.'

'Yes, ma'am.'

'Certainly, ma'am.'

The cat leaped from her arms, landed silently, scooted away.

'Ooh, Manfred's hungry, please see to his brunch.'

'Yes, ma'am.'

'Certainly, ma'am.'

Leona motioned us to a ten-foot sofa adorned by silk shantung pillows. The facing Chippendale table bore a collection of black-and-white photos in gold easel-frames.

Two dozen or so glamour shots and stills from old movies, each featuring the same raven-haired beauty. In most she wore western clothes, in a few she posed on horseback.

Decades had passed, but no mistaking the subject. Leona Suss at her prime.

I said, 'George Hurrell?'

She settled in an armchair, drew her legs to the side, folding like origami the way very lean people are able to do. 'You knew Hurrell?'

'I know of him.'

'George was the greatest as well as a darling person,' she said. 'He could make anyone look spectacular. Combine that with the raw material they gave him – Jane, Joan, Maureen, then the young ones – Sharon Stone. My God, the result was earth-stopping. George and I discussed several times doing a sitting but something always came up, so no, unfortunately these are the work of lesser talents. The studios had their own in-house people and, of course, there were always legions of journeymen eager to freelance.'

She played with her big white sunglasses. Diamonds or rhinestones studded the joints of the sidepieces. Similar but not identical to the shades Mystery had worn at the Fauborg.

A silver-nailed fingertip pinged the rim of a frame. 'These are just your run-of-the-mill publicity nonsense.'

I said, 'Did you act for a while?'

She smiled. 'Some would say I've never stopped. Mark, for one. He enjoyed what he called my sense of drama, said I was his Little Movie Star, which, of course, is utter fooferaw. I made a grand total of eleven pictures, each a Grade C oater. Most typically, they used me as the brunette foil for the beautiful blond heroine. After that, I did oodles of episodic TV – you don't want to know about me, you're interested in Tara.'

She repeated the name, let out a low, breathy laugh. 'Tara is a house, not a name, right fellas? A couple of times, Mark called her Tiara, which is even tackier, right? Perhaps the old fool's memory was slipping. Either way I didn't care, it reeked of trailer park.'

Milo said, 'Do you know her last name?'

'No, sorry. Anything I know about her is limited to what Mark chose to tell me. Which was mercifully little.'

'Would you mind sharing what you do know?'

She studied a silver fingernail. 'You're thinking how bizarre, this woman is faking serenity or she's crazy. But you need to understand the relationship that Mark and I shared for forty-two years. He plucked me from the throes of Hollywood desperation when I was barely twenty-four. He was twenty-six but seemed oh so worldly to a girl from Kansas. We were inseparable. Then he had the nerve to die on me.' Brittle laughter. 'Even beautiful relationships have their ups and downs, fellas. Mark and I chose to endure the downs in order to luxuriate in the ups. That necessitated a certain degree of tolerance.'

Both of us nodded.

'Don't pretend,' said Leona Suss. 'You people are paid to judge.'

Milo said, 'We don't judge that kind of thing, Mrs Suss.'

'*Missus*. I still like the sound of that. I was Mark's *only* missus.' Waving a languid hand around the immense room. 'If the poor, benighted boy needed to cut loose from time to time, so be it. We were in the rag trade, I learned to be realistic.'

'About . . .'

'The trollops who model bras and panties and nighties happen to possess the most spectacular bodies on the planet. We ran a high-volume business, meaning new panties and bras and nighties three times a year. Meaning a new crop of trollops three times a year. Can you imagine the temptation Mark faced on a daily basis? I never went to college, fellas, but I'm not stupid. As long as Mark remained faithful to me, he was free to engage in little bits of recreation.'

I said, 'Adventures.'

'No, recreation. Mark was *not* an adventurous person. Didn't like to travel, didn't like to expand his comfort zone, it was all I could do to get him to take a Crystal cruise once a year. If you need me to be specific, what I'm referring to is inserting his little you-know-what into a variety of young, moist you-know-whats.'

'So Tara was just another chapter in a long book.'

She favored me with a solemn stare that slid into amusement. 'You do have a way with words. Yes, that's as good a way to put it as any.'

'Was she one of your lingerie models?'

'No, Mark found her after he retired. On*line*. Which I find hilarious because the entire time we were in business, you couldn't get him near a computer and we were forced to hire strange little autistic men to attend to our technical needs. So what does he do? Buys himself a *laptop* that he doesn't even know how to turn on. Sets it up in his *den* and begins spending more and more time with it. It got to a point where he'd disappear for hours. I suppose you could call it an addiction.'

Milo said, 'What else did he tell you about Tara?'

'Cut to the chase, eh? Well, good for you, it's refreshing to see civil servants who care about doing a good job. What else did he tell me . . . that he'd found some late-in-life amusement and promised not to spend too much on her upkeep.'

'By upkeep—'

'Her apartment, her living expenses,' said Leona Suss.

'That didn't bother you?'

'I said, "You old fool, if you're going to do it, do it right, just keep a lid on the budget." I couldn't have him gallivanting all over town and ending up in a ditch somewhere. Mark had the most atrocious sense of direction. The way I saw it, his being aboveboard about wanting to you-know-what gave me the chance to exert some proper judgment over his Viagra-induced enthusiasm. Besides, if he wanted to live out his last days being ridiculous, who was I to stop him?'

'He was ill?'

'Not in any formal sense but he was always talking about dying, his cholesterol was horrid and he refused to moderate his diet. Meat, meat, meat. Then more meat. Then cheese and sweet desserts. The last thing I wanted was for him to keel over and leave me with guilt over having denied him his fun.'

Milo said, 'I see your point, ma'am, but that's awfully tolerant.'

'Only if I allowed myself to see her as anything more than a toy. Mark loved me deeply and exclusively, he was emotionally faithful, we raised two wonderful boys, built a glorious life together. If he felt like swallowing little blue pills and ripping off some cheap tail, why should it bother me?'

I said, 'So you set the upkeep budget.'

'I suggested an upper limit,' said Leona Suss, grinning wider than ever. 'Six thousand a month, and that was far too generous. Not that I was in a position to dictate, Mark had put aside a little personal retirement fund – some tax thing on the advice of our accountant. Everything else was in the family trust with both of us as trustees. He was free to crack his little piggy bank at will but he told me my figure was appropriate.'

Milo said, 'To some people six thousand a month would be huge money.'

She gestured around the room again. 'To some people, all this would be a big deal but one gets used to everything and to me this is just a house.'

'Everything's relative,' I said.

'Precisely.'

'A Frieseke, a Hassam, and a Thomas Moran isn't sidewalk art.'

Lavender eyes narrowed. 'A policeman who knows his paintings? How refreshing. Yes, those pictures are pricey by today's standards but you'd be amazed at how little we paid for them thirty years ago. The secret to being a successful collector, fellas, is have exquisite taste then grow old.'

I said, 'So six grand was a drop in the bucket.'

She placed the sunglasses next to one of her photos. Moved the frame so that we could see the image better.

Beautiful brunette with long, wavy, windswept hair peering up at a cloudless sky. A smile that could be interpreted a thousand ways.

'I'm going to say something that's going to sound disgustingly snobby but it's the truth: I can easily spend more than that on a single excursion to Chanel.'

'So all things considered, Tara was a cheap date.'

'She was cheap in *every* sense of the word. Liked to talk to Mark in a phony British accent. Like she was Princess Di. He laughed at her.'

Milo said, 'Do you know where her apartment is?'

'West Hollywood, Mark didn't want to drive far. If you wait here, I'll fetch the address.'

She was gone less than a minute, returned carrying a three-by-five card that matched the apricot couches. The cat padded several paces behind her, tail up, ears perked, eyes unreadable.

'Here you go.' After copying the information on a scrap of paper, she handed it to me.

From the Desk of Leona Suss

An address on Lloyd Place written in elegant fountain-pen cursive.

'I drove by exactly once,' she said. 'Not to stalk the old fool, to make sure he was getting his money's worth. Nice place, at least from the outside.'

Milo said, 'How much of the six went for rent?'

'I couldn't tell you. One thing I did insist should come out of the total was testing her for diseases. I couldn't have Mark infecting me with some gawdawful plague.'

Cocking her head and batting her lashes. Wanting us to know she'd remained sexually active with her husband.

I said, 'You saw the results of the tests?'

'A couple of times. Not the most pleasant of tasks but one needs to safeguard one's health.'

'Do you remember where she got tested?'

'Some doctor on San Vicente. And no, I didn't save the reports, I'm not one for tawdry souvenirs.'

'You saw the reports,' said Milo, 'but you don't know Tara's last name.'

'The reports came with a number code.'

'You took it on faith that the code was her.'

'Of course I did, I trusted Mark. Without trust there's no relationship.'

She unfolded herself, pranced to the mantel, pushed a button. The Slavic maid appeared. 'Ma'am?'

'I'd like some Diet Snapple, Magda. Peach – how about you fellas?'

'No, thanks.'

Magda curtsied and left.

'She's from Kosovo, lost a lot of her family,' said Leona Suss. 'My ancestors were immigrants from Bulgaria, settled in Lawrence, Kansas. Father worked building church organs for the Reuter Company until he was eighty. I find immigrants the best workers.'

Magda returned bearing a cut-crystal tumbler on a silver tray. Lemon, lime, and orange wedges rode the rim of the glass.

'Thank you so much, Magda.'

'Ma'am.'

Leona sipped. 'Mmm, yummy. How does the kitchen look, dear?'

'I need to do the oven.'

'Excellent idea.'

The maid danced off.

Milo said, 'Is anyone else in your family aware of Mr Suss's relationship with Tara?'

'Absolutely not, why would they be?'

'Seeing as you were open—'

'That was a specific openness, between Mark and me. Why in the world would I draw my boys into something so silly?'

She put her drink down. Glass thudded on silver. 'Why are you bringing up my family?'

'Just trying to be thorough, Mrs Suss.'

'It doesn't sound thorough to me, it sounds intrusive.'

'I'm sorry, ma'am—'

Leona Suss stared at him. Turned her head toward a garden-view window and offered her profile. The light did wonders for her skin. George Hurrell would've approved. 'Forgive me. It's not every day the police spy on my house.'

'Sorry to bother you.'

'You haven't, as a matter of fact you've been somewhat . . . I suppose the word would be therapeutic. Talking about it, I mean. Up till now, I've never really had the chance. So who do you think killed her?'

'That's what we're trying to find out, ma'am.'

'Well,' she said, 'if I was the detective, I'd look into her past life because someone like that would have to have all sorts of unsavory characters in her past.'

'Someone like—'

'Who'd sell herself.'

Milo showed her Steven Muhrmann's photo.

Blank look. 'Rather thuggish. Is he someone from her past?'

'Possibly.'

'Possibly,' she said. 'Meaning mind my own business, you need to keep everything close to the vest. Fine, then. Is there anything else I can do for you?'

'No, ma'am, thanks for your time.'

'My pleasure. I'll see you fellas out.'

Crossing the marble rotunda took us past a demilune table bearing a single photo.

Larger than the others but the same subject, again in crisp, pre-digital black-and-white. Leona Suss had abandoned cowgirl duds for a white dress and matching kerchief that encircled her head and showcased beautiful bone structure.

Unsmiling pose. Not sad, something else in the eyes. Tentative – waiting?

She and Milo were nearly at the door when I said, 'This is a particularly good one, Mrs Suss.'

She turned. 'That dreary thing? I should get rid of it but it was Mark's favorite and anytime I contemplate tossing it I feel so disloyal.' Sniffing. 'His clothes are still in his closet. Sometimes I go in there and feast on his smell.'

She flung the door open. 'I'm sure you fellas can take it from here.'

22

MILO PAUSED to study the Suss mansion before slipping into the Seville. 'The style to which she's become accustomed. Would you ever get used to living like that?'

I said, 'The option's never come up.'

'Six grand at Chanel – you buy Leona's whole blasé bit?'

'She didn't seem to be holding back. Still, it is a stretch. Either way, her knowing about the affair doesn't alter the botched-extortion motive. You saw how she got when you mentioned the rest of the family.'

'Mama Lion,' he said. 'It's one thing for Mark to play around with some bimbo he found cybersurfing, a whole other ball game if Leona learned her daughter-in-law set it up.'

The closed-circuit camera rotated toward us and held fast.

Milo harrumphed. 'Tara's a house, not a name – we're outclassed, c'mon.'

I drove away.

He said, 'To Leona, six a month is chump change but to Tara it would've been serious dough. Her getting killed nine months after Suss bit it could mean she was living off savings, finally ran out, tried to replenish by leaning on Connie, and paid big-time. Be nice if I had a real name for her.'

'Try Tiara. Sometimes slips of the tongue are meaningful.'

He ran *Tiara Sly* through the banks. Still nothing. Stretching, he fooled with his notepad.

A mile later, I said, 'Are you open to an alternative scenario?'

'Alternative to what?'

'Connie and Muhrmann as the killers.'

'Huff and puff and blow the whole damn house down and return to square one? Why wouldn't I welcome that?'

I didn't speak.

'Spit it *out*.'

'Leona just told us she met Mark when she was twenty-four. That's the exact age Tara claimed to be on her profile. On top of that, the photo in the entry showed Leona wearing an outfit nearly identical to Tara's the night she died. Consciously or not, Mark may have been looking for Leona the way she used to be. Everything Tara did was calculated to exploit that.'

'And to learn that, Tara had to be in contact with someone who knew the details of Mark and Leona's life. Like a daughter-in-law. So why the need for an alternative?'

I said, 'I buy Connie setting up the relationship but that doesn't necessarily make her a murderer. In order for Leona to endure forty years of Mark's escapades, she built up a carapace – an elaborate system of rationalization. Mark's flings with thruway sluts were simply the price of doing business, she was his true love. That kind of thing and a walletful of credit cards get you through the night but they take their toll. Suppose Leona had pinned her hopes on Mark's retirement. Finally, the horny old fool would keep it in his pants and take her on a cruise. Instead, he stocked up on little blue pills and started frittering his golden years with a vixen whose virtues highlighted Leona's deficiencies. Leona pretended to exert control by suggesting the vixen's allowance. Then Mark died and his finances were examined and she learned he'd been giving away a lot more than six a month. Or worse, he'd made plans to leave Leona and run away with said vixen. If Tara had the gall to approach Leona with financial demands, I can see the dam bursting.'

'What leverage would Tara have over Leona?'

'The threat to humiliate Leona publicly with a lawsuit that would drag in her sons.'

'That would only be worth something if the family didn't know about Mark's shenanigans. You really think he could cat around shamelessly for four decades without the sons figuring it out? Especially if they spent time at the business. In fact, if we're saying Connie was the one who pimped Tara in the first place, it's proof she knew plenty.'

'Lots of families engage in conspiracies of silence but fall apart when the wrong rock's lifted. Leona could cope as long as she could pretend to be Mark's "little star." Being confronted by Tara would've made her feel like a bit player.'

'Pushing the widow until she's anything but merry,' he said.

'I don't see Leona fooling with a shotgun or a .45, but she's got the resources to hire a pair of killers.'

'Mama Lion pounces.' He rubbed his face. 'So how does Muhrmann being around that night figure in?'

'Like you said before, co-conspirator or victim.'

'If Leona's angry enough to put out a hit and somehow found out Connie was part of the lure, Connie could be in serious jeopardy. Or not. But there's no obvious way to find out.' He cursed. 'Princess to Mystery to Tara to maybe Tiara. Next I'll be finding out she was born Theodore and used to shave twice a day.'

'Whatever Leona's involvement,' I said, 'she gave you two good leads: an address on Lloyd Place and a doctor on San Vicente who does STD testing.'

He pulled his phone out aggressively as if dislodging a burr, punched in speed dial for *Rick*.

Dr Richard Silverman answered, 'Big Guy.'

'You home or at work?'

'Work. You miss me?'

'Always. Free for a sec?'

'Perfect timing, I just finished operating. Semi-necrosed gallbladder, brink of explosion, a life was saved, cue in the triumphant beating of medical breasts.'

'Congrats.'

'Now that I've painted that appetizing picture, how about coffee? Where are you?'

'On the road. Sorry, jammed up.'

'Oka-ay . . . planning to make it home for dinner?'

'Hard to tell. Alex is here.'

'Ah.' Two beats. 'Hi, Alex. See if you can send him home for dinner.'

'I'll do my best.'

'Like he's a movable object.'

Milo said, 'Who in a building on San Vicente tests for STDs?'

'Any physician can test.'

'How about someone who specializes in it?'

'And here I was thinking this was a pleasant domestic chat.'

'Forget I brought it up.'

'Toothpaste back in the tube?' Rick chuckled. 'I have no idea who's on San Vicente and I don't imagine anyone who tests would breach confidentiality.'

'You're right, it was stupid.'

A beat. 'I'll ask around.'

'Thanks.'

'Thank me by being home for dinner.'

The next call was to a friendly judge whom Milo beseeched for a warrant on the Lloyd Place residence.

Friendliness only goes so far.

'Are you *on* something, Lieutenant?'

'Sorry to bother you, sir, I just thought you might be interested.'

'Why would I be interested?'

'Particularly nasty case, sir. Your tough line on crime.'

'How do you define nasty?'

Milo filled in details.

The judge said, 'It does sound ugly. Anyone else living at this address?'

'Not to my knowledge, Your Honor.'

'No one to squawk to the ACLU. All right, these are the parameters: You must establish or prove you've made a serious attempt to establish your victim's identity prior to verifying that she actually lived at the address. Upon your satisfying that contingency, consent to enter the premises will need to be granted by any current permanent occupant, including tenants, and the objects of your search will be limited to personal belongings and body fluids left behind by said victim.'

'Thank you, Your Honor.'

'Yeah, yeah, knock yourself out. With all the suit-crazy cretins running around, I probably still gave you too much.'

Dipping toward Sunset, we passed the raspberry-sherbet bulk of the Beverly Hills Hotel. Heading east, I turned onto Doheny, rolled down-hill, and searched for Lloyd Place.

Milo's GPS put it closer to Santa Monica than it was and I nearly overshot. One of those easy-to-miss turnoffs dead-ending just short of West Hollywood's border with Beverly Hills.

Narrow and shady, Lloyd was packed with small pride-of-ownership houses, many of them blocked by ivy-covered walls and hyperactive landscaping.

I said, 'Marilyn Monroe lived around here during her early days.'

'How do you know stuff like that?'

'Some lonely kids read a lot.'

I cruised up half a block before finding the address. One-story front–back duplex, nearly concealed by palm fronds. Green building; not philosophically, literally: mint-hued stucco below the midline, lime wood above.

Quiet, seldom-traveled street. Perfect for a love-nest.

The nest Mark Suss had feathered was Unit B, at the rear. No name on the mailbox. Unit A was marked Haldeman. An old black Mercedes convertible sat in the driveway. Milo ran the plates. Erno Keith Haldeman, Malibu address.

We walked past the car, along an oleander-shrouded brick path littered with fronds and seeds and pods and toxic pink petals. The air smelled like Tahiti. If Erno Haldeman was in his front unit, he wasn't letting on; no one interrupted our progress to B.

Plain wooden door, blinds drawn. The *Welcome!* mat was vacuumed spotless. No one answered Milo's knock. He called the county assessor and asked who owned the property, scrawled something, and pointed to the front unit.

We retraced our steps to Erno Haldeman's double-width door, elaborately carved, with an elephant centerpiece that spanned both panels. A brass knocker hung from the pachyderm's trunk.

Milo used it, four times, hard. The wood – teak or something like it – responded with a dull thud.

He tried again.

A male voice, deep and boomy, said, 'Go away.'

'Mr Haldeman—'

'Not interested in what you're selling.'

'We're not—'

'That includes salvation if you're Jehovah's Witnesses.'

'Police, Mr Haldeman.'

'That's a new one.'

'It's true.'

'Read off your badge number and I'll verify with the Sheriff's.'

'LA police, sir. Lieutenant Milo Sturgis.' Reciting his stats.

Ponderous footsteps preceded the crack of the door. A gray eye peered out from a spot well above Milo's sight line. 'For real?'

'Very real, sir.'

'What's this about?'

'Your tenant.'

'Tara? What's up with her?'

'She's dead, sir.'

The door swung open on a mountain of white linen.

Midforties, slope-shouldered, as broad as two men and stretching to an easy six six, Erno Haldeman had hairless pink hands the size of rib roasts, a bullet head shaved clean, a fleshy ruddy nose that drooped to a petulant upper lip, hound-dog cheeks that vibrated as he breathed. Straw-colored eyebrows were big and coarse enough to scour greasy pots. The gray eyes were rimmed with amber, disproportionately small, bright with curiosity.

The linen was a two-piece ensemble that had to be custom: blousy V-neck shirt, drawstring pants. Mesh sandals barely contained massive, prehensile feet. Haldeman's toenails were yellow and ridged, the consistency of rhino horn, but his fingernails were impeccably shaped and coated with clear polish.

'Tara?' he said. 'You're kidding.'

'Wish we were, sir.'

'What happened to her?'

'Someone shot her, sir.'

'Around here?'

'No, sir.'

'Here I was thinking you caught her doing something illegal, wanted my input.'

'She impressed you as someone who'd engage in illegal activities?'

'I trade grain futures, Lieutenant. Trust isn't a big part of my emotional repertoire. But no, she was never anything but neat and pleasant when she lived here and someone else was paying the bills. It was after the money ran out and she kept making excuses that I began to wonder. She claimed to be looking for a job but I never saw any sign of that. Not that I was paying attention to her comings and goings and half the time I'm out of town, anyway.'

'When did the money run out?'

'She owes for three months.'

A white shape larger than Haldeman drew our attention to the front of the house. FedEx truck pulling in behind the Mercedes.

He said, 'One sec,' signed for the package, returned reading the label. 'Great price on a Château Margaux premier cru from a dealer in Chicago, ten years old, should be ready pretty soon. Normally I don't buy blind but I'm familiar with this bottling and John can be counted on to temperature-control.'

Milo said, 'Cheers. So you carried Tara for three months.'

Haldeman shifted the package to one hand, grasping it between thumb and forefinger as if it were a bit of foam.

'Okay, come inside, I'm done making money for the day.'

23

ERNO HALDEMAN lived in a small space set up for a big man. Any nonbearing walls had been eliminated and the ceiling had been lifted to the rafters. Floors were black granite, glossy as fresh shoe polish, walls were high and white and bare. Scant furniture, all of it chrome and gray felt. A ten-foot slab of plate glass supported by three metal sawhorses hosted a bank of computers and modems and printers.

Haldeman placed his package on a white-marble kitchen counter.

'Why did I carry Tara for three months? I felt bad for her. And no, it wasn't because of any personal relationship. I'm happily married and even if I wasn't, pedophilia doesn't appeal to me.'

I said, 'You saw her as a child.'

'My wife's an acoustical engineer, has two degrees from MIT. I went to Princeton. One gets used to a certain degree of intellectual stimulation. To me, Tara was a child.'

'Dumb blonde,' said Milo.

'Must be the neighborhood,' said Erno Haldeman. 'Marilyn Monroe used to live around here when she was starting out.'

'Doheny and Cynthia.'

Haldeman blinked. 'A cop versed in Hollywood lore?'

Milo said, 'What surname did Tara give you?'

'Sly. Why? It's bogus?'

'We can't find anyone by that name.'

'Really,' said Haldeman. 'I won't insult you by asking if you've checked all the databases available on the Web.'

'Thanks for that, sir.' Milo sat down.

I did the same.

Haldeman said, 'Alias, huh? Well, no matter to me, she was a great tenant.'

'Until three months ago.'

'Nothing's forever. What else do you need to know?'

'Everything about her tenancy.'

'She's the only tenant I've had. My wife and I bought the place three years ago intending to combine the two units. By the time we got estimates, Janice's work took her overseas. Her firm's consulting to several of the large European opera houses, including La Scala in Milan, which is where she's been for most of this year. Then some trades paid off and I bought a condo in Malibu and we figured we'd make that our main home and keep this for rental income.'

He gave a tree-trunk thigh a light slap. Same sonic response as the teak door. 'Cutting to the chase, we decided to keep the units separate, converted A to what you see here because it's larger and the light's better, put B up for rent. Tara answered the ad, showed up, liked it, didn't quibble over the rent, and returned the following day with enough cash for six months plus damage deposit. That was more than a year and a half ago. She did the same thing every six months. Twice.'

'How much is the rent?'

'Eighteen hundred a month,' said Haldeman. 'She never worked so obviously I wondered, but gift horse and all that. Later, it became clear some old guy was footing the bill because he'd drop in two, three times a week, mostly after dark. Sometimes they'd go out together, sometimes they'd stay in. All night.'

Shrugging. 'The walls aren't that thin, but sound can get through. Maybe she was faking, but he seemed to be doing all right for his age.'

Milo showed him Markham Suss's picture.

'That's Daddy Warbucks, all right.'

'You ever talk to him?'

'Hello, good-bye. He was always pleasant, not a trace of embarrassment. Just the opposite, actually. I'd see him leaving and if he noticed me, he'd wink.'

'Proud of himself.'

'Maybe at that age that's the only score you need to keep. For me, right now, it's how much money I make.'

'What made you figure he was paying Tara's bills?'

'All that cash?' said Haldeman. 'Plus she never worked but was always decked out in fine duds.'

'Couture,' said Milo.

'I don't know from couture but she always looked put together. She was into jewelry, too. Old-fashioned stuff, not what you'd think a girl her age would go for. Obviously she was dressing for him.'

'What kind of jewelry?'

'Again, I'm no expert but I did see her put on some serious-looking diamonds. I remember thinking if she ever runs into financial difficulties, I can always hock one of those.'

'But she did and you didn't.'

'What can I say? She kept promising to come up with the rent. And crying. One look at her and she'd burst into tears. I figured it for histrionics, lost my patience, said, "From the way you're going on, you'd think someone died." That really uncorked the dam. That's when she told me. Her patron had died – that's what she called him. "My patron." As if she was Michelangelo and he was a Medici. She just broke down and sobbed for I don't know how long, said she needed time to get herself together, if I'd just give her time, she'd make it right.'

I said, 'Did she ever offer nonmonetary payment?'

'Such as – oh,' said Haldeman. 'Yeah, that would've been a nice porn script. No, she didn't and had it come to that I would've refused. If that sounds self-righteous, so be it. Janice is my fourth wife and I'm determined to make it work.'

Crossing a leg, he massaged an ankle. 'She was good-looking but there was nothing particularly sexy or seductive about her. At least from my perspective.'

I said, 'What was her demeanor?'

'Quiet, pleasant.'

Milo said, 'Unless her patron came over and the house was a-rockin'.'

'Yup. Till he kicked,' said Haldeman. 'Good for him. Getting some fun, I mean.'

'Did Tara have any other visitors?'

'Not that I saw.'

The shot of Steven Muhrmann elicited a head shake. 'Looks mean. He's the one who killed her?'

'We're not even close to a suspect, Mr Haldeman. In fact, we were hoping you could tell us her real name.'

'Tara Sly's what I knew her by.'

'What else can you tell us about her?'

'Nothing. I'm up early to catch the international markets, generally asleep by late afternoon. Weekends I go to my place in Malibu. Once a month I fly to Milan to be with Janice and sometimes I stay longer than I should. If I saw Tara once a week that was a lot.'

'Her mail came to Tara Sly?'

'Whatever she got went into her box, I never saw it.'

'Mystery woman,' said Milo.

'You could make it sound like that in retrospect. To me she was a dream tenant. Minded her own business, paid half a year in advance, never threw a party, never even played music that I could hear.'

'She have a car?'

'BMW – the smallest model. Silver. It had a rental sticker on the bumper.' Haldeman brightened. 'Here's something: It came from the Budget place in Beverly Hills, maybe that'll help you.'

'Appreciated, Mr Haldeman. Is the Beemer still in her garage?'

'Oh, no, she cleared out. Not just the car, everything.'

'When?'

'Sometime during my last visit to Italy, which lasted four days – three

180

weeks ago. Janice wasn't happy about the rent situation and I came home resolved to collect or else, knocked on Tara's door and when she didn't answer, I let myself in with my key. Place was empty.' His lips parted. 'Was she dead by then?'

'No, sir.'

'So she did rip me off.'

'Place is still empty?' said Milo.

'Completely,' said Haldeman. 'Feel free to see for yourselves.'

24

MILO TOOK the master key from Erno Haldeman's giant mitt, slipped his own paw into a rubber glove, and turned the doorknob.

Blank white space. The smell of fresh latex pigment.

'You've painted?'

'Don't worry, there was nothing worth preserving. Not a speck in the closet and she took every bit of furniture – here, I'll show you.'

Milo held him back. 'I'd like your permission to send a crime scene team over to dust for fingerprints and other evidence.'

'You're saying she was killed here?'

'We know she wasn't.'

'Then what's the point?'

'We want to identify any visitors she had.'

'I told you, there weren't any besides the old guy.'

'But if you saw her once a week that was a lot.'

Haldeman scratched the top of his hairless dome. 'Are we talking an invasive process?'

'No, sir. And the crew will do their best to clean up.'

'That's unpleasantly ambiguous, Lieutenant.'

'It'll be fine.'

'But if they find something creepy, they'll do damage.'

'I don't see that, sir.'

'No good deed goes unpunished, huh?'

Milo's favorite credo. He remained impassive. 'It'll take a day, Mr Haldeman, and then we'll be out of your way.'

'Do I have a choice?'

'You do.'

'But if I refuse you'll get a warrant or whatever paper's involved and the end result will be the same except you'll be pissed off that I delayed you so the floorboards will end up being pried off.'

'Not unless there's some reason you're aware of that we should pry them.'

Haldeman gaped. 'Good Lord, no.'

'Then I don't see a problem. There'll be some dusting, perhaps some spraying with chemicals. But all of it comes out readily and I'll take special care to ensure you get your property back exactly as we found it.'

'Man, you take life seriously.'

'Kind of an occupational hazard, sir.'

'Guess it is. All right, go ahead. Just let me know when your crew plans to show up. I want to make sure to be here.'

'Will do, sir. Thank you.'

Haldeman smiled. 'All this civic cooperation and you're not going to tell me who killed her.'

'We don't know, sir.'

Haldeman studied him. 'I think you're telling me the truth. Tsk, tsk. The agony of uncertainty.' His grin was wide, sudden, playful but malevolent. 'I make my living off it.'

The young, male clerk at the Beverly Hills Budget Rent A Car office wasn't impressed by the badge. Or the request. 'We've got four silver 1 series.'

'This one would've been rented long-term, maybe as long as a year and a half, two years ago, possibly by a man named Markham Suss.'

The clerk typed. 'I've got a Markham Industries renting a 1 series twenty-two months ago.'

'For who?'

'Just says Markham Industries. And it got returned . . . five days ago.'

'By who?'

'I'd assume Markham Industries. Says here it was dropped off after hours with none of the required paperwork. There was a month to go on the agreement and no damage, so we let it ride. If there was damage, we'd pursue to recover.'

Milo said, 'Markham Industries went out of business before the car was rented.'

'Okay,' said the clerk. 'So that's why you're here.'

'What do you mean?'

'It was used for something illegal, right? We get that all the time. People coming into Beverly Hills for their rentals thinking it's going to make them look respectable when they do something illegal.'

'Like what?'

'Drugs, mostly. Last year, these guys come in from Compton, think they're pulling off some big con 'cause they're wearing suits. We're real careful about our screening.'

Not careful enough to check on Markham Industries. Or maybe Mark Suss had kept a corporate account going after dissolving his company.

Milo said, 'What kind of background did you do on Markham Industries?'

The clerk typed some more, peered at his computer.

When the revolution comes, machines will talk to machines and people's vocal cords will atrophy.

'Doesn't say much, guess they checked out okay. We don't rent without proper documentation . . . looks like it was initially a two-week rental, then they renewed for a month . . . then three . . . then another three then – whoa, after that was a whole year – that's super-long for us.' He scanned the fine print. 'Looks like they asked for the long-term preferred rate, looks like they got it . . . whoa, they got it retroactive, big rebate for the first six months.'

'How was payment made?'

'Corporate Amex.'

'Signed by who?'

'Says here M. Suss.'

'Card number, please.'

'I'm not sure I can do that.'

Milo leaned forward. 'Trust me, you can.'

The clerk deliberated.

Milo said, 'M. Suss is dead, therefore he has no right to confidentiality.'

The clerk's fingernail pinged his keyboard. 'It's your responsibility.'

Milo copied the number. 'Anyone else co-sign the lease?'

'Um . . . doesn't appear to be.'

'If Mr Suss was renting the car for someone else would you need the driver's signature?'

'Not for the rent part if he was the only one paying. We would need a valid driver's license for the operator's part.'

'Do you have one on file?'

'Hold on.'

Crossing the reception area to a bank of steel cabinets, he opened and shut several drawers, finally stood away, examining a piece of paper smiling. 'Not bad.'

New Mexico license photo.

Tiara Melisse Grundy, five four, 105, brown and brown.

Long, dark, lank hair, no discernible makeup. But the lovely face above the white scooped neckline matched the girl who'd sold herself as Mystery.

She'd told SukRose the truth about her physical stats but had lied about her age: The DOB put her at one month shy of thirty.

Needing to be twenty-four because Leona Suss was being psychically cloned.

Even minimally groomed and wearing the borderline-sullen expression that comes from standing hours in line, Tiara Grundy looked young and fresh enough to pull it off.

Milo said, 'Why'd you smile?'

'Guy renting for his chick.'

'You get a lot of that?'

'Enough,' said the clerk. 'Costs a lot more than just leasing from a leasing company but they can go short-term and there's no down payment.'

'We talking married guys?'

Smirk. 'We don't ask about their home situation.'

We left the office with Milo muttering, 'Tiara Grundy,' as if he'd identified a new species.

I said, 'Mark Suss eased in with a two-week rental, she built up his trust, he stretched it to a month, kept stretching, finally sprang for a full year. At that point, a conventional lease would've been cheaper but this was easier to hide, so he asked for a rebate.'

'Mr Operator.'

'Even with a discount we're talking serious money on top of the six thousand a month. Plus jewelry. There were probably additional supplements – money Leona Suss never knew about. That says Suss took the relationship seriously. Maybe Tiara did, too.'

'Love blossomed out of the mulch of sin?'

'Poetic.'

'Catholic,' he said. 'Transgression's always lurking in the shadows.'

His index finger stabbed the address on the license.

Post-office box on Cerrillos Road, Santa Fe. He was on the phone before we reached the car.

The first call was to the crime lab, where he requested a go-over of the unit on Lloyd. His next quarry was Detective Darrell Two Moons of the Santa Fe Police Department.

Two Moons said, 'Hey, LA, long time. Bet you haven't had decent Christmas chili since you were here.'

'Nothing close,' said Milo. 'How's everything, Darrell?'

'Kids are growing,' said Two Moons. 'So's my belly, unfortunately. Katz's, too, we're starting to look like your typical waddling detectives on one of those true-crime shows.'

'Try Pilates,' said Milo. 'Tones up the core, improves posture, dissolves the body fat.'

'You do that stuff?'

'I'd rather drink battery acid.'

Two Moons laughed. 'What's up?'

'Got a New Mexico ID on a victim and a box address.' He gave Two Moons the barest essentials of the case, recited the info.

Two Moons said, 'Don't know her by name, so she's probably not one of our chronic troublemaking hookers. I do know the address, shopping center just south of St Michael's. Could be the Mailbox Incorporated or the office supplies store or maybe there're still renting POB's at the organic pharmacy. You want me to, I'll have a uniform stop by to find out.'

'That would be great, Darrell.'

'How'd she die?'

'Shot in the face.'

'Not nice,' said Two Moons. 'Someone didn't like her technique, huh?'

'Something like that.'

We headed back to the station.

Milo said, 'Tiara Grundy,' as if the name imparted wisdom. 'Grundy can't be that common of a name. If I find a local relative, I'll let you know where and when the notification's gonna be.'

I said, 'I'm tied up tomorrow until the afternoon.'

'Court?'

'Nope.'

'Changed your mind about picking up new therapy cases?'

I smiled.

He said, 'Mona Lisa, again? What's the big deal, I'm not asking for clinical details.'

'Good.'

'Oh, man, if I ever had secrets worth keeping, I'd leave them with you. Okay, fine, you're gonna heal some maladjusted type and it has nothing to do with me so I need to keep my mouth shut and concentrate on doing my own damn job.'

I said, 'There's a plan.'

25

THE FOLLOWING morning at eleven I was pushing Gretchen Stengel's call button. A female voice, too upholstered around the edges to be Gretchen's, said, 'One moment,' and buzzed me in.

The condo door was open by the time I got there. A chubby gray-haired woman in a loose floral dress smiled then held a finger to her lips.

When I got close enough, she whispered, 'Sleeping. Finally.'

She motioned me to the edge of the landing, held out a hand. 'I'm her sister, Bunny Rodriguez.'

'Alex Delaware. Bad night?'

'It was tough. Thanks for being here for Chad.'

'Is Chad here?'

'Napping also,' she said. 'Snuggled up against Gretchen.' Her eyes watered. Blinking. 'He's a sweet boy.'

As if I needed to be convinced.

I said, 'It's good that he's got you.'

'I've always loved Chad.' She breathed in and out and her body quivered like aspic beneath the thin, rayon dress. The print was hydrangeas and wisteria, green tendrils running amok. Her eyes were soft brown, bloodshot around the edges. Indentations on both sides of a thin straight nose said glasses were a regular thing. 'My own kids are grown. Guess it'll be an adventure. Hopefully not for a long time.'

Her smile fell well short of happiness. 'Nothing like denial, right?'

'Whatever it takes.'

'Yes, that's true.' Bunny Rodriguez leaned in closer. 'Her oncologist told me he can't believe she's still alive. I think she's running on love for Chad. He's the first . . .' Head shake.

'The first?'

'I was going to say the first decent thing in Gretchen's life but I'm horrible to judge.'

'Gretchen's led a tough life.'

'Yes, she has. If she'd – let's concentrate on Chad, that's what you're here for. He's the sweetest thing on two feet, always has been. The funny thing is my own kids weren't sweet. Good, yes. Morally sound, absolutely. But sweet and compliant? Not on your life. I was the obedient child and I produced two feisty rascals and Gretchen produces Chad.'

'That's why it's called a gene pool,' I said. 'We dive in, never know what's going to surface.'

She studied me. 'I like your way with words. Words are my thing, I teach English. This is going to be a nightmare, but we'll pull through, right? One way or the other.'

'We'll do our best. Is there anything you want to tell me about Chad?'

'Actually . . .' She thumbed her lower lip. 'This time he's being a little standoffish. Almost like . . . I think I know the problem. Gretchen asked me to tell him she was going to die, she couldn't bear dealing with it. So I did. After reading a couple of books. At his age, they said, he'd be concerned with separation from Gretchen. I didn't have the heart to tell him he'd never see her again, so I just used the word. Death, I mean. He seemed to get it. Was that wrong?'

'How'd he react?'

'He didn't react at all. Just stared at me as if I was talking in tongues.'

'You got through,' I said. 'He told me.'

'Does he hate me? Killing the messenger?'

'Not at all.'

'He seems to be shutting me out.'

'Maybe he needs to concentrate on his mother.'

'Yes. Of course, I'm thinking like – I'm being self-centered. I guess I'm just concerned about laying a good foundation now, so when the time comes . . .'

'It'll work itself out.'

'I suppose it will. In the end,' she said. Shuddering. 'What a repulsively profound word.'

A harsh 'Hey!' drew our attention to the condo door.

Gretchen, hooked up to her portable oxygen tank and bracing herself against the doorpost, flipped a flamboyant bird and shot a rotten-toothed grin.

'Hey, you two! Cut the chitchat, this is all about *me!*'

Bunny tried to support Gretchen but Gretchen shook her off. 'I'm not a cripple, go stay with Chad, he's waking up, you know how slow he does that. If he wants milk or juice give it to him, but no fucking soda.'

Bunny complied.

Gretchen laughed. 'She's older but I could always push her around.'

'How's Chad doing?'

'What if I want to talk about that instead of him? Manipulating Bunny. What if that's what's floating my boat today?'

'Talk about whatever you want until Chad's up.'

'Ooh,' she crooned. 'Tough guy. So tell me, did Sturgis appreciate my *ahem ahem* anonymous tip?' A phony throat clear led to coughing, then to the real thing, then a series of nasty-sounding barks topped by a paroxysm that doubled her over.

When she finally was able to breathe smoothly, she wagged a finger. 'Poor cancer patient nearly asphyxiates and you just stand there?'

'Last I heard you weren't a cripple.'

'Oh, man, you are – you must be hell in a relationship. Got a wife?'

'How's Chad doing?'

'Shine me on? Sure, why the hell not, I'll be dead and you'll be watching *Jeopardy!* or whatever you brainy types like.'

I waited.

She said, 'Chad's fine. Did you tell Sturgis the tip came from me?'

'Has Chad—'

'Blah-*blah*, blah-*blah*, blah-*blah*.' She placed a hand on my shoulder. Pressing down, but diminished strength made it feel like a butterfly alighting between nectar gulps. 'First the website, then Stefan. So what do you think, should I give him even more?'

'Up to you.'

'Like you don't give a shit.'

'Let's talk about Chad.'

The hand on my shoulder clawed. Oversized, predatory moth digging in for takeoff. 'Tell Sturgis little Ms Mystery was no mystery back when she was turning tricks. Tell him she used to be just plain Tiara from the trailer park, had no clue how to dress, how to talk, how to walk. How to give a decent blow job. Tell him to feel free to call me for more and guess what? If he does, I'll say fuck off, fatso. Because I'm not dancing to that rude fag's beat. He could've treated me like a human being, instead he treated me like shit.'

The hand took flight. She stabbed air. 'Lady G does not forget.'

I scoured my memory for something I'd missed about the meeting between her and Milo. Nothing.

People with personality disorders bruise easily.

For all the comic flaunting, it really *was* about her her her.

Tough way to live but I couldn't help wondering if it might be a good way to die.

Defying the mortality odds because she was fueled by rage and high-octane egotism.

I said, 'When you're ready, we'll talk about Chad.'

Her teeth drew back in a brown, fetid snarl. 'You're starting to really piss me off.'

She moved forward quickly. Kissed me hard, on the lips. Bruising me with the oxygen tube. Assaulting my nose with the reek of disease.

Pulling away, she took my arm and sang out, 'Let's have a nice civilized chat, God knows we could both use one.'

She sank into a chair with obvious pain, coughed some more, held out a protective palm when I approached her. 'Leave me alone. Fine.' Gasp.

A few minutes later: 'I should be nice to you. One session with Chad and he's better.'

'Better . . .'

'Sleeping through the night.' Her chest heaved. She adjusted the oxygen. 'Cuddly. I love when he's cuddly. It's like nothing's wrong and we're the way we used to be. Come here. Please.'

I sat down next to her.

'Closer. I promise I won't bite.'

I shifted nearer. She took my hand. Kissed my knuckles. 'Sorry for the other one. Kiss. That was gross.' Massaging my fingers. 'This is a nice one. This is how I *really* feel: You're a lovely man.'

She began to cry, reversed it abruptly when Chad bounced in announcing, 'I'm thirsty, Aunt Bunny says I can have choco-milk if you say so.'

'Sure,' said Gretchen, grinning. 'Look who came to visit.'

Chad's eyes shifted to me.

'Say hello to Dr Delaware, angel.'

'Kin I have choco-milk?'

'I said sure. Don't you want to say hi to Dr Delaware?'

Shrug.

Bunny Rodriguez came in. 'I told him what you—'

'Chocolate milk's milk so it's healthy, go pour.'

Bunny trudged to the kitchen, filled a four-ounce glass. The boy drained it. 'More.'

Bunny said, 'Gretch?'

'Whatever.'

Glass number two disappeared just as quickly. So did three. Milo-in-training.

I walked over to Chad. 'Feel like drawing again?'

'Guess.'

'Or we can do something else.'

'Draw.'

Gretchen said, 'Have something healthy, too, on top of the chocolate milk. Everyone needs to be healthy.'

'No.'

'Whatever, angel.'

In his room, Chad said, 'Mommy wakes up all the time. She's wet.'

'Wet on her face?'

'All over. Her jammas.'

'She's sweating.'

'I guess.'

'Know what sweat is?'

'It comes out of your body when you're hot.'

'Exactly. Do you ever sweat?'

'When it's hot.' Flicking the corner of a drawing pad. 'She does it when it's cold.'

'Even if it's not cold, she may feel cold.'

'Why?'

'That happens sometimes when people are sick.'

'Her skin,' he said. 'Then she coughs and I hug her. She like bounces.'

'From coughing.'

'I hug her.'

'You want to take care of her.'

He thought about that. 'I don't want her to fall.'

'Off the bed?'

'Anywhere.'

'That would be scary.'

'It would hurt.'

'Like falling on the floor.'

'I did it once,' he said. 'It hurt. Mommy kept sleeping. I put myself back in the bed.'

'You're good at taking care of yourself.'

'Let's draw, I'm gonna win.'

Six bouts of frantic, page-ripping black circles later: 'Mommy's not gonna die.'

I said nothing.

He said, 'That's what I think.'

26

IT TOOK a couple of days but Darrell Two Moons came through.

The POB Tiara Grundy listed as her New Mexico address had been housed in a now defunct stationery store. Grundy had been arrested three times in Santa Fe, twice at eighteen, once at twenty. Misdemeanor possession of marijuana, two public intoxications. All charges dismissed, not an hour of jail time served.

I said, 'Maybe another rehab candidate.'

Milo said, 'Possibly, but the drunk busts could be less than they seem. Darrell says back then they were doing regular sweeps of the Plaza, basically vacuuming up kids because merchants were complaining about a bad atmosphere. So just hanging out could get you swept up and seeing as she never got arrested again, that might've been it.'

'Maybe she left Santa Fe and got in trouble elsewhere.'

'Listen to the pessimist. You don't believe in personal redemption?'

'I do but she worked as a prostitute here in LA before she went cyber.'

He turned to me. 'You know that because . . .'

'I'd check out people who were running high-priced call girls five to ten years ago.'

He wheeled back his chair. 'You would, huh.'

I said, 'It might also lead you to Muhrmann. He seems like the kind who'd hire out as muscle to a pimp.'

'A pimp who has to hire out muscle because of a lack of testosterone?'

he said. 'Maybe someone like Gretchen Stengel? Now that I think about it, she used to hire bodybuilders.'

'Like Gretchen, but I wouldn't waste time with her.'

He pushed back some more, hit a wastebasket. As the receptacle spun and pinged the vinyl floor, he watched me.

I watched back.

'Okay,' he said, 'what other bush do you want to beat around?'

'We can discuss the secret of eternal happiness.'

He laughed. I did the same but there wasn't much joy in the air.

Tenting his hands, he studied a crack in the ceiling. 'I'm thinking this connects to your mysterious appointment yesterday.'

I didn't answer.

'I'm thinking it could also connect to that tip about SukRose.'

I pretended to brush a crumb from my sleeve.

'Gotcha! There's a reason they pay me the big bucks.' Gripping his desk, he drew himself back, ending up so tight against the rim that his gut overlapped. 'You want me to go pimp hunting, I will defer to your superior judgment. Even though Vice has never heard of Tiara Grundy or Tara Sly or anyone calling herself Mystery. But first, I'm following a juicy lead of my own.'

Flipping the murder book open, he drew out a photocopied mug shot.

'Meet Maude Grundy aka Momsy.'

Maude Stella Grundy had been twenty-five at the time of her arrest, looked nearly twice that.

A New Mexico penal code I didn't know.

Dark, stringy hair framed a thin but flabby face. Sunken cheeks and puffy addict eyes said her life had been ravaged by bad decisions. But lurking behind all that was the delicate bone structure and symmetry of a woman born pretty, and if I looked hard enough I could see Tiara's lineage.

Or maybe I was looking too hard.

Maude Grundy's birth date made her fifteen years older than Tiara.

I said, 'She could be an older sister.'

'Could be but isn't. Darrell found Tiara's birth certificate. St Vincent hospital, the main one in Santa Fe. Daddy unknown, Mommy the minor known as. Recommendations were made for adoption but it never happened. Nothing like pedigree, huh? On all Maude's arrest forms, she listed an address in Española, which is a working-class town thirty miles out of Santa Fe. Darrell traced and it used to be a trailer park, is now a Walmart. Tiara may have avoided conviction but Maude wasn't so lucky, has a whole bunch, some jail time, but no prison. Check kiting, dope, shoplifting, and, big shock, getting picked up on streetwalker stings.'

He took the paper back and stood.

I said, 'Where to?'

'Hey, I've got secrets of my own.'

'Oh, boy.'

He slapped my back. 'Nah, I'm lying. No confidentiality in my business. I learn nasty secrets, someone's life changes big-time. C'mon, let's go mommy hunting.'

One long stride propelled him out of the tiny office. He whistled his way up the hall.

'Maude lives in LA?'

'Pico near Hoover. No driver's license but last year she got pulled in for shoplifting downtown. Trying to boost crapola from one of those stalls the Central Americans set up in the old theaters on Broadway. She pled to petty-t, got a thirty-day at County, was out in ten due to over-crowding. I couldn't find any landline or cellular account and she doesn't pay taxes, but I might as well give it a try. No matter what she is, she deserves to know.'

I said, 'Tiara lives large on Mark Suss's dough but Mommy holes up in the inner city.'

'Maybe the kid didn't appreciate her pedigree.'

The address matched a decrepit, four-story, hundred-year-old apartment building neighbored by similar masterpieces and besmirched by gang graffiti: Stompy, Topo, and Sleepy celebrating some kind of victory in greasy black Olde English lettering.

Rusting fire escapes ended raggedly in the middle of the second story. A lot of the windows were boarded with plywood and the ones that weren't were dark. No external mailboxes; anything out in the open would stay unmolested for an eyeblink.

A group of shaved-head Latino teenagers who might've been Stompy or Topo or Sleepy slouched away when we got out of the car. Women with Rivera-mural faces pushed babies in strollers as if nothing but motherhood mattered. A shrunken old man in gray work clothes sat on a bus bench in front of the building, watching the traffic on Pico. The vehicular roar waxed Wagnerian on both sides of the boulevard.

Milo scanned the wall art. 'Why exclude Dopey and Sneezy?' He rang the shabby building's bell.

No bell or buzzer sounded and when he nudged the button, it fell to the sidewalk. 'Let's check out the back.'

As we headed toward the corner the old man on the bench craned. A voluminous white mustache spread wider than his face. 'Hey, police.'

Milo said, 'Hi there.'

'You looking for someone in that dump?'

'Yes, sir.'

'Sir. I like that.' The mustache was waxed, curlicued at the ends. His skin was the well-worn brown leather of a scholar's desktop, his eyes black and avian. Rough but clean hands. Same for the work clothes. An oval over the left pocket said *Jose*.

'You ain't gonna find anyone.'

A double-long bus rumbled up to the bench. The man sat there. The bus cleared phlegm from its craw, lurched forward just as the light turned red, crossed the intersection to a blare of horns and obscenities.

Milo said, 'Why's that, sir?'

'No one lives there, it's condemned.'

'For how long?'

'Few months ago, maybe three. There was a fire, some immigrant cooking on a illegal hot plate. They put it out but it wrecked the foundation. Building and Safety came and closed the place up.'

'You live around here?'

'Not around. There.' A callused finger jabbed at a building two lots east.

'There's no notice posted,' said Milo.

'How 'bout that,' said the man, chuckling. 'Maybe someone needed scratch paper.'

'Anyone hurt in the fire?'

'The immigrant's two kids died and I heard she got turned into something you don't wanna look at. Couple neighbors got sick from smoke and one of them died, too. Go call the fire department, they'll tell you. You wanna go back there see for yourself, go 'head. It's all black and hollow and you can't get in unless you get through the fences of the other buildings. They say they're gonna demolish but they don't do it. Can't figure out why it just don't fall down.'

'Who owns the building?'

'The kind of folk own buildings. Who you looking for?'

Milo said, 'A woman named Maude Grundy. Forty-four years old but she looks older.'

'Dead,' said the man.

'You knew her?'

'Knew she was Maude, she never gave a last name. Even if I didn't know her I'd know she's dead because the person who died in the fire was the only white woman living in the place. She woulda stood out even if she didn't behave like she did.'

'How'd she behave?'

'Drunk, walking around like she was crazy. Trying to sell herself.' He huffed. 'Like anyone would buy *that*. You say she was forty?'

'Forty-four.'

'I'da guessed seventy. Maybe sixty-five if she put on lipstick and she didn't. I'm seventy-seven and to *me* she looked old.'

'How'd she pay her rent?'

'Maybe she was a brain surgeon,' said the old man. 'How should I know? I worked fifty years doing landscaping, made the mistake of doing it for private companies not the city so I got no bloated-up pension and now I'm stuck living here. My building, everyone pays rent, we got families, mostly good people. That place? Lowlifes. Everyone was happy to see it burn. There was all sorts going in and out, never no manager. Anyway, she's dead. Ten-dollar Maude. So don't waste your time looking for her.'

'Ten dollars is what she charged?'

'So they say. She gave me the look, I went the other way. Poor can mean unlucky but it don't mean stupid.'

A call to the coroner pulled up Maude Grundy's death certificate. Two months and two weeks ago, pulmonary failure due to smoke inhalation. The body had been signed out by Tara Sly of Lloyd Place in West Hollywood and sent to a mortuary on Mission Road, across the street from the crypt.

Milo said, 'I know what that place is,' but he phoned anyway.

Undertaker's school, conveniently located. Maude Grundy's remains had ended up as a teaching tool for the freshman class.

'Donating Mom to science,' he said, 'and not even to a med school. With Suss's dough, Tiara could've managed some kind of funeral, at the very least a cremation. Instead she relegates Mommy to the formaldehyde gang. Okay, let's find the mysterious flesh peddler who's not Gretchen.'

Rubbing his face. 'Anything you want to say about that?'

I said, 'I wonder how far our princess progressed from ten-buck transactions.'

27

A WESTSIDE vice detective named David Maloney, who was old enough to remember, summed up the history of high-priced Westside sex-work after Gretchen's arrest. We met in the big D room, where Maloney commandeered a corner desk.

I'd seen Maloney before, in his long-haired, multi-pierce days. Now he had gray CEO hair and dressed like a pro golfer. Three holes in each ear were undercover souvenirs.

He talked fast, automatically, as if delivering a quarterly report to bored shareholders.

The first pimp managing the five-star hotel market was a woman who'd turned tricks for Gretchen named Suzanna 'Honey Pot' Gilder. Long suspected as a front for Gretchen during her boss's incarceration, Gilder was subjected to the same tax pressure that had ended Gretchen's reign. She endured two years before quitting and moving to Las Vegas, where she married the wayward son of a Mormon senator, self-published a confessional memoir, and raised babies.

Soon after Honey Pot's retirement, two Ukrainians and a Latvian working out of warehouses in Orange County ran slews of girls brought over from former Soviet republics. A few girls died and within a year, two of the men were found at the bottom of Lake Elsinore. The survivor shifted his business to Fresno and Honey Pot's stable resurfaced under the good graces of a woman named Olga Koznikov, who'd been Gretchen's longtime competitor.

Milo said, 'She have anything to do with the guys in the lake?'

Maloney offered his first smile. 'There's logic, then there's evidence. Olga's slowed down but she's probably running a small, select group. The big thing now is the Southeast Asians, all those massage parlors. But I'd start with Olga because she fits your time frame.'

Milo said, 'Thanks, I'll pull her record.'

'You won't find one. She has no bad habits and always kept her head on straight, including paying taxes.'

'How'd she launder the money?'

'Our best guess is by running booths at flea markets and antiques shows and importing furniture from China. She also owns a bunch of Russian restaurants. There's probably stuff we're unaware of.'

'She on or off the radar?'

'We're concentrating on the parlors.'

'How do I find this gem?'

'Easy as opening the phone book, she lists her business office. But I got it for you anyway.'

'You're a prince, Dave.'

'No prob. Sorry I couldn't help ID your vic. I triple-checked and no one knew any Tara Sly or Tiara anything and her picture didn't ring bells. But Olga's good at covering her tracks.'

Far Orient Trading and Design Modes operated out of a red, barn-like building at the rear of a complex of discount furniture outfits on La Cienega south of Jefferson. Quick, direct drive to LAX; easy to bring all kinds of things in and out.

Made-yesterday antiques were displayed in front of the barn. A row of parked vehicles included the silver Suburban that was Olga Koznikov's sole registered vehicle. No tinted windows, tricked-up wheels, or any adornment and the interior was impeccable. A baby carrier was belted to the middle row of seats.

As we approached the barn, a pretty Vietnamese girl in skinny jeans, a black turtleneck, and gold-lamé flats exited smiling.

'Hi, guys, can I help you with something?'

Milo fingered a huge, green funerary jar, then a mock-rosewood tansu that might last one dry summer. 'Nice. What dynasty?'

The girl giggled. 'Anything in particular you're looking for?'

'Is Olga around?'

The girl's smile froze. 'Hold on.'

She hurried back inside. We followed, watched her scurry up a narrow aisle lined with tables, chairs, cabinets, altars, and plaster Buddhas.

Before she made it to the rear, a man came out. Thirty or so, black, dressed in charcoal overalls over a white T-shirt, he had the height of a shortstop and the width of a defensive tackle. The girl said something to him. He patted her head, as if comforting a toddler, and she ducked out of sight.

He came toward us smiling pleasantly, thighs beefy enough to turn his walk into a waddle. The denim scrape was audible.

'I'm William. May I help you?' Boyish voice, Jamaican lilt, meticulous enunciation.

The overalls were stitched in orange, fit well enough to have been custom-tailored. His face was clean-shaven with glowing skin and his milk-white teeth were perfectly aligned.

The healthy, happy visage of O.J. before the fall.

Milo badge-flashed. 'I'm Lieutenant Sturgis. Is Olga here?'

'May I ask what it's about?'

'Reminiscence.'

'Pardon me?'

'Shooting the breeze about old times,' said Milo.

William's right thumb flicked the chest pocket of his overalls. He removed a pack of gum, slipped a stick between his teeth, and began chewing. 'I can't imagine what you mean.'

'No need to imagine.' Milo moved forward. William didn't budge. Then he did.

The woman eating a sandwich at her desk was white-haired, heavyset, looked older than the sixty-seven years her license claimed. The hair was curly as a poodle's show-do and cut mannishly short with ridiculous bangs. The face beneath the frizz was a near-perfect sphere, tiny-mouthed, hog-nosed, pale with pink accents. Droopy but unlined; fat's a good wrinkle filler.

The sandwich was an architectural masterpiece of pastrami, ham, turkey, coleslaw, white and orange cheese, red and green peppers. But the woman's aqua frock was spotless, as were her lips. Her eyes were soft, hazel, world-weary. The office was large, bright, unpretentious, set up with a photocopier, a small fridge, and an old gray PC that would've brought a sneer to the lips of the Agajanian sisters.

Olga Koznikov looked like a woman who accepted herself at face value, and that brought a certain serenity. Only longish nails, French-tipped and glossy as they clawed the sandwich, testified to tension and vanity.

'Hello,' she said, motioning us to the two chairs that faced the desk. 'It took you a while.'

She wrapped up what remained of the sandwich, lumbered to the fridge, and exchanged the food for a can of Diet Pepsi.

'Something for you?' Faint but distinct Russian accent.

'No, thanks.'

'You're here about Tara.'

'You know that because . . .'

Because Gretchen told you it was coming.

'I know because I hear she's dead.' Sigh. 'Poor little baby.' Another sigh. 'Sometimes I think of them as my babies.'

'Them being—'

'Young people looking for happiness,' said Olga Koznikov.

'You're the guide.'

'I do my best, Lieutenant Sturgis.'

Milo hadn't introduced himself.

'Tell us about Tara.'

'You want reminiscence. Too much remembering can be upsetting.'

William hadn't passed that along. Amid the clutter of the barn were mikes and cameras and who knew what else. And she wanted us to know.

Milo said, 'We're not Vice.'

'If you were,' said Koznikov, 'we wouldn't be talking at all.' She drank soda, reclined. 'Now please unbutton your shirt, Lieutenant Sturgis. Your handsome colleague, as well. Also, turn out all your pockets, if you don't mind.'

'If we do mind?'

'I'm an old woman. Memory fades.'

'First time I've been asked this, Olga.'

'I know, I'm sorry. But if you don't mind.'

'Do we get background music?'

'I could hit the desk with my hands if you like.'

When we'd buttoned back up, Koznikov said, 'Thank you. I hope it wasn't too embarrassing.' Winking. 'You both have nice chests.'

Milo said, 'Thanks for not taking it further.'

'There is a limit, Lieutenant Sturgis. I've always believed in limits.'

'Tell us about Tara.'

'What I will tell is a story. Like a fairy tale. It could *be* a fairy tale. Understood?'

'Once upon a time.'

'Once upon a theoretical situation. Okay?'

'Okay.'

'Then I begin,' she said. 'What if once upon a time a beautiful young girl comes to California and makes mistakes? What if she meets bad men who wait near bus stations and train stations and airports? It could be sad, no?'

'Tara got turned out by a street pimp.'

'What if this beautiful girl has several what I will call bad experiences? What if she is lucky to survive without serious physical injury?' Koznikov popped open another soda can and drank. 'What if she is more lucky and meets good people who take care of her? That would be happy, no?'

'Someone like a mother figure.'

'Mothers are good.' She rested a soft, liver-spotted hand on her left bosom. 'Everyone needs a mother.' Smiling. 'Maybe a grandmother.'

Milo said, 'Once she found proper guidance, what was her turf?'

'What if it was wherever the client desired? With limits, of course.'

'Outcall.'

'It's a big city.'

'What kind of limits?'

'It's a *very* big city. Gasoline is expensive.'

'She stuck to the Westside,' said Milo.

'The Westside is nice.'

'What other limits did she have?'

'What if,' said Koznikov, 'she got tested every month, always used condoms, and the people she met were screened to make sure they were nice and would not force her to use body parts she didn't want to use.'

Dr Jernigan's description of anal scarring flashed in my head. So did pictures I tried to shut off.

'Sounds like a good deal. Did the Westside include the Fauborg Hotel?'

Olga Koznikov blinked. 'Lovely place.'

'Did Tara work there?'

'If a client wanted a quite lovely place, that would be a good choice, no?'

Thinking of the Fauborg's typical guest, I said, 'Was Tara a favorite with much older men?'

She studied me. 'It's good you don't shave your chest hair. Men do that, now. I don't understand it.'

'Did older men—'

'You are asking me to remember things from long ago.'

Milo said, 'How about theoretically? Was she theoretically into geezers?'

Koznikov's hand pressed down on a heavy bosom. 'This is so long ago.'

'Olga, something tells me you remember everything you've ever done or thought.'

'A sweet thing to say, Lieutenant, but we all fade.'

'Tara never got the chance to fade. That's what we're here about.'

Koznikov flinched. For less than a second, a real person seeped through the kindly madam act.

As good as any therapist, Milo seized the moment: 'She didn't go easily, Olga.'

He placed a death shot on the desk.

Koznikov's face didn't change but the hand on her chest whitened.

'Help us, Olga.'

'She was so beautiful. Barbarians.'

'Any particular barbarians come to mind?'

'Why would I know people like this?'

Milo said, 'Any barbarians, a name, anything.'

Koznikov shook her head. Slowly, balefully. 'I would tell you. I'm sorry.'

'How long has it been since Tara worked for you?'

'Three years.' First time she'd strayed from theoretical. She realized it and her jaw tightened. 'Three years is nearly a thousand days. I like to count. For exercise. Mental. For my memory.'

Prattling.

Milo said, 'She left three years ago.'

One year before going cyber.

'I like crosswords, too. For the memory. But the English? Too elevated.'

'Why'd she leave, Olga?'

'People get tired.'

'Personal problems?'

'People get tired.'

'Did drugs or booze have anything to do with that?'

'People get tired without drugs and booze.'

'No substance abuse issues.'

'Some people have self-control.'

'Her mother didn't.'

'What mother? She had no mother,' said Olga Koznikov.

'She was born in a test tube?'

'Her mother died when she was a little girl. In Colorado.'

'What town in Colorado?'

'Vail. She grew up in the snow. Once upon a time.'

'That so.'

'Her mother taught skiing, died in an accident, she was raised by the county.'

'What about her father?'

'Swiss tourist, she never knew him.'

'She told you that.'

'She showed me a picture.'

'Of Vail.'

'A pretty woman with a baby. Snow.'

'Interesting,' said Milo.

Koznikov's cheeks fluttered.

'Olga, her mother was a woman named Maude Grundy. She was an alcoholic streetwalker from New Mexico who gave birth to Tara when she was fifteen. Tara's birth certificate says father unknown. Maude had a rough life, moved to LA at some point but we can't figure out exactly when. Whether or not Tara brought her here is unclear. If she did, they probably had a falling-out because Tara let Maude live in a dump that burned down two and a half months ago. Maude died in the fire and Tara didn't pay a cent to bury her.'

Koznikov had listened impassively. Now she took long sips from the can. Suppressed a belch and smiled. 'You are telling me this to make me sad.'

'I'm telling you in case Tara told you anything that was actually true and might help us find who murdered her.'

She turned to me. 'Your question I can now answer. Yes, the old ones liked her. I thought okay, she has no father, makes sense. This much is true, even if he was not Swiss.'

'What does having no father have to do with them liking her?' said Milo.

'They liked her because she liked *them*. That's all of it – love, sex, pleasure. You like me, I like you. One of them – what if once upon a time one of them, a very old, kind man, told me Tara was "patient"? That would explain it, no? That would help you understand.'

I said, 'Patience is a good quality in a young person.'

'Good and so rare.'

'How about a time line?' said Milo. 'When did she start working with you, when did she finish?'

'Three years is a long time to do anything.'

'How long have you had this place?'

'Eighteen years.'

'You don't get tired.'

'I am lucky.'

'Three-year stint,' said Milo. 'How long before that had she been in LA working for bad people?'

'A year.'

'So she arrived seven years ago.'

'You are good in math. I need calculators.'

'Did she talk about living anywhere else but Colorado?'

'Yes, but now I don't know what's true and what is not.'

'We can sift that out, Olga. Where else did she say she lived?'

'Texas, Arizona, Oklahoma.'

'Not New Mexico.'

'No.'

'What else can you tell us?'

'Nothing.'

'Nothing, huh?'

'Unfortunately.'

I said, 'What did she do after she quit?'

The hand left her breast and fluffed her hair. Curls expanded then sprang back like metal springs. 'The computer.'

'She started selling herself online?'

'Not selling,' said Koznikov. 'Advertising. For relationship.'

'She told you she wanted a relationship.'

'I don't meddle with the baby birds.'

'But you found out she'd gone online.'

'Things get around.'

'Did you talk to her about it?'

'The computer,' she said, 'is magic. It can be black magic.'

'No security,' I said. 'Unlike a face-to-face business with guys like William for protection.'

'William sells furniture.'

'Did you ever find out who she hooked up with online?'

'My guess is a rich man.'

'She never told you.'

'I don't meddle.'

'Things get around,' I said.

'They do.'

'You didn't resent her leaving.'

'Some jobs you can do when you are tired.'

'Not Tara's.'

'The cow with empty udders doesn't give milk.'

'Why do you guess she was with a rich man?'

'I saw her getting out of a car,' said Koznikov. 'Rodeo Drive, the fancy stores for the skinny girls. Nice little BMW. She carried bags.'

'From which stores?'

'Too far to read the bags.'

'Was she by herself?'

'Yes.'

'You assumed a rich boyfriend was paying for her shopping spree.'

'She didn't have an MBA.'

Milo said, 'I'm going to give you a fact, Olga. Because we value your help. The rich man she found was named Mark Suss.'

'Okay.'

'Old guy. Was he one of her regulars?'

'I don't know this Suss.'

'You know another Suss?'

Koznikov tugged a curl. 'I don't know him, I don't know what Tara did with him, I don't know anything.'

'She never talked to you about Suss?'

'How do you spell this?'

'S-U-S-S.'

'Short name,' she said. 'It's real?'

'Quite. Rich Beverly Hills family.'

'You think they hurt her?'

'Not at this point. How about the bad men she worked with before she found guidance? Would any of them still be angry enough to hurt her?'

Koznikov's laugh was the sputter of a faulty ignition. 'We are talking dirt.'

'Dirt can have a bad temper.'

Her eyes chilled. 'Dirt gets stepped on.'

'So no need to bother looking for her first pimps.'

'No need.' She rolled a hand into a fist. 'This Suss, you have talked to him?'

'He died.'

'Ah.'

'After she left, did she ever return to you?'

'For what?'

'A social call?'

She went quiet. Relaxed pudgy fingers.

'Olga?'

'Okay, I will tell you something. She came back one time. For advice.'

'When?'

'Maybe two years. Give or take.'

'A year after she retired.'

'Okay.'

'What'd she want advice about?'

'How to build a good relationship.'

'With who?'

'She didn't say. Later, I see her in her little BMW, the clothes.'

'Striking it rich and wanting to settle down?' said Milo. 'Every call girl's fantasy.'

'Big joke to you,' said Olga Koznikov, 'but not always funny.'

'It happens, huh?'

'I could give you names. Girls acting in movies, wives of rich men. Even lawyers.'

'Even.'

Koznikov grinned. 'Not everyone knows how to use the mouth right.'

I said, 'Tara wanted to build a relationship. Something more than sex.'

'She was happy, I was happy. She was a nice girl.'

'What else can you tell us about her?'

'Nothing.' Staring at us. 'Now it's *really* nothing.'

Milo said, 'Did William know her?'

'William sells furniture.'

'Even so.'

'Even so, no.'

'Back in the theoretical days, you had others like him. To set limits.'

Koznikov held out her hands.

'Was one of your musclemen a guy named Steven Muhrmann?'

Koznikov yanked a curl hard enough to shake loose several snowy hairs. They floated midair, wafted onto her desk. She brushed them away. 'Why do you ask about him?'

'So he did work for you.'

Her fingers drummed the desk. She picked up the soda can, crushed it with one hard squeeze. 'Briefly.'

'When Tara worked for you.'

Silence.

Milo said, 'Were he and Tara close?'

'*No.*'

'You seem sure.'

Koznikov rubbed her forehead.

'What, Olga?'

'Him,' she said. 'I told Tara, she agreed with me.'

'You told her to stay away from Muhrmann.'

'All the girls,' said Koznikov. She pitched forward, bosoms intruding on the desk. 'You are saying he's the one?'

Milo said, 'We're saying he associated with Tara after she retired. We'd like to speak to him but haven't been able to find him. Any ideas?'

'Did he do it?'

'We don't know, Olga.'

'But it's possible.'

'Anything's possible but no, he's not a suspect and I don't want you to act on that assumption.'

'I don't act.'

'I'm serious, Olga.'

'Fool,' she spat. 'He is the actor.'

'He wanted to act?'

'Probably.'

'Probably?'

'He lied.'

'So?'

'Lying is good practice for acting.'

'What'd he lie about?'

'Goofing around, not working.'

'Booze, dope, rock and roll.'

'Loser,' she said.

'How'd you find him?'

'One of my properties, we did construction. He was digging foundation. Big muscles. I thought maybe he'd be okay, because he's gay.'

'Muhrmann's gay?'

'I thought,' she said. 'Taking care of the body like that, the yellow hair, very tan.'

214

Milo smiled. 'Only gay men do that.'

'Gay men are the best,' she said. 'Take care of the girls, no problems.'

'Muhrmann didn't take care of anything.'

'Bum,' she said. 'Loser.'

'Did he have a particular thing for Tara?'

'No. Fool.'

'Not a smart guy.'

'I'm talking about *her*,' said Koznikov.

'She was stupid for hanging with Muhrmann.'

'You play, you pay.' She rubbed her hands together. 'Okay, I'm finished.'

Hoisting herself out of her chair, she pointed to the door. No more than five feet tall. Thin, tight lips gave her the look of a venomous toad.

Milo said, 'If you could direct us to any girls she worked with, that would be helpful.'

'I don't know any girls, I don't know anything.'

'You knew Tara was dead.'

'I watch TV,' she said. 'Mostly Home and Garden network, sometimes Do It Yourself. Good-bye.'

'Olga—'

'Good-bye. Please don't come back.'

She flung the door open. William stood inches from the jamb, chewing gum energetically.

'Hey,' he said.

Koznikov said, 'Take them out.'

Milo said, 'If you think of anything else—'

'I am old, I do not think well.'

William made a move toward Milo's elbow, thought better of it, and gave a small bow and stepped back. 'After you, sirs.'

Milo proceeded up the aisle but I was restrained by Koznikov's hand on my wrist. Hard grip, just short of inflicting pain.

Tiptoeing, she placed one arm around my waist, pushed her mouth an inch from my ear.

I tried to move away but she held fast. Put her mouth near my ear. Hot breath, then a whisper:

'Thank you for helping Gretchen.'

I peeled her arm off, walked away.

She laughed. 'That's what I figured you'd say.'

28

WILLIAM TRAILED us through the barn. When we hit daylight, Milo said, 'We'll take it from here, friend.'

William's stance widened.

'On the other hand, friend, let's see some ID.'

'May I ask for what reason, sir?'

'You may ask but you won't receive an answer. Show me some paper.'

William chewed fast. 'Of course.' Out came a billfold. Gold dollar sign clamping a brick of cash.

Milo said, 'Marcy William Dodd. Park La Brea Towers, huh? Nice.'

'I like it, sir.'

Milo pointed to the row of vehicles. 'Which is yours?'

'The Hyundai.'

'That your only drive?'

William stopped chewing. 'You were expecting a stretch Escalade, sir? With a gangsta lean and a fur hat on the headrest?'

'Why would I expect that?'

'You know how it is, sir.'

'Did you know Tara Sly?'

'No, sir. Before my time.'

'When did your time start?'

'Obviously after this person you're asking about left Madame's employment.' Teeth flashed like strobes. 'You know what, sir, I'm not feeling these questions and the law says I don't have to answer them. You take care, now.'

He strode back to the barn.

By the time I started the Seville, Milo had run his name, found nothing beyond the address.

'Cleanest bunch of felons I've ever met.'

'They sell furniture,' I said.

'And I'm an Olympic ice-skater. Okay, let's get out of here.'

As I turned onto La Cienega, he said, 'What'd she whisper in your ear?'

'Sweet nothings.'

'Seriously.'

'She really likes my chest hair.'

'The old charm never fails. You give her your number?'

'Oh, sure,' I said. 'Dinner and a movie.'

'Be a new experience for you,' he said.

'Cheating on Robin with an elderly psychopath? Gee, that's enticing.'

'Personal sacrifice in service of the department.'

'Unlike Muhrmann, I've got limits.'

'Mr Bad Behavior,' he said. 'And he goes way back with Tara – Tiara. Yeah, it firms him up as my prime.'

He pulled out his pad and pen. 'Time to fill in the time line before she snared Mark Suss. She splits from Santa Fe after her third arrest, which would be no longer than nine, ten years ago. Travels around, heads west. Maybe she even landed in those places she told Olga. A couple of years later, she's in LA, probably low and grubby because she gets nabbed off the bus, works the street. A year later she signs up with Olga, becomes a high-priced spread, lasts three then she retires at the ripe old age of twenty-six. After meeting Muhrmann and maintaining some sort of relationship. Am I missing anything?'

'I find it interesting that she stopped paying her rent right around the time her mother died.'

'What, traumatized into fiscal irresponsibility?'

'Maybe that motivated a life change.'

'Skipping out on the rent is psychological growth?'

'Starting to save up for the future could be,' I said. 'She was ready for a move. Did she go somewhere between the time she cut out and the time she was found?'

'Shacking up with someone?'

'Or living by herself.'

'Where?'

'Good question.'

'I've already been through real estate records and she doesn't own anything. If she had a new landlord, you'd think they'd call in if they saw her face on the news.'

I said, 'Unless whoever she was living with had a vested interest in not calling.'

'Muhrmann. Or Connie Longellos. Or both. There's a secret fun-pad somewhere.' Frowning. 'Or neither. Time to follow the money trail.'

We grabbed jet-fuel coffee from the big detective room, walked to his office, and played computer games.

With no legal way to access bank and brokerage accounts, the best bet was real estate records.

Philip Suss and Connie Longellos-Suss owned four commercial parcels in LA County plus the house in Encino and a Huntington Beach condo. Property taxes had been paid faithfully, no liens or major encumbrances. A warehouse in the toy district and a Tarzana facility rented to a sports club carried mortgages, but nothing substantial compared with assessed value.

Milo toted up the most recent appraisals and whistled.

'Twenty-four million bazoongas.'

I said, 'It's probably an underestimate because the properties haven't been assessed for years.'

One property had been sold last year: the building housing Connie Longellos's art gallery. Forty percent short-term loan on that one, but profit from the transaction had taken care of that and Phil and Connie had netted just short of a million dollars.

'Connie didn't go under,' he said, 'she wanted to clean up on the real estate. Oh, man, there goes my motive for her, goddamn rich people, yet another reason to hate 'em.'

He switched to Franklin and Isabel Suss's holdings, came up with the house on Camden Drive, an office-condo on Bedford Drive where they both saw patients, a second home in a gated community in Ventura, a six-unit apartment building in West LA. Mortgages on everything except the primary residence, but once again, nothing crippling. Value of the package: nine million.

'Nice,' he said, 'but only about a third of what his brother's worth. Frankie goes to med school, Philly ends up the tycoon?'

I said, 'Med school, internship, and residency create years of lost income. Phil could've used the time to be entrepreneurial. Or Frank's motivated by something other than amassing money.'

'Like?'

'Practicing medicine.'

'A straight line between two points? Talk about far-fetched.' He laughed.

'For all we know, Frank's just as rich as Phil but he has his money in other investments, like the stock market.'

'Maybe . . . hey, what if they look good on paper but one of them recently blew some serious dough on the market or some other scheme?'

'If either of them was in acute trouble, you'd expect them to sell off properties or take out additional loans. Neither is mortgaged to the hilt and most of Phil's properties are flat-out paid for.'

He rubbed his face.

I said, 'Even if they are financially secure, there could be a non-economic motive. Tiara decided to squeeze the family and they opted for damage control.'

'Defending the castle.' He logged off. 'I need to find a way to get closer to these aristocrats.' Placing a palm against a pitted cheek, he grinned. 'Maybe I should start with the doctors. Go in asking about dermal sandblasting or whatever the hell they do with a train wreck like this. Hell, maybe liposuction, too, if they've got industrial hoses.'

I said, 'Mr Rogers loves you just the way you are.'

'Plus my health insurance doesn't cover demolition and renovation and Connie Longellos is a drunk who hung with Muhrmann, so let's start with the goddamn obvious place.'

'Straight line between two points.'

'No longer far-fetched, lad.'

'Why's that?'

'I said so.'

We drove back to Encino. The house on Portico Place was pretty under afternoon sun, ocher face kicked down to a serene buttermilk hue, trowel marks lending depth to the finish, bougainvillea blossoms glowing like garnets.

Just as before, the white BMW and the bronze Lexus occupied the cobbled motor court.

Milo directed me to a spot up the block with an oblique view of the gates. We sat for a while before he phoned John Nguyen and asked about a subpoena of all Suss financial records.

Nguyen said, 'Why are you doing this to me?'

'What?'

'Making me the bad parent. The answer's no, now go clean your room.'

Ten more minutes passed, during which Milo polluted the Seville with cigar smoke and returned a message from Rick. A clinic that tested for STDs and genetic disorders was situated in a Cedars-affiliated building on San Vicente. Rick had phoned the director, an immunologist he knew casually, only to be barked at.

Any breach of patient confidentiality would be fought aggressively and Rick should know better.

Milo said, 'So much for professional courtesy. Sorry.'

'Guy's always been a dick, don't worry about it.'

'That's why I love you.'

'That's the only reason?'

'You want me to start listing?'

'Nah. Wait until you're home and have time to expound.'

After another quarter hour, Milo decided to ring Phil and Connie Suss's gate buzzer.

'Not that I have any idea how to explain my interest.'

'You can always take the soft approach, see how they react.'

'Meaning?'

'Apologetic, self-deprecating, the name *Suss* came up in the personal effects of a victim, if they'd be kind enough to spare a few minutes.'

'Genuflect and kiss ass,' he said. 'I'd rather get my face sanded.' A beat later: 'Okay, sounds like a plan.'

Just as he was reaching for the door handle, Connie Suss-Longellos stepped out her front door, wearing a black-velvet tracksuit and running shoes, no makeup, blond hair tied in a high pony. Starting up the Lexus, she lowered the hardtop and drove to the gate.

Filigree parted electrically. She turned south.

Milo said, 'Oh Lord of Detection, lead us to the Promised Land.'

A previous trip had taken forty years.

I kept my mouth shut.

29

CONNIE LONGELLOS-SUSS drove to a nail salon on Ventura near White Oak.

Milo said, 'Don't see the river Jordan anywhere.'

She stayed inside for thirty-two minutes and he took the opportunity to murder a chili dog from a nearby stand and slurp two Cokes. When she stepped outside examining a silver manicure, he was rubbing a greasy lapel stain with soda water.

Down came the top on the Lexus for a half-mile drive east into Sherman Oaks. She parked in front of a boutique named Poppy's Daydreams.

No additional spaces.

Milo said, 'Circle the block.' Then: 'Damn.'

'What?'

'There's an Orange Julius and I filled up on the brown stuff.'

I drove around the block, was nearing the clothing store when Connie reappeared, checked her parking meter, fed coins, continued on foot.

One block east to a bistro named Max Cuisine.

Milo said, 'Wonder if that means portion-sized. Hang a U and park across the street.'

By the time we reached the restaurant Connie had been served. Her plate said the portions were anything but generous: something small and pale and vaguely fowl-like floating on a cloud of green wisps. Bottle of designer water at her elbow, untouched bread basket. Her fork hung midair as she perused a copy of *Modern Painter.*

Too late for the lunch crowd, too early for dinner, and she was the only patron. But for the lace-trimmed streetwalkers and absinthe-addled boulevardiers inhabiting a collection of Toulouse-Lautrec prints, the only other human face in sight was a heavy woman in a chef's toque smoking at a far table while scanning *Le Monde.*

When we entered, Connie Suss ignored us. When we got two feet away she paid attention.

Milo's badge unhinged her mouth. 'Is everything okay? With my husband?'

'Everything's fine, ma'am. May we sit down?'

'Um . . . I guess so. What's going on?'

She put the fork down, then the magazine. Handsome woman, with clear blue eyes and clean, symmetrical features. She'd managed to maintain the tan while avoiding conspicuous damage. Maybe the color was spray-on. Or something her brother-in-law or sister-in-law had provided. Did doctors do that kind of thing? In Beverly Hills, probably.

We sat on either side. The table's small size enforced intimacy. She scooted an inch from Milo's bulk, found herself closer to me, and grimaced. I gave her some space.

'What's going on, guys?'

'Sorry to bother you – is it Ms Suss or Ms Longellos?'

'Depends.'

Milo raised an eyebrow.

'What I mean,' she said, 'is I use Longellos professionally but legally I'm Suss. When I met my husband I was already established so keeping my maiden name seemed easier.'

'What kind of work do you do?'

'Did, I'm retired. Finance, investment banking, that's how I met my husband, I managed money with a company that handled his family's finances. Then I got into art – why is this important? Why am I talking about *anything* to the *police*?'

'It's really nothing,' said Milo, 'but we need to be thorough. Your name came up in the personal effects of a victim.'

'A victim? What kind of victim? I don't understand.' She inched back.

'Homicide, ma'am.'

Connie Longellos's head shot forward as if she'd been shoved brutally. '*What?* What on earth would my name be doing with a – this is crazy, you must be mistaken.'

'Connie Longellos,' said Milo. 'We traced you through that name.'

'Well, that's crazy, that's really totally insane.' She fingered the zipper of her track jacket. Lush velour, tiny logo on the sleeve. An Italian brand I'd never heard of. 'Who is this victim?'

'A woman named Tiara Grundy.'

'Now I know it's insane. I have no idea who that is.'

'She also went by Tara Sly.'

'Same answer, guys. *That* one sounds like something a porn actress would use. No, you're totally mistaken, I don't know any Tiara or Tara anybody. How'd my name come up – was it on a piece of art? I've sold a lot of art in my day, I suppose she could've been a customer.'

'No, ma'am,' said Milo.

'Then what? Where was my name?'

'Personal effects.'

'What are you talking about?'

Milo didn't answer.

'You come barging in but won't tell me?'

'At this point, we need to be discreet, Ms Suss. What about Steven Muhrmann?'

'Who?'

'You don't know Steven Muhrmann?'

She chuckled. 'You guys are wasting your time, this must be a computer mix-up.'

225

'How about Stefan Moore?'

'How about not,' said Connie Suss. 'That sounds like a movie monster, one of those Japanese films.'

'Stefan?'

'Merman. Merman Invades Tokyo.' She laughed.

Milo didn't.

'Sorry, I'm sure you're doing your job,' she said, 'but you have to admit it's weird coming in here while I'm trying to have my dunch – that's a made-up word I use for dinner and lunch. I get GERD – reflux disease. So I like to eat early. Like a senior citizen.'

She eyed the ghost of the stain on Milo's jacket. 'You come in and throw names at me, that's pretty darn weird.'

She reached for her magazine.

Milo said, 'Markham Suss.'

Her hand withdrew. 'My father-in-law? What does *he* have to do with this?'

'Tiara Grundy knew him. Well.'

'Mark passed away a while back.'

'You don't seem surprised by the relationship.'

'Of course I'm surprised.'

'Honestly, you didn't seem surprised, ma'am.'

She exhaled. 'Okay, you're obviously talking about one of Mark's sluts, but that has nothing to do with me. What, she got herself killed and she had my business card or something? Maybe Mark recommended my gallery to her. Though I can't recall his ever having an interest in the gallery. Or bringing any of them in – I used to own a glass gallery not far from here but I closed it down because we got a terrific offer on the building and frankly I was tired of working.'

'One of his sluts,' said Milo. 'So there were a lot of them.'

'Sluts were pretty much a fixture in Mark's life, it's no big secret, Officer – is it Detective?'

'Lieutenant.'

'Excuse me. Lieutenant. Once my husband and I got serious, before

226

he took me to meet his parents, he warned me to expect some strange things.'

'Such as?'

'A little more . . . freedom of expression than some folk.'

'Extreme tolerance?'

'Mark might've called it that,' she said, 'but to me it was extreme ostrich-in-the-sand-ness. The unspoken truth, you know?'

'Denial.'

'Denial implies pretending. Mark made no pretense – I'm sorry, I feel disloyal talking about this. Now could you please let me dunch in peace?'

I said, 'Everyone was aware of Mark's behavior but no one acknowledged it.'

'If Lee – my mother-in-law – could live with it, what was it my business?' She frowned. 'Not that any of this is your business, Mark's been gone for nearly a year so he obviously had nothing to do with anything happening to this Tiara person.'

Milo said, 'And you've never heard of Steve or Stefan Muhrmann.'

'Asking me again won't change the facts, Lieutenant.'

'Hmm.'

'Hmm what?'

'Your name was associated with Muhrmann a little more directly.'

Connie Longellos-Suss's blue eyes bugged. 'What are you *talking* about?'

The chef in the corner looked up from her paper.

Milo said, 'Ma'am, I'm terribly sorry to upset you but a terrible crime's taken place and when evidence surfaces I'm obligated to follow up.'

'I don't know any Merman. Or Godzilla or Rodan. This is unreal.'

'You're not curious about how your name came up with his?'

'No, because it's ridiculous.' Sagging. 'Oh, no, you're kidding.'

'What?'

'Could this be another identity theft thing?'

'You've had identify theft problems?'

'A few years ago someone ran up bills on one of my credit cards. Idiots, they used a platinum card to buy fast food and computer games. I closed the account and there've been no problems since. But once stuff hits the Internet – are you saying this Merman is pretending to be me?'

'Steven Muhrmann used you as a reference to rent a house. And someone using your name actually sent a letter.'

'That's *psychotic*.'

'The house is on Russell Avenue, in Los Feliz,' said Milo.

'You might as well be talking Greek. At least that I'd understand, my father was Greek.'

Milo paged through his pad, read off the POB in Pacific Palisades.

She said, 'I've never owned a post-office box in my life.'

'Ma'am, I have to ask you a somewhat . . . difficult question, so please don't take offense. Have you ever been in rehab?'

She stared at him. Burst into laughter. 'In rehab? What on earth for?'

'You do have a DUI.'

'That? Oh, man, you guys are like . . . that was totally stupid.'

'Stupid, how?'

'Don't your police files give you details?' she said. 'About what actually happens at arrests?'

'The file lists you with a DUI conviction.'

'Then let me give you the facts: It was one of those New Year's Eve things. When *you* people do those random stops. The irony is my husband and I weren't even partying, we decided to stay home, enjoy some peace and quiet.' Laughing softly. 'We drank some wine. Riesling. I had two glasses and then I needed some . . . I got my . . .'

Peach-colored blush seeped into the corners of her tan face. 'What the heck, you've already ruined my meal. I needed a *feminine* product and I'd run out, okay? Normally it's Phil – my husband – who does nighttime runs to the pharmacy or the Seven-Eleven or whatever, but that kind of thing makes him squeamish so I went. And got pulled over randomly about a half a minute later. And –' she sighed – 'failed a stupid Breathalyzer. But like at one-tenth of a percent, the whole thing was ridiculous. I tried to explain to those morons – and yes, you people acted like morons – that I'd just gone out to get some darn tampons, all I'd had were two glasses of Riesling. They looked at me like I was a criminal, said I'd *blown* .09, which was more than the legal limit of .08. Then they arrested me. I went hysterical. So how did you geniuses handle that? Cuffed me and shoved me in the back of a police car. At that point, I totally lost it, started screaming, begged them to let me call Phil. They ignored me. The stress got me bleeding heavily and my hands were cuffed so I couldn't do anything about it.'

Her eyes pooled with tears. 'Just remembering it is utterly humiliating, but what the heck, you want details, I'll give you *details*. I bled all over their stupid car and when they saw it they freaked out, thought I'd cut myself. If they'd taken the time to listen, all they needed to do was hand me a darn tampon, but no, that was too logical. Instead they called in the paramedics, who showed up and checked me out and ended giving me a stupid *tampon*. By that time, I'd been gone from the house for over an hour and Phil was worried. He got in his car, drove toward the drugstore, saw my car, pulled over. Guess what they did?'

Milo said, 'Gave him a Breathalyzer.'

'Bingo,' said Connie Suss. 'Random, my butt. There must be some manual you people have about harassing honest, taxpaying citizens. Luckily, Phil passed. Even though he had *three* glasses of Riesling. He weighs a lot more than I do and I guess the time lapse helped. In the end, Phil convinced them not to take me to jail but I got a ticket and had to do community service. I ended up giving classes in art appreciation to some inner-city kids. You guys promised me my record would be wiped clean. What, you lied? Figures.'

She picked up her fork, plucked a tine, and set off a tiny musical tone. 'Now I've told you about the most humiliating experience of my life. Now you can leave.'

Milo said, 'Sorry you had to go through that.'

'Don't apologize, just give me some peace and quiet.'

Milo hung his head.

Connie Suss said, 'What are *you* so sullen about?'

'The questions I have to keep asking.'

'Good Lord, *now* what?'

'Your name came up as a patient at a rehab program. Where Steve Muhrmann was also in treatment.'

Her hands gripped the table. 'This is *psy-cho-tic*. Where is this supposed place?'

'Pasadena. Awakenings.'

'The only thing that takes me to Pasadena is the Rose Bowl, and the last time we attended the game was four years ago. This *has* to be an identity theft thing.' Her brow furrowed, then smoothed. 'Maybe it's one of those Medi-Cal frauds, where they bill for services that never take place? I will swear on a stack of Bibles that I have never ever been in any kind of rehab, nor do I have a drinking problem, nor do I know any of my father-in-law's sluts by name, nor have I rented a post-office box.' Pausing for breath. 'The same goes for any relationship with a Mer-Man.' Giggling. Shrill. She turned a hand into a swooping jet plane. 'Watch out, Tokyo.'

The chef peered our way.

'Hilarious,' said Connie Suss.

Milo said, 'Tiara Grundy's face was on the news.'

'I never watch the news, too depressing.' She patted Milo's cuff. 'Thanks, Lieutenant.'

'For—'

'Totally eradicating my appetite, I've been trying to take off a few pounds, you made it easy.'

Sliding bills from an alligator purse, she walked over to the chef. 'It was delicious, Françoise, but I'm going to take this home.'

'Certainly, Connie.'

Françoise took the plate into the kitchen. As Connie Suss waited, she kept her back to us.

Milo said, 'Thanks for your time, ma'am.'

No answer.

As we left, she said, 'You *should* thank me. It's people like me who finance this comedy routine you pretend is a job.'

30

A SERIES of calls to Valley Traffic confirmed the details of Connie Suss's DUI.

'I hate when they're credible,' said Milo. 'You feel anything deceptive about her?'

'Anyone can be fooled,' I said, 'but she seemed real.'

'So scratch one family member. Along with the whole damn case I've been building. Maybe she's right and it'll come down to a scam – and that psychiatrist Manlow was in on it. She also seemed straight, but like you said.'

I said, 'If Manlow was involved in fraud why would she let on that someone using Connie's name had entered the program?'

'She actually didn't come out and say it, Alex, she just didn't deny it.'

'Basically, she told us without having to come out and say it.'

'That could be because we caught her off guard. Or she's one of those liars who figures it's best to sprinkle in partial truths.'

He phoned the medical board, got voice-mailed to the ethical complaints section. Nary a gripe about Elizabeth Allison Manlow.

I said, 'Someone could've registered and paid as Connie without Manlow's knowledge. As long as insurance wasn't billed, there'd be no reason to check ID.'

'That much cash,' he said, 'means someone with plenty to spare. Like any of the Susses.'

'Using someone else's name would be a good way to hide the fact you're getting treatment. But it's also an act of aggression, so maybe we should look for someone who resents Connie.'

'Could be anyone.'

'Families are emotional cauldrons but posing as a woman almost certainly means a woman,' I said. 'That leaves Leona and the sister-in-law – Isabel. I don't see Leona putting herself at that kind of risk. Isabel's also a doctor. Easy access to drugs and that could've translated into addiction. And as a physician, exposure could've meant losing her license, so she'd have good reason to hide her identity. And like Connie, she'd be familiar with Mark's sexual hijinks.'

'She checks herself in under Connie's name, makes friends with Muhrmann, tells him about her crazy family.'

'Rehab encourages confession. A guy like Muhrmann would hear Big Money Old Guy Young Chicks. He flashes on Tiara, says, I've got a great idea.'

'Naughty Dr Isabel.' He pressed both hands to his temples. 'Or we're all wet and the fake Connie could be someone outside the family who knew enough to make trouble. Like a staff member, Lord knows how many people it takes to run those households. Some maid or butler thinks he can rake in a few thou, that could be enough motivation.'

'Millions beats thousands.'

'Stick with the family, huh?'

'Maybe it's *my* occupational hazard, but that feels right.'

He called the medical offices of Drs Franklin and Isabel Suss. After enduring a recorded mini-lecture on sun exposure recited over new age music, he reached a human voice.

'Doctors' office.'

'I'd like a consult on some dermabrasion.'

'Are you a patient, sir?'

'No, but I might wanna be. Anything tomorrow?'

'Let's see . . . Dr Frank's booked but Dr Isabel's got a cancellation at three.'

'Perfect.'

'Could I please have your insurance information?'

'Don't have it with me but I promise to bring it.'

'Please do, sir. It's important.'

He clicked off. 'This could turn bad if Connie's already bitching to the rest of the family about her screwed-up dunch.' He snorted. 'Traffic geniuses sure primed the pump for me. One-tenth of a percentage and they treat her like a criminal.'

'Put rules in place and some people stop thinking.'

'Ain't that the truth, amigo. Rick and I know a guy, used to be a tennis pro, developed heel pain so his doctor prescribed a handicapped parking permit. A few weeks later, the heel gets better but Jean-Georges is still putting his Jaguar wherever the hell he pleases. Meanwhile, some poor guy with one arm and a screwed-up leg has to borrow a pal's wheels and parks in a handicapped slot. When he comes out, the parking Nazi's writing him up. Fair enough. But what's the chance the Nazi, seeing the one arm and the screwed-up leg, tears up the ticket?'

A big hand slapped the dashboard. 'About the same as my being invited to the next Suss reunion.' Shaking his head. '*Dunch*. My thing's *cluttony*.'

'Chronic gluttony?'

'I was thinking "constant" but that'll do.'

I took Benedict Canyon over the mountains as Milo checked his messages. A sheriff named Palmberg had phoned ten minutes ago.

Squinting, he made out the number. 'Malibu station. Can't think of any reason for a day at the beach.'

The Malibu desk officer said, 'No one by that name works here.'

'He called me from there.'

'Hmm.'

'Lieutenant Sturgis. LAPD.'

'Hold on.' Moments later: 'He's from Downtown but he was here this morning. Here's his cell.'

One beep before a bass rumble said, 'Larry Palmberg.'

'Milo Sturgis returning your call.'

'Milo,' said Palmberg, as if digesting the name. 'Got a murder out here in Topanga I thought you might be interested in. Less than a mile north from where you had one last week and the body seems to be about from that same time, give or take. Might not be related, then again.'

'Male or female?'

'Male, two gunshot wounds to the back, magnum load. Blew out his spine and everything in front of it.'

'Any sign of a shotgun?'

'Nope, just two bullet wounds. There's a good amount of decomp but what I can tell you is he was a decent-sized fellow, dyed his hair blond, his driver's license claims his mama named him Steven Muhrmann. I looked him up, fellow's got a checkered past. Know him?'

'I know of him, Larry,' said Milo. 'Can't wait to make his acquaintance.'

Sheriff's Homicide Investigator Laurentzen Palmberg was six four, two hundred and fifty solid pounds, in his midfifties, with a gray crew cut and firm, rosy cheeks. Gold-rimmed, small-lens eyeglasses creased a serious nose. He was smoking enthusiastically, snubbed out his cigarette as we stepped out of the Seville.

Introductions were quick. Palmberg took out a hard-pack of Parliaments, kept passing it from hand to hand. Otherwise, he looked serene. Deputies in tan uniforms abounded, Palmberg was the only person in civvies: well-cut gray pin-striped suit, white tab-collar shirt, orange tie patterned with the noble heads of Irish setters. One dusty-toed black loafer tapped the eastern edge of the road.

He pointed to where white-clad crime scene techs fussed over something, around thirty feet down. The object of their attention lay on a ten foot mini-mesa chunked out of the hillside by eons of erosion. If the body hadn't landed there, it would've rolled another hundred feet into dense brush.

'Here's where it started.' Palmberg walked to a nearby evidence marker and nodded at a large brown patch spreading over asphalt, dirt, and grass. Clumps of what looked like pemmican littered the brush.

Once vital organs, drying in the sun. We all end up nonvital.

I said, 'What's he wearing?'

'Black suit, what used to be a white shirt. Black tie. Guess his last night was fancy.'

Same outfit I'd seen outside the Fauborg. I waited for Milo to comment but he just said, 'Who found him?'

'Helicopter,' said Palmberg, 'some real estate guy checking out large plots of vacant land. The pilot got as low as he could to verify it was what he thought it was, then called us.'

'Good eye.'

'He used to fly traffic for you guys, guess old habits die hard.'

Palmberg smoothed down an already impeccable lapel. 'The movie that's playing in my head until something better comes along is this: Muhrmann was with someone in a car, they stopped to enjoy the view. He's looking out that way, the shooter gets behind him, does the deed. Muhrmann either rolls down by himself or gets a little push. There's no sign of any big struggle and no drag marks so I'm figuring gravity was on the shooter's side, it really wouldn't take much propulsion once you put things in motion. Body stopped where it did because it snagged on some branches. Without that, we'd never have found him.'

Milo said, 'Any idea how far the shooter was standing?'

Palmberg gazed at the white-suits. 'Their best guesstimate is ten feet away, give or take. Due to the decomp it's hard to be sure, but no obvious stippling, so probably not a contact or close-up. I can see the shooter suggesting they stop for the view then making some excuse to go into the car where he gets the weapon and blasts Muhrmann before Muhrmann knows what's up. Your vic was shotgunned, huh? But you're here?'

'Shotgunned but also nailed by a .45.'

'Two bad guys?' said Palmberg. 'No sign of that with mine and the shell we recovered was a .357. So what do you know of *this* guy?'

Shadowing his eyes with a palm, Milo peered down into the crime scene. 'He was a prime suspect in my murder but now I might have to recast my own movie. How'd you know about my vic?'

'What do you think?' said Palmberg. 'I'm a dedicated detective, pore over the daily stats like it's my cholesterol report.' He rumbled a long, deep laugh. 'Nah, I saw it on TV, then when I found out where this one was dumped, I started wondering. So tell me, Milo, if Muhrmann was your prime, how come he wasn't mentioned on the news?'

'All I had on him was a feeling.'

'Feelings are good, I've closed a lot of cases with feelings.'

'Tell the bosses that,' said Milo. 'The ruling was I didn't have enough to go public.'

Palmberg clucked. 'My bosses would probably say the same. Anyway, it wouldn't have helped much, seeing as Muhrmann's been down there rotting for days, maybe got nailed the same night as your Jane Doe did.'

'Jane's got a name, now. Tiara Grundy, did some call girl work and ended up as a mistress to a Sugar Daddy.'

'Daddy on your radar?'

'Also dead, half a year ago, natural causes.'

'Boy, this town chews 'em up. What kind of natural?'

'Heart, he was pushing seventy, didn't watch *his* cholesterol.'

'Any leads at all?'

'Muhrmann's body could be a lead, Larry. He was seen with Tiara the night she died and we're thinking she was on a date but not with him.'

He nodded at me.

I recapped the scene at the Fauborg.

Palmberg said, 'Fake movie star with a fake bodyguard. Some sort of game, huh? You're thinking another rich mark?'

Milo said, 'A rich sociopath mark who colluded with Muhrmann to shoot Tiara, then took care of Muhrmann a mile later in order to tie up loose ends. Any tire tracks around here?'

'If there were any, they're long gone.' Palmberg removed his glasses, checked the lenses, scratched away a speck of something. 'Any specific candidates for this crafty death dealer?'

'We've been looking at the Daddy's heirs, thinking maybe Tiara tried some extortion when she lost her means of support.'

'Rich folk like to delegate.'

'They sure do,' said Milo. 'Problem with a contract killer is how do I access the money trail?'

Palmberg put his glasses back on. 'Sounds like we're both in great shape. You have problems sharing your file?'

'Soon as I get back, it's faxed to you.'

'I'll do the same, buddy. Once I have a file.'

They exchanged cards.

Milo said, 'My file has Muhrmann's mother's info in there, lives in Covina, nice lady.'

'Aren't they all,' said Palmberg. 'Your lucky day, missing out on notification by a mile.'

'Aw shucks.'

'Best part of the job, huh? We talking regular nice or *real* nice?'

'Real nice.'

Palmberg cursed cheerfully.

Milo took in the crime scene again. 'You been down there yet?'

'Twice. The second time my pants got ripped up, I had to change suits. You might think twice.'

Milo said, 'You keep spare duds on hand?'

'All the years of body fluids?' said Palmberg. 'You don't?'

Palmberg waited on the road, talking into his cell phone, as Milo and I climbed down, walking sideways but still slipping several times.

The flat area turned out to be a shallow crater, larger than I'd estimated, closer to twenty-feet wide. The sky above huge, deep blue silked by cirrus. The earth was hard-pack, gray where it wasn't brown, and carpeted with wild sage, mustard, wilting poppies, the odd struggling pine seedling.

Gorgeous spot, wide open and sunny. All that sweet air couldn't conquer the decomp reek. We reached the body just as the coroner's crew finished bagging.

Three techs, a woman and two men. They'd rolled down a snap-open gurney, looked unhappy about the prospect of getting it back up.

One of the men said, 'Hey, Lieutenant.'

'Walt. Could I have a look at him before you take him?'

Walt unzipped the bag to waist level. An abstractly humanoid mass, part leather, part oozing headcheese, caught light from the glorious sky. The eyes were gone, canapés for resourceful birds. Some kind of carnivore had feasted on the neck, extruding blood vessels and muscle fibers and tendons. The white shirt was shredded, the black tie turned to bloody ribbon. Splintered ribs protruded from a massive exit wound. The rotted sponge of lung and the degraded rubber of heart littered the ravaged chest. Dead maggots dusted everything like a hideous toss of wedding rice.

Milo turned to me. 'Any way that's remotely recognizable?'

I said, 'The hair's the same. So are the clothes and the general size.'

Walt said, 'You bring witnesses to scenes now, Lieutenant?'

'This witness is authorized.' He introduced me as a police consultant but didn't explain my link to Muhrmann. All three techs were puzzled but no one said anything.

The woman said, 'If he's on record, we can verify the ID. Printable left thumb and ring finger, the rest is gnawed to the bone.'

Walt said, 'Anything else you need, Lieutenant?'

Milo said, 'No, thanks. Zip him up.'

Walt did so without looking at the body.

The second man, younger, darker, said, 'Now the fun part, shlepping him up there. We shouldn't have to do it but the drivers are stuck in traffic and Detective Palmberg wants transport A-sap.'

Walt said, 'This was TV, they'd send us a copter, do that flashy basket thing. A copter found him in the first place.'

'TV,' said the woman, 'I'd get a makeup artist and fake boobs out to here and talk like an idiot.' She batted her lashes. 'Cee Ess Eye at your disposable, let's do an ultrasonic magnetic cross-section of the left lateral dorsal fibrio-filamental inclusion. Then we'll know who his great-grandfather was, what he ate for Thanksgiving six years ago, and what his first cousin's schnauzer thinks about kibble.'

Everyone smiled.

The younger man said, 'You ask me, using the gurney's a bigger pain. You guys take the body, I can do the gurney.'

The woman said, 'Anything to avoid the corpus delecti, Pedro.'

Pedro said, 'You want to do the gurney, Gloria, I'll do the body.'

'Kids, kids,' said Walt. To Milo: 'Can't take them anywhere.'

Milo said, 'If you can use two more sets of hands, we're at your service.'

Pedro said, 'That's okay, we're CSI studs, can handle it all by the first commercial.'

Walt said, 'Speak for yourself, action hero. As is, my back's gonna bitch for a week, they want to help, God bless 'em.'

Milo scanned the slope. 'Anything else down here other than him that I should be concerned about?'

'A little blood,' said Walt, 'but most of it's on the road and the first ten feet of the drop. We tagged and bagged skin fragments but all you're going to get is more of this guy, there was no struggle.'

Milo checked the area anyway, nostrils flaring, then compressing. 'How about two of you do the gurney, the rest of us will form the funeral procession.'

'It's a plan,' said Walt.

We began the climb.

Pedro said, 'The Lord is my shepherd. Too bad *this* ain't a sheep.'

31

I DIDN'T hear from Milo the following day and my call to Gretchen asking how Chad was doing went unanswered.

Robin and I went out to dinner at an Italian place she'd heard about. Little Santa Monica Boulevard on the western edge of the Beverly Hills business district. Family-run, the wife cooking, the husband hosting, two teenage girls serving. Homemade everything, good wine.

Garlic breath for both of us, which is as good a definition of diplomacy as any.

When we got home and took Blanche out of her crate, she licked my hand with special enthusiasm. Did the same for Robin and belched. Now we had a consensus.

The doorbell rang.

Blanche raced to the front of the house and sat there, tail-stub wagging.

Robin said, 'Someone she's eager to see.'

A voice on the other side bellowed, 'Must be my looks.'

She let Milo in. 'Hope I'm not interrupting, kids.'

A cheek peck caused him to grimace. 'Spaghetti con olio y mucho garlicko.'

'Master detective. I'll go use mouthwash.'

'I was just thinking we could all go out. Alas.'

'We're happy to feed you.'

He threw up his hands. 'The sacrifices I make for friendship.'

As we walked to the kitchen, Robin said, 'How's Rick?'

'Meaning how come I'm dining solo?'

'No, darling. Meaning how's Rick.'

'Busy,' he said. 'On call and probably honing his scalpel as we speak. I'm busy, too, only difference is he's going to actually accomplish something.' He stopped. 'But don't let me destroy your happy, wholesome domestic ambience. In fact, I should probably take leave before my mope-virus infects anyone.'

'Don't be silly,' said Robin. 'What can I get you? Hopefully something with garlic so we can all be social.'

Three hastily snarfed mixed-meat sandwiches and an equal number of cold Grolsches later, he let out his belt a couple of notches and beamed up at her. 'You're a ministering angel – who needs Prozac?'

'Bad day, Big Guy?'

'Nothing day.'

I said, 'No go on Dr Isabel?'

'If she was any sweeter, I'd need insulin. She sat down with me for over half an hour, took a careful medical history, looked at my hide and pretended it wasn't so bad, then spelled out the pros and cons of dermal abrasion and a whole bunch of alternative treatments. By the end I was feeling so guilty about scamming her, I nearly signed up.'

Robin said, 'We're talking about one of the daughters-in-law?'

'Yup. The other one wasn't as friendly, but considering the way we barged in on her and dredged up unpleasant memories, she was damn near saintly. Bottom line: They both come across as honest and solid and utterly un-criminal and there's nothing in their backgrounds to suggest anything nasty.'

'How come you looked at them rather than their husbands?'

'Because someone used the first daughter-in-law's name to check into rehab, meaning another female.'

'Dr Isabel,' she said. 'What's the other one's name?'

'Connie Longellos.'

Robin said, 'Connie can be a man's name. Connie Mack used to manage the Yankees.'

'How do you know stuff like that?'

'Daddy's girl.' She dropped her eyes, the way she does when remembering her father.

'I'm impressed,' he said. 'Unfortunately, the landlord said it was a woman.'

Robin said, 'Did I just complicate your life, Big Guy?'

I said, 'Actually.'

They turned to me.

'The landlord may have assumed it was a woman from the name on the reference. He never spoke to anyone.'

'Indeed,' said Milo. He winced. 'Maybe you prevented some serious tunnel vision. I'd thank you for thinking outside the box but anyone who blabs about outside the box has obviously never been there.'

Robin patted his hand. 'Would you like some dessert?'

32

I WALKED Milo down to his car.

'Thank Robin for the meal.'

'You already did.'

'Do it again. For dessert.'

'We didn't have dessert.'

'I sure did,' he said. 'Sweet insight.' Shaking his head. 'Connie Mack. Why the hell not? Those brothers get looked at tomorrow.'

I said, 'Fake Connie's POB was in Pacific Palisades, which isn't that far from both murders. En route, actually, if you're coming from BH.'

'Gotta be some kind of tie-in . . . okay, brace yourselves, Phil and Frank. If I can get backup, I'll have them both watched. If not, I'll start with Phil because his hours are more flexible. Plus, he's married to the real Connie and I can see some disgruntled husband pulling something like that.'

'No DUIs on Phil's record.'

'None on Frank's, either, but big deal, could be luck. Like Phil's the night he passed the Breathalyzer.' He laughed. 'Luck on top of the sperm club. Okay, sweet dreams, if there's something to clue you in on I will.'

The call that came through at eleven a.m. wasn't from him. Blocked number, straight to my private line.

'Doc, this is Moe Reed. L.T. asked me to tell you he got called downtown, doesn't know for how long.'

244

'Trouble?'

'If you call a statistics meeting trouble.'

'He's been avoiding that for a while.'

'Chief calls you personally and . . . expresses his opinion, you don't avoid.'

'Thanks, Moe. Anything else?'

'Chief woke him at six a.m.,' said Reed. 'Some way to start your day.'

I plugged each Suss twin's name into several search engines, cross-referencing with Topanga, Pacific Palisades, Malibu, a couple of West Valley towns. Nothing.

At noon, I walked down the kitchen stairs, crossed the garden to Robin's studio, stopped to feed the fish. She was studying the same guitar top, holding it to the light, tapping at various spots, running a finger along the outer contours. To my eye, she hadn't done much to it. Ten feet away, Blanche snoozed on her doggy bed.

'What's up, honey?'

'Milo's tied up, I thought I'd take another look at Philip Suss's house.'

She picked up a chisel, wiped the blade, set it down. 'I'll keep you company – don't be so shocked. Why not?'

'For one, it'll be boring.'

'With me to keep you company? Now I'm insulted.'

'I'll be fine, you'll be in a stupor.'

She looped an arm around my waist. 'I shouldn't be carving, anyway. Too distracted.'

'By what?'

'Her. I know there's no rational reason, but sometimes I get tired of ignoring how I feel. What's the second reason?'

'What second reason?'

'You said "for one." What's two?'

I had no comeback.

She said, 'There you go. With me along, we can pass for a loving couple, you'll be less likely to be mistaken for a weirdo snooper.'

'Guess I won't need my greasy raincoat and my Groucho nose.'

'The nose could be cute but definitely no coat.'

She propelled me toward the door. Blanche awoke, stretched, yawned, flexed her ears, then bulldog-bounced after us.

'You're sure you want to do this? It'll probably end up a whole lot of nothing.'

'Cheer up,' said Robin. 'It'll be fun. Or at least different.'

'Ann and Andy, huh?'

'I was thinking Nick and Nora.'

'We taking Asta along?'

She thought about that. 'No, she bores easily.'

We reached Portico Place shortly before one p.m. Crows squawked and squirrels raced up trees but no sign of human habitation, which is routine for any high-end LA neighborhood. The same vantage spot was available but I parked south of the house and farther away to avoid a pattern.

Oblique view but good enough to make out the BMW and the Lexus in the cobbled court.

Robin said, 'Nice place. For one of those.'

'McMansions?'

'No, it's better than a McMansion. Nice proportions. But new trying to fake old never really works, does it? Still, this one's a valiant try.'

She handed me one of the sandwiches she'd prepared.

Roast beef on rye, horseradish-flavored mustard, wrapped precisely in foil. Potato chips, pickle slices, sweating cans of soda. Everything packed in a mini-cooler.

'This is way too civilized,' I said.

'What does Milo eat?'

'Burritos are a favorite but anything quick and massive and oily.'

'Well,' she said, 'why not kick it up a bit, class-wise? Even when doing something uncivilized.'

'What's uncivilized about watching?'

'We're not watching, we're hunting, angel. Praying for someone to end up helpless and thrashing in a snap-jaw trap.'

'That bother you?'

'Not at all.'

We finished the food and the drinks, sat another twenty-three minutes before the gates swung open.

Connie Longellos nosed her Lexus to the street and turned south. Passing right by us but staring straight ahead.

'Pretty woman,' said Robin. 'But kind of grim, from what I could see. If her husband did that to her, being pretty obviously isn't enough.'

Fourteen minutes later, the BMW exited. Philip Suss sat high at the wheel, lips moving, smiling as he talked.

Robin said, 'Nothing grim, there. Whoever he's chatting with is making him happy.'

Suss headed south, too.

I waited awhile before following.

Robin said, 'This isn't one bit boring.'

When Milo and I had followed Connie Suss, she'd driven east on Ventura Boulevard to Sherman Oaks. Her husband took that same thoroughfare west, avoiding the freeway and slogging through turgid midday traffic. Easy to follow, as he nudged his way toward Encino's business district. I stayed three car lengths behind, closed the gap occasionally before drifting back, caught glimpses of his still-moving mouth.

He remained on Ventura through Tarzana and crossed into Woodland Hills where he turned left on Canoga Avenue, left again on Celes Street, right onto Alhama Drive. Stopping in front of a yellow, forties-era one-story cottage, he strode to the front door, rang the bell, was admitted.

Robin said, 'Nice white linen shirt, tailored slacks, polished shoes, and his hair's all shiny. He sure ain't playing poker with the boys.'

'Nora strikes.'

'Never knew what you were missing, huh? Seriously, Alex, didn't he look duded up to you? As in hot date? And check out the Mustang in the driveway. That's a girl-car.'

Pale blue fastback, white interior. A bumper sticker bore what looked to be a Japanese character.

I copied down the tag numbers. Robin took a sheet from my pad and sketched the character.

Driving up the block, I turned around, set up a watch spot to the north. Cutting the engine because Phil Suss might not be interested in a quick drop-in.

Seconds later, he emerged, followed by a woman.

Then another.

Two tall, shapely females in their late twenties or early thirties, each crowned by a mane of long, thick, dark hair that loved the breeze.

Phil Suss walked arm in arm with both of them, laughing and sauntering toward his car.

I was too far to make out ethnicity but both women wore tiny, tight tops – one red, one black – ultraskinny jeans that worshipped forever legs, and spindly heels high enough to turn walking into a balancing act.

Phil Suss held the passenger door open and bent the seat forward to give one of the women access. As she crouched and squeezed herself into the back, he patted her butt. The other woman rolled her hips and did the same for his rear. He kissed her. She returned the favor.

Robin said, 'Pretty *definitely* wasn't enough.'

I waited until the BMW returned to Celes before following. Reached the intersection with Canoga just in time to spot Phil Suss speed south.

248

After a quick right onto Dumetz, he drove less than a mile before merging onto Topanga. Fifteen minutes later, he veered onto Old Topanga Road and pulled into the gravel lot of a wood-sided restaurant.

Satori.

Robin said, 'Well, look at this.'

She and I had eaten here a few times, when we had time to spare and romance on our minds. It had been a while. Too long?

The setup was a loose collection of leaf-sheltered patios and cozy, stone-floored dining rooms. Some of the outdoor areas offered views of Topanga Creek. I remembered the menu as organic minus the self-righteousness, nudges toward vegetarian but some animal protein, good wines, high prices.

Lovely, when you were with the right person and the bees weren't swarming. The last time Robin and I had been here, a mama raccoon had tended to a litter of mewling pups creekside.

Phil Suss and his women entered under a wooden arch, arms around each other.

Robin and I watched from the Seville, close enough, now, to make out ethnicity. And prevailing mood.

Caucasian.

Happy verging on giddy.

Both women were gorgeous, with the toned voluptuousness of creatures who lived by their looks.

I thought of Tiara Grundy, wondered if she'd ever been here with Mark Suss.

Or either of his sons.

Robin said, 'The sandwiches weren't that big, let's do lunch.'

'You must be mistaking me for Milo.'

'Being Milo has its advantages, hon. C'mon, let's go in, I told you I'd provide cover. A single guy spying on them would attract attention. We're in love, everyone will rejoice.'

She opened the passenger door, paused. 'Do we need a plan?'

'Just be unobtrusive and learn what we can.'

'I can do unobtrusive,' she said. 'We can hold hands, pretend there's nothing on our mind but us.'

The restaurant was mostly empty, which worked to our advantage as the hostess consolidated her seating strategy.

Escorting us to a pine-shrouded patio, she led us to a table that offered privacy and a sweet view of babbling water.

Charming. But it put us too close to the rear booth where Phil Suss and the curvy brunettes had settled. Positioned our backs to the festive trio.

Robin said, 'How about there?' and pointed to a less favored station with a clear frontal view of Suss's party.

The hostess's eyebrows climbed. 'Whatever you prefer.'

'Thanks for the first one but that one's our special table,' said Robin. 'We were here on our last anniversary, happened to be driving by and decided to be spontaneous.'

The hostess smiled. 'Spontaneous is good.'

Phil Suss ordered two iced teas, one that he drank, the other that he covered with a folded napkin. The women opted for flutes of champagne.

Giddy girls, with all the right moves: hair tosses, lip licks, strategic touches of Phil Suss's shoulders and arms and cheek.

The one in the red top – a halter that exposed a flawless, velvety back – had dense, wavy black hair artfully streaked with bronze.

Black Top's ironed-straight locks were bronze-highlighted ebony.

As if the two of them worked as a team, had coordinated a joint pheromone attack.

Both women displayed traces of augmentation at all the strategic spots: chest, eyelashes, cheekbones. I revised my age estimate: midthirties to forty.

Phil glowed, loving the attention.

Robin and I picked up our menus, hid behind the oversized, hemp-bound litany as we continued to sneak peeks.

Refills of champagne, girlish giggles.

Robin said, 'Hmm, vegan duck. They didn't have that before.'

'Didn't know ducks were that philosophical.'

She laughed. We touched hands, ordered salads, continued to spy.

From the rapt expressions on the brunettes' flawless faces, Phil Suss was the wittiest man on the planet.

Another man walked past us.

One of the women called out, 'Baby!'

Robin and I continued to peruse but let our eyes drift.

Dr Franklin Suss, bald head glowing, wearing a slate-blue Nat Nast shirt embroidered with billiard balls, cream linen pants, and brown calf-skin loafers, kissed the woman wearing the black top, then her friend.

Then he walked to his brother and both men embarked on a garrul-ous ritual of hugs, double-cheek kisses, more hugs, back pats, power shakes.

Red Top said, 'Enough, you two, I'm gonna get jealous.'

Black Top said, 'Or we'll think you guys are *really* weird.'

Frank and Phil kissed again. Frank wiggled his hips in a parody of girlishness.

Everyone laughed.

Frank slid into the booth next to Red Top.

His arm snaked around her shoulder with the ease of habit. Phil's arm did the same for Black Top.

Phil uncovered the second iced tea and slid it over to Frank.

Frank high-fived air, raised the glass. 'Thank you, bro.'

Phil did the same with his tea. 'Bro.'

They stretched in front of the women and clinked.

Red Top said, 'Here we go again. Boys, pay attention: There are beautiful, sexy women here.'

'Brotherly love beats that,' said Black Top, pouting.

Frank said, 'Brotherly love. Guess we should live in Philadelphia.'

Red said, 'Huh?'

She turned to Black, who shrugged. 'What do you mean, Frankie?'

Phil said, 'Forget it, Lori, let's order.'

'Is it some kind of joke? Philadelphia's like nowhere.'

'Ever been there?'

'No, but there's no beach.'

Phil said, 'Now you're a geography expert.'

Frank snickered.

Black said, 'C'mon, Frankie. What's the joke?'

Frank did a slow eye roll. 'It was a bad joke, baby. So what're we having?'

Red said, 'Why would you tell a bad one?'

Frank's face tightened. 'I didn't know it was bad until I said it.' Speaking slowly, as if to a dull child.

Red said, 'Oh. Okay.'

Phil said, 'Think of it this way: When you guys put on the wrong bikini it takes you by surprise, right? It looks good on the rack, but then you find out it doesn't work on the bod.'

Lori pouted. 'Everything's right on *this* bod, Philly.' Puffing a substantial chest.

Her friend did the same. Then she brightened. 'Oh,' she said, 'I get it: Philly from Philadelphia.'

Titters.

Black said, 'But Frankie from Philadelphia doesn't fit.'

Dr Frank Suss said, 'There you go, always a bridesmaid, never a bride.'

Puzzled looks.

Phil Suss said, 'Enough of this bullshit. You guys are the hottest thing on the planet and Frankie and I dig you and I'm hungry.'

33

PHIL, FRANK, Lori, and the woman finally identified as Divana punctuated their lunch with frequent kisses, cheek strokes, and some not-so-subtle under-table gropes.

The couples paired off loosely: Frank with Divana, Phil with Lori. But I remembered the ass-patting back on Alhama Drive and doubted it was as simple as that.

Robin and I picked our way through a couple of salads and tried to look casual. As the meal wore on, her smile began to look like a decal.

But she was relaxed as we left Satori moments after the foursome departed.

Brothers in the middle, arms around each other's waists, laughing. Mute women flanking.

Phil and Lori got into the BMW. Frank ushered Divana into a black Cadillac XTS.

I said, 'Any suggestions if they split up?'

Robin said, 'I'd stick with Phil. It was his wife whose name got used.'

Girl detective.

Both cars edged out of the lot. North on the canyon would take them back to the Valley, south, past the spots where Steven Muhrmann and Tiara Grundy had died.

The Suss twins chose neither, staying on Old Topanga and proceeding deeper into the wooded, quiet corners of the canyon.

Two brothers, two cars.

Two brothers, two guns?

Easy nonverbal twin communication could lead to a perfect two-man firing squad. The synchronized wounds that had puzzled Clarice Jernigan.

Ready, aim. *Bro.*

They'd probably done it a thousand times as kids, using peashooters, toy pistols, water guns.

Adulthood changed the game, as the big thrill became aping Daddy's approach to women.

Taking on Daddy's Sweetie as a cruel inheritance.

A foolish, naive girl who had no idea she was chattel, easily disposed of like any other liquid asset.

Phil's white car slowed.

Frank's black car did the same.

The surroundings changed to tucked-away houses, many of them trailers and shacks and do-it-yourself follies, set well off the road. The brothers turned onto an unmarked dirt strip that angled acutely. A rural mailbox tilted on a stake. Shaggy cedars and drought-loving oaks drooped over the passage.

Both cars were soon enveloped in darkness, then gone.

I drove another twenty yards, kept the Seville running, got out.

'Where are you going?'

'For a look.'

'I'll go, too.'

'Inefficient,' I said. 'Take the wheel and keep the motor on. If I need to make a run for it, you'll be ready.'

'A run? How about neither of us goes and we just give Milo the address.'

'I'll just check for a second, it's no big deal.'

She held my wrist. 'Too much testosterone, baby, and now we know what they're capable of.'

'Testosterone will work in my favor. They're thinking fun, not felony.'

'You can't be sure of anything, Alex.'

I removed her hand, left her there.

Dried-up stick-on address numerals curled on the side of the mailbox. I memorized them, checked the box. Empty.

Thirty feet in, the dirt driveway S-curved, explaining the cars' quick disappearance.

Pressing to the left side, so I'd be facing any surprise oncoming vehicle, I continued, sinking into leaf litter that squished and hissed. Stopped to listen. Heard nothing.

A few more yards: laughter.

Fun, the best distraction of all.

As the driveway snaked to an end, afternoon sunlight flashed hot and white.

I inched forward. Stopped twenty feet back from a tamped-soil clearing, half an acre or so in diameter.

Aqua flash of swimming pool. Behind the pool, the log-sided flanks of a low, wide house. Behind the house, forest.

The Suss brothers' cars were parked carelessly in front of the pool, providing partial barriers.

Hums, thrums, laughter.

A male voice said, 'Oh, yeah, baby.'

I made my way behind the Cadillac, gazed through both windows, was hampered by tinted glass.

I hazarded a look above the hood of the car.

Phil Suss sat on the rim of the pool, naked and tan, bulky muscles blunted by a coating of suet. Eyes shut, mouth agape as one of the women lay across the deck and tended to his lap. Across the water, at the shallow end, Frank Suss, pallid, thin but paunchy, embraced the other brunette. Her legs clasped his waist. The synchronized movement of their hips created a languid stroke never tried at the Olympics.

As I turned to leave, Phil pumped air with one fist. 'Yes!'

Frank opened his eyes. Smiled dreamily. 'Bro!'

'Bro!'

Both girls laughed. But it sounded rehearsed.

Robin rolled the Seville toward me and I got in. Before I could belt up, she was speeding away, passing Satori without a glance.

Hands clamped on the wheel, unsmiling.

'You okay?'

'Anything earthshaking?'

'Nope.'

'What, then?'

'What you'd expect.'

She frowned. 'All of them together?'

'Separate but equal.'

'Right in front of each other. It's almost incestuous. And those two hotties don't have a clue what they're dealing with.'

'Now they'll have a chance to find out,' I said.

She put on speed, passed Steven Muhrmann's death site. No reason for me to point it out to her. Same for where Tiara had lost her face.

The ride emphasized how close the two locations were to each other. Fast-action night of blood and surprise.

Robin said, 'I wonder what that bumper sticker means. *Has* to be something lewd.'

It wasn't.

A website on *japanese bumper stickers* translated the character as 'peace' in a style of lettering called kanji.

Robin said, 'Okay, time to get back to what I'm good at.'

lori divana combined with the Suss brothers' names pulled up nothing.

I phoned Milo to give him the address on the log house's mailbox.

Voice-mail, again. Ditto at Moe Reed's extension.

I tried Milo's other acolyte, Detective I Sean Binchy.

'I think he's downtown, Doc.'

'Must be a long meeting.'

Binchy said, 'A lot of them are.'

'If you see him, have him give me a call.'

'Will do, Doc. Listen, could I ask you something?'

'Sure.'

'My sister's sister is thinking about going into psychology. Can she talk to you about it, one of these days?'

'Sure, Sean.'

'Thanks. I'll give Loot your message.'

'Could you look up a couple of addresses to see who pays taxes on them?'

A beat. 'Doc, all these new privacy regs, they're really clamping down on personal use. Some guys think the brass even has spy programs on us, recording all our keystrokes.'

'The info's not personal, Sean, it's part of Milo's case.'

'But he hasn't officially authorized it, Doc. I don't want to be a wienie, but . . .'

'I don't want to put you in a spot,' I said. 'But we're not talking confidential information, I could go downtown and access the data myself.'

'That's true, hmm,' he said. 'We're talking the face-murder?'

'Yup.'

'That poor girl . . . tell you what, I'll look it up and leave it on his desk. Along with a note saying you suggested the search based on . . .'

'Something I observed an hour ago.'

'Okay, consider it done. And I'll give Dorrie your number.'

I said, 'Once it's on his desk, Sean, would passing it along to me be a problem? Seeing as it's right out in the open?'

Silence.

'It'll save him time, Sean, I promise he won't mind.'

'Oh, man,' he said. 'Yeah, you've always been straight with me, Doc. What addresses are we talking about?'

34

THE HOUSE on Alhama Drive was owned by one Oral Marshbarger.

The Web produced only a single person blessed with that name: an accountant at a firm in St Louis.

Late to be calling over there, but I tried.

Voice-mail coughed up a long list of extensions. *'For Mr Adams, dial 101. For Mr Blalock, dial 102.'*

I waited for the alphabet to glide by, punched 117.

A man answered, 'Marshbarger.'

Misrepresenting yourself as a cop is a serious crime. Con-spieling while glossing over the details is hazy legal territory. It's also an easy carney trick because most people pick up on buzzwords and don't process details. Marshbarger, being a CPA, might mean he was the exception, but nothing ventured.

'Mr Marshbarger, this is Alex Delaware working with the LA police on a case. Some question came up about a property you own in Woodland Hills on Alhama Drive.'

'Police? Don't tell me they used it for *that*.'

'For what, sir?'

'Porn shoots, what else? When they showed up looking like that, all sweetness and . . . I guess you'd call it seductiveness – of course I was suspicious. I wanted to come right out and ask them if they were scouting for some porn outfit but I got worried there'd be some sort of sex-discrimination suit.

Like would you ask us that if we were *men*? Nowadays everyone sues everyone for everything.'

I said, 'When did their lease begin and what did they tell you about themselves?'

'So they *did* use it for that. Jesus.'

'You're not in trouble, Mr Marshbarger.'

'Why should *I* be in trouble? I'm the victim. The point is, it's disgusting. And fraudulent, the house was clearly advertised as a personal residence. Did they trash the place, someone complained?'

'The house appears to be in fine shape.'

'Did they plant flowers?' said Marshbarger. 'They promised to, that was part of the deal.'

'The garden looks great, sir.'

'I assure you, if there was some way I could've screened them, I would've, but what were my options?'

'Absolutely, sir.'

'There was exigency,' he said. 'I bought the place, figuring I'd live there myself. Three months later the firm transferred me here. I asked for compensation until I could rent the house at fair market and the firm agreed but the unspoken message was *Do it quick, Marsh*. Those bimbos were the first to show up with real money and good credit. Which makes total sense, I suppose, if they were fronting for some porn outfit. That industry grosses more than Hollywood, right? And lots of it never gets reported – is *that* what this is about? Some tax thing, you figured I'd know about it because I'm a CPA? Sorry, no, nothing. And that's all I want to say.'

'Mr Marshbarger, there's no tax issue and your tenants aren't suspects in anything. Including pornography.'

'What, then?'

'They've associated with what we call persons of interest.'

'Organized crime? Oh, Jesus—'

'No, sir, you've got absolutely nothing to worry about in that regard. I just need some information.'

'What kind of information?'

'Basic facts for verification. What names did they use on the lease application?'

'Apparently their real ones,' said Marshbarger. 'That's what the credit check company said, believe it or not.'

'You had your doubts.'

'Divana Layne? Lori Lennox? Those sound real to you?'

That from Oral Marshbarger.

I said, 'What job history did they list?'

'Models. They said they worked mostly in Japan.' Snicker. 'Those Asians go for the voluptuous ones, don't they?'

'And they both had good credit histories.'

'A-plus. Six-figure incomes for both of them. Maybe the yen–dollar exchange worked in their favor.' He chortled again. '*Models.* Maybe for *Hustler* but not for one of those fashion rags my ex used to read, with those stick figures.'

'Who were their previous landlords?'

'Real estate companies in Tokyo, they showed me letters of reference. In Japanese but they also had translations. Kind of hilarious, actually. Like those manuals you get with cameras and stereos?'

'You verified.'

'I made a couple of long-distance calls, got taped messages in Japanese, left my own message, never heard back. I didn't have time to be doing all that international calling, I needed to move, they had the money. And they haven't missed a month. In fact, if they're taking care of the place and there's no criminal activity, maybe I'm glad I rented to them. Why's this information so important, anyway?'

'How'd the girls find you?'

'Craigslist,' said Marshbarger. 'I tried ads, agencies, all that did was attract losers. And like I said there was a time element, so I did what everyone does nowadays. I didn't expect much. But they showed up with the goods. Financially speaking.'

'Anything else you want to tell me about them?'

'So I shouldn't evict them.'

'No grounds I can see, Mr Marshbarger. You shouldn't contact them, period. They haven't done anything wrong.'

'Porn's okay?'

'There's no evidence they're into porn.'

A beat. 'So why are we talking?'

'They know some people who've come to the department's attention. Speaking of which, let me run some names by you. Steven Muhrmann.'

'Never heard of him.'

'Tara Sly?'

'Now, that's a porn name,' he said. 'Or a stripper name – is that what they are? Pole-riders?'

'Markham Suss.'

'Nope.'

'Anyone named Suss?'

'Nope.'

'What's the rent on the house?'

'I wanted two thousand, we settled for sixteen hundred plus they handle all the utilities and gardening. And plant flowers and keep them up nice. The place looks okay?'

'Charming. Do they pay by check?'

'Auto-pay account through Wachovia,' said Marshbarger. 'They never miss. So it's okay for them to stay?'

'Yes, sir.'

'Okay . . . what did you say your name was? Just in case things do get complicated.'

'Phone West LA Division and ask for Lieutenant Sturgis.'

I gave him the number.

He said, 'That's not you.'

'Lieutenant Sturgis is the boss.'

'Sure, but—'

I hung up, silently thanking Robin for insisting we get a blocked number. Left a detailed message at Milo's private cell, plugged in *divana layne lori lennox lingerie.*

The computer spit out five Japanese websites and two from Bangkok. Canned translations turned the text into malaprop-laden gibberish that elevated camera manuals to Shakespeare.

Not a problem; the images said it all.

Page after page from Asian trade shows. Divana, Lori, and other similarly endowed beauties strutting Tokyo runways in various combinations of satin, lace, rayon, fishnet.

Name recognition for underwear models. They'd achieved minor celebrity in a culture with a genius for micro-delineation and exquisite refinement.

The most recent show was three years ago. Both women were old enough to have begun modeling over a decade ago.

That gave them plenty of opportunity to hook up with any combination of Suss males. A few years on the other side of the planet, then back to LA where they'd reunited with the twins.

So far they'd made the grade.

Tara's fate said they'd better hope that continued.

The house on Old Topanga Road was owned by one Olna Fremont.

I turned the name into a keyword. The information highway spread out before me.

I sped. Slowed to rubberneck.

Screeched to a halt.

35

LORI LENNOX née Lorraine Lee Bumpers came to her door, hair in curlers, wrapped in a white terry bathrobe lettered *Hilton* on the breast pocket.

Female Caucasian, five seven, 121, a DOB on her license that made her thirty-two.

A genuine birth date on a twenty-one-year-old LAPD arrest form made her thirty-nine.

Only one arrest in LA County, but a sealed juvenile record implied priors. The solicitation for prostitution charge was nothing glamorous; she'd worked Sunset and Highland as an eighteen-year-old runaway, got nabbed her first week, was sentenced to a group home and counseling. A year later, she'd been picked up on a similar charge in Vegas but since then had stayed out of legal trouble.

The six-figure income she'd claimed was real but limited to the five years she'd modeled in Japan, buttressed by residuals from a few TV commercials filmed there and partial ownership of an apartment building in Laughlin, Nevada. Since her move back to LA, a yearly gift of twenty-six thousand dollars from unnamed sources filled in some blanks. Gift tax was exempt for only half that amount, so most likely a pair of donors.

This morning her feet were bare, toenail polish chipped, face stripped of makeup. A reflexive smile corroded when she saw Milo's badge.

'Morning,' he said.

'I thought it was.' She looked at her wrist. Pale band on a tan arm where her watch usually sat.

'Eight fourteen,' said Milo. 'Hope it's not too early, Ms Lennox.'

She worked up another smile, produced uneasy dismay. 'Actually, it kinda is.'

White teeth were flawless. Her breath was stale.

'Is Divana awake yet?'

'Just,' said Lori Lennox. 'What's going on?'

'Can we come in?'

'The police? It's a little . . .'

'No big deal, Lori, all we want to do is talk.'

'About?'

'Phil and Frank Suss.'

Slate-blue eyes shuttled back and forth like ducks in a shooting gallery. Wanting to lie but insufficient smarts to come up with a good one. 'Okay.'

'You know them.'

'Yeah.'

'That's why we want to come in,' said Milo.

'Are they okay?'

'They're great, Lori. Coupla happy campers.' He pointed to the pale strip of arm. 'Nice tan. I'm betting real rays, not bronzer.'

'Yeah, it's natural.'

'Not a tanning bed, either,' he said. 'More like a swimming pool.'

She relaxed. 'I wish.'

'I'm not saying you own a pool, Lori. You've got something better. Access but no maintenance bills.'

'Huh?'

'Old Topanga Road.'

Her eyes fluttered.

Milo pulled out his pad, searched, read off the address. He knew it by heart but using paper makes it official, can kick up the intimidation level.

Lori Lennox began playing with the sash of her robe.

Milo said, 'Three p.m. yesterday.'

No answer.

'Black bikini. Not that it stayed on very long.'

She blushed from sternum to brow. I liked her for that. 'You have no right.'

'To what?'

'Spy.'

Milo thumbed his chest. 'Us? God forbid. Then again, it could be worse. So if you don't want to talk—'

'What do you mean worse?'

'Tara Sly.'

'Who?'

'Cute little blond girl.'

'Lots of those,' said Lori Lennox.

'Now there's one less.' He showed her his card. Tapped a finger next to *Homicide*.

She gulped. Made a third attempt at smiling, stopped midway, and stood back to let us in.

The house was bland, bright, kept up meticulously. Glass tabletops gleamed, cushions were plump, fresh flowers overflowed vases, bad poster art hung strategically. The nugget of garden on the other side of sliding glass doors was overplanted but green and glowing. Oral Marshbarger would be pleased.

Lori said, 'I'll go get her,' and returned wearing a baggy beige blouse, faded nonskinny jeans, flat sandals. She'd taken down her hair, put on hoop earrings. Divana Layne née Madeleine Ann Gibson trudged behind her in a gray *Power Gym* sweatshirt and black yoga pants.

No prostitution record for her but her young adulthood had been marked by a trio of shoplifting episodes and she'd ended up at the same group home as Lori.

Milo said, 'Hi, ladies. Please sit.'

'We're okay,' said Divana. No reason to laugh but she did. Same throaty glee I'd heard from the deep end of the pool.

Milo said, 'Please sit anyway. So I don't have to stretch my neck.'

The women looked at each other. Settled on the edges of blue-velvet chairs, ankles crossed demurely.

Milo said, 'So who wants to start?'

'Start what?' said Divana.

'The saga of Phil and Frank.'

Lori said, 'We're friends, that's all.'

'Swimming buddies,' said Milo.

'Is it against the law?'

'To what?'

'Do a married guy,' said Divana. 'If you think that, maybe you should live in Arabia or something.'

Lori said, 'It's a good deal. Keeps everyone happy.'

'Twenty-six grand a year keeps you happy.'

Divana twisted a ring. Small stone, maybe real.

She said, 'We keep the peace, you guys should thank us.'

'Keep the peace and pay your rent,' said Milo. 'Not that fifty-two grand a year means much to guys like Phil and Frank.'

Both women bristled.

Divana said, 'Why are you here?'

'Steve Muhrmann.'

Blank looks.

'And, of course, Tara Sly.'

Divana's nose wrinkled. Baffled.

Lori said, 'Who are these people? You're weirding us out.'

'Maybe you know Tara by her real name. Tiara Grundy.'

Divana giggled. Lori turned to her.

Milo said, 'Something funny?'

Divana said, 'Grundy sounds like an old lady. Like from a movie or something.'

'Unfortunately for Tiara, she'll never get old.'

'Bummer,' said Divana. 'What does that have to do with us?'

Milo showed them Tiara's SukRose bikini shot.

Divana's smugness vaporized. Lori said, 'Oh. Omigod.'

Divana said, 'That's crazy – I need a drink. Anyone else?'

'Coke Zero,' said Lori.

'We're fine,' said Milo.

'I'm not fine,' said Lori. 'I'm freaked out.'

Half a Bloody Mary later, Divana licked brick-colored grit from her lips. 'Yeah, we know who she is, she's their father's girlfriend, so what?'

'You met her.'

'No, they told us about her.' Pause. 'Showed us her picture.'

'In what context?'

'What do you mean?'

'How did she come up?'

'Hmm,' said Divana. 'I think it was at Cabo . . . no, it was Sedona, right? Yeah, Sedona. Right, Lore?'

Lori drew her legs up, yoga-like, tapped a sandal. 'I'm thinking yes.' She nudged an earring. 'Yeah, definitely Sedona.'

I said, 'One of your trips with Phil and Frank.'

Nods.

'You do a lot of those?'

'Not enough, let me tell you,' said Divana.

'Their schedules,' said Lori.

'At least they don't have kids,' said Divana. 'Just business.'

'And wives.'

I said, 'Kids tie you down.'

'That's what they tell us.'

'Phil and Frank?'

'No, our friends who have them.'

'But even with wives, the brothers manage to get away.'

'The brothers,' said Divana, shooting a lopsided grin. As if she'd never thought of them that way. 'They're the best little boys.'

'How did the subject of their father's girlfriend come up?'

'Hmm . . . we were . . . I guess in bed. Right, Lore?'

'Probably.'

'We spend lots of time in bed,' said Divana. 'Room service, champagne, pay-per-view, what's better? That day, they went off to see some red rocks. Frankie and Philly, not us. We said suit yourselves, boys, we're staying here with Mr Moët and Mr Chandon.'

I said, 'But at some point all of you were in bed and the subject of Markham Suss's love life came up.'

'Love life?' said Divana. 'More like sex life. They said he was a total horndog, that's where they got it from.'

'Proud of their heritage.'

'Huh?'

'They liked taking after their father.'

'Yeah, exactly. And then one of them said – I'm not sure if it was Philly or Frankie – he said guess what, the old guy's hooked up with some piece he found online, he didn't even used to like the computer. They thought it was funny.'

'They knew that because . . .'

'I don't know,' said Divana. 'Maybe he told them.'

Lori said, 'Maybe he was proud so he told them.'

'At his age, Lore? Probably super-proud. Probably Viagra, but still.'

'One thing I *didn't* like,' said Lori, 'was their making a big deal about her being young.'

'Tiara.'

Nod. 'They were like, "She's fresh, not a wrinkle." I said keep pushing it, Bad Boys, and we'll kick you hard in the you-know-whats.'

'They like to be talked to that way,' said Divana.

I said, 'Submissive.'

'Not really, they just like when we have spirit.'

Lori said, 'That's what they call it. Spirit.'

'So they were impressed with how young Tiara was.'

Lori said, 'Philly started, I remember 'cause that time I was with Frankie and she was with Philly and Frankie started to laugh after Philly said it and his chin bumped me and I got PO'd, almost pushed him off.'

'That time you were with Frankie,' I said. 'Other times you're with Phil?'

Both women looked at the floor.

I said, 'There's no formal arrangement, everything's relaxed.'

Divana's eyes locked on mine. 'It's not illegal, okay?'

'You bet.'

'Think of it like a club. Fun Club, exclusive membership.'

I said, 'This may be a stupid question but do their wives know?'

'Maybe,' said Lori.

'I think so, too,' said Divana. 'Maybe.'

I said, 'Really.'

'They don't seem real careful. Use credit cards for everything and they're like gone a lot.'

'With us,' said Lori. 'Two months ago we went to Jackson Hole, hot-air ballooning. Private balloon. It was beautiful.'

'So was the Four Seasons,' said Divana. 'That fireplace. Yum chocolates.'

I said, 'What did Frankie and Philly really think about Tiara?'

'We just told you,' whined Lori. 'They were happy. That he was having fun. They thought it was funny. It didn't bug them.'

'They didn't resent her?'

'No way.'

'Any money their father gave her they'd never get.'

'They don't care about money,' said Lori.

'They've got tons of money,' said Divana. 'All they care about is you-know-what.'

'They never expressed any bad feelings at all toward Tiara?'

'They're not like that, they're happy. Like little boys.'

'Boys,' Lori echoed.

Milo spelled out the time of the murder. 'Do either of you have any idea what Phil and Frank were doing then?'

Lori said, 'C'mon, you can't really think they would do something horrible like that.'

269

'If we find out they had opportunity, we'll be after them and you won't be able to stay under the radar.'

'What did we do?' said Divana.

'Had the wrong kind of friends.'

'*You're* wrong. They're not *like* that.'

He repeated the time frame. 'Can you vouch for their whereabouts?'

Lori shook her head. 'But that doesn't mean anything.'

I said, 'It does sound like a fun club.'

'We're just having a good time, what they do with their wives is their problem.'

'Or don't do,' said Lori, giggling.

'About Tara Sly,' I said. 'What else did they tell you?'

'Just that.'

'Their father's girlfriend.'

'Yup.'

'It didn't bother them.'

'Not at all.'

Lori said, 'Who killed her?'

'That's what we're trying to find out.'

'How'd she die?'

'She got her face blown off.'

Divana said, 'With like dynamite?'

'With guns.'

'Oh, no,' said Lori.

'Yuck,' said Divana. Tougher timbre in her voice. But she was the first to water up. 'Why would someone do that?'

'Once we know that, we'll catch whoever did it. You'll notice I said "guns." Plural.'

Lori said, 'Two guys did her?'

'Looks that way.'

Divana's eyes got huge. 'You're kidding – no, no way.' She squirmed in her chair. Recrossed her ankles. Looked away from her friend. 'Actually,' she murmured.

Lori leaned toward her.

Divana gave a long, chest-heaving sigh. Two hair tosses.

'Divvy?' said Lori.

'It's no big deal, Lore.'

'What?'

Milo said, 'You know where they were that night, Divana.'

Nod.

'What, Div?'

'I know, okay?'

'That was the night you said you had to visit your mother.'

Divana's smile was sickly.

Lori's mouth dropped open. 'You – oh, wow, I can't believe—'

'It's not my fault, Lore. They *called.*'

'I was here.'

Divana said, 'I know, but . . .'

'But what?'

'It's them, not me, Lore.'

'I was right here!'

'I'm *sorry,* okay? They didn't *want* that, okay?'

'Didn't want *me?*' Lori clutched her abdomen.

'It wasn't like that, Lore. It wasn't not you, it was . . . they wanted to try something different, okay? It's no big deal, they still dig you, look at all the times since then – it was once, okay? *Okay?*'

Lori's jaw worked.

Divana reached for Lori's hand. Lori yanked it away.

'It's not my *fault,* Lore. *They* wanted it, *they* asked for it. Like specific.'

'Just you, huh? They said that? Or you *suggested* it.'

'Why would I do that, it would just be more . . . they wanted to *try* it, okay? For something different. It's. No. Big. Deal.'

Lori heaved her cola glass across the room. It landed on carpeting, bled brown, rolled still. 'I don't fucking believe this.'

'It's no big deal, Lore.'

'Maybe not to a total slut.'

271

'*I'm* a slut? You're the one made me watch when you—'

'That's *different*! You were *there*, everything was *honest*. What you did was . . . was . . . *cheating*!'

Divana crossed her arms. 'I don't see it that way.'

'Like hell you *don't*.'

'Okay. *I'm. Sorry.* Okay?'

'It's definitely *not* okay.' Lori stamped out of the room.

Divana looked at us. 'Now see what you've done.'

Milo said, 'Can you prove you were with Philip and Franklin Suss that night?'

'Why would I make it up and fuck up my thing with Lori? Yes, I can prove it. We checked into the Beverly Hilton at like eight, watched a porn, then another. Then . . . afterward we had room service, we didn't get out of there until early the next morning. I couldn't go home earlier because Lori thought I was at my mom's and she lives in Oxnard and I always stay until morning. Frankie had to leave first, he had work, had this procedure, this laser whatever, he put on his doctor stuff – scrubs, white coat – and Phil made some crack about how I could be the patient. Frankie laughed, said that would be a lot more fun than burning out some old broad's liver spots. We were all in Phil's car, so we all left and drove Frankie to his office, it was still early, probably around seven thirty. We had the room until eleven so Phil . . . it's not important.'

I said, 'You and Phil went back for some private time.'

'Whatever. The main thing is they were with me.'

'Neither of them left the entire evening.'

Divana grinned. 'Trust me, they were there. They were *totally* there.'

Lori never reappeared and Divana remained in her chair. Examining her pedicure as we exited the house.

When we were back in the car, Milo phoned the Hilton, verified the room and the payment with Philip Suss's platinum card. Records from electronic keys said no one had left until seven forty-eight in the morning, with re-entry half an hour later.

I said, 'Talk about an ironclad alibi.'

Milo's smile was wider than Divana's. 'Titanium-clad.'

'Bet that was more fun than your meeting downtown.'

'Death would be more fun than my meeting downtown. That was nirvana.'

We high-fived.

'Bro.'

'Bro!'

Next stop: a quarter hour east on the 101 to North Hollywood.

The old man lived in a calamine-pink bungalow just south of Victory Boulevard. Cutest house on the block. When we got there he was pruning a massive bird-of-paradise that nearly obscured his picture window. A back bent at birth lowered his stature so he needed a footstool to reach the middle of the plant.

I supposed he'd needed some kind of lift to work the bar at the Fauborg. All those years, I'd never thought about that.

When he saw us he put down his clippers.

'Can I help you?'

Teutonic accent. I'd never heard him speak.

Gustave.

I'd pulled a surname from an *LA Magazine* article on the city's best mixologists.

Milo said, 'Mr Westfeldt, we could use some help.'

The old man listened to the request. 'Sure, no problem.'

36

DRESS FOR success.

For this job that meant my best suit, a black Zegna I'd found on sale, a yellow tab-collar shirt with French cuffs, a black-and-gold Hermès tie purchased at the same closeout, Italian loafers so infrequently worn their soles remained glossy.

One hand swung free. The other clasped the handle of a chrome-plated case fitted with stainless-steel clasps.

'Very James Bond,' said Robin. 'Aston all gassed up?'

'With jet fuel.'

'Try not to eject.'

She walked me down to the Seville, touched an ancient Detroit-fashioned flank. 'Guess this'll have to do.'

'A boy can dream,' I said. 'Zoom zoom zoom.'

The mansion's copper pedestrian gate was locked. After I pressed the buzzer, the closed-circuit camera rotated. Seconds later, the front door eased ajar and the Slavic maid – Magda – studied me through the crack.

Manfred the cat sat by her feet, a plump bundle of feline confidence. I smiled and waved.

She pushed the door fully open, came forward. The cat remained in place. 'Yes?'

'Dr Delaware for Mrs Suss.'

'Doctor?'

'Dr Alex Delaware.' I checked my watch. *Things to see, people to do.* She studied me. 'You here before.'

'Sure was.'

Her forehead rumpled.

I let her study my faculty card. The venerable med school across town prints nice-looking credentials, replete with an impressive gold seal. My appointment's in pediatrics as well as psychology.

Clinical Professor, hoo-hah-hah. A couple of lectures a year, no salary, I get the title. Everyone figures they're getting a deal.

Magda said, 'Missus know you come?'

'You bet.' I hefted the chrome-plated case.

'She sick?'

'Just a checkup.' In a sense, it was.

I pocketed the card. 'I'm kind of in a hurry.'

Nothing like a good suit. She unlocked the gate.

Once we were in the house, Magda seemed unsure what to do with me. I left her pondering in the entry and saw myself into the same delft-blue room. Sitting on the same downy sofa, I placed the metal case next to me, released the clasps but kept the lid shut. Crossed my legs and sat back and enjoyed the art and the glorious view to the glorious garden.

Magda came in, flummoxed.

'Go get her,' I said.

'Doctor?'

'Delaware.'

'She sleeping.'

Hardening my voice, I said, 'She *needs* to wake up.'

Leona Suss racewalked into the blue room wearing body-conscious mauve velour sweats, rhinestone-spangled running shoes, and full-metal-jacket makeup. White fingers clamped a cell phone that matched the sweats.

Pale brown eyes zeroed in on mine. The lavender I'd seen last time was a contact-lens invention.

Artificial lashes fluttered like breeding moths.

'Morning, Mrs Suss,' I said.

'What do you think you're doing? I need you to leave.'

I rested my hands behind my head.

'Did you hear me?'

Flipping the metal case open, I removed a shiny black laptop, placed it next to me.

'I thought you were a cop.'

'Nope.'

She said, 'Well, I don't care who you are, I'm calling the *Beverly Hills* police.'

She began punching a number on the mauve phone.

I said, 'Suit *your*self, Olna.'

Her fingers stopped moving. Her chin jutted forward like a switch-blade. The phone lowered to her side. 'What do you *want?*'

'To reminisce.'

'About what?'

'Old Hollywood,' I said. 'Ancient Hollywood.'

She recoiled as if slapped. 'Don't be rude.'

'I didn't mean you,' I said. 'I just like vintage cinema.'

Opening the laptop, I gave her a direct view of the screen.

Out of the case came a cordless mouse that I rested on the lid.

Click.

The screen filled with opening credits. Garish green letters over black. A film title.

Guns of Justice.

Leona Suss said, 'You need to leave my house at once.'

But she made no effort to enforce the command.

I said, 'Treat yourself – c'mon, make yourself comfortable.'

She remained on her feet. 'You have sixty seconds and then I am going to call *my* police.'

Click.

Close-up of a black-haired beauty wearing Hollywood's improbably haute version of cowgirl garb. Rifle in hand. Sneer on glossy lips. 'End of the line, Goldie.'

Camera shift to manicured fingers around trigger.

Ponderous music.

Then a long shot offering a full view of the brunette standing in front of a log-sided cabin. Obvious matte painting of mountains in the background.

New shot: rear view of two figures facing the femme with the rifle.

Shift to their POV: fresh-faced blond girl, equally pretty white-Stetsoned young man.

He said, 'Don't do this, Hattie.'

The brunette sneered, 'Breathe your last, Rowdy.'

The brunette shouldered the rifle.

The blonde screamed.

White Hat quick-drew a six-shooter and fired.

A blossom sprang from the brunette's left breast. A cardiac surgeon couldn't have placed it more accurately.

She looked down at the spreading splotch. Flashed a crooked, oddly engaging smile. Relaxed her fingers.

Dropped the rifle.

Fell to the dirt.

Close-up on beautiful dying face. Murmurs.

'What's that, Hattie?'

'Rowdy . . . I always . . . loved you.'

The blonde said, 'Reckon she's gone now.'

White Hat said, 'But you're here.'

Long, searching look. Longer kiss.

Fade to black.

Leona Suss said, 'And the Oscar goes to . . . '

I said, 'It does have a certain charm.'

'It's swill, I told you that the first time. Now get the hell out.'

I clicked the mouse.

Another title page.

Passion on the Pecos.

Same dark-haired girl, different weapon.

Long-barrelled revolver. Her turn to quick-draw.

Bam.

A man dropped from a tree.

Bam.

A man dropped from the roof of a saloon.

Bam.

A man darted from behind a wheelbarrow, managed to fire. Ricochet whistle.

The girl shot him off his feet.

Click.

Saloon interior. A white-bearded geezer put down his whiskey glass. 'Where'd you learn to shoot like that, Miss Polly?'

Across the saloon table, the brunette spun the barrel of her gun, blew at the tip of the weapon. Licked her lips. 'Aw, Chappie, it was nothing.'

'Sure looked like somethin' to me. Who learned ya?'

Soft, feminine giggle. 'A girl does what a girl needs to do.'

Shift to swinging saloon doors. White-Stetsoned man with oversized badge on his tailored vest.

The girl sneered, 'You!'

'Now, just put that down and go peacefully—'

Bam.

Fade to black.

Leona Suss said, 'I'll give you an autograph and we'll call it a day.'

Click.

'Enough!' she shouted.

I froze the frame.

The cat trotted in.

'Manfred,' she said, 'this fool is boring me, go scratch his eyes out.'

Manfred sat there.

I said, 'Guess he took the no-cruelty pledge at the pound.'

'Oh, shut up.'

'How about "Shut up, punk"? One of your best lines, in my opinion. In fact, here it is.'

Click.

'You're *boring* me!'

'This one's different,' I said.

And it was.

37

No MOVING images. Text.
I recited.

www.iluvnoirflix.com

Death Is My Shadow (1963)
Starring Olna Fremont as Mona Gerome
Stuart Bretton as Hal Casey
Plus an assortment of eminently forgettable
mugs, molls, mopes and miscreants

This is one of those obscure treasures, hard to find but well worth the effort even if it means having to use a VCR (try the reissue lists of sites like blackdeath.net, mollheaven.com, entry-wound.net).

In addition to being a budget-noir masterpiece released at least a decade too late, Death Is My Shadow is the swan song for Olna Fremont, ebony-tressed bad-girl queen of the oaters. And a glimpse at how Little Miss Evil's career could've developed had she been born twenty years later. It's also the only non-western Olna ever filmed and we think that's a shame.

I mean think about it, can't you just see Olna's pheromone-dripping sensuality, Cruella de Vil persona and uncanny ability to – let's be delicate – make ahem love to objects of destruction, placed in the capable hands of a Tarantino or a Scorsese?

We're talking hot.

As in legs. As in lead.

The plot of this one doesn't bear retelling in depth but suffice it to say that Olna's at the top of her psychopathic game, shifting allegiances like the sexy chameleon she is and engaging in enough firearms foreplay to get an entire NRA chapter off. The climax – and we use the term near-literally – is an explosion of hot . . . bullets – that leaves the audience spent.

Unfortunately, Olna ends up permanently spent, herself. As usual. Because in the self-righteous morality game that Hollywood has always pretended to play, bad girls aren't allowed to win.

But Olna doesn't bite it before she blasts the inevitably wooden and incomprehensively cast Stu Bretton off his brogaloned feet. Not to mention a whole bunch of other slimy, bug-eyed denizens of the underworld straight out of the Grade D playbook.

Olna's moist, gotta-do-you lips, nose-cone breasts and outrageously masturbatory gun antics (we especially appreciate the scene where she kisses her derringer) are worth the price of admission. Heck, just seeing Bretton's dead face when it's actually supposed to be lifeless justifies the eighty-six bloody, oft-moronic minutes you'll spend with this unintended but no less entertaining masterpiece of grit, sleaze, and cardboard characterization.

Utterly lacking in redeeming artistic value.

Five Roscoes.

I said, 'Everyone's a critic.'

Leona Suss pointed her cell phone at me and mouthed *Bang*.

She glided closer, seemed to be studying the top of my head. Settled smoothly and silently on the sofa, inches from me. Flaring her nostrils, she tamped her hair and secreted Chanel. Close to seventy years old, beautiful, ageless.

'You're a cutie,' she purred, mussing my hair. As she released her hand, she snuck in a quick, painful tug. 'I still don't get it, are you police or really some kind of doctor?'

'Bona fide psychologist,' I said. I recited my license number.

'Cop psychologist?'

'I work with them from time to time but I'm not on their payroll.'

'What does from time to time mean?'

'Complicated cases.'

She chuckled. 'Someone thinks I'm crazy?'

'More like fascinating. I agree.'

She closed her eyes, sank back against downy cushions. 'So you're not on their payroll.'

'That's the point,' I said.

'What exactly do you do for them?'

'Get paid for deep psychological insight.'

'What's your insight about me?'

'That we can learn to play nice.'

She whistled silently. 'You're a playful fella?'

I said, 'I can be.'

One eye opened. Her right index finger traced the outline of the ring on her left hand. Round-cut diamond, huge, white, lots of fire.

'Nice.'

'D Flawless,' she said. 'I think the cut brings out its best qualities, don't you?'

She took my hand, placed it on the rock. Her skin was cool, soft. She'd used some kind of cover-up for age spots and the blemishes floated like water lilies in a deep vat of milk.

I said, 'I think everything about you works quite nicely.'

She drew away. 'Sonny, I've been bullshat by the best. Don't even try.'

'Aw shucks,' I said.

I angled the laptop toward her.

She said, 'If you've got a game, name it. If you're going to waste my

282

time by making me sit through the crap I did when I was too young and too stupid to know any better, I'm cutting this little chat short.'

She sprang to her feet. 'In fact, if you don't get your ass in gear right now, I'm going up to my room and fetching my Glock. I'm sure you know what that is, seeing as you're a police groupie.'

'Lightweight, well made,' I said. 'Model 19?'

'A 22 and I know how to use it. You may be cuter than most girls can stand – you may know how to play dress-up – what is that, Brioni – no, Zegna, I know the stitching, Mark bought them like candy. But to me you're a punk and you'll stay a punk and that's how *my* police will view you when I tearfully tell them how you wangled your way past my retarded maid then tried to attack me.'

I said, 'That sounds like one of your movies. So does the crack about someone thinking you're crazy. Wasn't that what Mona tried in *Death Is My Shadow*? Acting nuts so no one would suspect premeditation?'

'Piece of crap,' she said. 'That review was too kind.'

'I think you're being too hard on yourself.'

Click.

She said, 'Oh, Jesus, you're an idiot.'

But she stayed there, eyes fixed on the screen.

Once an actress.

Text gave way to a slide show.

Leona as Olna in a white dress. Malevolently lovely face wrapped in a matching scarf. Graceful fingers clutching the stem of a Martini glass.

Olive and pearl onion bobbing in a crystalline bath.

Olna wearing that same outfit plus oversized sunglasses.

Olna, bare-shouldered and strategically draped by a bedsheet, smoking a cigarette in an ivory holder. The barest suggestion of teeth between glossed lips. Heavy-lashed eyelids drooped in postcoital torpor.

Next to her, the 'inevitably wooden' Stuart Bretton lay staring up at nothing. Muscular arms pumped. Squarely handsome, wavy-haired visage blank as dirt.

Olna pointing a gun.

Close-up on the weapon: double-barreled derringer. Side-by-side barrels. Stubby, nasty-looking weapon, the snout barely long enough to extend past her gloved hands.

Close-up on Stu Bretton's face. Caricature of surprise.

Close-up on Stu Bretton's beefcake physique, facedown on the bed, a bloody blotch between his shoulder blades.

Close-up on Olna Fremont's face. Surprised.

Long shot of cops, uniformed and plainclothed and armed.

Olna. Beautiful, peaceful. The bullet hole centering her smooth, white forehead the period on a final sentence.

I said, 'Life imitates art but only to a point. They let you keep your face.'

Leona reached for the laptop.

I drew it out of reach, continued to give her a full view of the last scene she'd ever filmed.

She said, 'Why the hell shouldn't I go get my Glock?'

'I'm sure if you tried, you'd score a hit. Where'd you learn? Kansas?'

She smiled. 'Rural life can be wonderful. And daddies love little girls eager to learn. Did you know gophers explode like little meatballs?' She rose to her feet, tussled my hair again. Took the time for a harder yank and studied my reaction.

When I moved to stay her hand, she pulled out of reach, flipped her hand like a geisha fan, and slapped my face.

Smiling as if she'd pulled off a first-take masterpiece performance, she glided toward the door. 'Unless you've got a death wish, you'll be gone when I return.'

I said, 'Unless you've got a death wish, you'll cool it with the D-list acting and pay attention.'

She came toward me, fists at chest level, poised to strike.

'Bad idea, Leona. Family's the glue that holds society together.'

She stopped short but kept her arms up. 'What the hell is *that* supposed to mean?'

'It means you've done at least one thing well. Those boys of yours get along great. Be a shame to change that.'

One arm dropped, then the other. She gazed around her roomful of treasures.

Sat back down.

38

I SAID nothing for a while. Allowed her thoughts to take over.

Whatever drifted through her mind clouded her eyes. She sat trance-like. For a moment I thought she'd dissociate. She shook herself clear. 'If you have something to say, spit it out.'

'One thing we can agree upon, Leona. The cops aren't geniuses. Truth is, they're pretty limited intellectually. So sometimes when a case gets interesting, I go off on my own and discover things that elude them.' I shrugged. 'Sometimes my discoveries turn out profitable.'

'Ah, the inevitable,' she said. 'You're a whore but a high-priced one. Okay, let's get down to business: What do you think you might know and how much are you fantasizing you can get for it?'

'A whore?' I said. 'I'd like to think of it as freelance investing.'

'Think what you want. Spread your legs and let's get it over with.'

I let her stew some more. When her neck tendons grew rigid, I said, 'One thing I learned from this case is that life really does imitate art. If you can call what you used to do art. The first time we met you I found you interesting, so I did a little research. Learned about that fall you took from a horse five years ago. All that pain and the prescription drug problem it got you into.'

'It happens. Big deal.'

I said, 'Kind of ironic. You make all those movies, do all that serious riding and never get hurt. Only to get thrown by a twenty-year-old nag at a charity moonlight walk for the actors' hospice.'

'No good deed,' she said. 'So what? I'm fine now.'

'You tried to get fine by yourself, but when that didn't work you had the smarts to check yourself into rehab. Awakenings, out in Pasadena, near the racetrack. You knew what you needed but going public was humiliating so you borrowed Connie's identity and paid cash. Or maybe you just don't like Connie, figured it was a way to stick it to her. Either way, the staff at Awakenings ID'd your picture. They remember you fondly. Only thing they didn't like was your choice in new friends. Steven Muhrmann, your basic shiftless LA lowlife, pugnacious, no capacity for insight, and no motivation to change because he was there by court order. The staff was concerned he might corrupt you.'

I laughed. 'Talk about a bad clinical guess, huh? Stevie couldn't play in your league in every sense and from the moment you and he hooked up you called the shots. But he ended up as more than a boy-toy. When you confided your plans for Mark's retirement, he said, "I know just the girl."'

She sat there, inexpressive.

'And Stevie's girl turned out to be perfect, Leona. Beautiful, pliable, not too bright. Exactly what Mark had always gone for. I was puzzled by your motivation. Why would a woman, even a tolerant woman, encourage her husband to troll the Internet for a mistress? And Mark had always been capable of finding his own bimbos. A fact you made sure to tell Lieutenant Sturgis and me minutes after we met you. We figured you as long-suffering. But that wasn't it at all, Leona.'

No answer.

I said, 'My first guess was logical but wrong – occupational hazard of being a shrink. I figured you assumed Mark would fool around anywhere, you might as well attempt some sort of control. Pure Hollywood: Everyone wants to direct. And maybe by getting involved, you could keep an eye on how much money he paid her.'

Her eyes had turned dead. A cheek muscle twitched.

'Who better to know which of Mark's buttons to push? Hence Cohiba, adventure, et cetera, all those buzzwords. All the misspellings and grammatical errors to make the essay sound like a bimbo's literary output. Because Mark always liked 'em dumb and you'd already read *his* essay – hell, Leona, I wouldn't be surprised if you worked the keyboard while Mark sat there like the horny old cyberdummy he was. You let him think he'd discovered "Mystery." After you'd planted Stevie Muhrmann as a gopher at SukRose so he could embed the cues in Mystery's profile. Elegant, Leona. But the more I thought about it, the more that seemed like going overboard just to play Hitchcock. Then there was the expense of setting Tiara up as Mark's mistress. Even if you did ride herd on it. Even if Stevie took a big chunk and rebated some back to you. Why encourage Mark in the first place? There had to be more.'

She blinked.

'Want to hear my second guess, Leona? The one that panned out?'

She swiveled toward me. 'I should do your work for you, you weaselly little scammer?'

I said, 'Gustave Westfeldt.'

'Who?'

I repeated the name.

She threw back her head, laughed. Got back up. 'Now I know you're full of shit. Get the hell out of here.'

'Something funny about Gustave Westfeldt?'

'What's *funny* is I never *heard* of him and you're utterly full of shit. *Out!*'

'You do know him, Leona.'

'I don't need you to tell me who I—'

'Actually you do,' I said. 'And you'd better listen hard.'

Her mouth worked. Fingers clawed velour.

'You don't know him by name, Leona, but you *know* him. I was a little better informed, had picked up on the *Gustave* part but had no idea about *Westfeldt*. Despite all those years of first-rate libations—'

'What the hell are you *babbling* about?'

'Gustave Westfeldt,' I repeated, as if summoning a deity. 'Old guy, curly white hair and a tiny little mustache.' A beat. 'Hunchbacked.'

Color drained from her face.

I said, 'The bartender from the Fauborg Hotel. For thirty-three years, as it turns out. All those people who serve us, we never take the time to learn much about them. But I learned a lot about Gustave. He's eighty-four, happy to be retired. And sharp, mentally. He never learned your name. Or Mark's. Because you always took a booth, never sat at the bar. But he sure recalled your faces. And your drinks. Sapphire Martini for you, straight up, olives plus onions. Onions without olives would've made it a Gibson, but you wanted both. You drank an identical cocktail in *Death Is My Shadow*, guess it's been your favorite for a while. I have to tell you, Gustave didn't approve, said if someone wanted salad, they should order salad. He developed his own private name for it: Gibsini. He laughs when he says it. And that's how he filed you away. *The Lady Who Likes Gibsinis.* Mark went for eighteen-year-old Macallan, which is a commonplace order, so Gustave filed *him* as *The Man with the Lady Who Likes Gibsinis.* Then there was a third party who started showing up with the two of you, a couple of years ago. Blond, lovely, young – so young Gustave first figured she was your and Mark's granddaughter. He filed her as *The Girl Who Likes Rum and Coke.* With one exception. The last night of her life. That night she ordered a – you guessed it – a *Gibsini.'*

Her cheek twitched again. She turned to block it from view. Didn't see me nudge the laptop.

'Here's the thing about bartenders,' I said. 'Even when they seem not to be paying attention, they often are. And they notice all kinds of things. What Gustave started to notice was that Little Miss Rum and Coke always sat between you and Mark and that the second time she joined you, when Mark thought no one was looking, he slipped his hand between her legs. Kept it there. And the strange thing was, Rum and Coke endured it as the conversation continued. Gustave, being an upright type of fellow, was immensely offended but he'd seen all kinds of things that offended him, had remained steadily employed by keeping his mouth shut. His tolerance was strained even further when at the end of that evening, Mark moved his hand and *yours* took its place. And that's the way it tended to go when the three of you showed up on Sunday night at the Fauborg and retired to that nice corner booth. Mark's hand, your hand, Mark's hand, your hand. You were out of view from the other patrons but Gustave had a nice clear view. "Now I got it," he told me. "These are perverts, I wanted to spit in their drinks."'

She gave a start.

I said, 'Don't worry, he didn't, like I said, he's a man of discretion. And he never told anyone. Until he told me. Because I really am a good psychologist and I know how to ask the right questions. And –' rubbing my thumb and forefinger together – 'I know how to provide what we call positive reinforcement.'

She muttered something.

'What's that, Leona?'

'You're disgusting.'

'Don't you think that's a little harsh, Leona, coming from someone whose view of morality can be thought of as blurred? To be charitable.'

'So what?' she said, facing me. 'She was an adult, got amply compensated, no one got hurt, it kept us whole and healthy and intimate with each other. So what?'

'If that was the end of it, we wouldn't be talking, Leona. But she turned up dead and I watched your movies and learned that you knew your way around a gun. I'm not talking Actors Studio nonsense. Your relationship with firearms was real and intense and borderline erotic. I believe you could go upstairs and bring down that Glock and finish me off with one shot. But you won't. Because you're smart. Because you being a gun gal isn't the important insight. That one I got from your co-star.'

A hand rose to her lips, cupped around her chin, and squeezed hard enough to turn the surrounding skin rosy.

'The inevitably wooden Stu Bretton, Leona. He really did stink as an actor but what makes him fascinating has nothing to do with technique. It's his striking resemblance to someone.'

The facial tic slid down to her torso, eels running riot beneath her skin. Her entire body shook. Her head bowed.

I said, 'Stu was a big guy, beefy, handsome, that nice head of thick, wavy dark hair. Which describes your son Phil to a T. As a matter of fact, Phil could be Stu Bretton's clone. The timing fits: Phil was born a year after *Death Is My Shadow* was filmed. Nothing unusual about a leading lady bedding her leading man, it happens all the time. What makes Phil's paternity interesting is that he's got a twin who's the spitting image of Mark. Now, how could that be, Leona?'

She buried her face in both hands.

I said, 'Big puzzle, but here's where my training paid off. Take a look at this.'

I held out the same faculty card I'd flashed at Magda.

She did nothing at first, finally spread her fingers, peered through.

'I may be a whore, Leona, but I'm a highly educated whore and working as a med school professor has exposed me to all sorts of interesting things. The incredible fixes people get themselves into. You know what I'm talking about.'

She began breathing hard.

I said, 'Superfecundation.'

Her shoulders heaved. She moaned.

'Big word but a simple concept, Leona. A woman has sex with two men during a brief period of time and has the bad luck to drop two eggs during that particular cycle. The result is fraternal twins with the same mom but different dads. It's not that unusual in so-called lower animals, rarer in humans but probably not as rare as we think. Because what woman, even if she figures out what happened, is going to divulge her secret? I've seen it at least twice in a medical setting: people coming in for tissue typing and we get results that are . . . thought provoking.'

She hunched lower. Gustave Westfeldt's female counterpart.

I said, '*Your* problem, Leona, was that you couldn't keep it a secret. Mark figured it out. Probably when the boys started puberty and Phil started looking like a man and the resemblance slapped Mark across the face. Because he'd seen all your movies, maybe even socialized with Stu Bretton. *Big* problem for you, Leona. But also Mark's problem because by that time he'd come to love both boys and the thought of rejecting Phil because of your screwup was unthinkable. Good for Mark, very noble. But being good old *horndog* Mark, he also decided to capitalize on the situation. As in, we'll stay together, Lee, go on like nothing happened. But I get to screw all the girls I want and throw it in your face to my heart's content. In fact, Lee, not only do you have to *tolerate* it, if I want you to participate, you'll damn well *participate.*'

Her hands flew away from her face. She smiled. Wet-eyed. Wild-eyed. 'You think you're so brilliant? Mark didn't figure it out. I told him. *Before* Philip became a man, when the boys were seven. Because I'd seen pictures of Stu as a child, knew what was coming, knew I had to deal with it. And don't kid yourself, you stupid punk, Mark didn't need an excuse to jam his pecker in every available hole. He cheated on me during our *honeymoon.*'

'Then I stand corrected, Leona. But the result was the same. Your confession gave Mark a lifetime of leverage and molded the relation-ship you two shared for over forty years. Maybe it wasn't so bad. Once you get past those silly taboos, what's the big deal about a threesome, a foursome, an anything-some? Who cared what got stuck where as long as you ended up with the house, the cars, the toys? And, heck, Leona, you found out you like chasing youth as much as Mark did. Enter Steven Muhrmann. And Tiara Grundy. I am curious about one thing: Did Stu Bretton ever find out about Phil?'

She tightened up, readying a retort. Shrugged.

'He had no interest in paternity?'

'Stu was shallow,' she said. 'That's why he couldn't act his way out of a paper bag.' Wagging a finger at me. '*He* wasn't greedy. The only time he wanted to see Phil was after he got sick with cancer. Not to make trouble, just to see him. I took Phil to lunch at Spago. Stu had a table across the room. Stu was a ghost, didn't look like himself anymore. Philly and I had a lovely meal. Foie gras mousse on kumquat tart.'

Licking her lips. 'Fava bean bruschetta . . . Stu picked at a salad. He left first. Our eyes met. He blew me a kiss when Philly wasn't looking. A week later, he was gone.'

'Peaceful passing,' I said. 'Private room at the actors' hospice.'

'You bastard! You've *excavated* us?'

'More like surface digging. I found a picture of you and Mark at a fund-raiser for the hospice. Found Stu's obituary in *Variety*.'

'All that smoking we did on screen,' she said. 'It'll probably do me in one day.' She laughed. 'When the boys were real little, before I told Mark, Phil had always been his favorite. Bigger than Frankie, stronger, more athletic. "The kid's Hercules, Lee, where the hell'd he come from?" And I'd chuckle along with him. Then I'd go off to my room and cry.'

She demonstrated, let the tears flow silently. Maybe it was Method Acting. It seemed real. I could've felt sorry for her. If she was another person.

I said, 'Did Mark's attitude change after he knew?'

'Not one bit,' she said. 'Mark was a prince.'

'A prince who betrayed you.'

The tears ceased. She made an ugly, guttural sound.

I said, 'You orchestrated Mark's retirement, figured with enough fun for all, maybe he'd relax and take you on a damn cruise. Unfortunately, just the opposite happened. Mark veered from the script and improvised. He grew to like Tiara. She amused him. Even her fake British accent amused him. He started to see her as more than a sex toy and began sneaking around you. Funneling her more money than you'd agreed upon. Gave her a diamond watch *way* above her pay grade. And Stevie Muhrmann was no better, going along with it. A bigger cut for Tiara meant a bigger cut for him. The problem with improv, though, is that actors can run amok. A director's worst nightmare. But you never saw how serious the problem was until Mark had the poor judgment to die unexpectedly and you had the even worse judgment to cut off Tiara's funds.'

'I'm the bank?' she said. 'Fuck her.'

'Actually, you were the bank, Leona. And banks run into problems when they're faced with Too Big to Fail. Which is exactly how Tiara had come to see herself. Because Prince Mark had armed her with a *ton* of leverage by divulging Phil's paternity.'

I stopped.

She breathed hard and fast. Growled. *'Bastard.'*

Hard to know who she meant. Maybe everyone.

I said, 'Maybe it was pillow talk, maybe intentional mischief on Mark's part. Whatever the case, the damage was done and Tiara took the knowledge seriously. There's a pathologist who'd been testing her for STDs for years and she asked him if he also did paternity testing. She wanted science on her side in case you went into denial mode.'

'Bitch,' she said. 'Pushing me, pushing me after I warned her. She was trailer trash, cheap, clueless, stupid. Didn't even know how to order a drink when I met her.'

'The whole Pygmalion bit, down to the accent,' I said. 'Talk about My Spare Lady. Maybe her poor judgment had something to do with her own mother dying, some people don't grow up until they're orphans. Or maybe it was just the faucet turning off, no more style to which she'd grown accustomed.'

'Bitch.'

'Entitlement's a nasty addiction,' I said. 'No rehab for it and cold turkey sucks. Tiara's ultimatum was clear: Pay me a whole lot of money or I go straight to your sons and give them a little genetics lesson. Talk about button-pushing, Leona. Your crowning accomplishment was raising brothers who love each other. Would the boys' relationship survive the truth? Maybe, but you couldn't risk finding out. So you agreed to Tiara's demand but told her as long as I'm paying, I'm staying, honey. You slept with her a few more times. You even let her stay at your house on Old Topanga when she got tired of paying rent. Then you set up a final date. Back to the Fauborg, where you and Mark and Tiara had spent so many quiet evenings before retiring for fun. The hotel was going down forever, perfect metaphor. You wrote the script:

ingénue, bodyguard. Experienced older woman calling the shots. The inevitable merging of flesh. You even had Tiara wear the outfit you wore in *Death Is My Shadow*. Told her to order the same cocktail. Use the same cigarette holder and sunglasses. Because we know how that scheming character ended up. But perhaps there was another reason, Leona: Maybe you were finally eliminating traces of the persona you'd played your entire adult life. Bad girl pushed too far who inevitably loses. Time for a new you.'

I smiled. 'The Prime of Miss Olna Fremont.'

She waved that away.

I said, 'Tiara complied superficially, but once again, she improvised. Wore the watch Mark had given her. Talk about a subtle little fuck-you.'

She fidgeted.

I said, 'The plan was the three of you would "meet" in a dark cocktail lounge, go off together, end up somewhere – probably right here on satin sheets. Stevie was looking forward to a night of fun. Loved playing Secret Agent Man.'

She snickered. 'His brain was potting soil.'

'Two against one, Leona. You've got guts.'

'So I've been told.'

'How did it go down?'

'What's the difference, let's talk business.'

'Here's what I think: You kept Tiara waiting, finally phoned Stevie and told him there'd been a change of plans, returning to the main house was out of the question. Stevie said, "Bummer." You said, "No problem, we'll party at the other house. Where Tiara's staying, anyway." Your log cabin, you bought it with your own money, so it was unsullied by Mark. It appealed to you because it reminded you of all those western sets. You had the two of them meet you somewhere, picked them up in one of your cars. Not the Rolls, too delicate, not the Mercedes, too small. Had to be the Range Rover, perfect for mountain roads. You drove, they rode. A few miles before Old Topanga Road, you stopped and pulled over and said, "There's a great view spot, I want to see if the stars are out." The three of you got out, maybe you pointed out some constellations, it is beautiful up there at night. And then Tiara met the Asp.'

She studied me. Scooted closer, stroked my fingers. 'I take it all back. You *are* a smart boy.'

'Thanks, but you made it easy. That last scene in *Death* where that cop tries to wrest your weapon away from you and you get shot during the struggle. Little side-by-side derringer, the one you kissed in previous scenes. It's a distinctive-looking weapon. Ralston Firearms model XC324, aka the Asp. Last manufactured fifteen years ago, crude but flexible: Each barrel can take a .45 bullet or a .410 shotgun shell and any combination thereof. The coroner was puzzled by how evenly aligned the wounds were on Tiara's face because she's assuming two shooters. But one double-whammy from a single person would explain it perfectly. From what I've read, it's got quite a kick but nothing a gopher-blasting gal couldn't handle. Risky, though, because if you missed, you'd need time to reload. But you had confidence. Bye-bye pretty face. That was the whole point. Enough slavish devotion to youth and things that don't matter. How'd Stevie react?'

'What do you think?' Her mouth dropped like a trapdoor and hung slackly. She bugged her eyes.

Aping a dullard's surprise.

I said, 'You weren't worried he'd attack you?'

'Not a chance,' she said. 'He always did what I said.' Smiling. 'Guess that was the attraction.'

She played with her hair. 'It's not like I gave him time to think about it. I kicked her down the hill, got back in the car, and started it up. He stood there, looking like he was going to be sick. I said, "Are you going to keep staring like a jackass or can we finally have some real fun?" '

She walked her fingers along a seat cushion. 'I got a little specific about the fun. What *you'd* call positive reinforcement. He scampered right in, I touched him where he liked to be touched. Tossed *it* into his lap.'

296

'The Asp.'

'It was still hot,' she said. 'That's a problem with it, it gets hot. I wore gloves.' She broke into throaty laughter. 'When it hit his crotch, he shot up so fast he banged his head on the roof. I said, "Calm down, darling. We'll have a blast." No pun intended.'

Slapping her knee. Squeezing my hand.

I said, 'But it was intended. A mile later you stopped again, pulled out a second gun from where you'd been hiding it. A .357 that could be fired a whole bunch of times. You ordered him out of the car. Why didn't he fight back then?'

'Scared,' she said. 'Like a pathetic little girl. I almost wanted him to try, he'd have ended up with no face himself. But too much to clean up.'

'He got right out?'

'Dropped to his knees and begged.' Huffing. 'Pathetic. He started asking me why. "None of your business," I said. "Now get up and let's have an adult discussion."'

Laughing. 'He actually thought he was going to be okay.'

'Then you shot him in the back. Why twice?'

'What I wanted,' she said, 'what I'd thought about – was to have him drop his pants and shoot him where it counted. Watch the look on his face when he realized what I'd turned him into. Watch him realize he was oozing away. But a girl has to be practical. I needed to get it done and move on.'

She touched my cheek, let her fingers trickle toward my chest. I intercepted her. No way for her to conceal a weapon under the tight sweats but my heart was pounding and I didn't want her to feel it.

Being this close to her made me want to bolt.

Like holding a defanged snake. An asp. The cerebrum says *Safe*. The primitive brain, the one that kicks in when survival's at stake, says *Get the Hell Out of There*.

'Shame,' she said. 'You're evil but you are cute, we could have all sorts of fun.'

'Until you'd had enough.'

'Touché. Okay, what do you want for the story rights to your little drama? Make your best offer, I don't negotiate.'

I said, 'I'm figuring over a two-year period Mark paid Tiara close to a hundred and fifty thousand, probably more. Given the circumstances, I don't think twice that amount is unreasonable.'

She wriggled. I let go. She tried to slap me again. I backed away. Stood.

'You're out of your mind,' she said.

'How about two hundred, then? Less than you paid for the Rolls and Phil and Frank get to continue as best friends forever. Not to mention, you stay out of jail.'

'I'll never see the inside of any jail, darling. It's a story, nothing more.'

'A true story.'

'Prove it.'

'If you're that confident, why haven't you gone for the Glock?'

'That's obvious,' she said. 'The other thing.'

'Phil and Frank.'

'Even so, two hundred is ridiculous. Even half that's ridiculous.'

'I disagree, Leona. Two hundred's *my* best offer and if you don't meet it, I'll walk out of here and tell my story to Lieutenant Sturgis. Like I said, the cops aren't geniuses but they can connect dots.'

'And what will happen to you?'

'They'll thank me and pay a consultant's fee.'

'Fifty thousand. That is *my* best offer and you'd do well to take it.'

'A hundred.'

'You are tiresome. Seventy-five.'

'Split the difference,' I said.

'Eighty-seven five. Exorbitant, but fine. I'll have cash for you in three days. Give me that card of yours, I'll call you and inform you where to pick it up.'

'Don't think so, Leona. I'll set up the date. When you orchestrate the score, the band tends to go out of tune.'

'Not to my ear,' she said, gaily. 'It was beautiful music.'

'Three days,' I said. 'I'll call you.'

'All right,' she said. Far too quickly. Way too syrupy. Definitely time to leave.

Retrieving the laptop, I left the room, crossed the cavernous entry hall.

The photo of the woman in white was gone.

Leona Suss made no attempt to follow and that raised the short hairs on the back of my neck.

As I reached the door, my head whiplashed for a backward look.

She stood, hands on hips, at the foot of the stairs. Rubbed her crotch briefly. Said, 'Ta-ta.' I knew she was already screenwriting.

The cat purred by her feet.

I turned the knob.

The army stormed through.

39

INFANTRY CHARGE.

Milo.

Sheriff's Homicide Investigator Laurentzen 'Larry' Palmberg.

Three uniformed sheriff's deputies, an equal number of LAPD uniforms.

Twice that many from Beverly Hills PD, along with two BH detectives thrilled to be 'doing something exciting.'

Seven crime scene techs. Because of all the square footage.

Dr Clarice Jernigan, wearing a hand-tailored coroner's windbreaker over an expensive pantsuit, even though she rarely showed up at any crime scene and there was no dead body. Because, in the event the murder weapons showed up, she wanted an unsullied chain of evidence.

Last in: Deputy DA John Nguyen, clutching the search warrant he knew he'd be serving and the arrest warrant he hadn't been sure about before watching the feed from the laptop.

Because 'filthy-rich folk hire media-savvy loudmouths who spin like dervishes and I need to make sure nothing stupid happens.'

'Also,' Milo confided to me, 'everyone likes to see a fancy house.'

One person, wandering the mansion casually, could've found it.

In the living-room-sized closet of Leona Suss's Louis XIV bedroom, a push-door behind racks of Chanel, Dior, Gucci, and Patrice Lerange opened to reveal a six-foot-tall, bird's-eye-maple-veneered jewelry safe. Whatever treasures nested within would await discovery until a lock-smith arrived.

The adjoining stainless-steel gun safe, a foot taller and double wide, had been left unlocked. Inside, oiled and boxed and beautifully main-tained, were two shotguns, a rifle, and fourteen handguns, many of which bore original tags and had never been fired, including a massive, gold-plated Magnum Research Desert Eagle Mark VII.

Milo hefted that one in gloved hands. 'Work of art. But probably too damn heavy for her.'

Palmberg said, 'Yeah, it's a beaut . . . pretending she's our size, huh? Both my daughters were like that when I took 'em to the range. I'm guiding them to lower caliber, they want to go nuclear.'

'They still shoot?'

'Nah, too busy, they're surgeons. One does veins, the other does bones.'

'Nice.'

'You get what you put in.'

Weight issues, apparently, didn't apply to the Asp, squat and ugly and crude. Side-by-side barrels formed a nasty omega.

On a middle shelf, Milo found the Smith & Wesson .357 revolver later determined to be the conduit for Steven 'Stefan' Muhrmann's trip to eternity.

In a drawer at the bottom of the safe were still shots from Leona Suss's films. A few love scenes but many more featuring death, terror, or simply the star bad girl brandishing weapons. Later photos, the most recent taken the previous year, chronicled the story of a steadily aging but still fit and agile woman who'd never lost her attraction to firepower. Some pictures captured her target shooting; in others she nestled the weapons like infants.

Those, especially, caused her to smile.

'Like they're her kids,' said John Nguyen. 'This is an interesting lady.'

'She's got real kids,' I said. 'That'll make it more interesting.'

'What do you mean?'

'You'll never go to trial.'

'What if I want to?'

'Doesn't matter.'

No sign Mark Suss had ever shared his widow's passion for firepower.

No sign, either, of the Glock she'd threatened to use on me. That turned up at the log house on Old Topanga Road, fully loaded and resting in a bedroom nightstand drawer.

The room itself was pink, a lace-trimmed setup with a heart-shaped canopy bed. One-quarter the size of the suite in her mansion, frilly and redolent of lavender and sharply discordant from the house's rustic charm. The door was dead-bolted but yielded easily to a battering ram. No sign anyone had slept there for years.

A screen porch set up with a propane heater had been used recently. Feminine products were stacked on a windowsill. Casual clothes hung in a cedar-lined chest. DNA recovered from the cot pushed into a corner was later found to match Tiara Grundy's. For three weeks, she'd been living out in the country, maybe enjoying the creek out back. Maybe deluding herself the rules were anything but Leona's.

Two smaller bedrooms at the opposite end of the house were set up as lairs for teenage boys, with rock posters, renderings of race cars, unstrung electric guitars. Alternative light sources picked up copious amounts of semen on both twin beds. Same for pine flooring, hook rugs, a nearby bathroom.

In the same nightstand drawer that held the Glock was a Patek Philippe Ladies' Calatrava wristwatch with diamond bezel. Thirty-five grand retail. Mark Suss had gone way off budget.

Swabs from the back of the watch also matched Tiara's nucleic acid. Not a trace of Leona's. She'd resisted the temptation to inherit.

But she had expressed herself; the watch's crystal face was ruined, scored to a ragged, filmy grid by some sort of sharp object. The tip of an empty ballpoint pen stamped with Markham Industries' address and phone number was later found to match the tool marks.

Milo said, 'Love is fun but hatred's forever.'

Leona Suss hired a team of Beverly Hills attorneys who soared straight over Nguyen's head. A deal was struck quickly and quietly: The accused would plead guilty to second-degree murder, receive fifteen years with possibility of parole after ten, and spend her time at a medium-security prison that had decent psychiatric care.

No need to confess, no airing of any motive.

Nguyen said, 'Don't say *I told you so.*'

I said, 'Eventually, you'll be happy about it.'

'Why?'

'You'll shower and not feel dirty.'

40

THREE DAYS after the arrest, Robin and Milo and Rick and I went to dinner. The same family-run Italian place on Little Santa Monica.

Milo said, 'Sir Alex Olivier. You poured it on heavy, amigo. Cops are idiots, huh?'

'I sacrifice for my art.'

He laughed. 'Yeah, I can see the pain.'

Rick said, 'Idiots? That could be one of your lines, Big Guy. When you're in *that* mood.'

'Better believe it,' said Milo. 'Anyway, thanks for figuring it out, *Dottore*. Chief says this time you'll get some serious consulting dough. Soon as he figures out a way to make it kosher.'

'Sorry,' I said, 'but I turn blue.'

'What?'

'When I'm holding my breath.'

Everyone laughed. My head was elsewhere but I was pretty sure I'd done a decent job of faking sociable.

As our glasses clinked, my cell beeped.

Robin said, 'You didn't turn it off?'

I held the phone to my ear, did a few 'Uh-huhs,' clicked off, and stood and squeezed Robin's hand. 'Sorry, genuine emergency.'

'That hasn't happened in a while.'

'All the more reason I need to respond.'

She gazed up at me. 'Any idea when you'll be through?'

'Not for a while – enjoy, guys.'

'Least it's not another acting gig,' said Milo.

'No, this is honest labor.'

Bunny Rodriguez met me in the hospital lobby. We rode silently up to the ICU.

She said, 'I didn't want to bother you but it happened quickly. She just . . .'

Fighting tears.

I squeezed her hand.

'There's nothing here for a kid,' she said. 'Nothing age-appropriate, I mean. The nurses were nice enough to unlock a side room off the waiting area. My husband's with him, at least he had the presence of mind to bring a couple of books and the drawing materials. But it's pretty bleak.'

'What's Chad's understanding of what's happening?'

'I was going to ask you that. Developmentally, I mean. How he actually feels, I can't tell you. It was so sudden, I wasn't paying attention to Chad. Talk about dereliction of duty.'

'Your mind was on Gretchen.'

'Even though she told me it *shouldn't* be. Yesterday. When we were discussing Chad's schooling up in the Bay Area and I stopped to ask her how she was feeling. She nearly took my head off. Barked that I should mind my own fucking business and follow instructions.'

'That sounds about right,' I said.

'Feisty to the end . . . the almost-end. One moment she was sleeping peacefully, actually looked better. The next moment the hospice nurse came in and told us her breathing had stopped, she'd gotten it restarted but it was weak, what to do next was up to me. I know Gretchen wouldn't want to suffer but I forgot about that, it went right out the window because what I wanted to do was save my sister. As if. I hope I didn't create a mess.'

'Have the doctors told you anything?'

305

'They don't expect her to last the night.' Throwing up her free hand. 'So maybe it won't be a mess.'

The hand I held turned clammy. 'You did right, Bunny.'

'Why do you say that?'

'It came from the right place.'

'Road to hell and all that? No offense, but that's meager comfort.'

'One way or the other, it's going to end,' I said. 'She won't suffer needlessly.'

'I want to believe you.' Gripping my biceps. 'You come across believable, that probably works well for you.'

In all sorts of situations.

We walked toward the main entry to the unit. She pointed to a closed, unmarked door.

'In there. I'd better go see Gretchen.'

Chad Stengel sat facing a wall, arms crossed, legs splayed straight out, in a too-high chair pushed into a far corner. Books and drawing pad and markers were stacked neatly in an opposite corner. A white-bearded man in a plaid shirt and cords stood near the stack.

A casual onlooker might assume the boy was being punished for something.

The man muttered, 'Finally.' Then: 'Dr Delaware? Leonard Rodriguez.'

'Pleased to meet you.'

'You'll take it from here?' Moving toward the door without waiting for an answer.

I said, 'Sure.'

Rodriguez said, 'You'll be fine, Chad. The doctor's going to help you.' He left.

I brought a chair within five feet of Chad's.

We sat there for a long time. Or maybe it wasn't that long. I didn't time it. It didn't matter.

Eventually, he said, 'She's real sick.'

'Yes, she is.'

'She's *real* sick.'

'Yes.'

'I don't want to see her.'

'That's up to you.'

'Not dead,' he said. 'I want to see her good.'

I kept quiet.

'Dead is *bad*.'

'Bad and sad.'

'A lot bad,' he said. 'You're her friend? That's what she said.'

'It's true.'

'You're a doctor but you're her friend.'

'Your friend, too.'

'She's not mad.'

'No.'

'Not at me,' he said. 'Never at me.'

'Never.'

'She's a little mad at Bunny.'

'About what?'

'I don't know . . . she's good.'

The small round face looked up at me. Clear-eyed, solemn. 'Not healthy good. *Good*.'

'You're right,' I said. 'Your mom did some real good things.'